"Laura, I have two favors to ask of you."

Seth went on, "I'm sorry, but I have to ask."

"What?" Favors? What exactly could she do for him?

"If we run into the men, I'm going to fight them as best as I can. I need you to take Abby and run, okay? Through the river or wherever you think is the safest. But let me fight and distract them and buy you some time. Please?"

That was a favor for him? It seemed like a favor for her. But Laura knew why he was asking. The thought of leaving Seth to near certain death hit her harder than she would have ever imagined. He was a park ranger. A stranger.

And she did not want him to die.

"Okay. I'll try, Seth." She hoped that was good enough.

"The second favor is a bigger one. When you get out of this, I want you to get a message to my family. Will you please tell them that I'm sorry and that I love them?"

MOUNTAIN STANDOFF

VICTORIA AUSTIN
&
TERRI REED

Previously published as *Rocky Mountain Showdown*
and *Buried Mountain Secrets*

LOVE INSPIRED
INSPIRATIONAL ROMANCE

LOVE INSPIRED®
INSPIRATIONAL ROMANCE

PLEASE RECYCLE
THIS PRODUCT IS RECYCLABLE

Recycling programs
for this product may
not exist in your area.

ISBN-13: 978-1-335-23090-4

Mountain Standoff

Copyright © 2020 by Harlequin Books S.A.

Rocky Mountain Showdown
First published in 2019. This edition published in 2020.
Copyright © 2019 by Victoria Austin

Buried Mountain Secrets
First published in 2019. This edition published in 2020.
Copyright © 2019 by Terri Reed

This edition published by arrangement with Harlequin Books S.A.

For questions and comments about the quality of this book,
please contact us at CustomerService@Harlequin.com.

Love Inspired
22 Adelaide St. West, 40th Floor
Toronto, Ontario M5H 4E3, Canada
www.Harlequin.com

Printed in U.S.A.

CONTENTS

Victoria Austin lives in the American Midwest with her husband, children and dogs. Her kids write notes in the furniture dust and the family watches television with the closed-captioning on because the house is, um, loud. She likes chocolate, peace and quiet, chocolate, and silence. She gets too much of one and too little of the other. This explains the tight pants and the many, many, many gray hairs.

Books by Victoria Austin

Love Inspired Suspense

Rocky Mountain Showdown

Love Inspired Historical

Family of Convenience

Visit the Author Profile page
at Harlequin.com for more titles.

ROCKY MOUNTAIN SHOWDOWN

Victoria Austin

Fear not; for thou shalt not be ashamed:
neither be thou confounded; for thou shalt
not be put to shame: for thou shalt forget the shame
of thy youth, and shalt not remember the reproach
of thy widowhood any more.
—*Isaiah* 54:4

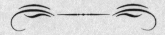

To my family—
I have everything because I have you.

ONE

The first thing Laura Donovan saw when she regained consciousness was the man leaning over her.

The first thing she felt was her fist connecting with his jaw.

"Hey!" the man exclaimed, stepping back quickly while holding his jaw. His hat fell to the floor.

Laura scrambled to her feet, trying to keep an eye on the man while desperately scanning the cabin for Abby. She didn't see her daughter anywhere. "Where's my daughter?" Laura was breathing hard like she had just run for miles, and she could feel her heart pounding in her chest. The muscles in her fingers tightened as she thought about fighting this man. She would do it if she had to. She would do anything to save her daughter.

The man's eyes widened and his hand moved away from his face. Instead, he held both hands in front of him, palms out, as if trying to show Laura that he was harmless. He was looking at Laura like she was a crazy person. "Your daughter?"

The man was dressed like a park ranger, right down to the ridiculous hat. Maybe he was a park ranger, since Mahoney's men had all been dressed in black from head to toe. Laura didn't care. She did not have time for this game. She had no idea how long she'd been unconscious, and she had no idea where Mahoney and his men were.

"Abby! Abigail!" Laura tried to sound calm, but there was no keeping the emotion from her voice. "It's okay, honey! Please come out. Please!" Laura ran into the cabin's first bedroom, flung open the closet door and dropped to her belly to look under the bed. Nothing. She ran into the bathroom and frantically pulled open the cupboard doors looking for the three-year-old. Where was she?

Please let her be hiding. Please let her be in the cabin. Please, please, please. Abby had to be terrified. What if she had run outside? What if Mahoney took her? What if he didn't, instead just killing the girl? Her baby.

No.

"It's okay, Abby! Mommy promises. Please come out." Laura ran to the closet in the second bedroom and threw the door open. She fell to her knees, crying in relief. Abby was there on the closet floor, arms locked around her knees pulling them tightly into her chest. She just looked at her mother, tears running down her cheeks.

"Abby. Oh, Abby. Come here, baby. It's okay, just come here." Laura pulled her sweet girl into her arms, then stood up while trying to press the child's warmth as close to her body as possible. Laura turned and swallowed hard when she saw the park ranger standing in the doorway.

He still had his hands held out in front of him, still had a confused look on his face.

Laura froze, trying to decide what to do. She had Abigail. Her daughter was okay. She was okay.

"Mrs. Donovan?" The ranger's voice was soft like he was trying to calm a wild animal.

Laura felt a whole lot like a wild animal right now.

"Get out of my way. Now." She sounded deranged, and that was not far from the truth. Laura needed to get her daughter out of the cabin. Off the mountain. And that man was standing between them and the door. His weapon was still holstered, and Laura decided he probably was a park ranger. One who had picked today to come check out the recluse living on the mountain.

"I don't know what I walked into, Mrs. Donovan. But I'm not the enemy here."

Laura's short laugh was bitter. Sure he wasn't. Even before this terrible, terrible day, park rangers had never been her friend. Laura couldn't tell if she was shaking or if the vibrations were from Abby, but either way they were less than stable. She needed to get it together.

Laura wished she could wipe her sweaty hands off on her jeans. Relax her shaky arms. Find some medicine for her pounding headache. But that would mean letting go of Abby and that wasn't happening. She sucked in a breath, trying to make the flow slow and steady. And subtle. The bright lights that had been floating in her vision faded. The haze of static in her head cleared.

"How do you know my name?" She sounded like she was accusing him of something. Because she kind of was.

"I told you. I'm a park ranger assigned to this part of Colorado. I know most of the people who live bordering the public lands."

"Great. You're not the enemy. Congratulations. Get

out of my way." Laura tried to sound as authoritative as possible.

The ranger took a step back but Laura did not move forward. He didn't look like any of Mahoney's men, and that uniform looked authentic, but Laura wasn't sure what was real anymore. Not after today. He was still too close for her comfort.

"Mrs. Donovan, I don't know what is going on. But I can help you. My name is Seth."

Laura snorted. "You think you can help, huh? Just wandered up here on the off chance I needed some help?"

His eyes were still wary and confused. "Yes. There's a fire out there. I got caught up in it while doing patrol. The only way out was up the mountain toward your land. I passed your cabin on my way and stopped to warn you. That's when I found you."

Laura bit her lip for a second. Okay. That rang true. And, more important, his vehicle sounded like a way to get off the mountain. Mahoney had slashed her tires earlier. Right in front of her. Just to show her how completely trapped she really was. "All right. Let's go." She jerked her chin, indicating that he should walk in front of her and she would follow.

Seth looked unsure. "Yeah. We'll go. But what did I walk in on? Why were you unconscious on the floor? Are you okay? I mean, what's going on?"

Laura swallowed, increasing the pressure of her arms around Abby even though she had already been holding the girl tightly. "It doesn't matter. We need to get out of here."

Bringing his hand back to his face, he rubbed the place where she had hit him and looked at Abby. Then he nodded and turned to walk through the living room and out the cabin door.

Laura took a deep breath and kissed Abby on the top of her head. "Okay, honey. Okay. We're going to go away from this now. It will be all right." Abby just pushed farther into Laura's front in response.

Seth had walked out. Laura needed to follow.

She exited the cabin's front door and saw a park ranger's truck parked in front. Seth really was a ranger. Once Laura was off this mountain, she would appreciate the irony of a ranger saving Malcolm Grant's daughter.

Seth was standing by the passenger side of the truck, holding the door open and waiting for her. She was a couple yards away, walking quickly, when the gunshot came from her left. Out of the forest. Seth was to her before she realized he'd moved. He grabbed her and began to pull. Away from the gunshot. Before Laura fully comprehended what was going on, she and Seth were back inside the cabin, and he slammed the front door shut.

"I only heard the one shot, but that doesn't mean there's only one shooter."

Seth didn't sound nearly as shaky as Laura felt. He had walked over to one of the windows and was peeking through the curtains with a gun in his hand. She hadn't seen him take it out. Belatedly, stupidly, Laura realized she was just standing there holding Abigail.

Reaching for an empty loop on his pants, Seth patted around his belt with a force that matched the intensity coming off him as he looked down. He let out a deep huff. Before Laura's brain could catch up with her runaway nerves, he was focusing all that intensity on her. "My radio must have fallen off when I ran. Please tell me you have one. I radioed in about the fire before I got here, but I need to call in for help with a shooter."

Laura was shaking her head before Seth even finished the question. "No. We don't get cell service this far up the mountain, and we don't have a radio."

"What about for emergencies? If you or Abby needed help?"

Laura's mouth tightened. "We rely on ourselves up here on the mountain. We don't like outsiders."

Laura watched his face, her stomach tightening. She knew the rumors surrounding her father. People said Malcolm Grant was the stereotypical ex-soldier turned recluse. Antisocial. Living off the grid and holding himself accountable to no law or authority. They were wrong, of course. But Laura had given up defending her father to people like park rangers long ago.

The man quickly moved back to the window, peering through the curtains. He spoke to her without looking her way, his voice curt but not entirely mean. "I think now is a good time for you to tell me what in the world is going on." He was moving as he talked, pushing the couch in front of the door.

The ranger moved through the living room, pushing the table against the back door. The cabin was really only four rooms—the living area/kitchen, two bedrooms and the bathroom. Now that both outside doors were blocked, Seth was looking out the windows again.

Laura didn't know where to start. Or what to say. "There is a man named Victor Mahoney. He is trying to kill me."

"Why?"

"I don't know."

Seth looked ready to argue with her when a second shot sounded. Laura heard it hit the outside of the cabin. She thought she could feel the walls shake from the impact, even though she knew that had to be her mind playing tricks on her.

Seth's face turned grim. "We need to get out of here."

How had all this happened? Laura didn't know. But she was trapped in the cabin with a park ranger. And Mahoney was outside still trying to kill them.

So now she was relying on the park ranger for help. He'd saved them. Maybe. Park rangers were always the enemy. Twenty years of being her father's daughter had taught her that. She'd watched park rangers harass, and even arrest on occasion, her father more times than she could remember. Her father refused to follow their rules. He wasn't hurting anyone, but the rangers couldn't let it go.

But, when faced with Victor Mahoney, this particular one was probably the lesser of two threats. Maybe.

Help us, Lord.

Laura had closed her eyes as she prayed. Habit. When she opened them, the ranger had this look on his face. An almost gentle expression, though the gentleness was offset by the tight lines around his mouth. As quickly as it had appeared though, it was gone. He went to check the other window again.

Laura's head hurt. She missed her dad. He would know what to do. From the day he'd adopted her, he had known what to do. She looked at the cabin door and could hear her dad's gravelly voice in her head. So rough and blunt, but never cutting. *"Get it together, girl. Be still. Assess. Plan. Try."*

"Okay, Ranger, let's make some plans." When she

spoke, the ranger turned from where he had been peering out the window.

"Seth."

Laura was jolted from her imposed calm. Disjointed
again. "Seth?"

His smile was slight and his voice did not betray the
urgency of the situation. "I told you, my name is Seth.
Seth Callahan. Maybe you can say it without the venom
you use with the word *ranger*."

The smile was absorbed by hard lines again as a
third shot came in through the window, sending glass
flying everywhere.

Yep, he had definitely walked into something. Something bad. His routine patrol had turned into an unexpected fire had turned into a detour onto Old Man
Grant's property. Seth had suspected that he might re-
ceive a hostile welcome when he walked up to the cabin
door, but this was beyond hostile. This felt like a siege.

Once Seth ventured another look out the now-broken
window, he could see at least two men out there. They
were dressed in black, wearing dark sunglasses, and
had earbuds. This wasn't good. Seth didn't need to rely
on his military training to recognize an assault team
when he saw one, though it certainly helped to solidify
the feeling of dread in his stomach.

At least they hadn't fired a second shot into the cabin.
Yet, anyway.

The doors were blocked. For now. But a couple
pieces of furniture were not going to keep those men
out for long. They needed a plan. And some serious
help. *Please, God. Show me what to do. Give me the
strength to do it.* That prayer had almost become a daily

plea when Seth had been in Afghanistan. And an hourly one when he was in the hospital and rehab center. And now it was back, seemingly his default mode when his life fell apart.

Seth took a deep breath, trying to be as calm as possible around Laura. Whatever this was, she was clearly hurt and upset. And, well, she should be, given their current predicament. He had left this morning for what was supposed to be a simple patrol, not a foray into an action movie. Seth had put combat behind him. Now, it seemed, it was back in his life.

Seth looked back out the window. The men were holding their position. For now. They were not firing their weapons. For now.

Laura was still clutching her daughter, who seemed to have snuggled up on Laura's chest. Seth just stared. It was rude and this was definitely not the time, but he couldn't help himself. The child looked...well, little. Seth tried to remember what his nieces had looked like before he left his hometown. The girl in Laura's arms seemed about the same age Beth had been when he last saw her. That would make her around three years old. Beth wasn't three anymore. And he had missed it.

Laura murmured something else to the girl, though Seth couldn't make it out. The tone was comforting and reassuring. She looked at him, indicating the girl with her chin. "This is my daughter. Abigail. Abby."

Seth moved from the window, trying not to be offended by the way Laura tightened her hold on Abby and shifted away from him as he approached. He walked past Laura and Abby to see what the situation was in the bedrooms. There was a window in each one, but no door. Looking out the bedroom window, he tried to make his voice low and calm. But he wanted to keep Laura informed.

Plus, he needed her. The public, including rangers, had not been welcome up here for decades. Old Man Grant excelled at keeping people off his land. Laura knew this mountain, and she knew what resources they had available inside the cabin. They were going to need her expertise to get out of this.

"I don't see anyone else—just the two men out front. How many men did this Mahoney guy have with him?"

Laura's dark eyes were serious and she kept one hand moving in a steady circle on Abby's back. "Eight maybe? I was more focused on him and the gun he had pointed at Abby."

"Why are they trying to kill you?" He looked at Abby, not wanting to frighten her. But he had to know, and the situation was beyond urgent. "Why did they leave you unconscious on the floor only to try to shoot you later?"

Laura's voice was a sound of anguish. "I gave them what they wanted. I gave them the key. Then he said he wanted our deaths to look like an accident. He hit me. I don't know how this happened."

What key was she talking about? Every instinct Seth had was screaming at him to quit talking and start acting. But he'd seen more than one mission go sideways because of bad information. Getting the details correct was often the difference between life and death. "I need you to back up. Start at the beginning."

"I found a safe-deposit key last week. This Mahoney came up the mountain today. With a lot of armed men. He said he wouldn't hurt us if we gave him the key."

"But he lied."

Laura actually rolled her eyes at him. "Clearly." Her voice was dry. Sarcastic.

"What's in the safe-deposit box?"

"I don't know," she said.

"How do you not know?" This was not the time for Laura to keep details to herself.

"I didn't even know the box existed. My husband, Josh, was killed eighteen months ago. I just boxed all his stuff up when we came back here. Last week was the first time I opened them. That's when I found it."

Seth had heard that Old Man Grant's daughter had moved back home. She'd stayed even after Grant had died.

Seth quickly walked to the front windows and tried to look out without being seen. The two men were still there, not moving or talking. Assault teams were very good at waiting. He made his way to the windows in the back of the cabin. Nothing but typical Colorado mountain terrain. Two men out front in plain sight. Nothing visible anywhere else. Seth's clenched stomach tightened even further. Those men had a plan and Seth knew he wasn't going to like it.

"Laura, we still need a plan. If we can't call for assistance, then we have to figure out some other way of getting it. Some other way to communicate that we are in trouble. We need help. Backup. More people with guns on our side."

Laura held her daughter closer to her body and shrugged her shoulders in an almost desperate manner. "I don't have any way to call for help. Believe me, if I did, I would have used it when the shooting started."

Seth blew out an angry breath. He hated this feeling. This trapped and useless sinkhole that he somehow found himself back in. His voice was harsh, but getting shot by the two men out front would definitely be harsher. "Well, think. You said you gave them what they wanted? So they just left? Then why are they back?"

Seth sounded accusatory. Too bad. It needed to be asked and being nice was going to get them killed if they didn't figure out how to get out of this situation.

Laura's voice was almost stiff. "They knew I had the key to the safe-deposit box. They said if I gave it to them, they would leave. I did." Her voice became even more brittle. "They lied. They said they had to kill us but it needed to look like an accident."

The fire. It had to be the fire. Seth had been completely surprised at the fire when he came across it while out patrolling. He'd assumed it was started by careless campers. Now he knew.

Laura wasn't done. "They said the smoke from the fire would kill me and Abby long before the actual flames. I panicked. They hit me, and the next thing I knew was you were there waking me up."

Seth exhaled deeply. He had asked and now he knew. The men must have been watching from somewhere safe to make sure the fire actually consumed the cabin. The cabin with an unconscious woman and a three-year-old little girl inside.

Seth looked out the window again. The men were still waiting. The more the men outside stayed still, the more Seth felt like he needed to be doing something. Standing and waiting for someone else to act did not sit well with him. He wouldn't—no he couldn't—play the victim and wait to see what his fate would be.

He wondered if something had gone wrong with the fire. While it was certainly healthy when he'd come across it, it wasn't moving terribly fast. It had run horizontally, blocking the road back down. And it would eventually reach the cabin and probably burn it down. But it wasn't going to do so in the next few hours.

This Mahoney must have started the fire far away from the cabin so it wouldn't look deliberate. But he'd miscalculated. And now it seemed that Mahoney would settle for Laura and Abby dying even if it didn't look accidental.

Seth really wanted to know more about this Mahoney and how Laura found herself in this situation. But not now—right now, Seth wanted a satellite phone and an extraction team. He wasn't going to get either. He needed to be smart and deliberate. And quick. He doubted the men would wait much longer.

Laura was just looking at him. Her hand was still making that steady circle on Abby's back. Her other arm must be hurting from supporting all of Abby's weight, but Laura wasn't showing any signs of stopping. The little girl was resting her head on her mother's shoulder, breathing into Laura's neck. One tiny fist clutched a stuffed yellow duck. She looked warm and sleepy. Safe. Seth glanced at the back door. The clear path into the forest. They could make a run for it, but it wouldn't work.

Laura spoke, her eyes also on the back door. "We won't make it, will we?" It wasn't really a question. Seth wanted to puff out his chest, flex his muscles and tell her that he would keep her and her daughter safe. That he could pick them both up and run them out that back door. Run them to safety. But Laura deserved honesty more than false assurances.

"No. If there are two men out front, then someone

has to be watching the back. Even if they aren't, the men out front would hear us. Chase us. And we—"

Laura finished for him. "Have Abby. We're trapped."

TWO

Trapped. They were trapped. Inside a cabin, surrounded by men with guns. Men who had been very clear about wanting to kill both Laura and sweet Abigail.

And Laura didn't even know what this was all about. Why?

Laura hugged Abby more closely to her body, breathing in the smell of children's shampoo, grilled cheese and that musky scent that came from playing in the forest. Abby's body was warm and slightly damp from when Laura had piled blankets on top of her and put her down for her nap. The fever she'd been fighting all week was gone for now.

One little foot was bare. Laura found her other shoe and put it on, feeling better that Abby was fully dressed. She ran her hands over the small feet, then went back to rubbing a circle on Abby's back, though that was more for her own benefit than the little girl's. Abby was asleep, but the repetition and physical contact soothed Laura. Grounded her. Reminded her that she and Abby were here together. Abby was the only thing Laura needed in this world.

Laura wanted to go look out the window for herself, but she made her legs stay where they were. She wasn't sure she would be able to peer through the curtains without being detected. And those men had already shown they were willing to shoot in.

She didn't want to put Abby down, and she sure didn't want to carry Abby closer to the window—to the men with guns. Laura wished again that her dad were still here. He would know what to do. How to make it right.

Laura smiled as she thought of what he'd say. His voice would be exasperated. Never out of patience with her, but his tone would have suggested that the answer was right there in front of her. Obvious and logical. *"Use the tunnel, girl. It's an escape tunnel. Escape in it."*

The tunnel. Laura sucked in a deep breath, her hand faltering in its circle pattern. How could she have forgotten? When she had first come to live with her dad, she'd been convinced he was some sort of alien. He lived on a mountain. A whole mountain to himself. He talked about not going into *their world*. And he had a tunnel. It made sense to a seven-year-old.

Laura had found it by accident about a month after coming to the mountain. She had refused to go hunting with Malcolm Grant, still stuck in the grief of losing her parents and the surreal timidity that came with finding herself living on a strange mountain with a new dad.

Mad at herself for crying, yet again, she had thrown her stuffed teddy bear as hard as she could. He'd landed in the closet. After a few minutes of telling herself she wasn't a baby and didn't need the silly bear, Laura had climbed off the bed and retrieved her only friend. And she had discovered the latch to the tunnel.

Laura smiled, remembering that moment so clearly. She had lifted the trapdoor, found a flashlight and jumped into the tunnel without thinking. Laura didn't know enough to be afraid. All Laura knew was that aliens were real, and she was going to take that tunnel to a different planet. She'd talked out loud as she explored, encouraging the aliens to come out and play. They never did, of course.

Her dad had been livid when he found her several hours later. It was the closest he'd ever come to yelling at her. "It's an escape tunnel, girl. Not a playground. It's secret. And we both need to pray to God that we'll never, ever need to use it."

And they hadn't. Until now.

Laura tried to take a deep breath, hoping it would calm her. *Please, God, let this be the right decision.* "I know how we can get out. There's a tunnel."

"A tunnel." Seth sounded like he had just been told that there was a teleportation device hidden in the cabin. Laura couldn't blame him.

"Yes, a tunnel. An escape tunnel. My dad made it, when he built the cabin. For situations like this." Laura's voice didn't betray the absurdity of those words. Incredulity might be an expected response to a secret escape tunnel, but Laura was loyal to her dad. Even though he'd been dead for a few months now, she was never going to betray him by mocking him. Especially not in front of park rangers.

"Your dad often find himself being shot at by random people?"

Laura tried to hide her wince. She had spent most

of her life hearing people criticize her dad, and she had learned to ignore them. Kind of.

"I'm sorry, Laura. I shouldn't—"

"Stop." Her voice was loud. Loud and tired and just a touch desperate.

Her little girl moved at the sound of Laura's voice, lifting her head and opening her eyes. Laura straightened her back, holding Abby more firmly to her chest. She placed her hand on the back of the child's head, pushed it back into the indent of her neck and breathed in deeply, her nose still in the child's hair.

She didn't have time for this, and she had more important things to do right now than defend her dad to this park ranger. Her eyes never broke contact with Seth. Her voice was softer. She didn't feel like forgiving him or being kind to him. She just felt…weary. Laura suddenly felt very, very weary.

"Just stop. You said we have to get out of here quickly. I'm telling you there's a way out. I'm going to take it. Are you coming with me?"

Before Seth could open his mouth to answer, Laura was moving again. She meant it about taking the tunnel out of here. Laura wasn't crazy about going alone, but she would if he didn't follow. She headed back to the small bedroom and opened the closet door. She got down on her knees, setting Abby on the floor.

"Here, honey, sit here for Mommy for just a second. Okay?" Laura took a moment to rub her hand over the sleepy girl's cheek. She nodded and leaned against the wall. Satisfied, Laura turned once again to the open closet.

Laura somehow found a latch in the floor—the trapdoor into a tunnel. Standing, she then reached up to the top shelf of her closet and pulled out a couple flash-lights. She handed one to Seth, who was standing close to her, just watching.

Then she opened the trapdoor and saw the ladder leading down into the dark. Cool air drifted up, along with the scent of damp earth. Laura didn't remember the tunnel feeling like a grave when she'd been a child. It did now, though.

The goose bumps that broke out on Laura's arm had nothing to do with the temperature.

Seth really did not want to climb down into that pit. That dark hole in the ground. But it was the only way out. And they needed it now.

"Here, let me go first," he said to Laura, stepping around her so he could be the initial one to descend into the hopefully stable unknown. He stepped onto the ladder and climbed down. At least it felt secure, not shaking or creaking as he put his full weight on it. That was a good sign.

Once Seth reached the bottom, Laura handed Abby to him. Then she climbed down the ladder after him. Seth handed Abby back to Laura and climbed halfway up the ladder so he could close the closet door and then the trapdoor. He wished he had a way to cover up the entrance. Hopefully the assault team wouldn't find the hidden passage right away. He and Laura needed all the time they could get.

"Here, let me help." Seth was surprised to see that Laura had set Abby down. She climbed up the ladder with him and focused her light on where the door had closed. There was a latch. And a lock. Seth was sud-denly grateful for paranoid men who built escape tunnels and thought to equip them with locks. They secured the door and climbed down.

Laura picked Abby back up and they turned to face the tunneled path in front of them. Their flashlights only illuminated the space about ten feet ahead. It was dark and cold. Damp. Seth couldn't see the walls surrounding them, but he felt them. "Okay. Guess this is the only way to go now."

They headed into the black. Laura scanned the interior of the tunnel with her flashlight as they walked. "I haven't been in this thing for years. I played in it once or twice when I was a child, but Dad was always worried it wouldn't remain a secret tunnel if I kept using it. He was pretty big on separating toys from survival tools."

Seth really couldn't think of anything to say in response to that. He supposed that if he had been a recluse with a secret escape tunnel, he probably wouldn't have wanted a child playing in it, either. It made sense in a hermit sort of way.

"All right. This should take us out of here." Laura sounded more hopeful than confident. She turned and looked at Seth, bringing her flashlight with her so that they could see one another. The expression on her face was a mixture of triumph and fear.

Seth knew the feeling. It was currently residing in his own chest. They had made it out of the cabin. The men with guns did not know where they were right now. But Seth also didn't know where they would be in a few feet. "Where does the tunnel end? I mean, will we be far enough away?"

Laura shifted her hold on Abby. The little girl looked more alert. Her big dark eyes, so much like Laura's, were watching him. Laura kissed Abby on the cheek and looked at him to answer his question.

"It's really long. I don't know exactly how long. I just remember it seemingly going on for forever when I was a child. It comes out farther up the mountain. Closer to the top. I'm pretty sure we'll be safe. I mean, I hope we will be."

Pressure expanded in Seth's chest as he thought about the chance that she was wrong. That they would walk out of this tunnel into something worse than the men at the cabin. Or that they would end up trapped here by the fire. Seth took a deep breath, set his shoulders and started walking. There really wasn't anything else to do, and they were wasting time.

The tunnel wasn't wide enough for two adults to walk next to one another. Thankfully, though, it was tall enough that Seth could stand fully upright. It made him feel less like some kind of underground mole. Or troll. "I'll go first and try to shine my light so you can use it, too. That way you can hold Abby with both arms. The ground looks clear at least."

Laura was keeping up with Seth's pace as he spoke. He hoped she understood that the tunnel was safe only for as long as it took those men outside the cabin to come inside and find it. Once that happened, it would become a prison. Or a tomb.

Laura shuddered, as though reading his thoughts, and looked at Abby. She was clearly terrified for her daughter, focused solely on keeping Abby safe. No, Seth vowed to himself, this tunnel would not become a tomb. Seth increased his speed, grateful that Laura followed fast enough that he was still right in front of her.

"That door was metal, and the lock seemed sturdy."

Seth knew he was trying to reassure himself just as much as he was Laura. He felt a bit like Pollyanna, trying to play the glad game. But his words were the truth and being optimistic always felt better than sitting in despair. "I'm not sure how prepared that team is, but I don't think they will have an easy time breaking through." He looked behind him and Laura jerked her head up and down once in a nod. "Your dad's paranoia is turning out to be a good thing."

Seth heard Laura's steps falter, but when he looked back her legs had resumed their prior movements. He'd regretted his words the moment he said them, but he regretted them even more when he saw that look in her eyes. It wasn't anger so much as sadness. Resignation. Seth didn't like the way that look made him feel. He breathed out through his nose, wondering why he couldn't have kept his judgment to himself. Criticizing her dad, a man she clearly loved, wasn't going to do a thing to help their situation. Moreover, he was the reason they still had a fighting chance against that army surrounding the cabin. *Lord, when will I ever learn?*

"He wasn't paranoid. Or crazy. Or a criminal." There wasn't any heat in her tone. Seth almost wished there had been. Surely hard anger would have been easier to digest than the resignation in her voice. Seth wasn't making her mad. He was hurting her.

He sighed. The man had been her father, so of course she would defend him. He didn't know what to say. He should apologize, but he still believed the words he was saying. He just wished they didn't upset Laura.

"My dad never hurt a soul in his entire life. All he wanted was to live on the mountain by himself. To be left alone. He never did anything bad to anyone, but people couldn't just let him be. They had to judge him. Question him. And make sure he knew that they considered him some kind of scary deviant."

She wasn't wrong. The stories of Old Man Grant were legendary in the park ranger office. They included tales of criminal behavior. But that behavior had been minor. Grant had not appreciated the restrictions governing use of public lands. Especially those pertaining to hunting or cutting down timber. He'd trapped animals and taken trees, but only what he needed to survive. At most, Grant was hostile. Rude. Protective of his land and more than a little frightening. Seth knew the conflict between Grant and the rangers in the office at the time had escalated to an unhealthy level on both sides.

A man who wanted to be alone. Much like Laura, it seemed. A man with a daughter. Also like Laura. "But he wasn't alone, was he? He had you for company. And your mother?" Seth was clearly prying for information. He couldn't help himself. He was speed walking through a tunnel, fleeing from an unknown threat, with a woman who had probably caused this mess to begin with. He was surprised by his curiosity, but it was a welcome distraction from what was behind them in the tunnel and what might be ahead.

Seth didn't want to get away from Laura. He wanted to know who she was and why she was on this mountain. She was also known for being hostile to the outside world. Why was that?

Seth wanted to know…her. Period. Laura didn't really fit with the vision of Old Man Grant's daughter.

"I think we better stop talking and save our energy. We're probably going to need it." Laura's voice sounded brittle. It seemed she was done talking.

Seth didn't say anything, but he did turn his attention fully on the stretch of tunnel in front of them. It had not changed in width or height but he thought he could feel it curving. Taking them somewhere.

He was walking in the dark. Again.

Seth had thought his days of battle were behind him. He had worked hard to put them there. Leaving the war had cost him everyone he had ever loved. Well, that wasn't exactly true. It was the way Seth refused to let his family help him after the war that had ruined everything.

Seth had so many regrets surrounding how he let war dominate his life. Now, it seemed, he had walked right back into it.

It was as awful as he remembered.

THREE

They walked and walked and walked. Hustling, Laura kept trying to listen over the sounds of their feet and breaths. She didn't know what she was listening for, exactly.

She thought she heard footsteps. Or voices. Or both. Her voice came out as a harsh whisper. "Do you hear something?"

Seth immediately stopped. He held up his hand, and Laura wanted to say that she didn't need him to tell her to be quiet. She didn't, though. As much as she did not want to be with Seth right now, she didn't want to be alone in the tunnel more. Well, not alone. Alone would be okay. It was meeting with a team of armed men dressed in black that she was looking to avoid.

Laura was glad she could hear Seth's ragged breathing as well as her own. It was nice to not be the only one feeling the pressure of this situation. Seth's whisper was soft, but not hesitant. "I don't hear anyone. I think we're still okay."

Laura looked at him and nodded. She readjusted Abby in her arms and jerked her head forward. Taking the hint, Seth started to move again. He might not have heard anything, but Laura noticed that his pace was slightly faster than it had been before she had asked her question. She was okay with walking faster.

This tunnel was not nearly as exciting and fun as Laura remembered. Instead of an adventure, the journey felt like a horror movie. She looked at Abby, who was dealing with this as though she went on trips through dark tunnels with her mommy every day. Laura made sure her grip on her daughter was firm and increased her pace, silently urging Seth along.

She had been frozen in the cabin. Unable to fully comprehend the danger, she had felt almost like she was sleepwalking. Now, however, her body thawed. She no longer felt like a statue. But it wasn't a relief. Instead of being frozen, her stomach was suddenly boiling with fear. Acid was bubbling, trying to burn its way up her throat. Her goose bumps were replaced with sweat. Her heart was beating again, but far too quickly. She tried to use Abby as an anchor, muffling a gasp into her sweet girl's hair.

She was probably scaring her daughter. Laura tried to stop. She couldn't.

When Seth suddenly turned and looked at her, Laura flinched. Her gasp must have given her away. He frowned and stopped midstride when she instinctively took the small step away from him. She didn't want to be weak. But, if she was, she definitely didn't want to be weak in front of him.

"Hey. Laura. It's going to be okay."

She looked at him like he had lost his mind, and he actually chuckled softly. "Okay, okay. It's not good. But we're not down yet, and I have faith." He smiled at her, his face warm and almost comforting. Then he continued walking down the tunnel.

Faith. Laura had faith. But faith wasn't always enough. Laura looked at her daughter and, as always, saw pieces of Josh. Abby's eyes were all Laura but Abby's dimples were all Josh. Tears welled up, and Laura closed her eyes as she kissed her daughter's head. Josh was dead from a mugging. Sometimes the evil in the world won. Laura swallowed, trying to clear her throat of the panic and excess saliva her now-burning body was creating.

Abby must have picked up on her mom's distress, because she reached those chubby hands up to frame Laura's face. Then she placed a smacking kiss on her mom's cheek, causing Laura to laugh out loud. Laura looked at Seth when she heard him chuckling, too. They shared a smile before Laura remembered that he wasn't her friend. No. He was one of those people who delighted in their supposed superiority over others.

Seth certainly wasn't the first person to say something disparaging about her dad. In fact, people had only bad things to say about the man who had shown her more love and acceptance in her life than she had ever found anywhere else. The man who had literally saved her life.

Josh had loved Laura. And Laura had loved him, and the family they created, in return. But the Laura who Josh met was relatively whole. She liked to think that it hadn't been too hard for her husband to fall for her. The daughter that Laura had been... Well that person was someone who was scared and hurt and bratty most of the time. And her dad had loved her in spite of it and during all of it. He had brought her through it.

Laura usually recognized that trying to defend her dad was a wasted effort. People saw Malcolm Grant—saw how he lived—and made their judgments. They weren't interested in the truth. They just wanted the most sensational story. They didn't care about the man who had survived in this world the best he knew how.

Her dad might have chosen to live apart from everyone, but he had been the best man Laura had ever met. He had sacrificed his solitude to raise her because he knew that she did not have any other family. Just him, an uncle who wanted to be alone. And her Uncle Malcom had put aside his wants for her needs and had become her dad. He deserved better. Laura couldn't keep quiet when people started telling the tale of Old Man Grant. If nothing else, the anger helped push away the loneliness. And Laura would much rather be angry than alone.

Her steps faltered and she squeezed Abby a bit too tight as she regained her footing. Seth turned to look.

"I'm fine. Keep going." He pressed his lips together, then turned and started on again without saying a word. Apparently, he didn't care for her demeanor just now. Too bad. Laura didn't care what he thought. So there. She viciously shoved down the guilt. This man was not her friend. He could not be her friend.

Even if she really needed one.

Nope. She wasn't going there. Not with this man. No matter how attractive he was. No matter how many times he was kind to her. She wasn't going there. She'd tried the real world once, and it had shattered every bit of her life.

"Does it feel like the tunnel is going up to you?"

Laura was startled by Seth's question. Embarrassed

that she had been caught so deep in her thoughts, she suppressed a sharp retort. Snapping at him might feel good in the short term, but Laura would eventually regret it. Instead, she focused on the tunnel. On her feet and her senses, trying to discern whether they were moving deeper into the earth or coming up out of it.

"I…I think we are! Moving up, I mean." It might be her mind playing tricks on her, but the floor of the tunnel seemed to be sloping upward. It was slight, but there.

Laura looked ahead and laughed. There really was a light at the end of the tunnel. Or at least a sliver of something that wasn't dusty and dank.

They reached the door, and Seth pushed. The wood made some creaking noises, but nothing else happened. It did not open.

Laura set Abby down and focused her light on the latch, trying to give Seth enough illumination to hopefully figure out how to open it. Her headache had only worsened with all the emotional highs and lows of the last hour. It seemed as though her body was flooded with adrenaline or dread every ten minutes.

"It's stuck, isn't it?" Laura was trying to keep her tone even, aware of Abby's little ears.

Seth didn't turn to look at her, using both hands to fumble with the rusty latch. "It'll be okay. If I can't get the latch to work, then we'll break it down."

"Break it down?" Laura heard the doubt and hope in her own voice. Was everything in her life so contradictory?

Seth's hands paused, and he turned and gave Laura an arrogant smile, knocking on the door in front of them. "Yeah. This is a wood door. An old, wood door. We can handle this."

Laura wanted to believe him. She wanted to argue with him. Before she could do either, however, Seth spoke with smug satisfaction. "Got it."

He pushed the door again, and this time it gave an inch. Then, nothing. Again. Laura made a sound of frustration. She was surprised when Seth turned and put his hand on one of her shoulders, squeezing it lightly. "Hey, hey. It's okay. It looks like there's a bunch of foliage growing on the outside of the door. Vines or something."

Laura felt foolish. Of course. The tunnel door wasn't exactly used every day. Nature had done what it always does. It had persevered, covering the ground and taking back what had originally belonged to it. She needed to get a grip. "Sorry. You're right. I don't know why I'm acting like this, but I'm done. No more hysterics."

Seth laughed and squeezed her shoulder again before letting go. He was reaching into his pocket as he spoke. "You're not being hysterical. I grew up with three sisters. Sisters who were all teenagers at one point. Believe me, I know hysterical."

Laura knew her expression was rueful. He made it sound like teenage girls were torture. Which, they probably were to a brother.

"Besides, I'd say you have plenty of reason to be upset. I'm not exactly calm myself."

Laura appreciated his efforts to make her feel better. She watched with growing excitement as he used the pocketknife to cut the plants that were visible through the one-inch space that the door had opened. Once done, Seth closed the pocketknife and put it back in his pocket. He looked at Laura and Abby, smiled and pushed the door open.

They climbed out of that tunnel and walked into

paradise. The sky was blue and the birds were singing. Laura could smell pine. It was a beautiful day. The kind of day for skipping and playing and laughing.

The wind blew, and Laura felt the tears threaten again. Smoke. She smelled smoke. Or at least she smelled the suggestion of smoke. She'd forgotten about why Seth said he came up her mountain, onto her land. "There really is a forest fire, isn't there?"

He was looking in the direction from which the wind had blown. Down the mountain. In between them and help. His voice was heavy with regret. "Yes, Laura. There really is a forest fire."

Seth's instincts were pushing against each other. The part of him concerned about a group of armed men coming out of the tunnel wanted to run down the mountain. Down meant people. Down meant safety. The part of him that did not want to get caught in a forest fire wanted to run up. Up meant no flames and no flashes of burning heat and no death by smoke inhalation. The one thing his warring intuition agreed on, however, was that they should not stand there and wait.

Seth heard Laura murmuring to Abby. He couldn't make out the words, but the tone was maternal and loving. He turned and shut the tunnel door. From the outside, the exit looked like a root cellar. He searched for a lock on the outside of the door, but there wasn't one. Old Man Grant's paranoia had apparently not gone far enough to encompass their current situation.

That was a shame.

Seth scanned the area and found some large fallen branches. Dragging them over to the door, he began to place them on top of it. He had just positioned the last branch when a small rock was tossed on top of his pile. Surprised, he looked up and saw Abby grinning at him. One chubby fist was empty and one was still gripping a small stone.

"I help," she said. She was beaming like she had welded the door shut.

Seth couldn't stop his smile. "Good job. You're a big help." His smile dimmed when he saw Laura walking toward them, struggling to carry a large boulder. Seth hurried to take it out of her arms.

She released it to him without a fight. "I thought some of these boulders would go well with your pile. They're certainly heavy enough."

Seth moved to place the boulder on top of the branches. Once he was done, Abby tossed her second rock. "One, two, three."

Seth laughed. "Yep. Three rocks. Let's get a few more, okay?"

Abby gave him a serious face. Or at least he thought it was supposed to be a serious face. "Get more." She started scanning the ground by her feet, exclaiming in delight when she found another pebble.

Seth went over to where Laura was, seeing several other large rocks. "Let's stack on a few more of these and then get moving. The weight will slow them down, but they'll get around it eventually."

Laura nodded, carrying a rock over and placing it in the pile. "Headed where? I'm not crazy about the idea of walking into a forest fire."

Her tone indicated that was an understatement.

"Me, neither. But we can't stay here. Those men will eventually figure out we're not inside the cabin. And since there are only so many places to search, they'll

find the tunnel. We need to get far away from here."
Seth looked into the forest as though that would provide some kind of answer.

Laura lifted her face and watched at him. Her expression wasn't exactly warm, but she didn't seem like
she wanted to punch him again. That was probably a
good sign.

Seth was comfortable in the woods. He was good
at navigating them. Surviving in them. But this was
Laura's mountain. She had grown up here. She was the
one with the expertise right now. "We need a plan," he
said. "Well, we need a safe place to go while we make
a plan."

"What about the fire?"

Seth considered what he had seen of the fire. The
way the scent of smoke wafted on the air, just hinting
at its existence. "I still think it's moving slow. Hopefully, firefighters are putting it out right now. Maybe
it will end up being a nonissue. Or a way for us to find
some emergency personnel to help us."

"It'll be dark soon. I don't know if that's a good thing
or not, but night is coming." Laura was sounding like
the practical and self-sufficient daughter of a mountain
man. Seth liked it.

"We really need to get away from here," Seth said. "I
don't like the idea of waiting around to see what comes
out of that tunnel. Any ideas?" Seth was willing to consider just about anything at this point.

Laura stared up the mountain. "Maybe." A pause.
"There's a creek not too far from here. Well, it's more
like a river actually. If we walk on its banks, it should
cover our tracks. Make us harder to find."

Seth felt savage satisfaction in his grin. "Yes. I like that idea. Lead the way," he said.

Laura picked Abby back up and started making her way through the forest.

"Do you want me to carry her? I don't mind." Seth asked the question to Laura's moving back.

"No. I've got her." Laura answered to the trees in front of her, not slowing or turning around. She was heading into a part of the forest that looked just like— well—every other part of the forest. Seth was suddenly very thankful. If he had to be trapped on a burning mountain with an assault team after him, at least it was with a woman who was raised in this wilderness.

Seth tried to think through their next steps, but he needed help. "Once we get there, we'll have to decide whether to go up or down the creek."

Laura turned around, surprise on her face. "What?"

"The creek. We'll have to decide which way to walk."

Laura continued through the trees. Her voice was contemplative when she spoke. "We can take the creek for a mile or so—long enough to lose any trackers. There's a place upstream where we should be able to get out without leaving too much evidence."

Seth nodded even though Laura couldn't see it. "That sounds good. Then what?"

"I know of a shelter not too far off. It was a place my dad used when he was hunting and didn't want to come all the way back to the cabin. It's sparse, but it's well hidden and has supplies."

"I like the sound of hidden and supplies." He hoped those supplies included weapons and ammunition. His service weapon was not going to provide a lot of protection against an armed team.

"I think I should head there with Abby."

Seth jolted. "You? With Abby?"

Laura did not turn around and look at him. "Yeah." She went on as though that was not a startling statement. "The creek is just over this rise."

Seth heard the creek before he saw it. It was perfect. Active enough to cover their tracks but shallow enough on the edges to allow them to walk without getting soaked.

They started trekking upstream, making sure to stay where the water would cover their tracks. Abby was watching the water, pointing at something every once in a while.

Laura spoke quickly, blurting her words out in a torrent of emotion. "Look. These guys are after me." She glanced at Abby, and the anguish on her face hurt Seth. "And Abby."

Seth waited. He did not see how agreeing with her would help anything. Laura continued, still talking quickly, her voice thick with sentiment. "You should go. You can probably make it back to town safely, especially if you're not with me. You don't need to get caught up in this."

Seth stopped walking. There was no way he could process what she had just said and keep moving at the same time. She thought he would leave her to save himself.

Filled with disgust at the very idea, Seth's voice was now heavy with emotion. "I'm not leaving you alone. I don't care what makes the most sense—I'm not leaving you two alone. We're going to get out of this mess together."

Laura looked at him. Oh, how he wished he could read that expression in her dark eyes. Did she believe him?

She opened her mouth, but Seth cut her off, angry that she thought he would be so cowardly as to save himself while letting a woman and child die. "No. I will march back to that tunnel and try to take care of that assault team by myself before I leave you two out here alone. We're all going to the shelter. We're all going to make a plan. We're all going to make it out of this."

She still looked like she wanted to argue. "Besides," he said, "they were watching the cabin and saw both me and my truck. They know we were in there together, and I'm sure they think you told me everything. I'm as big a liability as you are at this point."

Laura's voice was soft, but not defeated or angry. For that, at least, Seth was thankful. "All right. The shelter is this way."

They left the creek at the designated spot and headed up the mountain. Seth's legs started to burn after just a few minutes. He looked at Laura in front of him, Abby's arms wrapped around her neck.

Seth wanted to reach out and put his hand on Laura's shoulder to stop her but was afraid of destroying the fragile trust they seemed to have built. Instead he quit walking and coughed. Laura paused and turned to look at him. She had a question in her eyes, and he struggled to find the right words. "This is pretty rough terrain."

She waited, watching him. Probably wondering why he had stopped their progress to state the obvious. Seth felt himself becoming flustered, which made him want to snap. *No. That approach wasn't going to work*. He decided to just say it and wait for the rejection. "I was wondering if you wanted me to carry Abby for a little bit. She has to be getting heavy."

Laura looked at Abby, who seemed to be following the conversation with her sweet dark eyes. "She's been sick all week. I thought her fever had broken but it felt like it was coming back when I was carrying her in the tunnel. Are you sure you want to risk it?"

Seth couldn't stop the laugh. "I'm pretty sure, all things considered, getting the flu is the least of my worries right now."

Laura looked up at the sloping forest in front of them. She kissed Abby on the check and held her out toward Seth. "Thank you. A break would be nice."

Seth took the little girl, surprised at how light she felt. She was warm and wound her arms around his neck without hesitation. Laura began walking again, and Seth followed. The daylight was fading, and they needed to find a safe place to make it through the night. And they needed a plan for getting past both a forest fire and a group of armed men. *Help us to make the right choice, Lord. I don't want to let them down.*

FOUR

He was carrying her daughter. A park ranger was carrying her daughter. Her dad would be having a conniption right about now. This unexpected liaison with a park ranger was the most rebellious thing she'd ever done. Then again, Laura had never really had a rebellious phase. It was kind of hard to rebel when you lived alone on a mountain with a man who refused to get angry. She actually smiled at the thought of her father's face if he could see this.

"Mommy!"

Laura almost stumbled as she stopped and spun around. She should have known better than to place Abby in the hands of a park ranger. And then she had turned her back on them, not even watching what was going on.

The tension in her body evaporated as Abby blew her a wet-sounding kiss, Duckie clutched in her arm. "Wuv Mommy! Mwah!"

Abby wasn't hurt. She wasn't in danger. She was cradled in Seth's arms, grinning with those chubby little cheeks, and then sending big kisses to her mom. Seth's huge smile faded as he looked at Laura. That handsome joy was replaced with an expression Laura couldn't name. Defensiveness? Disappointment? He had surely read the accusation on her face when she had turned around.

Whatever it was, it made Laura look away from Seth's face. She focused her gaze just above Abby's head as she forced a smile.

"I love you, too, baby."

Her face felt too tight, and it was hard to maintain the upward curve of her lips. Abby seemed to buy the act, however, as she turned back to Seth and started babbling. Something about leaves and rainbows.

Laura chanced a glance at Seth. He was watching her, his face impassive. Unable to maintain his gaze, she turned to face forward again, navigating the path almost subconsciously as she thought about the man behind her. She couldn't figure him out. No, that wasn't true. Laura couldn't figure herself out.

"How far away do you think the shelter is?"

His voice was conversational, almost as though he was asking how she liked her coffee. Laura kept walking, trying to keep her pace steady. She was grateful for his effort at normalcy, but she didn't want to see that look in his eyes again.

"If I'm remembering right, it should be up here about three miles or so." Laura was proud of how evenly she answered him. She felt like a little girl playing dress up with a neighbor boy—both pretending to be mature and sophisticated. Two grand adults having a lofty conversation in adult voices about adult things.

A confident adult was the last thing Laura felt like right now. She might not physically be a child anymore, but right now she was scared and confused. But she knew she wasn't alone, no matter how much it felt like it.

Laura swallowed hard as a smile fought with the impulse to cry. She had God. She had Abby. And she had a park ranger.

They walked. And walked. Laura thought the forest fire had maybe moved to the muscles of her legs, concentrating its burn there.

"It's pretty up here." Seth's voice was still conversational, as though they had been talking the entire time. Two people out for a stroll, enjoying the scenery. Laura wanted to thank him for his effort, but that would kind of defeat the purpose of making this situation seem ordinary.

"Yes, it is." Laura didn't have to try too hard to infuse her words with warmth. It was the truth. "I love this mountain. I'm sure part of that is because it's home. But really, who wouldn't look at all this and fall in love?" Laura took a second and gave the scenery the respect it deserved. She had been focusing on escape. On next steps. On routes and plans and maps that existed only in her memory. Now she was focusing on the masterpiece that God had created. The one she had missed desperately when she lived in Denver.

The trees had brown, textured trunks and lush green leaves and sharp, precise needles, and they burst with life. The forest floor was covered in leaves and plants, a soft carpet. Moss looked soft and inviting. Rocks seemed to pop up here and there, little chunks of sculpture decorating the land.

The wind was blowing away from them, and Laura tried to find the familiar scent of the forest. She wanted to smell pine and wood and that musty, tangy, thick mountain smell. It was there. Along with the faint-est hint of smoke, unfortunately. But she couldn't see smoke yet, and that made her feel better. The sky was a color that, if she painted it, would probably be called unrealistic.

Laura's pace had slowed considerably. She felt her-self begin to blush as she stopped her staring and re-sumed their original steady pace. She hadn't meant to get so caught up, but she also didn't want that horrible silence to return. She turned and gave Abby a big smile. "The mountain is pretty, isn't it, Abby McDabby?"

Abby looked at her and smiled right back. "Pretty! Pretty mountain."

Laura looked at Seth. His eyes were warm. Happy. Not wanting to ruin the moment and lose the feeling of hope that was growing in her chest, Laura faced front again. She took a deep breath, and let it out slowly.

Thank You, God. We needed this.

Feeling reassured and rejuvenated, Laura checked her surroundings to make sure that they were still on the right path. The break from reality was nice, but get-ting lost was the last thing they needed. Seth must have noticed her change in demeanor.

"Um, we're not lost, are we?" He sounded hesitant. That made Laura smile. He seemed afraid the question would anger her. And scared that they might, indeed, be lost. Still basking in the relief of the carefree atmo-sphere they had created, she tried to make her voice as serious as possible.

"Lost? Umm…noooo. I just don't see the tree where we need to turn."

Silence. Then, still hesitantly, "Tree?"

Laura was glad she was still in front of Seth. There

was no way she would have been able to maintain a straight face. "Yeah. When we see this tree, then we need to make a hard left." She made of show of slowing her pace and looking at the nearly identical trees that surrounded them in the forest.

This time, his voice held a hint of dread. "What does the tree look like?"

Laura had to swallow quickly to keep the laugh inside. She waited a second until she thought her voice wouldn't give her away. Trying to sound as confident and nonchalant as possible, she responded, "It's tall. It has green leaves. The bark is a sort of brownish color."

Laura wished she could see Seth's face right now. He wasn't saying anything, and her mind was supplying all kinds of ideas about what his face might look like. His voice was decidedly thicker when he finally spoke. "Is there anything else? Anything that would make the tree stand out?"

Laura pretended to think for a second. "Oh! It does have some distinctive things on it."

"Distinctive? What are they?" Seth sounded relieved.

"It has moss on the trunk. Toward the bottom. And there are bird nests in the branches. And these squirrels. These certain squirrels live in it. They have bushy tails."

Laura heard Seth stop walking behind her. She put on her best poker face and turned to face him. "Is something wrong?"

Seth was looking at her with an expression that was probably half suspicion and half frustration. "Are you messing with me? We're looking for a tree that looks exactly like every other tree in this forest?"

Laura had to face the front and start walking again. She couldn't help but smile at how disgruntled Seth was.

"I mean, they look different to me. But, then again, this is my mountain." Laura continued her pace. She hoped that Seth would follow.

"Mama!" Laura turned to see Abby pointing at her. Abby wasn't upset, but she clearly wanted Seth to keep up.

With a huge sigh, Seth started moving again. "You're messing with me. You have got to be messing with me." He sounded like he was trying to convince himself. "You are messing with me, right?"

Laura's tone was probably giving her away, but she was enjoying this too much to stop now. "Messing with you? Oh, you mean about what the tree looks like?"

Laura heard a humph from behind and almost giggled. "I'm not messing with you. I mean, how else would I know where to go? There aren't any street signs or anything like that." She wasn't exactly telling a lie. Laura's dad had taught her about finding her way on the mountain, and part of that involved looking at the trees. Knowing the forest by sight.

Though he never put stock in memorizing where the squirrels with bushy tails were.

"So, we're looking for a special tree that is somehow different from all the other trees because it has bark and leaves and moss and nests and squirrels, even though every single tree I look at has all these things?"

Laura turned her laugh into a small cough. "Well, I don't know that I would call the tree special. I mean, isn't all of nature special?"

When Seth didn't respond, Laura's curiosity was too strong to ignore. She turned to see him muttering to Abby. He looked exasperated, but whatever he was saying was making Abby smile.

They rounded another tight clump of trees, and Laura realized that her fun was over.

"This is it. We're here."

Seth looked around, but "here" looked like every other place they had been since they got out of that tunnel. He was fairly certain that she was making fun of him. She had to be. She couldn't really be looking for a special squirrel tree. No. She was playing him. Probably.

Seth didn't normally enjoy being the butt of other people's jokes, but he found that he wasn't really upset with Laura. For one thing, he had seen her smile. Just for a second, but it was enough. Her cheeks had been pushed full, her eyes had seemed to come out from the shadows and she'd looked ten years younger. Seth had felt better, too.

Putting Abby down, he tried to discern where the shelter might be. He failed.

He looked to see Abby picking a flower that was growing near her feet and Laura standing there with her hands on her hips. The smile was still in place, though. So was the amused expression she had been wearing and trying to hide for the last ten minutes.

Seth threw his hands up in the air in a gesture of defeat. "Okay, okay. I give. Tell me your terms, and I'll surrender."

Laura looked like she was pressing her lips together, and the corners of her mouth were slightly curved upward. Oh, yeah, she was teasing him. She walked over to a group of bushes and pulled some vines away.

There was a door.

In the middle of the forest.

There was a door in the middle of the forest.

Seth was stunned. Yet, he had known somehow that Laura would come through for them.

The door looked old and rickety. As he walked toward it, Seth realized that the clump of bushes was not really a bunch of bushes growing together. Instead, it was a building of some sort. The shelter.

Seth walked inside, pulling out a flashlight from his belt as he did so. The interior of the cabin was similar to Laura's rustic cabin, though much smaller. It was basically just a room. The fireplace surprised Seth because he definitely didn't remember seeing a chimney outside. Of course, he didn't see the building, either. Seth spotted two windows, both with interior shutters closed over them. Seth guessed that if he opened the shutters, he would only see the dense brush that was covering the cabin. He noted a bed, a table with chairs and a kitchen that looked like it belonged on a campsite.

"Secret fort!"

Abby's excited voice drew Seth's attention to the door. She was pulling against Laura's hand, trying to get inside while her mother just stood in the doorway and watched Seth.

"It sure looks like a secret fort, doesn't it, Abby?" Seth was glad Abby was excited instead of scared. So far, she seemed to be calm or acting like she was on a grand adventure. Seth hoped it could stay that way. He didn't want the little girl to be afraid.

"Well, it's not much." Laura sounded resigned, like she had expected the worst and the worst is what they had gotten.

"It's perfect," Seth said. "It's hidden. It's dry." He opened cupboard and closet doors as he walked around the room, noting the precious supplies they held. "And it's got supplies." He was relieved to see a rifle with ammunition. He'd take that with him when they left.

Laura looked behind her, out into the open forest and then closed the door. "Do you think they are tracking us?"

Seth considered it for a moment. "I'm sure they will, eventually. But those men had a very urban look, Laura. I doubt they spend a whole lot of time in the wilderness."

Laura didn't look convinced.

"Even if they do, we have you," Seth said. She looked surprised. Maybe shocked that he was giving her a compliment. "You know these woods. You knew how to get us to this shelter with minimal evidence left behind." Seth recalled standing right in front of the shelter, knowing it was nearby, and still being unable to detect it. "And you led us to a shelter that is about as hidden in plain sight as something can be. In fact—" Seth stopped as the sound of a helicopter filled the small cabin.

Almost as one, they ran to the front door. Laura was reaching out, preparing to pull it open and run outside when Seth's hand on her arm stopped her. "No, Laura. Wait."

"What if it's help?" She sounded desperate. It hurt to hear.

"What if it's not?"

That did it. Laura dropped her hand and just stared at the door. Seth didn't have time to think. The chopper sounded like it was passing overhead right now. He needed to get a look at it. Barely cracking the door, Seth saw the chopper flying in the direction of Laura's cabin.

"Seth?" Laura's voice made some of the tightness

leave his face. He carefully shut the door and turned to face her.

"That was not a police or fire chopper. It looked private. All black."

Still frozen, Laura tried to get her tongue to work. "More men?"

Seth met her eyes. "Maybe. Or Mahoney's escape plan. But they didn't see us. Nothing has really changed."

Laura sighed. Seth didn't know if she was reassured or had just decided talking wasn't going to help anything. "Okay, so what now?"

Seth opened the door to peek out again. The sun was setting. "It's going to be dark soon. I think we should spend the night here. Rest, gather supplies."

Laura looked like she was going to argue. "What about the fire?" she asked. "I really don't want to wake up surrounded by flames."

It was a valid fear. And Seth didn't know anything for sure. "I think we'll be okay for now. I still think it's moving slow."

Laura looked at him, her face screaming that she was entirely unconvinced.

"Laura, I'll do whatever you want, okay? If you think we should keep moving, we will. But right now we just smell smoke. We don't see it and we don't see flames. None of our choices are good. But I think we should hide and rest for a bit."

Laura nodded. "We should go ahead and seal ourselves inside here as best we can. Try to hide the shelter as much as possible in case they come by."

Seth agreed, grateful that she was trusting his plan. Of course, that also meant anything that went wrong would be on him. A sharp pain shot across Seth's jaw and he realized he was clenching it.

There were no good choices, he reminded himself. They just needed to do their best.

Laura opened doors and drawers, much as Seth had done earlier. When she found a doll and a set of large blocks, she gave them to Abby. Abby promptly sat on the bed and began playing quietly.

Seth raised his eyebrows at the find. Looking at him, Laura smiled sheepishly. "Those were mine. Dad liked to keep me busy. I was quieter when I was busy."

"I bet." Seth pictured a rustic mountain man taking a little girl along on his excursions.

Laura went back to her exploration of the cupboards. She pulled several cans out and rummaged until she found a can opener. "Well, we'll have something to eat at least." She looked at the fireplace and then at Seth. "I don't think we should start a fire. The smoke would be a dead giveaway."

"Agreed."

Laura opened the first can and smelled the contents. Seemingly satisfied, she dumped the contents into a bowl. "I hope you like pork and beans. Cold."

Seth thought about some of the meals he had eaten in Afghanistan. "That sounds perfect."

Laura filled three bowls, found three spoons and they sat down at the table to eat. Even though they were near strangers, on the run, hiding in the woods and eating cold pork and beans, the meal reminded Seth of home. Of eating with his family at the kitchen table. He felt a pang of longing.

Seth was brought from his thoughts by Abby grabbing his hand. Her other fist gripped her mother's hand.

Laura held out her free hand toward Seth's. Her voice was quiet. Tentative. "Um, we always hold hands and pray before we eat."

Feeling a little foolish for not realizing earlier, Seth took Laura's hand.

Laura looked at Abby. "Go ahead, honey."

Abby closed her eyes and bent her head down. Seth did the same. "Dear God, thank You. Amen."

Seth smiled and looked over to see Laura's sheepish smile. "Her prayers are a little...short." She sounded amused and almost embarrassed.

Seth looked at Abby and patted her on the back. "That was great, Abby. I like a woman who knows how to be concise and efficient."

Abby smiled at Seth, likely not understanding all of his words but knowing she was loved and adored. She quickly remembered the food and concentrated on eating her dinner. Seth took a bite, pleased to find that the meal, while simple and cold, was actually quite good. "This is delicious. Thank you."

Laura chuckled. "All I did was open a can, but you're welcome."

After eating dinner, Laura put Abby to bed and then sat across from Seth at the table. The old oil lamp Laura had produced from somewhere made a nice glow. If it weren't for the armed men coming after them, this could have been a fun camping trip. Seth had certainly spent worse nights in his life.

Laura's voice was low when she spoke. Seth wondered whether it was because she didn't want to wake Abby or because of the subject of her question. "What are we going to do if they find us?" Laura turned her head and looked at Abby. Seth saw tears glistening in her eyes before she faced him again. "What are we going to do if they don't find us?"

Seth didn't want to give her platitudes about roses and bunnies. She was an adult. She was a mother. She needed to hear the truth and to know the risks of all their options. But, first, Seth needed to figure out what their options were. He wasn't exactly coming up with a long list.

"I don't honestly know, Laura."

"The smell of the smoke lessened as we walked to the shelter, I think. But that could have been the wind. Do you think we've walked far enough away from the fire?"

"I'm a little turned around after our adventure as moles, but we're farther up the mountain now than we were before, aren't we?"

Laura nodded.

"Okay. So when I saw the fire it was definitely spreading in such a way that it will block all attempts to get down this side of the mountain. The wind could change but—"

"We can't go down."

"Well, there's a chance that crews are fighting the fire right now. That if we walked toward the flames we'd also be walking toward help. But that risk makes me nervous. So I'd say the shortest route to help is probably out. I would hate to try it, hoping the fire won't block us, and then find out it is. I don't like that scenario at all."

Laura's gaze was steady. "And the men with guns might still be out there. Looking for us."

"Yes." Seth wanted to lie to her. But he respected her enough to give her the truth, even though he hated the expression that crossed her face. She looked, well, trapped. And it was a horrible thing to see on another person's face.

"How do you feel about us staying here?" Laura asked. "We have enough food for a couple of weeks. Maybe longer if we ration it. If it came down to it, I could leave to hunt. It feels safe here."

Seth thought about her question, appreciating the way she was treating him. The war between the park rangers assigned to this area and her family was almost mythical. But she was not digging into the conflict. Instead, she was dealing with the here and now. And, in this here and now, they needed to work together to get out alive. To get Abby out alive.

Seth froze when he thought he heard something outside. He had barely formed the thought when Laura extinguished the lamp and moved over to the bed where Abby slept. She had heard it, too, which meant it was real.

Seth knew there was a full moon and a sky full of stars out there. Bright and beautiful. He'd walked through the forest on nights like this before and had never even needed to pull out his flashlight. The cabin was completely dark, though, so overgrown on the outside that no light came in.

The sound outside became louder and more distinct. Something coming through the brush, breaking branches and crunching the leaves and needles that made up the forest floor. And voices. Male voices, loud and aggressive.

"This is pointless. We're wandering around in the dark getting eaten alive by mosquitoes for no reason. They could be anywhere."

"Shut your mouth. Boss says to get them—we get them."

Seth looked at the dark shapes that were Laura and Abby on the bed. He wanted to go over there. He wanted to wrap his arms around them and use his body as a shelter. He stayed where he was, though. He was afraid that he would bump into something or knock something over if he tried to get to them in the dark. The last thing they needed was for him to alert these guys of their location.

Instead, Seth looked at the door. Or, where he thought the door was. He thanked God that he still had his gun on him. He hoped he would not need it, but he felt better having it in his hand.

Seth stopped breathing when a small beam of light came inside the cabin. The men had powerful flashlights. And the cabin wasn't as protected from outside eyes as he had thought.

FIVE

The small beam of light almost danced as it moved along the far cabin wall. If Abby had been awake, she would have probably laughed in delight. That light should be beautiful. Instead, it made Laura feel like she was going to vomit.

"Yeah, well, I don't care what the boss says. If I see a bear, I'm getting out of here."

The man's voice was louder than before. Closer. Laura wanted to cradle Abby to her body, but she didn't dare wake the sleeping child. Abs was a heavy sleeper, but Laura was poised to hush her if it looked like she was starting to stir.

"Why are we even here? I'm telling you, man, they went down the mountain."

"Boss says the fire would have stopped them."

The light left the cabin. Where were they going?

"Then they're in the middle of fire, nice and crispy. Why are we looking for dead people?"

Laura winced. The man sounded pleased at the thought of three people burning to death.

"Yeah, well, this is pointless."

"I heard you the first time. I don't want to hear it a

third. Boss has us split up, covering the entire mountain. We'll find them. And, when we do, she's gonna watch her daughter die. Then she and that ranger are gonna get it, too. They've made this hard enough. Boss is done with accidental and humane."

The voices had been decreasing in volume as the men were hopefully walking away, but Laura clearly heard that last part. She swallowed rapidly several times, trying to fight the urge to vomit, which had become almost unstoppable as those men talked about hurting Abby. Hurting her sweet little girl who couldn't even conceive of such evil.

It was silent outside, but no one moved inside the cabin. Laura put a hand over her stomach, willing it to calm down. There was a time and place for everything, and this was neither the time nor the place for her to have a breakdown. She needed to save her daughter, then she could worry about hysterics.

When she felt like she had control over her body again, Laura looked at Seth. Well, she looked in the direction she had last seen him. He had been utterly silent ever since she had blown out the light, so Laura assumed he was still at the table. She would have heard him move.

Was he was looking at her, too? What was he doing? How long should they wait until those guys were out of earshot? Were more coming?

The questions were flying in Laura's head, and she realized her hands were squeezed into fists. No. No, no, no. She forced her fingers to relax and folded them together. She slid to her knees on the ground without making a sound and kneeled next to Abby's sweet little sleeping body. Laura leaned over, closed her eyes and began to pray.

It was a familiar prayer. Her favorite saying was one about why worry if you pray and why pray if you are going to worry. Laura loved that saying, but it was also her nemesis of sorts. She prayed. She tried to give her burdens to God. Truly. But, no matter how good her intentions, she always kept the worry. She obsessed. She planned. It made her prayers feel like a mockery and inevitably started a cycle of worrying and praying about worrying and worrying about worrying while praying.

But Laura still tried. Because when it came down to it, Abby was going to learn by watching what Laura did. No matter what Laura said. So Laura kept on trying. She prayed about her worries. And she prayed that God would help her release them to Him.

Here, in this dark cabin, Laura felt very much alone. Out of control. And absolutely terrified. So she leaned over her daughter, turned her fists into hands of prayer and tried to talk to her Heavenly Father. It was working, too. She was still anxious, but the absolute panic was fading. God was in control. God was in control. God was in control.

"I'm coming your way." Laura jumped at his whisper, but was thankful for the warning. She was so focused that she might have screamed if Seth appeared next to her without telling her first. He didn't make a sound as he crossed the room, and Laura didn't know he was there until she felt his warmth next to her. He placed his hands over hers.

"I'd like to pray with you, if that's okay?"

"Is it safe?" It felt almost sacrilegious worrying that they both should not pray at the same time. But practicality won out again. Shouldn't one of them be watching the door? Maybe they should pray in shifts. The thought made a wave of hysterical laughter bubble in Laura's throat, but she suppressed it.

Of course it was safe to pray. Especially now. This man wanted to pray with her. He wasn't scorning her for praying in such a dire situation. He wasn't being cynical about her prayer. No, he wanted to join her.

"Of course you can. I have to warn you, though. I'm not very good at this. I never have been. It seems that practice doesn't make perfect in my case."

Seth squeezed her hands, and this time his voice was slightly chiding. "Hey, don't do that. Don't be all self-deprecating. I'm scared, too. I was grateful when I realized you were praying, because I really need it, too."

"I, um…" Laura really didn't know how to respond to that. She went back to bowing her head, looking away from Seth's face, which was still hidden in shadows. Here, in the dark, it seemed intimate, yet right, that they should hold hands and pour out their fears together.

They didn't say anything, just interlaced their fingers. Kneeled side by side. Shared warmth and communion. Laura's mind calmed. Her body strengthened. She breathed out an "Amen" and looked up at Seth as he did the same. She removed her hands from his and pulled the covers back up around Abby as she slept.

Seth stood and moved to the cabin door. The longer they stayed in the complete darkness, the more Laura was able to see. Seth's eyes must have been adjusting the same way because he did not seem to stumble. Laura watched him put his ear near the door, though he was definitely a shadowed figure instead of a clear person.

He moved to the shuttered windows and did the same

thing. Then he came back to where Laura was still sitting on the floor next to the bed. "I think they're gone. I don't think they realized we were here."

"But they are going to keep looking, aren't they? Mahoney really wants us dead."

Seth crouched down, sitting back on his heels so that he was about face level with her. "Yes. It sounded like they are going to keep looking until they find us."

Laura noted that he said *us*. And he was right. He was in this now. She had done this to her daughter and to him. She was the one who finally felt ready to go through all the boxes of her husband's things. She was the one who had found the key. And somehow she was the reason Mahoney knew about the key. She had to be. Laura didn't know how Mahoney knew. But she found the key and less than a week later he was here. This was all her fault. Even though she had just prayed, she still felt helpless. That feeling of not being able to do anything to change an awful situation rose up again.

Like when her parents died. Like when Malcolm, her second dad, died. Like when Josh died.

Laura put her hands down on the bed and felt Abby. Abby.

And she sniffled back a laugh. Yes, she had been in many horrible, helpless places before in her life. Circumstances that she couldn't change, no matter how hard she prayed and wished and tried. But God had brought her through. Had given her a new father. A daughter. Reasons to keep going and ways to smile and laugh even after she'd sworn she'd never do either again.

Seth came back and Laura looked at him from her place on the floor. "What do you think we should do?"

"We need to sleep. We won't be any good in the morning if we're both exhausted."

That was a good plan in theory. In reality, though, Laura knew she would never be able to sleep with a forest full of armed men looking for her. And her baby. "I won't be able to sleep."

Instead of arguing with her, Seth just nodded his head. Laura liked how he did not dismiss her concerns as trivial. "I agree. I'd be too afraid of waking up with a gun pointed at my face."

Laura cringed at his bluntness. She really didn't need an image to go along with her fear.

Seth looked at the door and nodded. "Here's the plan. We'll take turns keeping watch and sleeping. We have about seven hours until daylight. You go to sleep now. I'll wake you up in a few hours and then I'll sleep."

It wasn't a bad plan. "You'll really wake me up? I'm going to be mad if you let me sleep all night and you stay awake." Laura wanted to get out of this alive more than she wanted chivalry. She was going to need Seth alert and awake tomorrow.

His smile was rueful in an adorable kind of way that confused Laura. "I'll wake you up. My goal is to keep you and Abby safe, and I need to get at least a few hours shut-eye to make that happen."

"Okay." Laura climbed into the bed with Abby, pulling the small child to her and smiling when little arms and legs automatically curled around her even though Abby was sound asleep. Laura saw Seth move closer to the door and sit on the floor, leaning against the wall. He didn't light the lamp again.

She closed her eyes and tried to breathe slowly and evenly, but gave up after a couple of minutes. She stared at the black of the ceiling and tried to listen to the forest, the sounds that had been her lullaby since the day Malcolm Grant took her out of that hospital. She only heard her blood roaring in her ears.

"Seth?" she whispered, hoping he would hear her.

"Yeah?"

"What are we going to do in the morning?"

He didn't answer right away, and tears rose in Laura's throat.

"When it's light outside, we'll make a plan. It'll be a new day."

Oddly, that helped. A new day. Yes. Things often looked better in the morning. Laura closed her eyes and slept.

Seth woke up and had absolutely no idea where he was. That never happened. Whether in the desert, in his bed or camping in the forest, Seth always woke up and knew exactly where he was.

But not today. There was someone in the bed with him. He blinked and tried to figure out where in the world he was. And how he got there.

Then he remembered. His eyes popped open and he saw the warm body next to him. Abby. She was on top of the covers while he was under them, but he still felt heat coming from her small form. And she had a little hand thrown across his chest, little finger slightly curled.

He turned his head and saw Laura smiling at him. She waved hello. Still slightly off-balance, Seth just waved back.

It was daylight. From the brightness inside the cabin, it had to be well after sunrise. Laura was standing at the little table doing something with cans and plates. Seth sat up and slowly moved away from the little girl, doing his best to not wake her. He folded the covers over her as he got up.

He walked over to where Laura was preparing breakfast of some sort. His stomach growled, and he knew he'd be grateful for the food even if it was more cold pork and beans. He looked at his watch. Eight thirty. He'd woken Laura up around three in the morning, hoping to get at least a couple of hours of sleep before sunrise.

He'd overslept. On the run from too many bad guys to count, stuck in a hobbit fortress, a forest fire probably coming their way and he'd overslept. Unbelievable.

"Why didn't you wake me?" He tried not to sound too accusing, but he was definitely having a surreal morning and that carried through to his tone of voice. Laura stopped what she was doing to look at him.

"I'm sorry. You and Abby were sleeping so soundly. I watched the sunrise and just felt," she paused and looked away, a blush rising on her cheeks, "peaceful. This is a peaceful place. I wasn't in a hurry to wake you and have reality come back to slap me in the face."

Seth understood that. He did. And he certainly felt better after five hours sleep than he would have after two and a half. Besides, they were probably about as safe in this cabin as they could be, given the current circumstances. "I'm sorry, Laura. I get that. I didn't mean to sound like I was mad at you."

She smiled a grateful little smile that made his heart feel funny, then went back to creating breakfast out of hermit survivalist rations.

"How did Abby get in the bed?" This time his tone

was all curiosity. He'd woken Laura and prepared to bunk on the floor, leaving the bed for the little girl. Laura had refused. To the point of almost yelling at him even though they were trying to be as quiet as possible. She'd picked Abby up and said she was going over by the door to keep watch and to snuggle with her baby and he better get his butt in bed.

Seth almost laughed as he remembered. Laura Donovan was fierce and more than a little scary when she got going. Which shouldn't surprise him too much since their introduction involved her punching him in the face.

Abby had slept through the entire thing, as content to sleep in her mama's lap as she had been in the bed. Seth wondered about that kind of trust. He had known it once. The knowledge that you don't have to worry, because there was someone there to take care of you. He was overcome by the intense longing to make sure the sweet child stayed that way for as long as possible. He vowed internally that this little girl was going to come off this mountain with that innocence intact. Yes, she was.

He was also a little worried. Abby had slept for a good chunk of their journey so far. Seth knew it was because she was sick. Laura had told him it was just a cold, just a slight fever. But she still deserved to recover in a nice bed. In a nice house. Free of the threat of violence.

"I put her down in the bed around sunrise," Laura said. "I'm sorry if she bothered you. I thought it would be okay since she was on top of the covers. And there seemed to be enough room."

"It was fine. I didn't even know she was there until I

woke up." Seth wasn't upset about what Laura had done, but he was shocked. Yesterday, he was the enemy park ranger. He'd had to talk her into letting him carry Abby even though Laura was exhausted. But today? Today she put her precious daughter with him.

Seth felt something like pride in his chest at the development. It was ridiculous, but he took it as a sign that she was beginning to trust him. To see him as one of the good guys. It had been a long time since Seth had felt proud of his character, but he did today. Laura thought he was a good man.

Please, Lord, let that be true. The plea was sudden and startling. He hadn't consciously thought it, but it leaped out of his soul. A cry for help, still waiting for an answer. The blanket of shame and regret Seth carried with him, the one that covered him and smothered him, lessened for a moment. He could breathe. Feel hope.

He'd been physically hurt in a war and then had hurt his family in return. Only, he'd hurt them emotionally instead of physically, which was almost worse. Then he'd left them, wounding them even more. Seth had somehow maneuvered himself into a dark corner with no light and no way out. It felt familiar to the current situation.

And yet he was starting to find hope.

Seth realized Laura was staring at him, and his ears started to burn. Yeah, he probably looked like a fool. Or a crazy man. She was probably back to wondering whether he was a reliable friend or not. "Sorry. I was just thinking. Can I help you?"

"I'm not sure there's much to do. I found some protein bars, but they look a couple years old. They haven't expired yet but that doesn't mean much when it comes to survival food. I thought we could take them with us. I also found some canned fruit. It didn't have an expiration date, and it smells okay. So..." Laura's voice trailed off.

"So, we're having fruit surprise for breakfast and bricks for lunch," Seth finished for her.

Laura laughed, a glorious sound that belied the danger they were in. "Pretty much. I'm going to wake Abby." She took a couple of steps toward the bed. Stopped. "She'll have to go to the bathroom when she wakes up. Do you think it's safe to go outside?"

Abby wasn't the only one who needed a little privacy. "I'll go check it out. I'll be back." He picked up his gun and cracked the door. He heard Laura murmuring quietly and Abby's sleepy voice, but he focused his attention on the outside. He didn't see anything. He didn't hear anything. The birds were singing as though they were the only creatures out and about in the forest.

Seth opened the door only as wide as was needed for his body to slip through. He stepped outside and shut the door, taking time to cover it up as much as possible with foliage. If there was danger out here, he wanted Laura and Abby to be as concealed and safe as possible. Seth walked around the cabin. He saw the footprints from the men last night. They had been close. Too close. Looking at the indentations in the mud just feet away from where they'd been hiding made Seth freeze for a second. Then he forced his body to relax and kept surveilling the area.

They were safe. For now. Well, at least from the men. The smell of smoke was stronger than it had been yesterday.

Seth took care of his business and went back to the

cabin, making sure to obscure all of their footprints. He called out softly before opening the door. Laura had seemed both ready and able to fight him yesterday, and he didn't want to catch her by surprise. Laura and Abby were both standing in the middle of the room. Laura had the rifle in one hand, though it was pointed down at the ground. Her other hand was holding Abby's little wrist, as though to keep her from pulling away. He closed the door as soon as he was inside.

Abby saw him and, indeed, began pulling at her mama trying to get to him.

"I think it's okay for now. I didn't see or hear anyone."

At that, Laura let go of Abby and the little girl ran to him and hugged his legs. He bent down to pick her up. "Good morning, Miss Abby."

She put both of her palms on his cheek. Her hands were sticky and Seth wondered if she had been sampling the canned fruit. She smiled at him. "Potty!" She said the word proudly, like she was announcing some great accomplishment. Seth laughed and looked at Laura, who set the gun down and walked over to pull her daughter out of his arms.

"Yes, yes. We're going potty. But remember, we have to be quiet."

Seth went back to the door and opened it, peeking out again. It was still quiet. "I'll go out with you, just in case." They went outside and Laura took Abby into the woods a ways. They came back quickly, Laura looking over her shoulder as she walked.

"Was it okay? Did you see someone?" Seth hadn't, but someone could have snuck up on them. The forest was large and there were too many places to hide.

"No. No, we're fine. Sorry. I'm just feeling especially paranoid this morning."

Seth understood that. He remembered past missions where he'd started seeing the enemy in every shadow. He was feeling that way right now. And this forest had a whole lot of shadows.

SIX

Back inside with the cabin door shut and camouflaged yet again, they ate the breakfast Laura had prepared. Well, the food she found. The mood was definitely lighter than it had been through the night, but Laura was now thinking about the day ahead. She wasn't hungry anymore.

"Seth?" He stopped chewing and looked at her. "What are we going to do? I thought about it last night after I woke up, and our options are all horrible. And limited."

"I thought about it, too. It was all I could think about, really."

"And?"

"And? Well, I'm sure headquarters is missing me by now. I bet they're looking. At least, I hope so. We can either stay here and wait for help to find us or we can try to go through the forest and get to safety."

"Go through the forest? You mean the forest fire, right?" Laura sounded scared to her own ears. Too scared.

"Ideally we go up until we can go around the fire," he

said. "Or we hope that they get the fire put out and come up to see if anyone needs help. But I just don't know."

Well, he summed that up. The options sounded limited and terrible, even though he was a law enforcement officer of sorts and even though it was daylight and even though her daughter was smiling and talking happily to herself. And even though *everything*—the options were still options in name only. "So what should we do?"

"I don't like sitting here. For one, we'd have to be still and quiet. And we're well hidden, but there is always a chance they could find us. Then we'd really be trapped. Plus, there's the fire."

Laura breathed in deeply, considering his words. He was…not wrong. Keeping Abby pinned up inside, spending every night terrified to move, waiting on help to find them? Laura thought she would lose her mind the first day, especially when she knew those circumstances were going to stretch out into the unforeseeable future.

Seth was watching her, waiting patiently. She liked that he let her process her thoughts and didn't demand instant answers. "I think waiting here is the worst of the two options."

Seth nodded. "I agree. Every way I thought it through, trying to get down the mountain made the most sense. But this is all going to be on you, and I'm sorry about that."

"What?"

"You know these woods. You know this mountain. I only know the public parts, but you know this part."

He was right. Laura remembered how many times her dad had made her walk their mountain. Map it. Learn it. Come to know it on an almost instinctual level where each tree and rock and call of bird was distinct.

She'd hated it. Complained endlessly about it. Been thankful when she had left this mountain and never had to do it again.

And now, here she was, sitting in her dad's shelter and thanking God and her father for all those lessons. Seth was right, she did know the mountain. More important, she knew every way off it. She just needed some information.

"What do you know about the fire?"

"It's on the east side of the mountain. It's wide. Moving slowly up."

Seth gave her all the information she needed because he knew exactly what she was asking. If she had to go through this, at least it was with a park ranger. A man who knew forests and fires.

Laura choked on air as she thought about how thankful she was that she had a park ranger here to help her. Her dad might actually be rolling over in his grave right now. Or, not. Malcolm Grant had understood so much more about the world than Laura had ever given him credit for. He would understand this situation with the same practicality that had helped him survive the Vietnam War and a hostile return to his country.

"We need to get off the east side, then."

"Yeah. You know about the breaks?"

"Oh, yeah. The mountain at its finest when it comes to protecting its own." The mountain was geographically set up so that a fire on one side would not spread laterally around it. There was a large river going down one side and a wall of barren rock cliffs on the other. Basically, the mountain was divided into two halves and a fire on one side would not spread to the other unless it came over the top. That had saved homes and people more than once.

"The fire looked like it was going to spread laterally as far as the breaks and then move up."

"So we can't go down. We can try to cross the river. Or the cliffs. Or we can go up and over, hopefully ahead of the fire."

Seth's eyes were serious, all sense of amusement and joviality completely gone. "That's pretty much the conclusion I came to, too. This is where I need your expertise. Which option is the best?"

Laura really hated that she was the one with the information to make this decision. She was terrified of choosing wrong. "Those men are probably trapped by now, too. Don't you think?"

"They have a helicopter, but they still need to hurry. The fire is spreading, and a helicopter is very noticeable up here, especially with all the firefighters and emergency personnel activated."

"Okay. So that means they need to find us fast and then try to get off, as well."

"That would explain why their boss had them search all night. He must know they are up against a ticking clock."

A burning clock, really, but Laura didn't want to make that distinction. "The cliffs are out. I've tried climbing them a couple of times before, and it was nearly impossible," she said. "And that was with climbing and safety equipment."

"Okay." Seth didn't question her assessment. "So the river, or up and over?"

She wanted to say neither. "I really don't like the

idea of the river. It's wide and usually has a nasty pull to it. Plus, it's raging right now."

"It is high. I saw it a couple days ago, and I'm not sure I've seen it that full," he said. "I don't suppose your dad left a raft or boat hiding somewhere, did he?"

Laura's lips quirked. "Not that I know of. I mean, he probably wouldn't have told me anyway for fear I'd go on a joyride."

Seth smiled slightly, too. Laura liked it. "So you think over is the best way?"

Laura hated the weight of this decision. "Maybe. I mean, yes. I do. Except we have those men looking for us, and I bet they are going to be picking the up-and-over route, too. It's the easiest choice, for whatever that's worth, and it's predictable that we'd head that way."

"I agree with you there, too." Seth sighed, long and deep. It was a weary sound. Laura felt a similar drag and they hadn't even started yet.

"I think we should head toward the river but plan to go up," she said. "We'll do the up-and-over path, but if we need to try to cross the river we'll be close enough to attempt it."

"You can do that? Lead us over the mountain, but also close enough to the river to use it as a Plan B?"

Laura thought about his question. There were three lives on the line. This was not the time for false bravado and ego. It was the time to assess. And be honest. "Yeah. I can. It'll be a little zigzaggy, because the river isn't straight. But we should have good cover. Yes. I can do it."

Seth didn't question her more. He nodded his acceptance and stood. "All right. Then we should start out.

The faster we get going, the faster we'll reach safety. Do you know if there are any bags or packs in here?"

Thankful to do something other than sit and worry, Laura stood. "Yes, we'll be able to take enough supplies with us to last the trip." If they made it, that was.

If it weren't for the armed men and the forest fire, this would have been a beautiful walk through the forest. Seth had always liked the woods and had spent much of his childhood exploring them with his family. When he'd been in Afghanistan, he'd almost craved them. Seth had walked out of that rehab center and demanded his dad take him to the forest. Any forest. While his dad waited in the car in the parking lot, Seth had limped into the cluster of trees and just breathed. It was the first time he'd felt like he could breathe since the IED had gone off. The forest in his home state of Oregon was every bit as pretty as the one they were currently walking through.

Even though he'd been released from rehab, Seth still wasn't able to live on his own. His injuries, both physical and mental, required almost constant care. Seth's pride hated being dependent on his family for everything. So, he lashed out at them. Yelled at them, called them names, told them that nothing they did for him was right or good enough. He had hurt the ones who loved him.

Then, he'd been ashamed. So very ashamed of the man he was to them. The man he had become. Of the months abusing them that he could never take back. When Seth had realized how badly he'd failed his family, he could not stay there with them anymore, so he had fled. To the woods.

And he had been in the woods ever since, it seemed. Sometimes they soothed him. Healed him. Helped him understand where he had gone wrong.

But today's trek wasn't a stroll with God and His beauty. Laura was busy navigating their course. Abby was doing her part by playing the quiet game with admirable determination. And Seth needed to be alert for the men hunting them down. He had to stop reminiscing and start focusing or he would add even more regrets to his list. Regrets so big that the list itself might just disintegrate.

They were moving fairly quietly, and Laura was doing a great job of keeping them out of exposed or open spaces. She was carrying Abby for now, though Seth intended to insist on carrying her later. He already had an argument prepared about how they were in this together, a team.

As two people comfortable in the outdoors, they were managing to move without leaving too much of a trace. There were no broken branches. Since they were hiking through the trees, the ground was covered with a thick layer of pine needles and leaves. Seth looked behind them every once in a while to make sure they weren't leaving obvious tracks.

Seth's stomach churned as he looked more closely. Though adept in the forest, there were still signs of their passing. Three people could not move with any semblance of speed without leaving some trace of their route. But Seth thought that speed was more important than erasing their tracks. Especially since he didn't know where those men were in their search pattern. There was a very real possibility that some of the men were ahead and that he and Laura would walk right into them.

A very real possibility that Seth wasn't going to harp on. Every mission had risks. All you could do was be aware. They were. Laura had apologized earlier for all the zigging and zagging, but she said she wanted to be close to the river and stay in the cover of the trees. She had grasped the possibility of the men being in front of them instead of behind them without Seth ever having to tell her.

Laura Donovan was many things. Stupid was not one of them. No. Watching her walk confidently in these woods, barely making sound, charting a course based on trees and trees and some more trees was the opposite of stupid. It was amazing. Seth was good in the woods. He was considered a skilled tracker. He was the one who went in to find lost hikers. And yet, these woods intimidated even him. They didn't have a map. They didn't even have a compass. They just had Laura.

Of course, they were on Old Man Grant's land still, and no one had ever been here before. At least, no one wearing a park ranger uniform. Seth was walking blind right now, in more ways than one.

When Laura suddenly stopped, Seth looked around in a quick three-sixty. He closed the distance between them and made sure to keep his voice low. "What is it? What's wrong?"

Laura shifted Abby in her arms and turned to look at him. "Nothing. I mean, I don't see or hear anyone. I just don't know where to go from here."

"You're lost?" Seth was more incredulous than upset. Laura moved like she was a part of this land.

"No. I know where we are. We're just out of cover."

Seth looked ahead and saw plenty of trees. "What do you mean?"

"The river is going to turn sharply up here. By almost half a mile. The tree cover doesn't turn. It's a beautiful stretch of open ground that seemed almost magical to me when I was young. It's where my dad would take me to fly a kite."

Seth smiled at the image of Laura as a child flying a kite on this mountain. Then his smile faded as the rest of the picture came into his mind. Laura with a mountain man. And that was it. Had she been happy trapped up here with only a grown man?

"Why do you look sad?" Laura's voice was curious, not accusing.

"I was just picturing you up here and thinking that it must have been very lonely."

"It was just me and my dad. And it was a great childhood." She sounded defensive. That wasn't what he wanted.

"I'm sorry, Laura. I'm really sorry. I don't know why my head is so thick, but I promise I'm working on it. Forgive me?"

Some of the warmth came back, though Seth could feel the distance she was placing between them. "Yeah. I'm sorry. I'm a little sensitive about my dad."

Seth could understand that. Family was family. And Malcolm Grant could not have been all bad if he raised a woman like Laura. Laura looked out ahead of her, and Seth wished he knew the layout of this part of the mountain. He hated that she had all the responsibility for this decision. She shouldn't have to be the only one weighing the risks and fearing making the wrong choice.

"A lot of my defensiveness is because I used to agree

with you." She was still looking away, and all Seth could see was Laura's back and Abby's sweet face, looking drowsy and flushed as she rested her head on Laura's shoulder. "My parents died when I was seven. Malcolm Grant was biologically my uncle." Seth felt his eyes widen and was glad Laura wasn't looking at him. For all the gossip about Crazy Old Man Grant, no one ever talked about the fact that Laura was not his biological daughter. "And Malcolm came to get me. I was hurt and scared and alone. I would have gone into foster care without him. You've heard about him—the last thing he wanted was a child. But he came and got me anyway."

Seth heard her sniffle and curled his hands into loose fists to keep from touching her. Comforting her. "He came and he did his very best. And you know what? It was good enough. More than good enough. I'm a functional, well-loved adult. The homeschooling education he gave me helped me excel. I was a well-loved child. But even though I loved him, and I did, I could not wait to leave this mountain. I just wanted to be normal. He was my teacher and my father and all I could think about was how I wanted more."

Her voice was thick with regret, a tone Seth recognized. One that tugged at him and made his own throat swell with longing for a chance to have done things differently. She sniffed one last time and Seth watched her straighten her shoulders and stand a little taller. Well, taller for her. She turned and looked at him then.

"Sorry. I'm done."

Seth started to tell her she never needed to apologize for her feelings but she shook her head, holding her hand up in a stop gesture. "I can't anymore, Seth. Let's just decide which way we're going."

Seth actually clenched his jaw shut for an instant to keep quiet. He was in no position to insist that anyone talk about their past or regrets. And she wasn't wrong. They needed to keep moving. "I hate to say this again, Laura, but it's your call. I trust you. Which direction do you feel better about taking Abby in? The meadow closer to the river or the trees farther away?"

She looked in two different directions, back and forth. Her hand was rubbing circles on Abby's back again. Slow, repetitive movements that were almost calming to watch. After a very long minute, Laura took a deep breath and pointed to the trees. "I feel better about the trees. If we need to, we can make a run for the river. But, like I said before, crossing the river is going to be hard. The trees at least give us a chance to hide."

That assessment was fair enough. "Okay. I agree. Let's head to the trees."

Laura took a step forward, and Seth reached out to touch her arm. He tried to ignore how nice it felt to make contact with her warm skin. Instead, he gestured to Abby. "You've been carrying her for a long time. Please give me a turn?"

There was no long, tense wait like there had been the first time he'd asked to carry her daughter. Instead, she gestured to his shoulder. "Okay. But only if you let me carry the bigger pack."

Seth wanted to say no. He really wanted to say no. But he'd been raised by a fierce mama and had three older sisters. Yeah, he knew exactly where a *no* would land him in this situation. Instead of answering, he just took off the pack and set it on the ground, reached out his arms and gathered the still-dozing little girl into his arms.

He was shocked again at how light she was. How her little arms wrapped around his neck. How her face nuzzled his shoulder without the slightest care in the world. Abby had abandoned the quiet game for a nap, and she seemed more than happy to use Seth as her mattress.

Seth had nieces and nephews. Several. He'd been deployed when they were born. Then, later, he'd been too broken to enjoy them. What did they look like now? Maybe he even had another one. One who would never know him. That was a small distinction since none of them really knew their uncle Seth.

Abby made a murmuring noise and shifted her head, and Seth realized he had increased the pressure he was using to hold her. He forced himself to relax. This wasn't the time. It was never the time to go down that road.

Laura shouldered the pack and started walking. She stopped after a few feet, bent over to pick up a large branch and began to use it as a walking stick.

"Have you walked over the mountain before? I mean all the way?"

Laura looked surprised at his question. "Yeah. Several times. It's been a few years, but I still remember." She gave him a goofy grin. Seth really liked that teasing look on her face. "If I'd been able to get school credit for it, I would have a PhD in walking around this mountain."

"All right, then, Doctor Donovan, do you have any idea how long it might take us to go over? To get to the nearest house or ranger station on the other side?"

"It's about fifteen miles until we start to reach civilization on the other side. I'm not exactly sure what we'll find, though, since Dad just stopped us at a certain point. But if he wanted to stop, that had to mean there were people ahead. And people means help."

Seth looked at his watch and considered the distance they had already traveled that day. "If we keep our current pace and don't run into any, um, troubles, it should take us about fifteen hours."

Laura sighed. "I agree. At least fifteen hours. This is going to be one of the longest days. Ever. And I say that as a woman who was in labor for thirty-one hours."

"Do you think we can walk straight through? It'll be dark before we get over the mountain. Do you think we can walk in the dark or should we camp out somewhere?"

"I think we'll probably need to camp, but can we re-evaluate as we get closer?"

"Hey, I'm not in a hurry. It's not like we have reservations or a check-in time to meet."

Laura bit her lip, eyes wide. "The fire?"

Oh, how he wished he had a sure answer to that question. "I don't know. But I think I'd rather hide and rest while it's dark and risk it. At least until the smoke becomes thicker or we see flames."

Their voices were low, hushed. It was probably wiser to be completely silent, but Seth couldn't make himself stop the conversation. He enjoyed talking to Laura. He wanted to know about her.

"Seth?"

"Yeah?"

"What's the plan after we get to safety?"

Seth liked that she was assuming they would make it. Belief in a mission could go a really long way. But she asked a good question. A hard question.

"I don't know, Laura. We need to go to the police. I'm

sure they'll protect you. They'll try to catch this guy. But with a forest fire, all resources will be stretched to the limit. Thackery is the closest real town, but it's still pretty small. I just don't know how much they'll be able to do, at least in the immediate future."

Laura didn't argue with him, and that said too much. She knew how small the police force was. And she also had a long history of the police being the enemy.

"Laura, I know I asked you before. But things were crazy then." His lips twitched. "Well, crazier than now. Do you have any idea what's in that safe-deposit box?"

"No." Her voice was a horrible cross between desperate and pleading. "I told you the truth. After Josh died, I moved home. I just boxed up his belongings and brought them with me. But I couldn't go through them."

"But you did eventually?"

"Last week. It's been eighteen months and I finally felt like it was time to fully move on. Deal with the past. I found the key inside a box Josh kept under the dresser. I have no idea what bank it goes to or what is inside."

"Mahoney didn't mention how he knew Josh? Or how he knew you had found the key? It can't be a coincidence that he showed up so soon after you found it. How did he know?"

"I don't know," Laura said. "It's all crazy. Impossible." She bit her lip, looking almost ill. "I keep thinking he must have been watching me somehow. But inside the cabin? Inside my home? That's the place I've always been safest. I just don't know."

"It still doesn't make sense, Laura. Even if they were watching you, they'd have to be really close to see a solitary key. That just seems like too much of a stretch."

Laura gasped. "I called Josh's old firm and asked them if they knew anything about a safe-deposit box."

"You did?"

"After I found the key, I went to town for supplies. I used the cell signal down there to call Josh's old firm to see if they knew about the key. Could Mahoney have been listening to my calls?"

"That sounds more likely than them visually seeing you find a key," Seth said. "What did they say?"

"They said no."

Seth had more questions. But he couldn't think of how to ask them without insinuating Josh had done something wrong—something to bring all this violence to his wife and child.

So he said nothing.

They kept on walking.

SEVEN

Laura was going to get three people killed, including herself, and she would never know why. Even though she was in excellent shape, she was having trouble keeping her breathing even as they walked up the mountain. The air kept catching in her lungs, and she felt like no matter how deep she sucked it in it just wasn't reaching her organs. Laura had never come close to drowning, but this had to be what it felt like. It just had to be.

Laura began moving them away from the river, into where the trees were thicker. The noise was louder in here, too. Or at least it should be. There should be birds and insects and squirrels and the noises from all the animals who lived in these wild woods. But all Laura could hear was her heart pounding.

Her despair was a train, roaring through and blowing its horn. The train really ought to slow down, but it wouldn't. It just gained speed and shot off steam and plowed through whatever might be on the tracks.

She stopped walking. She couldn't move another foot. Not right now.

"Laura?" Seth was there, with Abby, one of his warm hands on her shoulder.

She looked at the ground, afraid to meet his eyes. "Josh did this. Mahoney knew Josh. Knew about the key. Somehow the man I loved did something that is going to get us all killed."

Laura hated the tears running down her face. She wiped them off, trying not to sniffle too loudly. "I'm sorry," she said. "We don't have time for this. I'm sorry." Laura felt calmer just having her fears out in the open. "Okay. I'm done now."

Laura started walking again, away from Seth's warm hand.

"Will you tell me about your husband?" He was walking behind her again.

Laura smiled as a wave of bittersweet memories came over her. She found that she wanted to tell Seth about Josh. She had done a lot of healing in the last few months. "Sure. I left the mountain when I was eighteen. I went to college in Denver and met Josh my freshman year."

Laura flushed, feeling self-conscious at this next part. It made her sound naive. Too simple. But it was the truth, and Laura treasured the way it had all just seemed to happen. "He was the first friend I made. He was my first boyfriend. He proposed our junior year and we married the summer after we graduated. We had Abby two years later. He died eighteen months ago."

Laura's legs were moving on autopilot at this point. Her body was walking through the trees on her mountain but her mind was back in Denver. Back in that time of her life when things spiraled out of control. When nothing she did could make anything better. Her husband had been killed in a freak accident. Her daughter would never know her father, all because Josh was in the wrong place at the wrong time. That was when Laura had realized her dad was right and the outside world was not for people like them.

"My dad came off the mountain to get me. Again. He hadn't left since my parents died, except to buy supplies in town. When I called him, I thought I'd have to leave a message. Wait until he went to town and had a signal. But he was in town when I called." Laura smiled remembering her shock at hearing her dad's voice over the line. "When I told him that Josh was dead he said he was on his way. To hold on because he was coming. And, you know what, he did. He was there before it got dark, and I didn't have to face a night alone. He held me and told me he loved me and that everything would be okay."

Laura was jerked back into the present when Seth put his hand back on her shoulder. Suddenly, she wasn't in that awful time. No, she was on her mountain. She could hear the birds and smell the pine. And the faint scent of smoke from the fire that was coming up to get them.

"I'm sorry, Laura. You were right about Malcolm being a good man." It was the first time Seth had not called her dad Old Man Grant. "He sounds like a very, very good man. One who was misunderstood."

"He was. He was so gentle, Seth. And hurt. He was just a hurt man doing his very best. Trying so hard."

Seth nodded. "Tell me more about Josh?"

"He was a good man, too. He was. I know it sounds like I married the first man who gave me the time of day, but it wasn't like that. He took the time to get to know my dad. He came up to the mountain and appreciated the world my father had made. He understood that I was the product of how I was raised, and he never tried to change me. When I just wanted to stay home, not socialize, he stayed right home with me. Josh never made me feel weird. Or deficient."

There was a silence and then Seth's voice sounded almost choked. "I'm really glad you found a man like that." Laura wondered what he was feeling to make his tone sound like that. They walked for a bit, the quiet almost soothing after the rawness of her words.

Seth spoke again, his tone causal. "What did you two do for careers after college?"

"Josh was an accountant. He worked at a big firm in Denver. I majored in biology. I worked in a lab until I got pregnant with Abby, and then I stayed home."

"An accountant? Did he ever talk about his clients?"

Laura smiled. "He tried a couple of times, but it was honestly the most boring stuff I'd ever heard. And I say that as a woman who spent years studying single-cell organisms. It wasn't at all exciting or dangerous."

They walked in silence a bit more. Then Seth's voice was hesitant. Timid, almost. "Laura?"

She already knew she wasn't going to like this question. Laura felt the pieces of that brick protein bar she had eaten make themselves known in her stomach. "Yeah?"

"How did Josh die?"

The brick pieces swirled and then sank. Hard. "He was mugged. From what the police said, someone shot him while he was walking from his office to his car in the parking garage. His watch and wallet were stolen." She stopped and swallowed, slow and deliberate, trying desperately to calm the storm in her belly. "And his wedding ring. His wedding ring was also stolen."

"I'm sorry, Laura. I'm really, really sorry."

She had heard that a lot in the days after Josh died. From his coworkers and his friends. From her old co-workers. But from Seth it seemed genuine. And it actually helped a little. "Thank you."

"Thanks for telling me." He sounded sincere. Laura knew he was. It was nice.

Laura felt ready to leave the past behind and work on the right now. Plus, she needed to focus all her attention on her surroundings. If they were walking into a trap, or a fire, Laura wanted as much notice as possible. Her dad had always stressed the importance of focusing on the task at hand. And she had a major one right now.

She wasn't going to let anyone down.

"I know we're not close to the top," Seth said, "but I can definitely tell we're making progress. The ground is a lot steeper here. I feel like we're walking up a ramp."

Laura appreciated the change of subject. The lifting of mood. She was more than happy to play along with the subject change. Laura smiled at his observation. "Yeah, it's going to stay this steep until we get to the top." She had a sudden mental image of what they must look like, the three of them climbing up a mountain. Fleeing the bad guys. She started to giggle as her mind took the picture and added to it.

"Um, Laura, what's so funny?" He sounded almost scared, like he was afraid she had crossed that thin line between sane and not so much.

"Nothing. I just suddenly realized we probably look a lot like the ending of *The Sound of Music*. You know, fleeing through the mountains?"

Laura turned to look at Seth and saw that he was

also smiling. "Huh. Well, since that movie ended happily, I think I like the comparison. Don't ask me to sing, though."

Seth was smiling and playing along in their conversation about musicals and singing. Abby was still sleeping, and his arms were relaxed as they held her.

Sucking in a deep breath of air, he froze. Smoke. He was definitely smelling smoke stronger than before. He looked up, but could only see blue sky through the tree branches. Laura had done a great job of keeping them in the thicker parts of the mountain, so Seth couldn't see all around. He couldn't even tell which direction the smoke was coming from. He bent down and picked up a dry brown leaf. Letting it drop from above his head, he noted the direction it went as it fell to the ground.

Laura watched him, her expression some kind of grim understanding. It did not do anything to appease the dread building. "You smell it, too, huh?" She sounded like she knew the answer but dreaded hearing it anyway.

"The smoke? Oh, yeah. How long have you been picking it up?"

Laura shrugged. "Not long. I would get the occasional whiff here and there, but the strong hit of smoke didn't start until the last few minutes."

She looked at the ground where his leaf had fallen to blend in with all the others. "The wind is blowing the wrong direction."

He knew what she meant. If the wind was blowing the scent of smoke in, then it was wafting away from the fire, which should be behind them. Straight behind them as they moved up. But the leaf had blown to the side. From where the wall of rock cliff was. "Yeah. That can mean a couple of things."

Seth might not know this mountain like Laura did, but he knew about fires and how they spread. Traveled. Changed and charged and consumed. Destroyed. Killed. "One. Instead of moving up the mountain evenly, the fire has moved up a lot faster on the side bordered by the rock wall."

"And so it is almost racing us up the mountain. And winning."

Yeah, she got it, all right. "Two. There's more than one fire."

Laura's brown eyes darkened, and Seth knew that she understood him. Her voice was almost toneless when she spoke. "You think those psychos set a fire to try to smoke us out. Or burn us up."

"I know it sounds crazy, but it's actually pretty smart. With the big blaze going, their fire would not be noticeable. People will just think it's part of the original blaze. Plus, it's an efficient way to cover a large search area."

"And by cover, you mean it's a good way to force us out of hiding so they can kill us." Her voice wasn't toneless now.

"Hey, Laura, it's okay. It's going to be okay." Abby stirred as Seth moved closer to her mother, but he didn't stop. Holding the child with one arm, he used the other to reach out and pull Laura into a hug. She came easily, putting her arms around him, sandwiching Abby in the middle. Laura buried her face in Abby's hair, and Seth heard her breathe in deeply. Shakily. Abby's eyes opened. She moved her arms from around Seth's neck and turned to wrap them around her mom.

Laura turned the group hug into her holding Abby.

Once she had her daughter, Laura stepped away. Not far, but Seth could no longer feel her body heat. And he no longer had that sweet child against his chest. He found he missed both very much.

Abby was looking at Laura and Laura was murmuring something into Abby's ear. It sounded motherly and warm. Reassuring. Whatever fears Laura had, she set them aside for her daughter. She calmed her child and made her feel safe. Seth wished he had the ability to do that for Laura.

Abby kissed Laura's cheek and said something to her mom. Smiling, Laura kissed the girl back and then set her down on her feet, keeping hold of her hand. "Abby says she wants to walk for a while."

Seth looked at the ground, concerned. Laura smiled, seeming to read his mind. "She'll be fine. She's more than used to exploring the mountain with me."

Seth couldn't stop his smile. "Are you going to lead the way, Miss Abigail?" Seth kept his voice light and teasing, not wanting to undo any of the work that Laura had just done.

"Shhhh. Quiet game." She tried to whisper. Tried, because it was the loudest whisper Seth had ever heard. It made him smile, for real.

Laura's smile looked less real and more worried. The fire. "What should we do, Seth?"

"We know for sure the fire is behind us. It's also coming from the direction of the rock wall. That means the river is still our best Plan B. I say we keep going up the mountain, but maybe stay just a little closer to the river. Just in case."

Laura nodded and started walking. Seth noted that she headed more in the direction of the edge of the trees than she had been before. She was slowly angling them closer to the river. That thing was a beast the last time Seth had seen it. Just a couple of weeks ago. But if it came down to men with guns, a blazing inferno or that river, well, he picked the river.

He really hoped it did not come down to those choices.

Abby was keeping pace with her mom really well. And she wasn't making much noise at all. It seemed all the women in Malcolm Grant's family knew how to handle themselves out in nature. That made sense. For all she might have disliked her dad's hermit ways, Laura had proven to be very much his daughter. She was surely teaching her own daughter the same.

And Seth was beginning to understand the quiet dignity they all had as a result of this way of life.

They were at the edge of the tree line now. Still under cover, but Seth could see the open meadow Laura had talked about. It was beautiful. He couldn't see the river, or hear it, but he felt reassured knowing that it was there. Just across the open ground.

Just like God is. His heart was hit with the conviction and he missed a step. Laura turned to look at him, and he waved her on. Just as he had God. How many times had Seth assumed that God was not here simply because he could not see Him? Or hear Him.

Seth had been raised in the church. His parents had taught him better. Had shown him better. And still, he had forgotten too many times to count.

But Seth could feel Him now. Seth had come up this mountain, been shot at and was currently trapped by man and nature. If there was ever a time that Seth should have felt completely alone, it was now. But he didn't. He could feel the Lord walking with him. He just knew he, Laura and Abby were not alone in this thing. They just weren't.

The sun was out and shining, and Seth had to squint his eyes. The inner forest had been dark, even though it was the middle of the day. Coming to open ground was shocking in its brightness. His eyes adjusted, and Seth was able to pick up some of the finer details. The small plants growing in the open clearing were blowing slightly in the breeze. The same breeze that was sending one or more fires right at them. There was a sprinkling of color from the scattered flowers that were starting to bloom. The sun was reflecting off—

Seth didn't think, he just reached out and grabbed Laura's arm, the one that was holding Abby's hand. "We have to hide. Now. Quietly."

Laura did not waste time looking around, though Seth knew she must have wanted to see what was making him act like this. Instead, she picked up Abby and put a finger over Abby's lips. Her face was so stern that even Seth felt the urge to shush and stay shushed.

Laura began to walk deeper into the forest, quickly but quietly. Seth followed, turning frequently to look behind him. The trees were enveloping them and any view of that open area and light was gone. But Seth wasn't hiding from grass and light.

Laura stopped and looked at the trees, and Seth wondered yet again how she was able to know where she was based simply off of a bunch of trees. He was a skilled forester and they all looked the same to him. He could navigate using a compass. Rivers. The stars. But he did not see how one could navigate in a forest full of identical trees.

She turned sharply and it felt like she was backtracking a bit. Seth didn't care, so long as she was taking them somewhere safe. Somewhere hidden. Or at least somewhere that was not here. Seth turned and saw the shine. Again. Except it wasn't a shine. It was a reflection. Sun on something metal. Something that didn't grow on this mountain. And it was heading into the forest. With them.

Someone with a gun was coming their way.

EIGHT

Hide first, figure out what's going on second. Shelter. Then questions. Shelter. Shelter. Laura kept repeating the words in her head, because she really wanted to stop and figure out what they were running from. And how far behind them it was. And if it was going to catch them.

Seth had said *hide* and they had taken off. But she didn't know what they were hiding from. Probably not the fire since you didn't normally hide from fires. That meant men with guns.

Laura had Abby clutched to her chest and was moving as fast as possible without sounding like a woman running through the forest. Thankfully, Abby had picked up on the serious change in mood and was being quiet. When this was over, she was going to let Abby scream and play and giggle for a month solid. While on a sugar high. She certainly deserved it after being so good the last couple of days.

Laura's legs moved from memory, heading to a place she hadn't seen in years. *Please let it still be there. Please.* It should still be there. Her dad wouldn't have destroyed it, but nature itself certainly could have.

Laura turned to make sure Seth was still with her. He was. Of course he was. His presence was reassuring. The look of his face, however, was not. He still seemed worried. Almost afraid. And his gun was in hand, ready to fire. Laura moved a little faster, deciding that making some extra sound would be worth it if she could take that expression off Seth's face. Or at least figure out what it meant.

Laura looked up ahead and almost sobbed out her relief. It was still there. She turned to Seth, only to find he was closer than ever. She naturally slowed as she turned and he stepped up and held her arm. He was urging her forward. Taking the hint without any trouble at all, Laura decided to just get into the cave and explain it to him later.

She went toward the grouping of large rocks covered in moss and vines. The foliage looked tight, grown thick. Laura couldn't see the entrance but it had to be there.

Laura put Abby in Seth's arms, barely slowing down at all. He took her immediately, wrapping both arms around her. He also did not break stride.

Laura thrust her hands right into the overgrowth, pushing in up to her elbows until she felt smooth rocks underneath. She probed in the area where the cave should be. And found it. Bending down, she quickly ripped a seam at the bottom and along one side, creating a kind of flap door. Thankfully, the plant life was not thick enough that she needed to take precious time cutting it with her knife.

She lifted it as little as possible and crawled in. *Oh, God, I'm just not sure I can deal with snakes right now. Or bears. Or spiders. Or anything breathing and mov-*

ing, really. If You could just make this cave empty of the creepy-crawlies or things that want to eat us, I would really, really appreciate it.

Laura didn't get her flashlight on before Seth crawled in after her. He still held Abby tight, but he smoothed down the flap she had ripped as much as possible. If the person on the outside wasn't looking, he wouldn't even realize there was a cavern. Hopefully.

Laura turned on the light and slowly scanned the area. It was exactly as she remembered. The rocks were clustered together, almost in a U shape. There was a larger slab of rock on top. She'd always called it a cave, but it wasn't technically. That was just the closest description that fit the enclosure. The vines helped to seal it up and cement the effect of being in a cave.

It was tight for three people, especially since two were adults. But they fit. It was dry. And Laura did not see any animals or creepy-crawlies. Or slitheries. *Thank You, God.*

Seth held out Abby and Laura took her. She curved herself against the back wall of the space, sitting with her legs crossed and cradling Abby on her lap. She leaned down and pressed a kiss in the curve of Abby's neck while holding a finger to her lips. Abby hadn't made a sound, but Laura wanted to remind her to be quiet.

Laura moved her finger and Abby squeezed Duckie in her little arms. Her thumb was in her mouth. Laura had been working on breaking that habit, but she wasn't about to deny her girl any measure of comfort right now.

Seth was crouched down, balanced on the balls of his feet. He had his gun out again. Laura had not seen him draw it—it certainly wasn't in his hand when he passed Abby back to her. He had to have put it away to take Abby and then immediately pulled it out again. Because the danger was still real and right on top of them.

His hands went over the seams of the flap Laura had made, securing it again. To Laura's eyes, it looked as good as possible. They were very well hidden. If she could just quiet down her breathing a bit, they should not be findable.

Seth reached for the flashlight, turning it off. There was enough light to see, but barely. Hopefully, the vines were thick enough to conceal them. Please, let them be thick enough.

Laura swallowed hard and tried to even the rise and fall of her chest. It felt tight, like she needed to gasp for air. She fought the urge. She was fine. Her daughter was fine. Slowly the thundering in her ears quieted down and she didn't feel like she was huffing and puffing anymore.

Seth was still positioned in front of the flap with his back to Laura and Abby. His body was big and broad, completely filling the entryway. If someone did open that flap, they would only see Seth. And his gun.

Laura still had no clue what they had run from. What they were hiding from. But it had to be one of the armed men. The ones who were hunting them down. Why else would he have acted like that? If it had been the fire or an animal or pretty much anything besides a person, Seth would have talked to her while they fled. No, fleeing in silence had to mean fleeing from a man who wanted to kill them. Or men.

Seth was just staring at the wall of plants. Laura wanted to ask him if he saw anything. Or heard anything. Had they been quick enough? Was the man just coincidentally coming this way or was he actively pursuing them? Was it a man or men? And how many?

The questions flew through Laura's mind faster than she could process them. She had the overwhelming urge to run. To pick up Abby and just run and run and run.

They were going to die. Laura's fight-or-flight response was fully engaged, and the flight response was definitely winning out. Laura did not want to be here anymore.

They were going to die.

No. This was not truth. This was panic and despair. Laura closed her eyes and buried her nose back in Abby's hair, smelling her sweetness. Abby was warm in her lap. Soft. Warm. Alive. Her greatest gift from God. Laura started counting her blessings. Going through all the ways God had been with her. Reminding herself that He was faithful and steadfast. He did not give her a spirit of fear.

This was okay. This was going to be okay. She was a capable woman. She was Malcolm Grant's daughter. She could and would survive what this world threw at her. This was her mountain, her home. She would be safe here.

Laura opened her eyes and saw Seth's back again. She wasn't alone. He was here. He was strong and he was armed and he would not let anything happen to them.

Laura was overcome by the strength of her gratitude. After Josh had died, Laura had come back to the mountain. To be alone. She had decided that her dad was right and being alone was best. The world and its people was not for her. Right now, though, Laura was beyond glad that she wasn't alone. That she had Seth.

Whatever might happen, it wasn't just her and Abby against the world.

Laura's feelings for Seth were all caught up in the trauma of the past days and the relief that she was not by herself. He was a ranger. She was a widow with a small child. But Seth was here and Laura was extremely happy.

Laura saw Seth's back tense, his arms raising the gun and aiming it at the door. She murmured a reminder to Abby to hush and held her close. And waited.

Then Laura heard it. The leaves were crunching. Loudly. There was the sound of men talking. And the thump of feet on the ground. At first Laura thought she was imagining it, that she wanted to hear something to explain the running and hiding so her mind gave her something. But as it got closer and Seth seemed to get tenser and tenser, Laura knew it wasn't a hallucination. It was all too real.

She wished they had been running from the fire. Or a bear. She could make out the words the men were saying.

"Man, I'm about sick of looking at trees."

Laura did not think those were the men from before. Maybe. She didn't know. What she did know was their dash through the woods had been fast. And messy. Neither she nor Seth had taken the time to cover their tracks. If those men had any experience hunting at all, they could probably pick up the signs of their flight. And follow them to their hiding place.

Seth hadn't thought those men looked like outdoorsmen when he saw them at her dad's cabin. *Please, God, let him be right. Cover our tracks and don't let them find us.*

"Shut it, dude. Complaining isn't doing anything besides making me angry. I'm tired of hearing you complain. I'm tired and my feet hurt and I want a real bed and a real meal. But if I can't have that, then I want you to be quiet."

"Okay, okay. We're done here. Let's move on."

Laura felt her heart lighten.

"No, we're not done here. You heard the boss. There are not a lot of places they can be, but that woman is probably good at hiding in these woods. We have to search it all. He said to look under every rock, and I'm not going back there without following orders. He wants them dead and he wants confirmation that it happened."

And Laura's heart crashed into the ground.

The sounds got louder. The men were doing a lot more walking around and it sounded like branches were either being moved or run into. If they were looking under the foliage and forest growth, those men would find the cave for sure.

One of the men made a loud noise. "Hey, dude. Come here. Do you see this?"

Laura's heart stopped completely.

Seth was definitely going to have cracked teeth when this was all over. If it ended in such a way that he was alive to go see a dentist, that is. Seth had never hoped to visit the dentist before, but he was wishing it now.

These two men were doing a much more thorough search than the previous two had done. Of course, this rock-cave thing was a lot smaller than the cabin. Smaller was harder to find. And it had been so well hidden that even Laura, with her innate forest sense, had struggled to find it. So those were things in favor of them not being found.

But Abby was awake this time. Even though she had been admirably quiet, that could change at any time. From what little Seth knew about children, Abby had been beyond good so far. Probably because of her slight fever. That was bound to change sometime. No one was perfect, and Abby was only getting more exhausted and hungry. And probably sick and tired of this walking through the woods nonsense.

And also, this cave thing was small. Tight. Seth was prepared to fight his way out, but he didn't exactly have a lot of room to maneuver if the men found them. And there was absolutely no place at all to hide if the men just started shooting into the enclosure.

Seth wanted to spring at them. To jump out and get the men before the men found them. It went against everything in Seth's nature to sit and wait. To see if they were found. He had been trained to be proactive, and he was much more comfortable bringing the fight to the opponent.

But he wasn't alone. And the grim reality was that these men were not alone. There had been a lot more than two at the cabin. The others were probably close enough to hear gunfire if it came to that. And they probably had radios. No, Seth needed to sit and wait and pray that the men passed them.

"What is that?" They had found something. Hopefully not a trace of Seth, Laura and Abby.

"I don't know. Some kind of print."

No, God. Please, no. Seth's plea was almost guttural, and his hands wavered as they held the gun.

"Dude, what was that?"

"Some kind of animal. A bear maybe. Do they have bears up here?"

"How should I know? Do I look like Ranger Rick to you?"

"That's hilarious. Do you see any sign of the woman? Or that park ranger?"

"No. All I see are trees and leaves. That's all I've seen for two days."

"I'm so tired of this. Maybe they got away?"

"Nah. Boss is monitoring the radio in the park ranger's truck. There hasn't been any mention of them. No one knows they're missing and no one is looking for them."

Seth felt a jolt at that. He'd been gone for over twenty-four hours. Surely someone had noticed he never came back down the mountain? His boss or coworkers? Had it really come to this? He could disappear and no one would even notice?

"Well, that fire is getting closer. I know boss says he's got it under control, but that thing scares me. I don't know why he had to set it in the first place."

"Yeah, well, it's not your job to know why. Boss said this was the best way to kill the woman. They are trapped by the river and the fires will make them run to us."

"I don't know why we don't just set this entire mountain on fire and be done with it. Then we could get back to where they have restaurants. And cable."

"You know why. She knows about her husband's safe-deposit box. Boss needs to make sure she's dead. And, after the last two days, I think he wants to make it hurt." The man's voice took on a gleeful note. "I hope he wants to make it hurt."

Seth didn't know if he felt or heard Laura's gasp, but when he turned around to look at her she had her hand physically over her mouth as though she was muffling her own voice. He wanted to reach out and comfort her but this was the very definition of not the right time. He turned back to the entry and focused on where the men were. He wanted to have as much notice as possible if they started closing in on the cave's location.

The other man sighed loudly. "Fine. But can I be the one to shoot the park ranger at least?"

"Yeah, dude. If boss agrees, you can shoot the park ranger."

The men's voices faded and the sounds of their search also lessened. They were moving on, searching somewhere else. *Thank You, God. Thank You.*

Seth lowered his gun, but did not stop his vigil at the entrance. Thoughts were whirling around in his head, but he tried to push them away. First, he needed to be sure that the men were gone. And make sure Laura and Abby were safe. Then he could deal with the implications of the men's conversation.

Seth looked at his watch. He waited five minutes. Ten. At fifteen, his muscles started to relax. Well, not relax. Just lose some of their tension. He still had a really difficult conversation to get through. And then they had to leave the relative safety of this place and continue the journey off this mountain. No, it wasn't time to relax.

He sat back and leaned against the side of the wall. His legs ached in a good way as he stretched them out in front of him as much as the space allowed. He looked at Laura. She was still holding Abby in her lap. Her arms were wrapped around the girl like she wanted to cover her and protect her from the world. Both, at once.

Seth felt like he understood. He was struggling with some conflicting emotions and urges himself. His time overseas had taught him so much. One of those lessons was that it is always better to face the truth head-on than to deny its existence. If something was going to be hard and dangerous and risky, well, it was better to acknowledge that. Wade in the muck and deal with it. Pretending it didn't exist would only lead to ambush and unexpected casualties.

"Laura, are you okay?" It was a dumb question, he knew that. Of course she wasn't okay. He wouldn't exactly say he was okay and it was not his whole world being turned upside down. "I'm sorry. I know you're not."

Laura unwrapped her arms from around Abby. The little girl was sound asleep, and Seth envied her ability to leave the tension of this hiding place. Laura's voice was very quiet, but they were close enough together that Seth could hear her.

"They're going to kill you."

That wasn't what Seth had expected her to say. Not at all. Not even a little bit. "If they find us, they are just going to kill you."

"I heard." He wasn't really dwelling on that part, though.

"I mean, I know they're going to kill me," her voice hitched, but she continued, "and Abby, too. But I...don't know. I just don't know. They're calling dibs on who gets to kill you. And they are happy that Mahoney is going to make my death horrible. How did this happen?"

Seth didn't know how this had happened. He just

knew that it had. And now they had to deal with it. "It's okay, Laura. They're not going to find us. We'll make it off this mountain." Seth prayed that he lived to see the truth of that statement. It hit him that the worst part of being killed was that he wouldn't be there to protect Laura and Abby. He'd never know if they made it out okay.

No. That wasn't going to happen. He needed Laura to keep hope. To believe. She was smart enough to realize if he was telling her to do something he wasn't doing himself. So he needed to do it with her. For her. And for himself. It was one thing to be realistic and practical and aware of the dangers. It was another thing to get caught up in defeatist thinking. Seth wasn't going there. Not today.

They just sat there, held tight in the space that cave made. The men were probably long gone by now, but Seth wasn't in a hurry to leave this safe little place. He wished they could just curl up together, the three of them, and forget what was on the other side of that foliage.

But they had to leave. Their escape path was narrowing. They were scared. And it all just felt very pointless.

"Laura? Do you know what's inside that safe-deposit box? How Josh came to be mixed up with Mahoney?"

She bent her head down, breathing into Abby's hair. Seth hated that he couldn't read her expression, couldn't tell what she was feeling. Besides fear, that was.

"Laura, look at me." He waited until she did. "I know that was a shock. I believe you when you say you don't think Josh was involved with this. I believe you."

He wasn't sure if he did. But she needed her husband

to be a good man. And Seth didn't see any advantage to proving her wrong. At least not now.

Laura's voice was distressed. Pleading, as though she automatically expected him to disbelieve her. To call her a liar. Turn against her. "I'm sorry, Seth. But it has to be a mistake. Josh would not have been involved with a criminal."

NINE

Laura owed Seth an explanation. Actually, Josh owed both of them explanations. But he wasn't here and Laura just couldn't believe that he was anything less than the good man she knew. Seth was asking the same questions that were pounding inside her own head, though. Because they both needed to know why they were suffering like this.

And Laura could tell that Seth was trying very hard not to pressure her. To let her sit with the idea that this was all some kind of mistake. She appreciated that.

That is what made Laura try to answer his question. "I know it doesn't make sense. The key was in Josh's things. Mahoney came because of the key. The man is an awful criminal. But there is no way Josh was involved with him. It is just not possible." She held herself very still as she waited for Seth to respond. This was the part where he accused her of being naive and delusional.

"Okay."

Okay? He just said *okay*?

"I believe you, Laura." He leaned back fully and stretched his legs out a bit more. He did not look threatening and his posture was almost comforting. Inviting. "Tell me why you're so sure Josh was not involved."

Even though it seemed Seth was not going to become her adversary, she still felt completely unsettled. Laura took a deep breath and felt Abby slightly trembling in her lap. Regret overflowed in Laura's heart. She had wanted so much for her child. Safety and security. Giggles. Arts and crafts, and pudding and cookies. Friends. Instead, her girl had lost her father. She'd been yanked away from all she knew to live alone on a mountain. And now they were running for their lives. Even though Laura had not told Abby about the danger, the child was well aware that things were bad. And scary.

She began to run her fingers through Abby's hair, smoothing. In theory, the actions were meant to soothe the small girl, who looked confused and scared. It was something Laura often did when Abby was upset. But it worked both ways. Laura's own breath evened out. Some of the painful stiffness in her shoulders began to melt away.

"First, Josh wouldn't break the law. He was a Christian."

"Christians can mess up, Laura. They can make mistakes." He sounded like he was walking through a house of booby traps and Laura almost felt sorry for him. Except it was her life that was blowing up.

"I know. I know. Josh wasn't perfect. He was as human and fallible as the rest of us. But his faith was strong. He is the one who helped me come to terms with my own faith. He was a good man, Seth."

Seth was just looking at her. Watching. Laura kept moving her hands through Abby's hair. Soothing them both.

Seth nodded slowly. "Okay. In our current situation,

it doesn't really matter. There's a safe-deposit box out there that Mahoney wants bad enough to kill three people and set a mountain on fire. That's a good lead we can give to the police."

"If we ever make it to the police."

Seth slid over to where Laura was, angling his body so he was sitting next to her as much as possible in the small area. He took her hand in both of his. Her other hand slid out of Abby's hair and into her lap. Seth squeezed her hand gently and then let go to put his arm around Laura's shoulders. He was holding both her and Abby in a gentle, supportive hug.

The residual tension left Laura's body altogether and she rested all her weight against him. Her head fell back against her shoulder and she turned in to his body, breathing in his warm scent and listening to the steady beating of his heart. Tears welled up and spilled over.

Laura didn't want to cry. Not here, stuck in a literal hole. Not in front of Abby. Not when she felt so weak. But she couldn't stop the tears. It was all too much. She had not been safe out in the real world and she had not been safe back home on the mountain. There was nowhere she was safe. Worse, there was nowhere she could keep her daughter safe. Her daughter was in danger, it was somehow her fault and there was nothing anyone could do.

The only person who had ever been able to make her feel safe was her dad. And he was gone.

She muffled her sobs in Seth's chest and felt him wrap his arms to more completely embrace her and Abby. Abby's little hands patted her on the back and she cried harder that her sweet daughter was comforting her instead of the other way around. When it was over, and she could hear beyond the cries of her own heart, she became aware that Seth was murmuring to Abby.

"Your mommy is fine, honey. She's just feeling sad and sometimes we cry when we're sad. But she is okay. She loves you and everything is going to be okay."

Laura laughed and moved her arms to complete the group hug. She felt better, as though she had bled out some of her pain. "Seth is right, honey. I'm okay. I just got sad for a minute, but I'm okay." Laura lifted her head and looked at Abby, cupping her chin with one hand and stroking her cheek with the other. "Are you okay, baby?"

Abby nodded and hugged her even tighter. Laura looked at Seth. She didn't want to peer in his eyes and see whatever was lurking there, but she owed him that much. But looking made her even more confused. She thought she saw affection. And sympathy.

He should hate her for dragging him into this mess. But he didn't act like he hated her at all. Laura added that to the list of things to figure out once this whole mess was over.

"What do we do, Seth?"

His hand was rubbing her shoulder, and Laura was leaning into it. She had missed the touch of another person, of someone who was not Abby. She had not had physical contact with someone besides Abby since her dad died. It had been months. It suddenly felt like it had been decades.

"Priority one remains getting off this mountain. We keep on with our plan, staying in the trees as much as possible, tracking the river, heading over the mountain."

Laura nodded. So much had happened and yet they were still in the same place. They still had the same objective. The same plan. It was back to her. Her turn to step up and do her part, use her knowledge of this place to get all three of them to safety.

Laura had felt like throwing up when that man had called dibs on killing Seth. And when he talked about her forthcoming painful death. But she couldn't think about those things now. If she let fear cripple her, she might as well walk out there and turn herself in to Mahoney.

"How did you know they were there? I didn't see a thing." That part had really been bothering her. The first indication she had that something was wrong was when Seth made it clear they needed to get out of there and hide as fast as possible. How was she supposed to lead them to safety if she couldn't even tell when the enemy was close by? She was supposed to be the expert out in these woods. She should know when humans were present, especially since it was such a rare event. Yet, she had not even known for sure what they were running from.

"I saw a reflection. I wasn't positive it was them— I just knew the sun was hitting something metal out there. And I knew metal didn't belong in these woods."

"I didn't see that. I completely missed it."

"Hey, Laura, look at me. No, really look at me." She did. "That's not your fault. You had Abby. You had to map out our path. You had a lot to do. I'm not blaming you. It's not your job to do everything."

"I know." But she should have seen sun reflecting off metal. If she missed that, would she miss a more subtle sign? Would she lead them right to the men? Lead Abby and Seth to their deaths? If that happened, Laura would never forgive herself.

* * *

She said she knew it wasn't her fault, but Seth could see the truth in her eyes. Laura was feeling like a failure. She was blaming herself.

Seth had felt fairly helpless for the last two days. Unable to step up and make it right. But this was something he could try to fix. Something he needed to resolve, right now. "Laura, please listen. Really, really listen."

She looked at him and there was fear in her eyes. That was unacceptable. Completely unacceptable.

"It's not your job to do anything. I know you've been taking the lead on this. That we've needed to rely on you because you have the expertise on this mountain. But you're not alone. And I'm not helpless."

As he spoke, some emotions rose up inside that he hadn't been aware of carrying. Hadn't known were lurking in his heart. A kind of defensiveness. A need to prove that he was a capable man, strong and able to protect them.

He had hurt his family and had run because he could not figure out a way to make things right. He'd felt like a dog with his tail tucked between his legs for a very long time. But he wasn't that. "I'm a grown man who grew up in the Oregon woods. I'm a trained park ranger. I have outdoor skills, too. Hunting and tracking. Navigating in the forest."

She was looking at him, and he saw her throat move as she swallowed.

"You have the knowledge of this mountain, and I am beyond thankful for that. But no one person can do this, Laura. No one person should have to do this. I'm here, and I am more than just another body. I want to help. I need you to let me help."

She was still listening. Still looking at him. Here, in this enclosure, with that sweet child on her lap, Laura looked very small. Very alone. But she wasn't alone right now, and Seth suspected that she had been alone in the past for far too long. He knew all about that.

He'd been alone, too.

And Seth was tired of it. He had a family back home. A family who loved him. Wanted him. And he ran because he couldn't swallow his pride. Accept their help. Avoid taking his anger at his wounds out on them. Laura did not have any of that. They were both suffering from the same thing but Seth's was self-inflicted. He'd known he had made a mistake about a week after he'd left. Then, he had spent more than a year telling himself he needed to live with the choices he made. Now, though, after all this running, of watching this incredible woman, Seth decided that he was going to try to fix his mistakes. If God gave him another chance, he would not take it for granted.

Seth tried to put every ounce of his determination and sincerity into his voice. "You worry about keeping us on course and helping us find a safe place when we need it. I'll worry about whether the fire is catching up or where those men are. We're a team, and that means you can rely on me for some things. In fact, I want you to rely on me. Please."

"Okay." It was whispered, but Seth thought she was perhaps shy instead of hesitant. Something shifted in his soul; something happened in this space. He was more open. Hopefully that shyness on Laura's part meant she picked up on it, too.

But they had to get off this mountain. It was literally on fire. Their escape options were shrinking. And these men were not going to give up anytime soon. That was okay, because Seth was not going to give up, either. And he would put his will up against someone else's any day of the week.

Seth was feeling alive again, the blood pumping hard through his veins. But this time it wasn't pumping with fear. Nope. This time his body was surging with determination. "So this area was just searched again." His voice was brisk. No nonsense. It was time to set aside emotion and focus on the mission. They needed to get out of this cave. "That probably means it's safe, for now."

"Yeah, but they know the fire is closing us in. They are using it. The search area is getting smaller and smaller."

"You're right. So we need to up our level of caution. And that river is becoming much more viable as a Plan B."

"I really don't want to cross it with Abby."

"Me, either. But if it comes to that, we'll do it. And it will be okay."

"Okay. We have about four hours of daylight left. Traveling in the dark is sounding better and better to me."

"Agreed. So let's go. We'll be careful, but we're going to keep moving. If you know of any more of these hidey-holes, a route that takes us past them might be worth a slight delay."

"You think we're going to run into more men."

Seth paused. But he would not lie to her. "Yes. I do. But they seem to be completely lost in the woods, and that will definitely work in our favor. They don't seem to know how to track. Or how to move quietly. We'll use that."

Laura breathed in deeply and sighed it out. Seth almost smiled as he watched the slump leave her shoulders. He could practically feel her gathering herself up. She shifted, putting Abby on her feet, and whispered to her. Seth could hear her telling Abby that they were going to go outside again. That they still needed to be as quiet as possible. That it was dangerous, but Seth and Mommy were going to keep her safe from the bad men.

Seth couldn't see Abby's eyes, but he watched Laura look intently into them. Then she smiled and kissed Abby on the forehead. Laura looked at Seth. "Okay. We're ready. Let's go."

Seth lifted the flap up slowly, and peeked outside. He saw nothing unusual. Heard nothing but the normal sounds of the forest. The smell of smoke had become constant, but the sky still looked blue.

He held out a finger to Laura, gesturing for her to wait while he checked it out. He kept his weapon at his side, but was ready to lift it and use it if needed. He lowered the flap, concealing Laura and Abby inside as much as possible. After walking around for a couple of minutes, Seth felt confident that it was as safe as it could be in their current circumstances. He holstered his gun.

He opened the flap and saw relief take over Laura's face. "It's okay. We're clear."

Laura came out, and Seth automatically reached down to carry Abby. She came without hesitation, wrapping her arms around his neck and burying her face in the space between his shoulder and his face.

Laura started to walk ahead of them, but Seth reached out and took her hand. She looked surprised, but she didn't pull away. They moved forward then, a little group of three. Laura was still in the lead. Seth was looking all around, trying to make sure he would see if they ran into the men again.

He knew he was being ridiculous, but he was thankful Laura was going along with it right now. He was going into the territory of hypervigilance. There was a fine line between being aware and getting paranoid. Between observing your surroundings and stressing your body out so much that it began to misfire. Stopped functioning the way it should. Seth forced himself to take it back a step. He squeezed Laura's hand and then let go, wrapping both arms around Abby.

As much as he had liked walking with her warm hand in his, he knew this was better for their safety. He was able to keep up and observe their surroundings a little better. He could watch his footing while holding Abby.

Laura gave him a concerned look, and he just smiled at her. He tried to look reassuring, but was glad he didn't have a mirror to see if it worked or not. It must not have been too bad of an approximation, though, because Laura smiled back and continued leading the way.

She was going a different way than before. They were still in the cover of the trees, but they weren't on the route they'd been on when Seth first saw the shining reflection. He reached out and touched her back. "Why are we headed a different way?" His voice was as soft as he could make it and still have it be audible. He felt bad questioning her, but he wanted to understand where they were going as best he could without actually knowing what the land looked like up here.

"I'm still taking us in the same direction, but I want

to incorporate possible hiding places into our route."
Her voice was so soft that Seth only understood what
she was saying by looking at her lips while listening. He
nodded and gave her a thumbs-up sign, and she started
walking again.

For all that being a hermit's daughter had caused
Laura pain in her life, it seemed like it was the very
thing that would save theirs. Her knowledge of these
woods was so complete that it was almost unbelievable.
Even people who lived on the other side of the mountain probably didn't know their land as well. It was one
thing to live in a place. It was another thing entirely to
have that place be your whole world. This mountain had
been Laura's whole world for a very, very long time.

The trees thinned out and Seth tried to see if he
could tell where they were on the mountain. There were
small patches of snow that had not melted scattered here
and there, indicating that they were making progress
in their goal to go up. Even though it was spring, the
snow would probably get heavier the higher they went.
But snow was good because up was good.

The heavy canopy over them finally gave way and
Seth found he was ready for blue sky. A reminder that
there was a whole world out there for them. More than
tree after tree.

Instead, he saw smoke. Thick, heavy. The entire sky
was black.

TEN

This alternate route took them closer to the open fields than Laura would have gone otherwise. But she knew of a couple of hiding places this way and those things had proven to be really, really useful. So she chose this route.

Which meant that she took them right into the fire. In her effort to keep her daughter and Seth safe and alive, Laura had walked them right into the hot spot. Some guide she was turning out to be.

Laura didn't even try to force the shock off her face before turning to look at Seth. She was stunned and scared to her core and there was no way she could pretend otherwise. She simply wasn't that good of an actress. She would have said something, but all words had fled. The phrases had seen that smoke and understood its implications and run far, far away. She and her baby were stuck here, but at least her words were safe.

"I don't smell the smoke, so that's a point in our favor." Seth was not shocked. At least he did not look or sound shocked. Maybe he was better at suppressing his emotions, but Laura didn't see any signs of distress or panic in his demeanor. That was okay because she had enough for both of them.

"The smell of smoke is the same. Constant, but not overpowering. It's coming this way, though. That wall is definitely headed at us." He continued on as though he were talking to a functioning adult.

Abby looked at Laura and she flinched. Her daughter had the same shocked expression on her face that had to be gracing Laura's own. Her daughter was scared. Sick. She should be bundled up on a couch, watching cartoons and eating soup. With medicine.

Not okay. If Seth could focus, look at this newest threat objectively like it was just another obstacle, then Laura could, too. She would. She slowed her breathing. She knew how to handle this. Fires were not uncommon in the Colorado mountains. Her dad had not just taught her about what to do, he had drilled it into her head.

"The animals here aren't alarmed yet. I don't see a flood of them fleeing the blaze."

Seth looked around and slowly nodded. "That's good. That's really good. That smoke looks bad, but we're not in the thick of it." Yet. Laura absolutely heard that little word that Seth did not say out loud. She felt its echo in her soul.

"Yeah. And we don't want to be anywhere near it. The smoke is something else. That blaze has got to be a monster."

"Do you think we can still make it up the mountain? That smoke isn't just coming from the side. It's almost catty-corner in front of us."

Laura looked at the smoke. It seemed alive, and she could almost see it moving. Not just caging them in at their side, but coming at them somewhat head-on. She mentally went up the mountain, seeing the different paths they could take. The river was looking more and more appealing, so Laura concentrated on the routes that ran parallel to it.

Fires were dangerous, and they could move awfully fast in the right circumstances. Laura could conceive of three nightmare scenarios. One, the fire could chase them to the river and catch them before they made it to the water. Two, the fire could circle around them and somehow come between them and the river.

Or three, they would make it to river before the fire got them but then drown or be pummeled to death by the boulders hiding in the current.

Laura's stomach churned as all three scenarios played out in her head. No. No, no, no. This was not going to happen. *Please, God. Give me the wisdom and strength. Help us to get through this storm.*

"I don't know, Seth. I'm afraid it's going to cut us off. I'm really worried that it will circle ahead of us and come down between us and the river. We can't get caught in the middle. We just can't."

Seth shifted Abby to one arm and wrapped the other around her. This was not the time or place, but Laura couldn't stop herself from taking comfort from this strong man. She needed to soak up some of his strength. His confidence. His calm.

"It's okay, Laura. It's going to be okay."

She couldn't help but laugh, even if it was choked up and muffled. "You keep saying that. You've said that at least twenty times in the last two days."

"Because it's true. I have faith." Seth sighed, looking her in the eye. "Or at least I want to. I want to so much. I want faith, Laura. Faith in God. Faith in my abilities.

Faith in your abilities." Another sigh, but his voice was still sure. "We are going to be okay." He sounded like he believed it. Very convincing. And it helped. Hearing his firm belief that they could overcome any obstacle they encountered, including fires and guns and mysterious bosses, helped her to believe it, too.

He squeezed her then, increasing the pressure in such a gentle way that he was almost physically holding her together until she was ready to take over the job. He had a Donovan woman in each arm, and he still seemed strong enough to take on the rest of this mess. Laura had missed knowing someone else was there. Having someone she could lean on.

She had missed having a partner.

After taking a few selfish moments, and thanking the Lord that she was able to do so, Laura straightened and stepped away. She bent forward and put a hand on each of Abby's cheeks, leaning in to kiss the little girl's forehead, eyelids, nose and chin noisily. Abby laughed and Laura found it impossible to be scared when her daughter was giving off such joy.

Laura let go and looked at Seth. "Okay, I'm ready. I think staying within eyesight of the river should be priority number one. I'll feel a lot better if we can see our Plan B at all times and know it is still there and viable."

Seth didn't hesitate. "Sounds good to me."

"That means we're giving up some cover. And we're giving up access to some hiding places I know."

Seth nodded. "I get it. I'm with you that the river is the most important, though. We'll be as careful as possible, but we need to get off this mountain. Now."

The words weren't even fully out of his mouth before Laura started walking. There was nothing worse than standing around feeling uncertain. Anxious. Laura was ready to move in the right direction.

Her pace was faster than before, though she was still sure to not break branches or leave a very noticeable trail. She headed directly to the river, and some of the instinct to run lessened when she heard it. It sounded fierce. This time of year was when the river was at its fullest. The snowmelt swelled the rivers and they came crashing down the mountain, wearing down rock and anything else in their path.

It was a white-water rafter's extreme dream. And one of her worst nightmares. If they had to get in that water, then things were bad.

She stopped her direct path to the river and began moving back up the mountain, this time angling until the water came into view. The final bit of instinct telling her to run for the water died down then. She could see it. Plan B was as safe and as viable as a crazy Plan B could get.

She turned to make sure Seth and Abby were still with her, and of course they were. Just like before. They were right there and they were safe and she was safe and she was not alone. Her looking had less to do with wanting to make sure Seth was doing what he said and more to do with the way seeing him reassured her.

Abby was staring at the river, obviously enthralled by the rushing water and the loud roaring sound it made. She was pointing and saying something to Seth, but the sound of the river drowned it out. Laura could only see her daughter's smile. And Seth's gentle one in return.

Josh had died when Abby was just a baby, but Laura imagined that he might have looked like that holding his daughter. She felt the familiar pain that came when she thought about her husband, but it wasn't crippling anymore. She still had no clue how Josh was involved with Mahoney, but her husband had been a very good man. He would have been an excellent father. But he wasn't here. Laura liked to think that he was in Heaven, watching her. And she knew that he would not want his wife and daughter to spend the rest of their lives mourning him. He would want them to find happiness again.

Laura had thought happiness meant safety up on the mountain. Now she wondered about her plan. About the full life she might be denying Abigail. Mountain life had been the best her father could do, but Laura knew the man had settled for as much peace as he could find. He'd encouraged her to leave, to go to school. To start her family out in the world. Malcolm Grant had wanted a full life for her.

Laura's foot caught on a rock and she jolted back to reality. She had no idea where all these thoughts were coming from, but this was not the time. She could not afford to make a mistake because she was lost in her own head. Laura pushed those thoughts inside a box. She would take them out later.

She smiled. So far she had scheduled a nervous breakdown and an examination of how she felt about her dead husband for later. For when they were out of this situation. When she and Abby got to safety, Laura was going to be very, very busy. She was almost looking forward to it.

Abby thought the river was pretty. And loud. And pretty loud. Seth knew this because the little girl had told him. Several times. While pointing. Seth was grateful that the river was loud enough to cover her voice because the last thing Seth wanted to do was hush her, especially after she had been so good during the whole thing.

He'd seen Laura stumble a bit, but she regained her stride without any help from him. He'd been watching the expression on her face and her furrowed brow and had wondered what she was thinking about right before the rock caught her toe. Whatever it was, she had either stopped thinking about it or she was doing a better job of hiding her emotions.

Seth looked at the wall of smoke in the distance, then at the river that was almost startling in its strength. Violence. And then Seth saw a couple of blooming wildflowers against some large boulders. This would have been an amazing and beautiful picture. The kind of thing that made viewers wonder if it was Photoshopped or made up. In reality, though, standing between two of nature's deadly and powerful forces, knowing there were several armed men out there trying to kill them, it lost some of its appeal.

Laura started leading again, moving at a pace that impressed Seth. They'd been walking for hours, yet she was willing to carry on at the necessary pace. All without complaint. She managed to do it gracefully and without disturbing the ground she covered. He kept up easily, but he could feel his blood pumping from the activity. It seemed Laura had decided that speed was just as important as stealth, and looking at the black wall in the sky in the distance Seth agreed wholeheartedly.

She brought them back under the cover of some trees, and Seth relaxed a fraction. He could still see the river, and Seth wondered how long the cover lasted if they stuck to the strategy to stay in sight of Plan B. He wasn't going to ask, though. He didn't want to distract Laura. He didn't want to make any extra noise. And, truly, part of Seth did not want to know the answer to that question because he was guessing they would not have near as much cover as they needed.

It was a beautiful day, and they seemed to be making good time. The snow went from a splotch here and a splotch there to bigger patches. Seth could see large covered areas in the distance. The air was cooling down, but he didn't feel cold. Abby was dressed in layers and she did not seem to be cold, either.

The silence was peaceful and they walked in such a way that his feet were almost making rhythmic motions. All of it was soothing. The atmosphere felt almost like a prayer, that mood of contemplative quiet. Seth had not felt that atmosphere in a long time. Too long.

He was almost unnerved by it. Yes, he was keeping watch. He was vigilant and well aware that danger quite literally surrounded them. But he was also full of emotion right now. Feeling. It was like he was climbing up to God, and the higher he got, the more he shed the distractions of this world, and the better God was able to communicate with him.

That was a silly notion. God could communicate with him anywhere. Under any circumstances. Yes, the Lord was always present and speaking to him. The problem was, Seth did not always listen. He was able to fill his life with noise and distractions and tasks. He was able to avoid that still quiet voice in his soul. That nudging of his conscience. The gentle prodding of the One who knew all.

But it was almost impossible to ignore up here. Seth felt it flooding over him as strongly as the waters in that river would if they were forced to try to cross it. He smiled when he realized how fanciful his thoughts were. Ridiculous. Maybe they were farther up this mountain than he thought and the high altitude was getting to his brain. He was daydreaming like a child. Seeing what he wanted to see.

"Are you okay?" Laura's voice was hesitant. Almost with a hint of fear. That softened Seth's natural instinct to deny anything was wrong. Or resent her noticing that something was off. He wanted to be real with her. He did not, however, want to analyze that desire too much. This wasn't the time or place for thinking soft thoughts about this woman. They had a job to do.

"Yeah. Sorry. I was just thinking."

They were still moving at a decent pace, still under the light cover of trees. He shifted closer to her so that they could talk without raising their voices, though the roar of the river carried this far and helped to mask much of the sound.

"You looked like you were in pain."

Seth smiled. That was certainly one way to describe it. Thinking about how God had to get him on a mountain between a forest fire, a raging river and armed men with homicidal tendencies before Seth would listen to Him was kind of a painful realization. "I was just ruminating."

"It's kind of hard not to up here, isn't it?"

"That's probably understating it. My brain was just racing."

"Want to share?" The words left Laura's mouth and then she quickly turned and gave him a wide-eyed look. "I'm sorry. I'm not trying to pry." Her words were coming so quickly together that Seth felt like he was hearing her about two seconds after they left her mouth. "I just mean, you know so much of my messed-up life. You listened while I told you everything. I just thought, I mean, maybe, I don't know. If you want to talk, I'm here. If you want. I mean, you don't have to."

She sounded so sincere and afraid of upsetting him. It was such a sweet and beautiful thing. She should be focused solely on getting herself and her daughter to safety. But instead, she was finding the time to care about him. To worry about him.

Well, why not? Wasn't his desire to do everything himself what had gotten him in this mess to begin with? Not the mess of running from armed bad guys, but the mess of being away from his family. Being alone, even though he was in a world full of people.

"I was just contemplating how hard it is to avoid thinking up here. It's so open and quiet that a lot of the thoughts I had shoved away were coming back."

"About your time in the military?"

Seth stopped to look at her. "How did you know that?"

Laura's smile was almost rueful. "I recognized the look. You know a lot about my dad, but did you know that he was a Vietnam vet?"

"No. I had never heard that."

"Yeah. He had a hard time over there, from what I know of it. He came back and that's when he became, well, isolated. The hermit thing didn't start until he came back. I can remember my biological dad explaining it to me once. They were brothers. I remember asking why Uncle Malcolm was so weird and scary and my dad telling me it was the only way he found to keep living in this world after the war."

"And I remind you of him in that way?" Seth wasn't exactly insulted. There was a lot of truth in the comparison. For someone who used to make fun of the man, Seth was realizing much of Old Man Grant could be found in his own mirror.

"Just a bit. You come off like someone who served in the military. Who knows war."

"I did. I do. I did three tours in Afghanistan. Got hurt. Came back."

That was the very abbreviated version, but Laura just nodded and started walking again. Her manner was easy. All encompassing. She was good at accepting what a person could give. And Seth found that he wanted to give more. To her, at least. He suspected that she knew a lot about regrets. About being judged. About acting without knowing how or why.

"My family tried to help me. Nursed me back to health. Took care of me." His voice was rough and his chest was so tight that he thought it might split in two. How could talking about that time hurt worse than war? Laura kept walking at a steady pace. And that made it better. Not seeing her face. Not seeing her eyes. That helped.

And he was all the more a coward for it, but he accepted it gratefully.

"I hated it. I hated that I was a grown man who needed his mommy to take care of him. I hated the way all my friends and family looked at me with pity in their eyes. Like I was some kind of sympathy case. It was my ego. I know that. Now. It was all pride and ego and anger from feeling helpless."

"That seems like a very rational response to what you went through. Very human. Normal even." Laura's voice was soft, and she was still walking without looking at him.

"Yeah. Maybe."

They walked for another couple of minutes in silence. The words just kept building up inside Seth. He wanted to keep them in, but they wanted out. And really, maybe saying them out loud to someone would help. He'd certainly said them to himself enough times.

"I ran away. I couldn't take it anymore and I ran away. I was a grown man, but I left a note and got in my car and fled."

Silence. What was she thinking? Was she shocked? Disgusted?

"I understand that."

"You do?"

"Yeah. Things were hard after Josh died. A lot of pitying glances my way, too. So I came home. I phrased it like that. Coming home. But it was running away and hiding in the most isolated spot I could think of."

Seth thought there was a difference between her coming home and his hurting his family by running from them, but he didn't want to argue the point.

"They know I'm okay. I write them about once a month, to let them know. I don't include a return address, which is cowardly, but I just can't. I've asked them to give me this time, and so far they have. Still, I know I hurt them." He was still hurting them. There was no way his mother was not hurt every single day that went by without him calling. But, as more time passed, it just seemed like his mistake grew and grew and now it was so big that Seth didn't know if it was fixable.

Laura stopped, turned around to face him. Seth braced for whatever he might see on her face. He didn't know which would be worse, blame or sympathy. Instead, she looked alarmed.

"Seth. Look behind us."

He whirled around so quickly that Abby startled in his arms.

Black. Everywhere he looked was a wall of thick, black smoke.

ELEVEN

It had reached them too quickly. There had not been any sense of fire and now there was a blaze so intense it made the sky look like the dirtiest of nights behind them? No. That wasn't how forest fires worked. At least not naturally spreading ones. Not in these conditions.

"That's not the original blaze, is it?"

Seth's face was as dark as the air around them. "No. Not with these winds. It wouldn't have come up on us like that."

Yeah. She knew that, but she had really, really hoped he would say something different.

Seth did a slow full circle where he was standing, taking in all their options. Or lack thereof. Laura had thought she felt trapped since this whole thing began, but, looking at the current situation, she knew that had been a false perception. Now. Now she felt trapped.

"Seth?"

"They set that fire to chase us out. We have smoke on two sides and the river on a third."

"They're forcing us to go one direction."

"Yeah. And I bet they're up there waiting for us to walk right into their little trap."

Little trap? Right now it felt very large and very, very dangerous.

"What do we do?"

They both looked at the river. It was still raging. In fact, it seemed as upset as Laura felt. "We stick close to the river. But I'm not liking our odds any more now than I did a while ago."

Laura nodded. "Agreed. I really, really don't want to take Abby through there."

"Okay, let's keep moving forward. We just need to be as alert as possible. It's no longer a matter of if we run into the men, but when."

They walked. Slower. Quietly. Every hair on Laura's body stood on alert and her mind was buzzing. After several minutes, she almost wished they would just see the men already. The anticipation was almost too much to take.

"Laura."

They were walking close to one another now, almost as a single unit, and Seth's low voice carried to her perfectly.

"Yeah?"

"I have two favors to ask of you. I'm sorry, but I have to ask."

"What?" Favors? What exactly could she do for him? Especially now?

"If we run into the men, I'm going to fight them as best as I can. I need you to take Abby and run, okay? Through the river or wherever you think is the safest. But let me do that. Let me fight and distract and buy you some time. Please?"

That was a favor for him? It seemed like a favor for her. But Laura knew why he was asking. The thought of leaving Seth to a near-certain death hit her harder than she would ever have imagined. He was a park ranger. Rangers harassing her dad were the prominent theme of her childhood. They were not her friends.

But she did not want him to die.

Laura looked at Abby. Forced her throat to swallow. "Okay. I'll try, Seth." She hoped that was good enough.

Seth just looked at her, his face almost still. Probing. "The second favor is a bigger one. And it is very dependent on you doing the first. When you get out of this, I want you to get a message to my family. Their contact information is on file with the ranger service. Will you please tell them that I'm sorry and that I love them?"

Laura couldn't breathe. She had to stop walking, and Seth stopped right beside her. She felt his hand on her back, but the world around her was a blur. This man planned on dying. He fully expected to run into those men and to not walk away from the encounter.

That was not exactly shocking considering the odds they were facing. They were on a burning mountain and up against more men than Laura could count. All heavily armed.

Foreseeable or not, though, it still burned Laura's lungs.

And he expected her to survive? He thought, he really, really thought that she and Abby would get off this mountain alive and could get a message to his family? How? How could she pull that off? Laura intended to fight for her daughter until she had nothing left to give, but, deep inside, in the part of her that she hadn't wanted to acknowledge, Laura had fully expected to fail.

That was what turned the hot coals into a blaze in her lungs. She and her daughter were going to die. She hadn't even known that was inside her. That horrible ending that seemed almost unavoidable.

Except Seth really thought she could avoid it. He was earnest in his request. They were not empty words. He thought she could fix things with his family.

He trusted her to make things right. To help repair the relationships he valued the most.

Okay, then. Her voice was thick, but she put every ounce of determination she could muster into it. "Yes, Seth. Yes. If you can't tell your family, then I will. I'll tell them everything, including what an amazing man they created and sent out into the world."

Seth nodded, squeezed her shoulder and started walking. Laura moved, too.

She didn't know what else to say, but that was okay. Because sometimes you didn't have to say anything. Sometimes, you just understood. Her dad had taught her that.

The river curved up ahead, and they both slowed down. They did not want to round a corner and walk into the ambush that had to be waiting for them. Laura tapped Seth on the arm and started moving away from the river. She wanted to stay close to good old Plan B, but they also needed some kind of cover.

They entered the trees, which made them less visible. What if the men were waiting in the trees? That was the obvious place for people trying to hide to be.

No. Laura needed to stop this. She said a quick prayer. There. Laura truly believed that worrying about something you prayed over was pointless. She wanted to pray, give it to God and let Him deal with it.

But, oh, it was so hard. And she often failed at the giving it to God and letting go part.

Yeah, she failed at that a lot.

But she always kept trying. That was the only thing she could do. Try and try and try.

Blowing out a deep breath, Laura looked at Seth. He was watching her with an almost tender expression on his face. Her face grew hot and she shrugged her shoulders at him. He smiled back and nodded.

He got it.

And that was nice. Josh had always accepted her quirks with an easy understanding. That had been a precious thing in her life. Laura had assumed she would never have that again.

Maybe she was wrong.

They moved around the curve. Laura was holding her breath, fighting the urge to just run and see. If you thought there was a monster in the closet, waiting in bed and imagining it wasn't the answer.

No. Every child knew that you jumped out of bed and flung that door open.

And Laura really wanted someone to open this closet door. And turn on the light.

But the monsters in the closet weren't real and these men absolutely were. She would not put their lives in danger in the long term because it might make her feel better in the short term.

Seth's hand suddenly shot out and grabbed her arm. Pulled her to a stop. He never said a word, but his message was clear. There was something up ahead. Something bad.

Seth silently passed Abby to Laura, and she squeezed her girl. He moved to walk in front of Laura. They seemed to be creeping, not going forward at all.

But they had to be because they rounded the corner and saw it.

It was a trap.

And that trap was about to be sprung.

Seth led them to a group of boulders that formed a low wall. She set Abby down, and held her finger to her lips. The child had surely picked up on the tension in the air, but it wouldn't hurt to reinforce the need for silence.

Seth and Laura both peered over the little wall, and Laura could not stop her gasp. Thankfully, it was not loud. And the men were far enough away to not hear.

And they were not even looking.

It was amazing, really. For men who had gone to such great lengths to find Seth and Laura, they were almost lounging. Relaxing.

Laura saw seven or eight men. All armed. With multiple guns.

There were several Jeeps with boxes in the back.

The men were leaning against one of the Jeeps, laughing and talking.

Laura rested her forehead against the boulder and felt Seth's hand on the back of her head. She breathed in, trying to find the scent of this mountain she loved under the ever-present odor of smoke. This close to the boulder, Laura could almost imagine she was a child again, alone on her mountain.

Laura lifted her head back up. It was what it was, so she needed to deal. And Laura had a lifetime of experience at dealing with whatever was thrown at her.

She started on the left side of the camp and began to scan to the right, slowly looking and trying to see something, anything, that might help them.

She made it to the far right, and was about to give up, when she froze. How had she not noticed that right away?

"I'm hallucinating, right? This whole thing has finally gotten to me and now I've lost all touch with reality." Laura's voice was the lowest murmur, but she wasn't asking a question. It was more like she was muttering to herself.

"If you're talking about the small army of armed men standing right there, then no. You're not hallucinating."

Laura didn't look at him. She was still staring straight ahead like she had been hypnotized into some kind of trance. "No. Not that."

Seth looked at her profile, but she was dead serious. "No, you're not talking about all those men with guns?"

"No. Look, Seth." She sounded disappointed that he hadn't caught on yet.

He looked. Lots of men, too many to fight. Check. Guns, probably loaded with lots of bullets. Check. Laura reached out and gripped his arm. Not held. Not even pushed or pulled. No, she placed her hand on his forearm and dug her fingers in like she was clinging for all she was worth. She was still staring straight ahead and Seth was moving from confused to some combination of irritated and frightened. What was going on?

"Rafts, Seth. Look. By the river. Do you see a bunch of rafts, or am I just seeing what I want to see?"

Seth had been focused almost solely on the men themselves. They were the threat in his view and he hadn't really taken his eyes off them. Now, though, he scanned the surrounding area. And felt his heart jump.

She was right. There. Just over there. Rafts. Three of them. They looked like the kind you would go white-water rafting in for fun or recreation.

"Yes." He had to keep his voice calm and low. The last thing they needed was for the men to find them or for Abby to react to their excitement. "Yes, Laura. Those are rafts."

"I, I, I… What does this mean? Why do they have rafts?"

"This Mahoney is determined. He's prepared. If you're going to bring a small army to a mountain to kill one woman and one small child, you might as well make sure you have enough equipment for any contingency." It made sense in a sick kind of way.

"I want one of those rafts, Seth. How do we make that happen?" Laura's voice was pure determination. Seth had not ever heard her so focused. So intent.

"You think we can go down the river in one? We don't have life jackets or other safety equipment. Even if we made it over there, by the time we get a raft we will not have any time to do more than jump in and hang on." And they had Abby. Seth didn't say that last part out loud because no one needed to tell Laura that they had her daughter with them. She knew. She always knew.

"I can do it." Again, her voice was absolute. It seemed that Laura was going to use the sheer force of her will to make this happen. And from where Seth was crouched down behind a fallen tree, that will seemed absolute. He felt a military battle yell rising up in his chest. Oh, yeah. They were going to make this happen.

"Okay, then. Let's make a plan." Seth started counting men. There were eight that he saw. They were all clustered, almost loafing around. Of course, there wasn't much reason for them to be up and actively searching. They had done a masterful job of forcing Seth and Laura to come to them. Right to this camp of horrors.

The good news was that the men clearly did not know that Laura and Seth were there already. They must have moved faster than the men had planned for. Good. Real good.

"All I can think about is grabbing one of those rafts. They're calling to me like a homing beacon." Seth smiled, even if it did feel a bit grim. Zombie Laura was gone and his wonderful capable Laura was back. They had proven to be fairly unstoppable when practical and capable Laura was around.

"We need some distraction. Something big enough and far enough away to get all those men to run to it. We don't need much. Just enough time to get to the rafts, throw one in the water and jump in. Even if they follow us, it will be near impossible for one raft to catch up with another successfully in these rapids."

"Do you still have your knife?"

"I— Yes. Why?" She had sounded a little bloodthirsty when she asked and Seth was momentarily afraid that she was going to try to engage in hand-to-hand combat with these guys. When it came to protecting Abby, Seth wasn't sure he would put it past her.

"I'm going to stab the other two rafts. Deflate them. They won't be able to follow us."

Seth nodded his head slowly as he surveyed the area again. "They still have those Jeeps. They could drive alongside the river, catch up that way."

"Until they hit that fire they set. Can't drive through

that." Laura sounded almost smug and Seth smiled. She was right. Again. He handed her his knife.

"They can also shoot at us. The river will move us quickly, but bullets are fast, too. They could hit us. Or the raft. Both would be the end of our escape."

"This is outside my area of expertise. Any ideas how we get past bullets?"

Seth pulled out his gun. "I can try returning fire, but it's me against eight men."

"So, what do we do?"

There really wasn't a choice. They'd been backed into hard positions since this thing first started, but this was by far the hardest. The tightest corner. But it was the corner they were in and they had to just deal. "We try. We pray. We do our best and hope that it works."

"Okay." Laura's voice was not hesitant or unsure. Seth was so incredibly grateful that he was not alone in this mess. That he had her there with him to help him through. "So what kind of distraction are we going to do? I'm afraid I won't be any help with that one unless it involves me running and screaming. But I don't think that will get us what we want."

Seth smiled. No, that was not going to be the plan. "I don't know, yet. There are some crates and boxes over there. See them? I kind of want to check them out."

"What do you think is in there?"

"I don't know for sure, but I'm hoping weapons. Or maybe even something I could use for an explosion."

"An explosion? You can do that?"

Seth gave her a mock serious look. "Yes, ma'am. I can be real handy with explosions when I need to be." He'd used them more than once in Afghanistan. It had been a couple of years, but those skills were the kind that stayed with you for forever. Sometimes Seth had considered that to be a curse. Right now, though, he was viewing it as an asset to be grateful for.

Seth looked at their current location. "Do you think you and Abby will be safe here while I go check things out? Rig some kind of diversion?"

Laura looked behind her to the grouping of trees they'd been in before almost walking into this trap. "I think so. We might have more cover back there, but we'd have to actually walk that way. I feel safer here without moving."

"Yeah. We were fortunate walking in. Movement could catch their attention. Okay. You stay here with Abby. Be ready to go. I don't know how much lead time I can give us before whatever diversion I come up with, so we might have to move quickly."

Seth started to crawl away, not wanting to dwell on the fact that he was about to separate himself from Laura and Abby for the first time since this whole thing started. He was leaving them. Alone. If something happened, he would not be there to protect them. No, he needed to get on with it. Put their plan into action. It was the only way to get this done. If he lingered too long, thought too much, he probably wouldn't leave at all. Fear could be paralyzing, and the best way was for him to break on through. So he started to go.

But Laura reached out and grabbed his hand. Her grip was firm and her other hand came around so that his hand was clutched between both of hers. "I, um, you're leaving. You're going to leave."

He brought his other hand and added it to the pile so it was a mass of hands gripping and clinging. "It's okay, Laura. I'll be okay. I know how to move without being seen. This isn't the first enemy camp I've explored, though I wouldn't mind if it was my last." He smiled at her, trying to reassure her that this was not the end of the world. He might have a boulder in the bottom of his stomach right now, but he didn't want her feeling that way. Not now, not ever.

She blew out a shaky breath and her eyes still looked distressed but she stopped clutching him in that desperate manner. "You're right. I'm sorry." Laura looked at Abby, who was watching all of this with wide eyes. She reached over and pulled the girl into her lap, snuggling her neck. "I'm sorry. We're good. You go save the day and we'll be ready to run like crazy."

He didn't believe that she was good. But there wasn't anything he could do right now. The best thing for them was to get off the mountain. To get to safety. That was the goal Seth needed to focus on.

He turned from them then. Looking away from these two people who had come to mean so much to him. And he faced the camp. The men lounging around, large guns in their hands. Their barricade. Pushing everything out of his mind, Seth began to make his way to those boxes.

He was a soldier on a mission.

TWELVE

He was gone.

Seth was gone.

Laura had watched him as he moved away. He'd looked like he was going to make a wide circle around the camp, trying to get to those boxes by staying as far away as possible. Laura could not see him anymore. She kept looking at that grouping of boxes, forcing herself to breathe in and out as she waited to see Seth there. Exploring them, as he put it. But so far, she only saw those men with large guns who were waiting to kill them.

No. Getting caught by those men would be the end. Done.

Laura gripped the handle of the knife tightly, squeezing it almost like a pressure ball. She still had the rifle right next to her. Loaded. Ready. But using it would alert every man in this camp that she was here. If she was discovered by one man, she had a fighting chance of protecting herself and her daughter with the knife without bringing the rest of the men running.

The thought of what she was planning made her sick. It was almost too much. She had come to the mountain to be alone. To find peace and safety. And now she was contemplating how she could use a knife to hurt someone.

No. Not to hurt someone. To protect someone. To protect her Abby.

Laura moved Abby off her lap. She had quietly explained to the little girl that they were waiting for Seth and then they were going to run as fast as they could to the raft. Abby had been in boats before, but she had never been white-water rafting. She'd never even seen someone do it.

Laura had explained about holding on. About lying down on the floor of the raft. About staying right by her mommy so she could be safe. Abby had repeated the instructions back to Laura. Hopefully it would be enough.

Laura took her eyes off those boxes to scan the area again. It was the same. Too many men and too many guns. She looked behind her, and her fear ratcheted up another notch. The smoke was definitely closer. The fire the men had set behind them was working exactly as planned. It would eventually force them into the camp.

Laura wondered where Mahoney was. It seemed that the men had plans to get to safety by driving over the top of the mountains in the Jeeps. Or maybe rafting down the mountain. Laura still couldn't believe that there were rafts here. She supposed she ought to be grateful that they were the well-prepared type.

But would they be prepared with the things Seth needed? He was going around in a wide circle to reach those boxes. But there was no way they could make it to the rafts or the Jeeps without being spotted. And given how close the fire was, Laura hadn't even suggested trying to sneak past the men and keep on moving.

This entire plan hinged on some kind of distraction.

Away from the river. That was their only hope of reaching a raft and getting down the river in it.

Laura looked back to the boxes and gasped. Seth was there. He had a second knife out and was prying the lid off one. There were three men about fifty feet away. They were not facing Seth, and they were engaged in loud conversation. They were laughing. Happy. Laura felt sour disgust on her tongue as she watched the men who were waiting to kill them laugh and be merry.

She looked back to Seth and held her breath as he lifted the lid. He was moving slowly, and Laura prayed that he was able to be quiet as he dealt with the contents of the box. Laura saw him look inside. She couldn't read his expression.

Seth reached inside the box and began pulling things out, but Laura did not know what they were. Did he have what he needed or was he going to try to make do? Laura understood why she and Abby stayed where they were. It was easier for Seth to move around and not be detected. Laura and Abby were currently in the best location to make a dash for those rafts. Even so, Laura found herself wishing she was with Seth right now. Good or bad, she wanted to face the contents of those boxes together.

Seth filled his bag with the mysterious objects and then faded into nothing again. One minute he was in front of her and the next he was gone. *Please, God, be with him. Help him. Make this work.*

Laura quickly went through the pack and took out things she thought they could live without. It was heavy and would slow down their run to the rafts. She kept some food. Some basic first-aid supplies. Taking Abby's duck from her, she explained that Duckie was going to ride in the bag. It seemed silly, but odds were good that the cabin had been consumed by the fire. That duck might be the only thing her sweet girl had left, and she deserved to take her only friend with her.

Laura set the pack down, straps up and ready to go. She moved to her knees and told Abby to get ready to run. If Seth came to them already running, they would be ready to join him.

Laura kept her eyes on the area Seth had disappeared into when he left her and Abby. She assumed he would come back from the same direction. She hoped he would approach them slowly and steadily, the same way he had left. She hoped he would return and tell her everything was going to be okay. That the distraction would happen soon. She hoped he would pick up Abby, and she could shoulder the pack. Laura hoped they could hold hands and wait. And then run. Together. As one. As planned.

Hopes were nice. They had seen Laura through many dark times. But these hopes all died as the earth literally moved. Something big had just blown up. The men all jumped up. There was yelling. Questions. Smoke rose from the part of the forest where Seth had disappeared with the contents of that box. The men ran toward it then. All of them. The camp was empty and there was a clear path to those rafts.

But where was Seth? Was he hurt? Was he unable to make a delayed explosion and so he sacrificed himself for them?

Was she supposed to run to those rafts without him? *No, Lord. Please.* If she ran now and he was hurt or coming, then he would be left behind. If she did not run now and those men came back, then she and Abby would be caught. Those men had to know they were in the area. That explosion was clearly not an accident.

What am I supposed to do, God? Help me. I don't know what to do!

Laura was looking between the rafts and the place where Seth should be coming from. She stood up. Picked up Abby. Indecision ripped her soul into pieces.

It wasn't supposed to be like this.

And then she finally saw Seth. He was running, full steam, toward her. "Go! Go! Run, Laura!"

And she did. She started running, ignoring the shakiness in her legs from those moments where she thought Seth wasn't coming. Seth caught up to her and took Abby out of her arms without breaking stride.

They reached the rafts. Seth set Abby down and grabbed one. Placed it on the river bank and then put Abby inside. They were getting ready to push it in the water. To push and jump and hold on, when Laura heard the first gunshot.

Aimed at them.

She turned and saw several large, angry men running their way. And they were shooting as they came.

Seth didn't know if he was irritated his explosion didn't wait until he was back to Laura before going off or proud that he had managed to make it go boom at all. That crate had not been full of the ordinances of Seth's dreams. He'd had to take apart several smaller weapons and use their parts to make an explosive device. He'd also had to rig up some kind of fuse to get any delay at all.

He'd done his best, but he'd known, he had just known, that it would not be good enough. That was okay. When he was running back to Laura, when he heard the explosion happen much earlier than it should have, he had known that she would probably leave without him. And, with that knife, she would probably take away the option of him using another raft to follow.

And that was okay. He was running, using his legs for all they were worth, feeling the pain from the old injury jolt in his knees as he pushed even harder, and he was okay. Laura and Abby would make it to safety. They would go down that river and away from these guys and past the fire. They could ride until they reached help. And Seth would know that he had done a good and honorable job.

Dying was not a new concept. Dying in an unexpected and painful way wasn't new, either. Seth had come to terms with the choices he made in his life.

He had lost that peace for a while, back home. How ironic that it was the safety of home and the love of his family that had taken away his blasé acceptance of what was to come. And he had run. But he had fixed that as much as possible. Laura would help him make amends and his family would have some kind of closure.

So Seth had run and run and run. Even though it was pointless. Even though he was too late and he had missed his chance. But Laura would have hers. He ran, rounding that corner, fully prepared to see two destroyed rafts and one missing raft. And he was ready to thank God for that, to thank Him that Laura and her sweet girl would make it. To give thanks and then to fight until he couldn't fight anymore.

He'd almost fallen over when he took that corner and saw Laura and Abby. Standing there. They were just standing there looking at him. Why were they just standing there when the explosion had gone off minutes ago? He'd yelled, as loud as he could. There was no point in trying to be covert. Not if Laura and Abby never made it to the rafts.

They'd pushed the raft into the water, skipping the step where they disabled the other rafts. There just wasn't time.

Then the bullets came. One hit a rock that sat halfway in the water. The rock burst into little pieces, tiny shards of warning that their time was well and truly up. They needed to get in that raft and get speeding down the river or they would not be going anywhere.

Those men would catch Laura and Abby and they would kill them. That could not happen.

No.

Abby was on her stomach in the raft, her little body as close to the floor as it could be. She was holding on to some of the inner ties. Good girl. Laura must have told her what to do and she was doing it perfectly. Such a smart and good girl.

It took three shoves to get the raft in the water, and the shots behind them didn't stop. Seth did not know how none of them hit the raft or him and Laura. No, that wasn't true. He did know. He always knew who protected him in this world.

Laura and Seth jumped in the raft before the current could carry it away and Seth was thankful yet again for Laura's outdoor skills. She knew exactly what to do and Seth did not have to worry about her in that respect. They each picked up the oars that were lying next to Abby and began to paddle. The current was powerful, so if they could get the raft floating they would be okay.

They should be okay.

They would have a fighting chance at least.

And a fighting chance was all they needed to make it.

"Stay as low as possible." He had to yell to be heard over the noise of the water all around them. He could see the men running toward them, guns still pulled. The closer they got, the better their chances of actually hitting their target.

"I didn't think you were coming." Seth jerked his gaze away from the men and looked at Laura. Her voice was pure anguish. Absolute pain. She was…she was… crying.

Seth gripped the oar harder and used every bit of strength the adrenaline rush had given him to paddle, willing the raft to move faster. They needed to be away from these men. They needed to be down this river. To be safe, so Seth could hug Laura and reassure her and do whatever he needed to do to make that look leave her face. To make that tone go away. It was unacceptable that she was feeling this way. Unacceptable, and Seth needed to fix it.

They both jerked down at the sound of a gunshot that was much, much closer than the others had been. Too close.

He looked and saw a Jeep speeding along, tracking them on land while their raft tried to run away downriver. The Jeep was going very fast and the ground was bumpy, so the man standing up in the back and trying to kill them wasn't able to aim accurately.

Another shot. Seth flinched again.

He might not be able to get a clear shot off, but he was sure getting close enough. Seth pulled his own gun and returned fire. His shot didn't land, but the Jeep did swerve a bit, so that was good. Something. Better than nothing.

Seth turned and saw Laura struggling with the oar. He immediately put his gun back in its holster and resumed working with his oar. The current provided momentum. They were going plenty fast, and though Seth wanted to get away he didn't really want to go any faster. This raft already felt like an out-of-control amusement park ride.

No, they weren't using the oars for speed. They were using them to navigate around the obstacles in the water. Rocks, tree branches, rocks, rocks and rocks. They were high up in the Rocky Mountains and this part of the country was aptly named.

Abby was wet, very wet. Seth could see her shivering. All the water that sloshed into the raft as they pushed against rocks with their oars and encountered the churning liquid landed on the floor of the raft. Where Abby was. But she was still holding on. Laura was sitting with one leg over the child, helping to hold her in place.

Seth worried about Abby drowning, but she was on her side. Her face was clear of the water on the floor. And down there was safer than the alternative.

He flinched as another shot came from the Jeep. And then another.

This needed to stop. One of those shots was going to land. Seth knew it. Statistics said it would land eventually and the shooter was not giving up. Seth looked down the river, almost hoping to see the active fire. They needed to get to that part, where the Jeep could no longer follow.

Seth saw smoke, but no flames. The river was windy

at this part, so it could be around the next bend. It could be close. *Please, God, let it be close.*

"Seth!" Laura's scream was just as anguished as her last statement. He looked to where she was pointing. At a raft. Following them down the river. It had four men in it and they were close enough that Seth could see the murderous expressions on their faces.

And the guns in their hands.

THIRTEEN

When Laura had first seen those rafts, she'd thought they were God's way of answering her prayers. Now she thought they were the physical embodiment of every nightmare she had ever had. They should have tried to sneak around the barricade. Or to go through the fire. Either of those options suddenly seemed better and more reasonable to Laura than their current predicament.

It couldn't be possible, but it seemed like the men on the raft behind them were catching up. Even though they were in the same water, with the same type of boat, theirs looked like it was going faster.

Laura closed her eyes, squeezing the handle of her oar until the pain cut through the numbness. They had four large men in that raft. Each man had an oar. Those men were not using their oars to avoid rocks. They were using them to propel the raft through the water.

The raft was going to capture them.

It was going to catch up and then they would shoot Seth. They looked angry enough that they might shoot Laura and Abby, too, no matter what Mahoney had said.

This was going to end badly.

But she wasn't about to give up. "Seth, they are all using their oars to go faster. The raft is going to catch up with us."

Seth didn't respond to her yell, but the look on his face showed that he either heard her or he had realized the same thing.

The Jeep was still following on the side of the river. The man in the back was yelling into some kind of radio. He was talking instead of shooting. That couldn't be good.

What was he planning? Why had he stopped shooting?

"Laura! Look! The fire!"

Laura looked and saw. The fire. They had rounded several curves in the macabre pinball game they were playing, and the flames from the fire were now very visible. Laura thought she could feel the heat, but that was probably her imagination.

The flames moved and danced and Laura had to force herself to look at the river, to focus on the boulders there. Those large, hard obstacles were every bit as much a threat as the men with guns who followed them on land and water.

The only good thing about getting ready to raft through a fire was that the Jeep would have to stop. That would take away an attack from at least one side.

"Laura. Get down. Now." Seth's voice was somehow low and deadly and still loud enough to carry to her. She looked ahead and saw a second Jeep parked on the side of the river, at the spot right before the flames were consuming the mountain.

It was parked and waiting.

There were several men standing by it.

With guns.

Pointed at them.

That was what the Jeep man had been doing. Radioing for backup. Backup that wasn't hindered by being in a moving Jeep traveling over uneven ground. Backup that could probably hit its target.

And they were the target.

Laura got down as much as possible. She moved so that both of her legs were over Abby, and she could feel her child's heat under her thighs. Getting down to avoid getting shot meant the raft was going to hit more rocks.

Seth handed her his oar. "Hold this. I'll shoot better with two hands, but I don't want to lose my oar."

Laura clung to the handle, pairing it up with hers. She had them both pulled inside the raft, clutching them like some kind of shield. Too bad they weren't bulletproof. She crouched down as low as possible, shoving the oars under one armpit and holding them with one hand. Laura reached down with the other hand and held on to Abby. She tried to make her hand gentle and reassuring, but she doubted her girl felt anything but terrified.

This was not the kind of childhood a little girl should have. How had it come to this? All Laura had wanted to do was get off this mountain and live a normal life. Be a normal girl. Normal.

Yet, here she was. Back on this mountain. Widowed. Running for her life. Dragging her child through one traumatic experience after another. It wasn't supposed to be like this. It wasn't supposed to be like this at all.

She looked up from her crouch and saw Seth holding one of the raft ties in his fist. She knew he was hoping to secure himself to the raft, but the sight didn't make her feel better at all. He couldn't wrap it around his wrist or hand because if he went over that could really hurt him. But she didn't think he would be able to hold on, either. It was just too much to ask of a human being. Right now, the sight of him holding that rope felt very useless to Laura. Pointless. And depressing.

She flinched at the sound of the first shot. Suppressed a scream. Heard Abby cry out.

Then there was a second shot. A third. Coming from Seth. From that parked Jeep. From the raft behind them. Back and forth, and all too loud and too close.

The raft was jerking, bouncing off of boulders. Slamming into waves. Those movements were painful and terrifying and probably the only reason that the men on the riverbank or raft behind them had not managed to shoot them yet.

Seth fired one more time and then he stopped. He slid over to where Laura was and shielded her body with his. He was around her and over her and covering her and Abby much more than Laura would have thought was possible. "I hit the other raft, but I didn't do anything to the men on the shore. I'm out of bullets. We're almost to the fire line. Almost."

Almost. Almost. Almost. Laura chanted the words in her head. They were a plea. And a prayer. They had come so far, they had to make it through this, too. They just had to.

The weight of Seth's body increased and Laura was almost lying down on top of Abby. The water in the bottom of the raft was freezing and they were all soaking wet. None of that stopped Laura from feeling the heat, though. It came out of nowhere, though really it had been their end goal all along. They were past the fire line.

The bullets stopped. That horrible popping noise that made Laura tense every muscle waiting to see if a bullet would hit its mark. It was gone.

But it wasn't quiet. The fire was every bit as alive and growling as the water. The men in the Jeep had been intent on killing them. This fire seemed intent on killing anything. Everything. In its path or not. It was hungry, and they were nothing more than fuel.

About a minute after the last shot was fired, Seth sat up. He grabbed one of the oars that Laura was holding and moved back to the front of the raft. Now that they were done fighting the men, they only had to fight the river. And a fire.

The river was substantial, but the flames were jumping toward it. They needed to stay away from that side. Laura positioned her own oar and started helping. It was a relief to be proactive when it came to all these boulders. The repetitive jarring of slamming into rock after rock lessened.

Laura's arms began to ache with the effort she was expending, but it felt good. She was alive, and she was still fighting. Her eyes began to water, maybe from the heat. Maybe from the wind.

She gazed at the part of the mountain on the other side of the river. It looked dry. And, most important, not on fire. It was so tempting to try to navigate over there. To try to stop, get out, walk on her legs. Make Abby dry and warm.

But that was not an option. It wasn't safe to try to

land the raft over there. Those men were not giving up. How long would it take them to cross the river and come down the mountain? Though it was bumpy and cold and flat-out miserable, this river was still the fastest route down. It was still their best shot at getting off this mountain and to help.

Laura could only see Seth's back. And more fire. Up ahead, for as far as she could see, fire. Flames and heat and fire and the consumption of this mountain she loved so much.

Her dad's part of the mountain. His refuge.

Her part of the mountain. Her refuge.

The river curved and Laura actually sobbed when she saw that the fire had burned out up ahead. She hadn't even realized she was crying until those tears became a fountain of emotion. Seth turned to look at her, and she just pointed. His smile was somber, but it was there. He turned back around to face the front again and Laura reached down to pat Abby on the back.

She smiled at the girl. "It's going to be okay, Abby. We're almost done with the worst part."

As quickly as it appeared, that heat ended. Smoke was still heavy in the air, but Laura glanced over to where the sky looked blue. She imagined the town at the base. The town that this river was taking them to. The town full of people, and not the kind who wanted to kill them. The kind who could help to keep Abby safe.

This was going to be okay.

"Laura!" Seth's tone told her that she was wrong. This was not going to be okay. He leaned to the side, and she looked up ahead. There were several large trees lying across the river. There was no way to get around. Their raft would hit nature's equivalent of a brick wall.

* * *

This wasn't happening.

Okay, it was. And, frankly, Seth didn't know why he was surprised. This week was going down in history as one of the worst weeks ever. And he said that as a man who had fought in a brutal war, been injured and run away from his family. Yeah. This week had been that bad.

"Go right. Try to go right." He had to turn around to make sure Laura heard him. She immediately started trying to push the raft that way. He did, too. But it wasn't enough. Even with their combined efforts, their skilled efforts, the raft was resisting any attempt to go toward the side of the river that had not been burned by the fire.

"Seth, it's too hard. The current is working against us." She was right of course. He should have realized sooner. Much of their ride down so far had involved trying to stay away from the side of the mountain that was on fire. Because the raft wanted to list that way.

"The left. Go to the left." His aching muscles almost appreciated the change in exertion.

And it was working. It was absolutely working. The raft moved over to the bank, hitting some of the smaller rocks lining that side. They were in the right position now. They just needed to slow down.

Just.

"Seth, look. We can use that to ramp up on the bank." Laura was pointing to a place up ahead where the bank dipped in. Made a little inlet. Yes, this could work.

Seth tensed his arms as they approached the inlet. He used every bit of strength he could muster and pushed toward it. He heard Laura give a yell as she pushed, too.

And the raft was stopped. They were in the inlet. Seth quickly scrambled out, taking one of the raft ties with him. He pulled it taut and looked over to tell Laura to follow.

But she was already there with Abby. She pushed the child ahead of her, half carrying her as she climbed over the end edge of the raft onto dry land.

Once they were off, Seth started to pull the raft out of the water. He looked up in surprise when Laura stepped in front of him, grabbed the rope and began pulling, too. The raft came out of the water. Once it was fully on the ground, with no chance of it being sucked back in, Seth let go.

He sank down to his knees on the ground and watched Laura do the same. She held her arms out to Abby, and the little girl ran to her mom. Abby threw herself at Laura with such force that both mother and child ended up lying on the ground.

Seth crawled over to where Laura was and flopped on his back next to her. She was holding Abby on top of her body, the little girl looking almost like a blanket. A shaking blanket. Seth couldn't hear the crying, but Abby was clearly sobbing into her mother's neck.

And neither one of them said a word.

They just stayed there, breathing heavily, shivering, trying to soak up every sunray that was available.

After what felt like one minute and one hour all at once, Seth rolled over and looked at Laura. She turned her head toward him. "Well, that was fun," she said. "Let's do that again the week after never."

Seth smiled at her humor. All of this, and she was still here with him. "So, you're saying that you don't want to carry this raft to the other side of the wall of trees and get back in?" His tone was light, but his question was very much a serious one. They were not out of the woods yet. Neither literally nor metaphorically.

She looked at Abby, who was still on top of her. Laura's hands were back to rubbing again, more soothing motions that were probably also meant to help the child warm up.

"What do you think, Seth? I really don't want to get back in the raft. It's dangerous and cold. Abby is so tired, I'm afraid that she'll get hurt."

She wasn't wrong. Again. "We were really fortunate with that first ride. Really favored. I agree—let's walk."

Laura sat up, keeping Abby in her lap, the child still plastered to her chest. "Okay. Let's go. The sooner we start, the sooner we'll reach town."

Seth wanted to build a fire and warm them up. He wanted to get them out of those wet clothes. He wanted to let them rest. And he really wanted to take off his boots and take the world's longest nap. But he could do none of those things. He could only stand up, hold out a hand to help pull Laura to her feet and then reach out and take Abby.

He didn't ask this time. He just took the little girl, and she came without protest from either mom or child. She was trembling slightly in Seth's arms and he held her closer to his body, hoping his heat would both warm and calm her.

"I don't even want to think about how we spent the better part of two days walking up this mountain and we just undid all that work in minutes." Her voice sounded tired. Really tired.

"I know. But we're okay. And we're clear of those

men." He wanted to reassure her. "Plus, we're walking downhill now. This is good."

"We're past the point where the cabin was. It's probably gone, huh?"

Seth really wished that he was okay with lying to her. But he wouldn't do that. Not to anyone, but especially not to her. "I don't know, Laura. But you're probably right. It's probably damaged at best."

She was silent, and Seth tried to give her time to process, focusing on leading them downhill on the easiest path he could find. Abby had stopped shivering. Her head was heavy on his shoulder, and Seth looked down to see her eyes were closed. She was sleeping.

Something moved in his chest as he pondered the gift that was carrying a sleeping child. A little girl who trusted him enough to let go of any worry or fear. Who trusted that he would make everything okay and all she had to do was close her eyes and go to sleep.

I'm not going to let her down, Lord. I'm not going to let either one of them down. Help me. Let us feel your presence. Keep these three people safe.

"Seth?" Laura's voice was soft, and he thought he heard tears in it. He tightened his arms around Abby to stop himself from reaching out to Laura.

"Yeah?"

"I'm really glad you're here. I thought I wanted to be all alone with Abby, but I was wrong. I was really wrong. A person isn't meant to go through life isolated from others."

Seth stopped walking and closed his eyes. This woman reached right inside him and just pierced his heart. The one he had tried so hard to turn to stone. It wasn't stone. It was soft. And bleeding.

He opened his eyes and looked at her. "I'm glad I'm here, too, Laura." It was the truth. And it was the very surface of all the things he felt swirling around inside his heart and mind. He just needed some time, preferably off this mountain and somewhere safe, to consider them. Understand what they meant.

They walked, then. And walked some more. It was the continuing theme of this journey so far. Seth figured they had to be getting close to something. To the bottom or to people or to something. Laura's mountain was remote and covered a large area but it did not go down indefinitely. They had to be off it. He turned to ask Laura if she recognized where they were when Abby moved.

"Mama!" Abby lifted her head and reached out for her mom. Seth felt an intense sense of loss as Laura took the girl and she was no longer cradled against his chest.

"Hey there, pretty girl, did you have a nice nap?" Laura was murmuring into Abby's ear, but Seth could hear every word. And he could sense the maternal love that Laura radiated when she was with her child.

Seth felt the burn before he heard the shot. The impact of the bullet knocked him off his feet. He heard Laura and Abby scream, but all he could see was the sky. It was blue again. The smoke was blowing up the mountain, and from right here it looked like a beautiful day.

Laura was kneeling over him, pushing down on his chest so hard that he groaned. Why was she hurting him? He moved his hands to where Laura's were and felt something warm and wet. Blood. His blood.

"Laura. Run. You and Abby need to run."

Her expression could only be described as horrified. "No. No, Seth."

He grabbed her wrists. Pulled them away. "Go. The shooter will be coming. You have to save Abby."

His vision was blurring, but he saw the tears rolling down her cheek. She looked at him with anguish in her eyes, regret tightening her mouth. She nodded. "Thank you. I'm so sorry."

The she bent down and kissed him. It was the best thing he had ever felt. He wanted it to last forever.

No. She needed to run.

She lifted her lips and put her hand over her mouth. Seth turned his head and watched her pick up Abby and start to run.

The dark spots in his vision were dancing. Growing bigger. But he kept his eyes on Laura and Abby, willing them to run and run and run until they simply disappeared.

Laura made it twenty feet when a group of men stepped out of the trees right in front of her. She froze.

"Hello, Ms. Donovan. You've made this all much harder than it needed to be. Tried to ruin my plans. But you'll be glad to know that I think I can salvage them." The man standing in the middle spoke with a condescending tone. He wasn't armed, but he didn't need to be. The other men with him were armed enough for everyone.

Seth tried to yell, to distract them. To plead with them. To do…something. His words were a harsh whisper. They did nothing.

Seth watched the man walk up and put his hand on Laura's cheek. Reach over and stroke Abby's hair, even though Laura tried to jerk her daughter away from that touch.

Seth had messed up, and it was too late to fix it.

They should have risked riding the raft the rest of the way down.

Then black spots became all that there was.

FOURTEEN

Laura needed to stay calm to get out of this situation. Calm. She needed to be calm.

That was impossible. Seth was bleeding into the forest somewhere. Or not. Maybe he had stopped bleeding. Maybe he was dead. Laura bit the side of her tongue until the pain added to her tears. She wasn't going to think like that. Seth was okay. Seth had to be okay.

Except, she knew he wasn't. Mahoney had walked over to him, and Laura feared he was going to let the man who called dibs finish it. To kill Seth. Instead, he had laughed and said to leave Seth. To let him die a slow death.

No. Please, please, please. Please, God. Let Seth be okay.

Abby made a little squeak and Laura realized she was holding her too tight. She lessened the pressure of her arms. "Sorry, baby. Mama's sorry."

For so much. Much, much more than a tight hug.

They were sitting on what used to be a chair in her home. The boss's men had used their guns to get Laura and Abby into yet another Jeep. A gun pointed at her daughter made Laura startlingly eager to do whatever was asked of her. Whatever she was told—ordered to do.

Laura couldn't identify the emotions at seeing her cabin again. The forest all around was destroyed. But this cabin. It was safe. It was whole. Well, for the most part, anyway. The fire had come in. Touched some things. Left. But most of her belongings were salvageable.

Mahoney had laughed at her expression. "Yeah. I saved it. Couldn't have it going up in flames empty, could I? Good thing my guys were prepared."

He'd pointed to the chair and Laura had sat. Ten minutes later, she still felt…nothing. Numb. Too numb even for the terror to come through.

But it was there. She had Abby on her lap. Had both arms wrapped tight around her. Was clutching her and vowing to protect her daughter with everything she had.

Right now, Abby felt an awful lot like a shield. Like whatever tried to hurt Laura would have to go through Abby.

Laura hated that. Numb or not, she could feel her skin crawling with the realization that her daughter was protecting her in a very real way. She wanted to move Abby from her lap. From in front of her chest. But where would she put her? Wasn't she safer in her mother's arms than anywhere else? That should be the safest place in the world for a little girl.

But if this man chose to shoot her, to shoot her in the same place where he shot Seth, that bullet would have to go through Abby to get to her.

Suddenly, Laura wasn't numb. She was feeling everything all at once. Hot and cold and terror. The urge to run. To flee. To hide. The need to fall to her knees, both to beg God and to beg this man.

Please, please, please. Don't hurt my baby. Not my baby.

Laura wanted to offer herself. To see if she could be enough of a sacrifice to appease this man. But, if she was, if he chose only to hurt her and not Abby, then where would her daughter be? How could she survive left alone on this mountain?

They had spent days, literally, trying to get away from Mahoney. Running and hiding. Praying. Planning. Using every bit of physical and mental energy that they had.

It didn't matter. None of it mattered. Laura and Abby were right back where they started. And, Seth. Seth was, well, not here. Maybe not alive.

No. No, no, no.

This was not happening.

Laura stood up, still clutching Abby. All the men in the room turned toward her. All with guns drawn. Laura swallowed, but she just knew she would go insane if she had to sit and wait and wonder. She couldn't take the possibilities anymore.

"Sit back down, Mrs. Donovan. Right now." Mahoney did not sound upset, but he still sounded deadly. His hand held the gun like he knew what he was doing with it. That hand wasn't shaking. It looked awfully sure and ready.

"Why? You're just going to kill us anyway, aren't you? Like you did Seth?"

"I am. But I would really prefer it looked like an accident."

Anger rushed a course of fire across Laura's face.

"Yeah. And I'd really prefer that someone knows we were killed. That someone looks for our killer. That someone comes after you."

Laura swallowed a sob. She could do this. She had to. It had come down to this, and it was time for her to leave Abby in Jesus's hands and trust that He would protect her. Laura swallowed again, determined to not talk to this man with a trembling or weak voice. He probably knew that he had gotten to her, but she refused to give him the evidence of that fact.

"Besides, you already shot Seth. The authorities are going to know there was a murderer up on the mountain."

Mahoney lowered his gun and smiled at the man standing to his left. Laura noticed that none of the other men had lowered their weapons even a fraction.

"Oh, I disagree, Mrs. Donovan. Killing the ranger wasn't ideal, but you're the one who brought him into this. And when the authorities look into his death, they will have no reason to ever connect him to me. Especially since you and your daughter will have died in this unfortunate fire."

Laura felt herself glaring, but this wasn't an ideal time to physically attack the man. For one, she'd have to put Abby down. For two, well, she didn't have a two. All she cared about, all she knew, was that she had to figure out a way to save Abby.

That wasn't true. She still cared about Seth. So much. He was also struggling with his own regrets. He'd had been with her these last few days. She did not want him to die.

And for a woman who had wanted to sit in the dark and hide after her husband died, Laura found that she cared very much about her own future, too. But she could not help Seth. She couldn't even help herself. Maybe, just maybe, she could help Abby.

Please, God. Please let this work.

"I want my daughter to survive this. She's young. Too young. She'll never remember what happened. Or what you looked like. Your name. If you drop her off in town, make sure she is found, she can still live a full life. And she won't be any kind of threat to you."

Laura swallowed several times in a row. Her daughter. Her baby. She hopefully wouldn't remember the terror of this week. But she wouldn't remember Laura, either. She wouldn't remember that she was wanted and loved. That her mother did not leave her willingly.

"Ah, Mrs. Donovan, you're touching my heart. Really, I'm feeling it right here." He tapped his chest, where his heart would be. Laura didn't think he had one, though. He couldn't. "And what would convince me to take your child to safety after I kill you?"

Laura forced herself to ignore the part where he confirmed that he was actually going to kill her. She already knew that, but it still didn't feel good to hear him say it out loud. "Because you're not an evil man." He was. He really was. But she was desperate.

Mahoney crossed his arms over his chest and looked at Laura. His eyes were narrowed and his mouth was a rigidly straight line. "I do not like being manipulated, Mrs. Donovan. I like to be in charge. I am always in charge."

Laura met his gaze. She wasn't going to look away from this man. And, if she was going to die, she wanted to know why. "How did you know Josh? What did you do to him?"

Mahoney smiled. "Oh, your Joshua was one of my best employees."

Laura sat down. She was breathing as slowly as possible, trying to stop the tears.

Mahoney sat across from her. He leaned back in his chair, crossing the ankle of one suit-clad leg over the knee of the other. He looked comfortable, as though they were discussing the weather instead of her husband's attachment to a criminal. "I'll be brief, Mrs. Donovan. I've had an eventful few days, and I'm actually quite ready to get back to the comforts of my home. I'm a drug dealer. A really, really good one."

Laura stared at him with her eyes so wide that her skin felt stretched.

"I'm also a man of business. And I like things to be—" he quirked his lips at Laura and she swallowed back even more bile "—neat. I needed help with my money, and so I hired the best."

No. Laura knew where he was going now. He had hired Josh?

"Ah, you're catching on. My private detectives told me that you were smart. I can see they were correct. Yes, I hired your husband's firm. He handled my account. He was excellent at what he did."

"Josh wasn't a criminal. He wasn't." It seemed ridiculous to argue this point, but Laura couldn't help herself. This man would never convince her that Josh had been involved with the drug trade.

"No. Sadly for all of you, he was not. He worked for me for several years, and all was well. Then, somehow, he realized something was, shall we say, amiss. I did not know it at the time, but he started gathering evidence of my misdeeds. He was going to turn me in to the authorities."

Yes. That was the Josh that Laura had known.

"Thankfully, I discovered what he was doing. I'm a careful man. I have certain, ah, safeguards in place. And they protected me."

Laura was back to glaring. He sounded so proud of his criminal system.

"Once I became aware, I took actions to eliminate the threat. I had an associate kill your husband."

There was a roaring in her ears. It sounded like a train. And a wail. He'd just told her he killed her husband. He said it like it was nothing. Like he washed his car and picked up pizza for dinner.

"Unfortunately, my associate was a bit hasty. He killed young Joshua before finding the papers."

"Papers?" Laura didn't know what he was talking about, but that might have been because her brain was stuck back on the part about how he killed her husband and destroyed her life.

"Keep up, Mrs. Donovan. I dislike having to repeat myself. Your husband collected papers proving my guilt. It would be quite difficult for me if those papers landed in the wrong hands."

"Like the police."

"Exactly."

"The safe-deposit box," she whispered. That key she had found.

"We had looked everywhere. We even searched your home."

Laura's throat was almost too tight to talk. "My home?"

Mahoney looked almost rueful. "Oh, yes. While you

were at young Joshua's funeral. We did not find the papers anywhere."

Laura was going to throw up. "I've been wanting to know. How did you know about the key?"

Mahoney's face tightened. "We've been watching you. Waiting. Thinking that eventually you would take the papers to the authorities. But you never did."

They had been watching her, even up on the mountain. Seth had been right. Of course he had been. The logical answer was usually the true answer. Was the feeling of safety ever real?

"We've been monitoring calls—both your phone and Joshua's firm," Mahoney said. "You called them last week, asking about the key."

She really was the reason Mahoney was here.

"Once I knew you had the key to the box that held those papers," Mahoney continued, "I had to plan a way to get to you. It turned out that my preparation really paid off." More anger in his voice. "You and that park ranger made this much more difficult than it needed to be."

Laura's own anger bubbled and roiled.

"But I have you where I want you now. And this will all be over in a minute."

The bubbling and roiling froze and Laura's blood was ice.

For a second, Seth thought he was stuck in yet another dream about Afghanistan. The only thing he could feel was the acid inside his body, eating away at what was left of his soul. And he was alone, all alone.

Seth opened his eyes and sucked in a ragged breath. Smoke. Wetness. Rocky ground. He wasn't in his bed having another nightmare. He was up on Laura's mountain. And she and Abby weren't here.

The men. Seth jerked as the full implication hit him. Those men had Laura and Abby. They took them. Why did they take them if they were just going to kill them? Where were they now?

Slowly, Seth turned on his side. He took a couple of deep breaths and tried to assess what his body was telling him. Beyond the pain. Beyond the shock. After a minute, he sat up. He saw Laura's pack on the ground not too far away. It had either fallen or been thrown there. Seth tried not to picture that scene, what it had looked like when those men had taken them.

Seth crawled to the pack and opened it. Laura had lightened it up before making that run to the rafts. He rummaged around and smiled. The first-aid kit was still in there. That woman was an expert survivalist and she knew how to prioritize. Thank you, Laura Donovan.

Hs hand froze when he saw Abby's Duckie. That sweet girl was scared somewhere. She needed her Duckie. She needed Seth.

Seth groaned and slowly took off his shirt. The bleeding had slowed and the entry wound was crusty on the outside. How long had he been out? Seth tried to reach his hand around to his back, but that wasn't happening. He could feel blood running down his back, so the bullet had exited. At least it wasn't still inside.

Seth shouldn't be alive. Those men were pros. Why wasn't he dead?

Seth looked down and felt his breath catch. His dog tags. He'd had them on under his shirt. They'd been a part of him for so long, had seen him through so much.

He still wore them every day, even though he had left military service far behind.

They were a mess. Not just covered in blood, but... dented? Seth quickly took them off, examining them with his eyes and fingers. They'd been hit. With a bullet.

It was impossible that they saved his life. But here he was, alive. The bullet should have killed him. They must have slowed it down. Maybe changed its path. He didn't know. All that mattered is that he was still alive.

Seth bandaged his wounds as best he could and then crawled to where he saw a large stick. Using it as a makeshift cane, he slowly stood up. This was doable. Seth knew what it felt like to be dying, and this wasn't it.

He wouldn't say he was in good shape, but he was much better than he should be, all things considered. Leaning on the stick, Seth looked around. He did not see or hear anything except the normal forest sights and sounds.

Mahoney must have taken them back to the cabin. To kill them there. That was the only thing that made any kind of sense.

Seth looked up the mountain. That's where Laura's cabin was. That's where the fire was. That's where Mahoney had wanted to kill her and Abby to begin with. He swallowed and took a couple steps in that direction. That was probably where Laura was. The helicopter could have left while Seth was unconscious. But if it hadn't, then Laura and Abby were up there.

Seth took a few more steps and had to stop again. Going uphill was not easy at the best of times, but especially not with a hole going through his body. He'd have to go through the fire again. And when he got there, then what? It would be him against a large number of armed men. Men who were not injured.

Seth wanted to go up. He wanted to charge up that mountain and save Laura and Abby. Save the day. He wanted to know that they were safe because he made them safe. That the bad guys were captured because he captured them.

Seth wanted to climb the mountain and be the hero. Do it all himself.

He sat down on a large rock, dropped the stick and leaned forward, resting his elbows on his thighs and holding his head. It hurt, bent over like this, but it hurt even more when Seth realized what he was thinking.

Do it all by himself. Isn't that how he got here in the first place? Isn't that what he counted as one of his greatest regrets? He didn't want his family to help him recover. He didn't want to admit weakness. No, he left so he could do it all by himself.

And it had been a mistake. He should have stayed. He should have leaned on those who loved him. He should have let them help.

No. He wasn't making that mistake again. He needed to go down the mountain. Away from Laura and Abby.

It felt an awful lot like he was running away and leaving them to take care of themselves.

But it was the right move. The hard move, but the right one. It gave Laura and Abby the greatest chance of surviving whatever it was they were enduring right now.

Seth stood and started walking down the mountain. He turned each step into a prayer.

Let me find help.

Let Laura and Abby be okay.

Don't let them be afraid.

Comfort them.
Help them feel loved.
Don't let me be too late.
Please, God.
Please.

The prayers were a rhythm, his heart bleeding into his pleas to God. He didn't feel the pain of his injuries. He didn't consider how far away help might be. He didn't look at the setting sun or the dark shadows that surrounded him. He only looked at the ground about three feet in front of him. Made sure he placed each foot securely. Firmly on the ground. Held on to his cane and begged God to find Laura and Abby in this mess and be with them.

His mom would have chastised him for that prayer. She believed that God was always with you. No one needed to ask God to be with a hurting person, because He never left. Ever. Instead, she would have told Seth to pray for the hurting person to be aware of God's presence. To open themselves up enough to feel it and to take comfort in it.

Seth almost missed a step as a longing for his mom caught him off guard. He should have called her. He'd written that his leaving was his fault. Not hers. His demons to face. Not her mistakes. Not her anything. But he should have called his mother.

Seth coughed and intentionally cleared his head. No. Laura and Abby didn't need his regrets over his past mistakes. They needed his prayers. And his help. Both came with him taking this next step. Then the one after that. And the next one.

Seth walked for forever. He started to wonder if he was maybe still on the forest floor unconscious. Maybe this was a nightmare where he walked and walked and walked but never reached his destination.

Maybe he should have gone up the mountain. To the fire at least. There might have been emergency personnel there, fighting the blaze. They could have helped.

The fire was closer than the bottom of this never-ending slope.

He should have gone up.

Seth stopped walking and looked back up the mountain. The scent of smoke had faded. He could not see any. Had they finally managed to put the blaze out? Or was he that far away?

Should he continue on? Maybe he should reverse course. Maybe going down was yet another mistake, but he still had time to fix it.

Seth was frozen. He didn't know which way to walk, but he needed to move somewhere. Do something. Soon.

Seth was all alone in the forest.

FIFTEEN

Laura needed a plan. And a weapon. Her dad. Seth. Pretty much anything. And everything.

"Well, Mrs. Donovan, I won't say it's been fun. But I'll certainly remember you and all your spunk."

That compliment made Laura's skin crawl. He was going to get up, leave, and then they were going to die. The situation was unbearable. Laura was more afraid of watching her daughter be hurt than she was of dying. That's just how bad life had become. Death was the preferable outcome.

No. That was not true. She was her father's daughter. She was her Holy Father's daughter. She was a mom. Laura was smart and capable and more than willing to fight for her child's future. She needed to come up with a plan. Which was exactly where this crazy internal monologue started.

Stall. She needed to figure out how to stay alive as long as possible. If there was any way at all that Seth was alive, he would come for them. Laura knew in the depths of her being that Seth would bring help. If he was alive.

If he wasn't alive. Well, then she needed to just try

to stay living, and keep Abby alive and unhurt, for as long as possible. Maybe something would happen in the future to give them a fighting chance. So they needed a future.

The plan was to stall.

Now that she had a plan, Laura needed to figure out to how to execute it. And quickly, because Mahoney was getting ready to leave.

"Mr. Mahoney." It was the first time she had addressed him as anything formally. For a few extra minutes of life, she would be respectful toward this man. With her words at least, if not in her heart. "You're making a mistake. I can help you."

Mahoney moved to get up out of his chair, so Laura began to talk faster. "You're going to need me to get inside that safe-deposit box."

Mahoney smiled, fully standing. It was not a nice smile. "I have a copy of your husband's death certificate. I have a copy of your identification. And I have a woman who looks like she could be your twin. I don't need you at all."

"You're wrong," she said.

Mahoney settled back down into his chair, and some of the tension left Laura's muscles. Sitting was good. Sitting meant listening which meant taking up more time which meant stalling. The plan was to hold things up, and Laura intended to work that plan until something better popped into her brain. *Please, God, give me something better. Help me to think my way out of this situation.*

Mahoney's eyes were narrowed and he looked like he doubted her words. Well, she doubted them, too. But it was all she had.

"What makes you say that?"

"I found a letter from my husband warning me that the box was very important. I called the bank and told them to make sure not to let anyone but me inside. There's no way your woman looks enough like me to pass careful scrutiny." That was a lie. All of it. Laura hoped she was convincing.

"We've been monitoring your phone, Mrs. Donovan. You did not call the bank. In fact, you told Joshua's former secretary that you didn't know what bank the key was from."

Laura told herself to stay calm. Steady. And hopefully very convincing. "I found an envelope with a bank name on it the next day. I went back to town to make a call. My cell phone was dead, so I used Mr. Miller's phone at the general store."

Laura had gone back into town the very next day because her generator had died. She'd purchased the necessary part to fix it at the general store. But she had not made any phone calls.

Mahoney opened his briefcase and pulled out a large cell phone with a long antenna, probably a satellite phone. He made a call. "Yeah. Give me the rundown on what Laura Donovan did the day after she called the firm about that safe-deposit key."

Laura saw spots in her vision and forced herself to take a breath. She was thankful she had kept her lie close to the truth. The report Mahoney was hearing should match what she said. Should.

"Got it." Mahoney did not sound happy. He pushed a button on the phone, presumably disconnecting the call. Then he looked at her and his eyes were blazing. "Okay. Let's say you're telling the truth."

He bought it. "Take me with you. I'll get you the papers if you'll leave us alone after that." He wouldn't. Laura knew whatever he told her would be a lie. But it would buy them some time and that was good enough right now.

"And why didn't you mention any of this before?"

Laura's shame was not faked at all this time. "You told me that all you wanted was the key. You said if I gave it to you, that you would leave. That no one would get hurt. I believed you." Like a fool. She had given the man the thing he wanted without a second thought. He'd had a gun and he'd had her daughter and she had just caved. She was determined to be smarter this time.

Mahoney didn't say anything. He just stared at her for a long moment. Then he was back on his phone. "Yeah. I need to know about the phone calls made from that general store the second day that Laura Donovan went down there. From the owner's phone, too." Mahoney looked at Laura. "Last name Miller. Specifically, any banks that were called."

Laura forced her face to remain confident. Why had she been so specific? And how quickly would Mahoney get the information and know she was lying?

Mahoney ended the call and leaned back in his chair. "We shouldn't have to wait too long. I don't think I believe you, but it never hurts to check. I've had men working since last week to track down the bank. That should be easier now that I have the key." Mahoney pulled out the gold key Laura had given him days ago. He waved it in front of her face before putting it back in his jacket's inside pocket. "I'm still thinking it will be best for all if you and your daughter die in a tragic accident and are quickly forgotten."

He planned to make it as though she and Abby were never here. Never lived. Tears rushed up behind Laura's eyes as she realized that she truly would disappear. No one would notice her absence. Or Abby's. Her family was all dead. Josh had been an only child of only children. His mom passed before Laura met him, and his dad passed their first year of marriage.

And Laura was really, really good at being alone. At not making friends. At pushing the few people who tried far, far away. Really, it was a wonder that Laura had ever met Josh. Known him. Loved him.

If she and her baby died, no one would visit their graves. Laura didn't even know if they would have graves.

This had been what she wanted. To be left alone. Loving people hurt, especially when they died and left. Her parents. Her dad. Josh. Everyone she loved had left her, and that was okay, because she wanted to be alone. Except she didn't. Laura didn't want that kind of life anymore, and she definitely did not want that for her sweet girl.

Laura wanted to attack this man. Her fists were aching with the pressure she was using to squeeze them into tight little balls. Abby was shaking, her head buried into Laura's shoulder, her arms squeezing Laura's neck tight. It almost felt like Abby was trying to climb inside Laura's body and hide there. Laura would let her if she could.

But Laura could not attack this man. She had to keep stalling and have faith. Faith in God. Faith in Seth. That was her mission right now.

Mahoney's cell phone rang, and he answered it. He

was talking in a low voice, and he sounded pleased with whatever he was hearing.

Laura looked out the window, feeling desperation rising like a tsunami wave ready to wipe her out. She blinked hard at the shining reflection she saw.

A shining reflection. Like what had warned Seth about the men earlier. The warning that had allowed them to hide.

Laura knew her mountain, and she really knew her dad's cabin and the surrounding land. There wasn't anything out that window that would reflect light. And, since it was dark, there shouldn't be any light to reflect in the first place.

Maybe it was Mahoney's men. He had certainly brought enough men and equipment with him.

But maybe it wasn't.

Something was out in the woods. There was light. And it was reflecting. In a pattern. A very subtle pattern.

Laura looked away. At Mahoney. He was still on his phone, talking quickly and not paying any attention to her. Good.

Laura looked back out the window. That same reflection.

Could it be a clue? A signal? She didn't know if that thought was blind hope or a reasonable conclusion. Either way, Laura was going to assume it meant something.

Mahoney put his phone back in his pocket and glared at her. "It seems you have a problem with your story, Mrs. Donovan."

It was a signal. Laura tightened her grip on Abby, and pictured all the ways out of this cabin. All the places she could hide. Something was going to happen. When it did, she would be ready.

"Problem?"

"Yes. There is—"

Her world exploded. Again. There were gunshots. Men yelling. Flashes of light and strange smells.

Laura jerked out of the chair, clutched Abby to her chest and ran. It was pure chaos, but Laura could navigate this cabin blind. If this was her chance, Abby's chance, she was going for it.

Seth was actually rocking back and forth on his feet to keep from running in. Joining the fight. The past two days had challenged him in ways that Afghanistan had never managed to do. But this? This standing here useless while others went in and fought to save Laura and Abby—this waiting—might be the greatest challenge yet.

But waiting was best. He was here, but he was in no condition whatsoever to be fighting. The firefighters he'd encountered on his never-ending trip down this mountain had tried to make him go to the hospital. They'd called an ambulance and everything. Seth had thrown a fit he would not be proud of in the morning, refusing. Besides, he knew Laura's cabin better than any of them. He knew more about these men than they did. Bringing him along for his knowledge was the smart play.

Seth had stood by impatiently while the police arrived. While the necessary manpower was finally assembled. He had waited during that drive up to the outskirts of the cabin. He had waited while the SWAT team had done their reconnaissance. He had waited for them to come back and say whether Laura and Abby were even up here. If he was even in the right place. Then Seth had waited while the police had made their plan. And now? Now he was waiting while the good guys went in and fought the bad guys.

A fight where Laura and Abby would be caught in the middle. Caught in between flying bullets. Breaking glass. Smoke bombs.

Best-case scenario was they were hiding, terrified, waiting to see who won. Worst case involved that boss killing them to cut his losses. Or using them as hostages. Or them getting hit by a stray bullet. Or, or, or. It was too much.

Seth took a step forward. The jolt of pain made him stop. No. This was not about him. This was not about his pride or his ego. He would not be an asset right now. He would be a distraction. A liability. The best thing was for Seth to stand by.

Seth looked down at Duckie in his hands. The stuffed animal he wanted to put back in Abigail's arms.

Seth was absolutely sick of waiting.

And then, he wasn't waiting anymore. The shooting stopped. The area became as bright as day as the lights the police brought with them were turned on. Seth walked forward, taking in the scene.

There were a lot of men in cuffs sitting on the ground. The police were bringing more out of the house. More from behind the house.

And there was Mahoney. He had to be the boss. While all the other men were dressed in black gear, this man was wearing a suit. He did not have the look of a mercenary. No, he had the look of a sleazy businessman.

Seth took another step and made eye contact with the

leader of the SWAT team. He nodded and Seth stopped hesitating. He rushed into the cabin as fast as his injured body would allow him.

Laura. Abby.

They weren't out front. Where were they?

He entered the cabin and ignored the destruction. He didn't care about broken furniture. No, he only cared about the two people who were hopefully safe inside.

"Laura! Abby! It's Seth. If you can hear me, come out now. It's safe." Seth took in another breath, preparing to yell again. If that didn't work, he would take this cabin apart and find every hidey-hole Malcolm Grant had put in it. He would find them.

"Abby! Wait!" Seth heard Laura's cry about a second before Abby came running into the room. She didn't slow down or pause before throwing herself against Seth's legs. Laura was right behind her.

Seth's legs gave out and he was on the floor. Abby crawled up his body, wrapping her arms around his neck and pressing her wet face against his cheek. He hugged her to his body, pushing Duckie into her hands. Laura leaned over and was suddenly pressed against him, too. Seth didn't know if she was trying to hug Abby or him, but it didn't matter. He opened his arms to include her, hugging both of them as hard as he could.

He sent one hand up to cup the back of Laura's head. He wanted to check them over to see if they were okay. He wanted to hold tight and never let go. He didn't even know what he wanted. This moment was all feeling.

"Seth, you're alive." Laura's voice was thick and Seth leaned his head back enough to see her face. She was crying. Sobbing. Her entire body was shaking with the force of it.

"Yes. I'm alive, Laura. I'm so sorry I let you down."

"Let me down? You saved us." Her voice was muffled because she had moved to press it back against his chest.

"I didn't save you."

"You did." She looked up then, tears still pouring down her face. "I don't care. I don't even care. All I care about is that you're here. You're alive. Abby is here. She's alive."

"And you're here. Alive." His own voice was shaky. It had been very, very close. Those statements were not a given. They could have easily all three been dead.

"Yes. We're alive!" Laura's sobs were now a laugh. A celebration of triumph.

Laura's smile fell away. "Did they catch him? Mahoney? Did they catch him?"

"Mahoney? Is that the man in the suit?"

Laura nodded.

"Yeah. They caught him. He is out front, in handcuffs, right now."

More tears. So many. Too many. "He killed Josh, Seth. It wasn't some random mugging. He told me. He killed Josh on purpose."

"What? Why? Did he tell you why?"

Laura pulled away then and Seth felt the cold even though he still had a very clingy Abby in his lap. "Yeah. Mahoney is some drug king. Josh found evidence about him, and Mahoney wants that evidence."

"That's what was in the box?"

"Yeah, he realized what Mahoney was, so he gathered some documents that will incriminate Mahoney. That's what this whole thing has been about. Josh wasn't a criminal."

Seth reached out and took Laura's hand. It wasn't as good as hugging her, but he would take contact with this woman any way he could get it. "You were right, Laura. Josh was a good and honorable man. Your husband was a hero."

Laura squeezed his hand. "Thank you. I'm so glad."

Seth saw the lead officer standing in the cabin's doorway. He didn't know how long the man had been there, or how much he had overheard, but Seth appreciated him waiting. At Seth's look, the man walked in. "Laura, this is Lieutenant McCoy, the head of the local SWAT team. He's the one who rescued you."

Laura let go of his hand and stood up. Seth also managed to stand, though it was made more difficult by Abby's body still clinging.

Lieutenant McCoy reached out and shook Laura's hand. "It's real nice to meet you, Mrs. Donovan. And I couldn't have rescued you if Seth here hadn't found us and told us what was happening."

"Well, thank you. Both of you. Thank you very much."

"Ma'am, you and your daughter are okay? Not hurt?"

Laura reached out and rubbed Abby's back. "No. Somehow, we're both okay."

It wasn't just some random somehow, though. It was because God had laid His hand over them and protected them. He had seen them through this storm. And He would see them through the next couple of weeks, too.

Seth intended to mention counseling to Laura. Both she and Abby would probably benefit from talking about everything that happened. Finding a sense of safety again. And him, too. Seth wanted to talk to someone. Clear his head. And make sure he learned all the lessons God had taught him the past few days. The past few years, for that matter.

SIXTEEN

"Seth. Go see Seth." Abby's little voice was insistent, full of energy now that her fever was gone. If this was any indication, Laura was going to have a very strong-willed teenager on her hands in a few years.

"Yes, Abby. We're going to go see Seth." Laura tried to infuse her voice with patience, but she had already said these words at least a dozen times today. And it was still early morning.

"Now." Laura wanted to smile when she saw Abby with her arms crossed and a scowl on her little face. It was a pose that Laura often assumed when she was trying to be stern with Abby.

It seemed that Abby was trying to reverse the process. Yep, Laura was going to be in serious trouble when this little girl got older.

Laura looked at the clock and then stood from where she had been sitting on a bed in the hotel they had stayed at last night. It was still too early for visiting hours at the hospital, but Abby seemed to be done waiting in the small room. So was Laura, for that matter.

"Okay, baby. Let's go run some errands, and then it will be time to go see Seth."

"Seth." Abby's voice was definitive. A statement of fact. Trouble.

Laura took Abby to a big-box retail store to pick out a gift for Seth. It wasn't ideal, but the store was open and it was large enough to distract Abby until they could go to the hospital. Once there, the girl had stopped demanding to go see Seth every ten minutes. Instead, she wanted to walk up and down every single aisle, determined to find the perfect gift.

Two hours later, Laura was finally driving toward the hospital. Abby was secured in the back in her car seat, a stuffed bear sitting next to her. The bear was every bit as large as Abby. Abby loved him, and Laura found the gift hilariously appropriate. She was as excited as Abby to see Seth's reaction to her gift.

Some of Laura's mirth faded, though, as they parked the car and entered the hospital. The somber lobby and slow elevator ride to Seth's floor emphasized the events of the past few days. Laura found Seth's room, set down the massive bear and peeked inside, hoping he was awake. Now that they were here, she wasn't sure anything could keep Abby away. And, if she were honest, Laura wanted to see Seth just as badly. She knew, logically, that he was okay. That he was going to be okay.

He had given Abby the hug she requested yesterday. He hadn't wanted to come to the hospital, let alone take an ambulance there, but the police had insisted. So had his boss, who had arrived on the scene sometime during all the chaos. With a sigh, Seth had climbed into the ambulance and gone to the hospital. The police said he would be admitted for the night just as a precaution.

Laura mentally kicked herself when she remembered

how she had just stood there yesterday. Her brain unable to comprehend all that had happened.

Her husband's death wasn't an accident. Victor Mahoney had been watching her for months. A criminal had been a part of her every move for months and she hadn't even known. And then, in the course of days, Laura had been shot at, had taken her daughter on the run, had been captured and had thought that she and Abby were going to die. It was too much.

Far too much if she factored Seth into the whole complication. Seth the park ranger. Seth the critic who had judged her father. Seth the hero who had saved them. Seth the man. The man who had awakened feelings in Laura she had thought were gone forever.

With those feelings churning in her stomach, Laura saw Seth sitting in the hospital bed watching television. She knocked lightly on the door that was slightly ajar.

Seth looked over at her and smiled. "Hey. Come in, come in." He turned off the television and set down the remote control. Laura stood there looking at him. She had known he was okay, but a wave of relief hit her when she saw him awake and smiling.

"Seth!" Abby ran over to the bed and held out her arms. Seth was leaning over the bed railing to pick her up when Laura realized what he was about to do.

"Seth, wait. Don't pick her up." He already had Abby sitting in his lap by the time Laura made it to the bed. "Seth, you shouldn't have done that. You could have hurt yourself."

"I'm fine, Laura. This whole thing is an overreaction by the doctors. I should get sprung from this place today." Seth turned and winked at Abby, who promptly tried to jump off his lap. Seth wrapped his arms around her. "Whoa there, Abby McDabby. Where're you going?"

"Present, Mama!"

Seth was looking at Abby and Laura with a smiling question on his face.

"Abby picked out a present for you."

Abby nodded and then reached up to cover Seth's eyes. "No peeking."

Laura could see that Seth had obliged Abby and closed his eyes. She retrieved the bear from the hallway, and brought him into the room. When she was holding the bear in front of Seth's face, Abby moved her hands and spoke. "Okay, Seth. Look."

Seth opened his eyes and took in the giant Smokey Bear. His eyes traveled from the tan hat to the plastic shovel the bear was holding to the blue pants. Laura saw him bite his lip. Hopefully, he thought it was as funny as Laura did.

He looked at Laura. "Was this your idea?"

Laura tried to talk through her smile. "Nope. Abby walked up and down every single aisle and picked this out herself."

Abby looked proud. "It's a bear."

"Yep, it's a great bear, Abby. Thank you."

"Welcome." With that, Abby turned to snuggle into Seth's chest.

Still grinning like a loon, Laura set the bear down on one of the chairs in the room. She sat in another chair.

"So, you're really going home today?"

Seth nodded. "I should be released this afternoon." He looked at Abby. "She's asleep."

"She didn't sleep very much last night. By the time

we spoke with the police, it was pretty late. Then she was excited about being in a hotel room."

Seth's voice was all tease. "I bet. She was probably awed by the electricity and running water."

Laura felt herself blush. "Very funny, Mr. Park Ranger." He looked pleased with himself.

"Were you all able to sleep in this morning at least?"

Laura snorted. "Hardly. Abby woke up at the crack of dawn, all eager to see you." She leaned forward in the chair to brush a piece of hair out of Abby's eyes. "You're fortunate the hospital has set visiting hours, or else she would have been here to see you before the sun rose."

Seth reached out and took hold of Laura's hand. "I wouldn't have minded." He looked at her for a long moment before speaking in that same serious tone. "I was worried about both of you. I missed you."

Seth couldn't have kept the admission inside. It was the truth. He had been missing them—ever since he had stepped inside that ambulance. Once the initial rush of being admitted to the hospital was over, he'd been able to sit and think. About his past. About his future.

Laura pulled her hand from his. She put her hands beside her, gripping the edge of the chair so that Seth could see the color of her skin change where the pressure was the greatest. She looked scared, and it made a lump of fear and panic rise up in his throat.

"Laura—"

"I'm sorry." She blurted it out before he could finish his question.

"Sorry? What in the world are you sorry for?" Seth couldn't think of a single thing she needed to apologize for.

Laura had tears in her eyes. "I'm so sorry for everything. This is all my fault."

Seth opened his mouth to reassure her, but she held up one of her hands. "Wait. Let me say this. Please." Seth closed his mouth and nodded.

"Thank you. I know you're going to disagree with me, but I'm right. Victor Mahoney came here because of me. You spent all those hours being hunted in the woods because of me. You got *shot* because of me." Her voice cracked on the word *shot*, and it broke Seth's heart. She took a shaky breath and continued. "I have brought nothing but trouble and turmoil into your life. I'm so sorry." Laura looked down at her lap, not meeting Seth's gaze.

"I'm not." He said it quietly. With as much certainty and conviction as he could possibly put into two little words. Laura lifted her head and looked at him, but he couldn't read her face. Seth knew without being told that this was one of those life-altering moments. *Give me the words, God. Please, let her understand.* "I'm grateful." He ignored Laura's skeptical face and continued. "I've spent most of the morning thanking God for what He did."

Laura's face was still blank. Unreadable. So was her voice. "What He did." She made it a statement, not a question.

"Yes. What He did."

Laura looked at Seth then, met his gaze and held it for several long seconds. "What did He do, Seth?" Her voice was a whisper, full of emotion.

"He led me to you." With a smile to the little girl sleeping against him, he added, "And Abby."

Laura just watched him. Seth hoped she was listening with an open heart. "I was so alone before I met you, Laura. I know you think that you were the recluse. The only one hiding. But that's not true."

Slow tears began to roll down Laura's precious face. Seth reached out and wiped them away with his fingers, loving the feel of her skin.

"I've been hiding. From my family. From God. From my future."

More slow tears.

"You changed all that. You woke me up." He smiled. "You and this wonderful little girl made me realize what I can have." Seth swallowed. "And I want it."

Laura's eyes widened slightly. She covered her mouth with one hand, as though to hold in more tears. Seth hoped they weren't the sad kind.

"I want it with you, Laura. It's been crazy and incredibly fast, but I have fallen in love with you. And I don't want to let you go."

A sob escaped from behind Laura's hand, and Seth felt like his heart would break. He couldn't tell if she was upset or overwhelmed.

"I need to go home. Back to my family."

She nodded and looked down at her lap again. Seth cringed as he realized he was bungling this. He grabbed her hand and held tight, determined to get it all out as quickly as possible. "But I'm coming back. For you. To you."

Laura looked at him, blinking the tears from her eyes. "What?"

"I meant it when I said that you're it for me. And I want to be it for you. That means I need to step up and become the kind of man who could possibly be worthy of you and Abby."

"Worthy? Seth, you don't have to prove anything to me."

Seth smiled. "Maybe not. But I need to prove something to myself. I want to be proud of who I am. I need to go back to my family and make amends. I need to tell them that I'm sorry I rejected them, ran from them. I need to try to repair our relationship." His smile grew. "And I need to tell them about you and Abby."

Seth sat up as straight as he could while in a hospital bed with a toddler on his lap. "And then, Laura Donovan, I'm coming back here. I plan to court you. To show you that I would make a good husband to you and a good father to Abby. I'll wait as long as it takes to make you both mine."

Laura stood and walked toward the windows. Seth wished he could see her face. At least then he would feel like he had a shot at guessing what she was feeling. Was she happy? Was she trying to find a way to let him down easy? Seth was pretty sure she was scared. He could deal with her fears. With enough time and patience, she would realize what he already knew—they were perfect together. They weren't perfect people, but they could create something wonderful together.

"I won't be here."

Laura's voice was quiet, but Seth heard her. "What?"

"I'm leaving." She was still looking out that blasted window.

"Okay, where are we going?"

Laura did turn then. "We?"

Seth tried to impart every bit of his intention and will into his words. "Yes, we. I meant what I said, Laura. Unless you flat out reject me, I intend to pursue you romantically. I can't do that if we're living in two different places."

Laura just looked at him like he was nuts. Seth felt a little crazy, to be honest. But he was meant to be with this woman. So he would put his trust and his faith in God and accept whatever this relationship brought his way.

"I—I don't know where. I just know I need to go somewhere new. I was hiding. I went out into the world and it hurt me. So I ran home, to a place where there were no people to break my heart."

Seth tried to be patient and let her finish.

"But that's not living. Life is scary and hard. And wonderful. My dad never wanted me to stay on the mountain. He pushed me to go to college. He encouraged me to date. To experience the world. And I did. I met a wonderful man and we created an incredible daughter."

Looking at Abby, Seth had to agree.

"And Josh wouldn't want me to close myself off from the world. He would want me to be happy. For Abby to have the fullest life possible." Laura looked upward and snorted. "I bet they have both been watching me from heaven. Probably yelling at me. Telling me to get up and go find happiness."

She looked back at Seth, meeting his gaze directly. "I'm ready to do that. I'm going to find a nice place and I'm going to live there. *Live.*" Laura's face looked intense, a fire in her eyes. "You said that you will go wherever I am. Me, too. I need you to know I would do the same for you."

Her, too?

Laura moved to stand directly in front of Seth. She

still looked determined, but also vulnerable. "I want to go somewhere and live again. With you."

Seth felt all the tension leave his muscles. He reached out and held her face, palms of his hands resting on her cheeks.

He wanted to let her finish.

He wanted to kiss her.

"Abby and I want to be with you."

Seth leaned forward and gently pressed his lips against hers. "I love you, Laura. I want to go slow. I want to be careful with you. But I don't need time to know that I love you. And Abby."

Laura's smile wasn't the least bit vulnerable now. "I love you, too, Seth. We both do."

Seth didn't need anyone to point out God's hand in this development. He sent up a burst of gratitude. He dropped his hands from her face, moving them to hold hers between their bodies. "You know, I'm from a place in Oregon called Carter City. It's a small town, but the people are wonderful. All in all, it's not a bad place to live."

Laura smiled her beautiful smile again, squeezing both of her hands. "Really, now? Tell me more."

EPILOGUE

Two Years Later

Laura sat in the passenger side of the Jeep thinking about circles. Circles and cycles and circumstances that seemed random but had to have been preordained.

"What are you thinking about so hard, pretty girl?"

Seth's voice was teasing and warm and happy. Laura loved that he sounded so incredibly joyful. He reached out and held Laura's hand, keeping his other on the steering wheel of the SUV he was driving. He ran his thumb over a wedding ring. Her wedding ring. The one he had placed on her finger two days ago.

"I was thinking about the first time you drove up this mountain."

Seth squeezed her hand. "If I ever needed proof that God exists, I have it. He surely sent me to find you."

Laura snorted. He could be such a sap at times.

"That's one way to look at it, I suppose. The other way would be that you drove up a mountain, found a crazy recluse and almost died." She was teasing. Mostly. Though she had found peace and happiness since their ordeal on the mountain, she would never be able to entirely joke about the terror of those days.

"Laura." Seth's voice was loving and almost chiding. "I drove up a mountain alone and ashamed and came back down complete and free."

Laura was silent for a moment. "You know, for a park ranger, you sure can say the sweetest things."

"They're true." He looked at her face briefly, then returned his gaze to the road. "I miss Abby. Maybe we should have brought her with us."

Laura laughed. She couldn't help herself. Abby had Seth wrapped around her little kindergartner finger. Like Laura, Abby had been blessed with a biological father who loved her. Like Laura, Abby had lost that biological father. And, like Laura, God had sent Abby a man—a new father—one who would love her with every bit of his being. Laura frequently gave Seth a hard time about his mushiness where Abby was concerned, but he would just smile and shrug his shoulders.

Of course, Seth wasn't the only one. Abby was staying with Seth's parents while he and Laura had their honeymoon at the cabin. They spoiled Abby about as much as Seth did. Actually, all of Seth's family spoiled Abby. And Laura. From the second Laura and Abby had come to Carter City, they had been surrounded by grandparents and parents and brothers and sisters and cousins and nieces and nephews. It was unfamiliar and overwhelming and often exhausting. It was also wonderful. Laura delighted in the fact that Abby was growing up in the middle of such a large, loving family.

The terrain got slightly rougher and Seth let go of Laura's hand so he could use both hands to drive. "Hey," he said with a grin, "you wanna reenact our first meeting?"

Laura crossed her arms in mock irritation. "Very funny, *Ranger*." She rolled her eyes at his satisfied smile. Feeling like her heart was almost too full of joy, Laura closed her eyes and said a prayer that had almost become instinctual.

Oh, God, I can't believe You gave us this man. Thank You.

* * * * *

Terri Reed's romance and romantic suspense novels have appeared on the *Publishers Weekly* top twenty-five and Nielsen BookScan top one hundred lists, and have been featured in *USA TODAY* and *RT Book Reviews*. Her books have been finalists for the Romance Writers of America RITA® Award and the National Readers' Choice Award, and finalists three times for the American Christian Fiction Writers Carol Award. Contact Terri at terrireed.com or PO Box 19555, Portland, OR 97224.

Visit the Author Profile page at Harlequin.com for more titles.

BURIED MOUNTAIN SECRETS

Terri Reed

Trust in the Lord with all thine heart;
and lean not unto thine own understanding. In all thy
ways acknowledge him, and he shall direct thy paths.
—*Proverbs* 3:5–6

Thank you to my editors, Emily Rodmell
and Tina James, for your patience and
encouragement through a difficult time.
I appreciate you all so much.

Thank you to Leah Vale for your endless support
and to my family for your endless love.

ONE

"Maya! Maya!"

The *crack* of the office door bouncing off the back wall reverberated throughout the hardware and feed store.

At the front counter, Maya Gallo braced herself and gave the customer she was helping an apologetic smile. "Excuse me, Ethan. Apparently, Brady has something to tell me."

"No worries, dear," the older gentleman replied and wandered off toward the tack room. There was no pity in his voice, but Maya could feel the empathy and sympathy radiating off of one of Bristle Township's most stalwart citizens.

Maya's fifteen-year-old brother, Brady, skidded down the aisle between the bags of goat and backyard flock feed of the Gallo Hardware and Feed. Their parents had opened the establishment shortly after Maya was born. She couldn't remember a day when she wasn't in the store. She missed them so much.

It had been ten years since that tragic night when her mother and father were on the road coming down from a day of skiing on Eagle Crest Mountain, Colorado, and hit a patch of ice. The resulting car accident had taken both their lives, leaving eighteen-year-old Maya to raise her five-year-old brother.

Brady's almond-shaped eyes danced with anticipation as he halted in front of her and Maya's heart filled with love for her little brother. Though he had Down syndrome, he functioned at a high level and was smarter than most people gave him credit for. He was also a hard worker, opinionated and determined. But, more important, full of joy. A joy that at times broke her heart.

She could guess today's excitement meant another clue in the "Treasure Hunt of the Century" had been uploaded to the blog of the wealthy and eccentric Patrick Delaney.

Knowing if she tried to stall, he would burst with his enthusiasm. "Okay, what is it?"

"Another clue," he said, confirming her suspicion. "A piece of a map. I need to hike up Aspen Creek Trail. Can I, please?"

A pang of sorrow and grief hit Maya square in the chest. The trail was on the lower half of Eagle Crest Mountain. The other side of the mountain was where the skiing resort and runs were located. And the road on which her parents had perished.

The urge to remind Brady that finding the Delaney treasure was a hopeless cause rose up strong within her, but she bit the words back. They'd gone down this road so many times over the past few weeks, ever since the peculiar billionaire, who lived on the outskirts of Bristle Township, had put out to the world that he had hidden some sort of treasure somewhere along the Rocky Mountains.

The man hadn't said where in the Rockies. And considering the mountains ran from Canada down to New Mexico, that was a lot of territory to cover. Towns all along the Rockies were being overrun with seekers of fortune and fame who ate up every clue, and then spent hours and hours searching the canyons, forests, peaks, hills and valleys of the rugged mountain range. Bristle Township and County was no exception.

Not that the townsfolk didn't appreciate the business the fervor stirred up, but for Maya it was a constant worry. Brady loved puzzles. The more challenging, the better. He'd glommed on to the treasure hunt with both hands.

She glanced at the clock. Just after nine in the morning. If he left now, he'd be at the trailhead in fifteen minutes. She doubted Mr. Delaney had hidden his prize along such a well-used hiking path, but following the clues made her brother happy. Thankfully, Brady wouldn't be alone out there. Even in the fall when the air turned cool, there were sturdy souls who hiked the trail every day.

"Are you done with class and homework?" He went to classes three days a week at the local high school and worked with a special education teacher. The other two days a week, he did an online course and homework.

"All done. And turned in." He grinned. "Mrs. Vincetti wrote that I was a rock star."

He was so eager to learn. It broke her heart that the school couldn't afford the special education teacher on a full-time basis. But he was excelling at his studies. "What time do you need to be back?"

He thought for a moment. "By lunchtime."

"Which is?"

He tapped the large round watch on his arm. "Noon."

"That's right. So that means you need to be aware of the time to see how far you go in so that you know when to turn around to be back by noon. If I have to worry, we won't be doing this again." She made this speech every time.

"I won't make you worry, Maya. Do I ever?"

Oh, had he. When she'd first started to loosen the reins, letting him have some freedom, she'd known it would be a learning curve for them both. But Pastor Michael Foster and his wife, Alicia, had insisted it was time to let Brady grow up, and Brady's doctor had agreed.

Because Maya respected and cherished the older couple and Doctor Brown as well, and relied on them for sound counsel, she'd done as they'd suggested and given Brady more control and allowed him to make his own decisions.

But he wasn't good with directions or managing his time, something they'd been working diligently to change.

This would be his fifth outing seeking treasure in as many weeks. She was pretty sure he understood the concept of time now and knew how to use his compass, but that didn't stop the little flutter of unease from curling in the pit of her stomach.

For her own piece of mind, she'd filled his small backpack with a first-aid kit, insect replant, sunscreen, reflective thermal blanket, a compass, a walkie-talkie, a cell phone and a flashlight, along with a water bottle and snacks.

"Your house keys?"

Brady unzipped the front pouch and pointed to a set of keys dangling from a carabiner attached to the inside of the bag. A small square wireless tracker covered by a sticker of Brady's favorite cartoon character hung next to the keys. She had the corresponding GPS tracking device in the office.

"It's packed and all set to go, Maya." Brady zipped the pack closed and secured it over his shoulders on top of his blue down jacket.

"Hat?"

He yanked his baseball cap from the pocket of his jeans and secured it on his head. "Okay?"

Her heart squeezed. "Be careful. And stay on the path. No straying."

With a salute, he ran out the side exit, the echo of his booted feet ringing in her ears.

She hurried to the front window in time to see him pedaling his bike down the sidewalk toward the far end of town where he'd turn onto the road that would take him to the trailhead. He waved to people on the street who waved back.

She touched the glass pane and said a prayer of protection for her younger brother.

A stab of guilt ate away at her. Her gaze lifted to the white snowcapped peaks of the mountains. If she had prayed for her parents that long-ago winter night instead of being angry that she'd been stuck at home babysitting her brother while they went off and had fun, maybe they'd still be alive.

Movement across the street drew her gaze to the tall good-looking sheriff's deputy lifting his hand in a wave, his dark-eyed gaze locking with hers.

Embarrassment flooded her and she snatched her hand away from the windowpane. She quickly stepped back. Great. The handsome officer probably thought she was flirting with him. *Ugh*. The next time he came in for tack would be uncomfortable.

The last thing she wanted in her life was romance. There'd been a few men over the years who'd shown interest but she had her hands full with Brady and the store.

To complicate things with a relationship... The thought was overwhelming. What if she fell in love and then something happened to the guy?

She had Brady, her friends and the town. What more did she need?

At noon, Maya had watched the back entrance, expecting Brady to come racing into the store any moment. At one o'clock, she paced by the front window, her gaze searching the main street of Bristle Township for signs of him. She checked the GPS device. The red dot showed he was on the Aspen Creek Trail. Most likely he'd found something or was digging beneath a bush with no clue how worried she was waiting for him to return.

By two, when the red dot hadn't moved, dread that something had happened to him set in. She flipped the open sign over, jumped in her Jeep and drove to the trailhead. Brady's bike was sitting in the bike rack.

Trying to keep her breathing even, she told herself not to panic, even though her heart rate was way faster than normal, making her chest hurt. She checked the handheld GPS device, glad to see the little red dot indicating that Brady was still on the trail but worry poked at her. He hadn't moved in a long time. Had he fallen and was injured?

The thought galvanized her into action. She hurried up the dirt path. "Brady!"

On either side of the trail, tall aspens and pines grew, their branches spreading out to form a canopy that only allowed intermittent shafts of sunlight to stream through, while otherwise shrouding the path in gloom. The thin air was crisp and a shiver prickled the fine hairs at Maya's nape.

"Brady! Answer me," she called out, praying that her search wasn't futile.

Where were all the other hikers? She could only guess because of the later hour in the day that most had already made their treks up and back down the mountain path. She rounded a bend in the trail. According to the GPS tracker, she should have been right on top of Brady. But the path was empty.

With her breath lodged in her lungs, she searched the bushes on the sides of the trail. A patch of blue snagged her gaze. She dived for the bramble of tangled foliage. "Brady?"

Horror closed her throat. It was her baby brother's favorite backpack. She tugged the blue backpack from beneath the thorny bush. She hugged the bag to her chest, her heart thumping as fear clouded her vision. Where was her brother?

Had he strayed off the path? Was he hurt and needing help?

She put on the backpack so that her hands were free to push back the low branches as she made her way into the thick forest.

The snap of a branch breaking sent a bird flapping from a tree branch above. Maya's heart jackknifed as she froze, unsure from which direction the noise had come. "Brady?"

Something hard and heavy slammed into her from behind, sending her sprawling forward on her hands and knees. Dirt and debris bit into her skin. Rough hands grabbed at her. She rolled away, landing awkwardly on the backpack. A hooded person with a strange mask covering their face rushed toward her.

Terror had her rolling again into the bushes. She scrambled to her feet, ignoring the ripping of her jeans on a branch. The hooded figure yanked on the straps of the backpack. Maya delivered a low fisted shot to the person's gut, knocking the assailant back several steps, enough so that Maya could twist away with her brother's pack still on and flee into the woods.

She ran as fast as the terrain would allow, dodging branches that scratched at her hands, tore her coat and plucked at her hair.

Behind her, she heard the thrashing of her attacker through the underbrush, quickly gaining on her.

She had to find safety. She darted around a copse of trees and spied a downed trunk. She jumped over it and hunkered down, out of sight.

Please, Lord, protect me. Protect Brady.

Why was someone trying to hurt her? Where was her brother?

"There's been another injured treasure hunter outside Denver," Deputy Kaitlyn Lanz announced in grim irritation.

Deputy Alex Trevino shook his head. "That makes five in the past week." He rose and headed to the sheriff's office. Pausing in the doorway, he addressed the older man sitting at the oak desk. "Sir, we really need to do something about Patrick Delaney and his treasure hunt."

Sheriff James Ryder ran a hand through his silver hair. "If I thought there was something to be done, I'd do it. I've talked to Patrick. Mayor Olivia has talked to Patrick. Even the feds have talked to Patrick. The old coot won't relent. He's the town's biggest supporter so there's only so much pressure we can exert on him. He's within his legal rights."

Frustration beat a steady tempo at the back of Alex's head. "It's only a matter of time before we have issues here in Bristle Township."

"Don't borrow trouble, Trevino," the sheriff said. "How are your plans for the festival coming along?"

Alex was in charge of the security measures for the upcoming Harvest Festival and parade. "Good. The auxiliary volunteers have committed to patrolling Main Street. Between the volunteers, Kait, Daniel, Chase and me, we'll have the festival covered."

"What about the parade?"

"That, too."

The outer office door to the department banged open. Alex spun, his hand going to his holstered weapon. The other three deputies on duty rose from their desk chairs and took similar on-guard stances.

An older man with wisps of gray hair covering his head and a panicked expression rushed into the station house. Ethan Johnson.

"Mr. Johnson, can I help you?" the station receptionist, Carole Manning, hurriedly trailed after him.

"Come quick," Ethan said to the room at large. "It's the Gallos."

Though he relaxed his stance, alarm threaded through Alex's veins. An image of a dark-haired beauty rose in Alex's mind. He'd seen Maya Gallo just this morning standing in the window of the hardware store. Though he didn't know the woman well, he found her to be pleasant when she helped him with tack and such for his horse, Truman. "What's happened?"

"I was there this morning, but I had to come back because I forgot to get some bedding for the nests in my chicken coop and the store is closed. Only the door is unlocked. It's not like Maya to leave the store unattended. Something's happened."

The sheriff stepped out of his office. "Now, Ethan, I'm sure Maya and Brady are fine. Maybe they are at the diner having a late lunch or have gone home for the day and forgot to lock up. Let's not jump to unnecessary conclusions."

Ethan shook his head. "No, Sheriff. I tell you, this isn't like Maya. And Brady was all riled up this morning about something."

"Probably the treasure," Carole stated with a sage nod. "Brady is big into finding the treasure and a new clue was released this morning."

Alex glanced at his superior, then back to Carole. "But the clue could be anywhere in the Rocky Mountains."

"True." She walked over to his desk and sat at the computer, her fingers flying over the keys. "Here. Take a look at this. Mr. Delaney put up a partial map."

They all huddled around the desk to look at the computer screen.

"That could be Eagle Crest." Deputy Daniel Rawlings towered over them at nearly six-three and pointed to a spot on the screen.

"Or it could be any number of mountains from Canada to New Mexico," Kaitlyn pointed out, flipping her blond ponytail over her shoulder. "There's no way to be sure that's our Eagle Crest Mountain."

"Well, whatever the case," the sheriff said, "we need to do our jobs and make sure our citizens are safe." He pinned Alex with a hard look. "Find the Gallo siblings."

Glad to be put in charge, Alex nodded. "Yes, sir."

"Ethan, let me walk you out." The sheriff gestured for the other man to leave with him.

"Okay, you heard the sheriff," Alex said. "Kait, get the Gallos' home address from Carole and see if the Gallos are there. Daniel, you go to the store and check it out. See if there are signs of a struggle or something that will tell us why Maya closed up early."

"What do you want me to do?" Deputy Chase Fredrick asked. He was the youngest and newest of the deputies. Medium height and lean with sandy-blond hair and dark blue eyes, he had a boyish face hidden by a well-trimmed, close-cropped beard.

"You're with me," Alex told him.

"Got it." Chase went back to his desk to grab his jacket.

"What are you going to do?" Kaitlyn's hazel eyes filled with concern and curiosity.

Grabbing his jacket and shrugging into it, he said, "If Brady and Maya are out hunting for treasure, they most likely started at the Eagle Crest trailhead."

Alex brought his sheriff's-department-issued SUV to a halt in the parking lot at the lower trailhead of

Eagle Crest Mountain. Chase pulled in next to him in an identical SUV. Alex noted five other vehicles in the lot. His gaze zeroed in on a mountain bike in the bike rack near the trailhead kiosk.

Brady's bike. The teenager had ridden down Main Street this morning. Alex hadn't thought much about it at the time. Now it made sense. Brady was trying to find the Delaney treasure. The map that had been released this morning, though pretty generic, could arguably have some similarities to the mountain trail ahead of him. Alex climbed out of the SUV and met Chase at the bike rack.

"What now, boss?" Chase asked.

Alex tried not to flinch at the word *boss*. He wasn't the boss. He knew there were those in the department and in town looking for Alex to step into the role of sheriff when the old man retired, which he'd been threatening to do for the last three years that Alex had been on the force.

That the sheriff put him in charge of this investigation didn't mean anything. Sheriff Ryder usually picked one of his deputies to take point.

The sun hung low in the sky. Shading his eyes, Alex gauged they had only a few more hours of daylight left. "We'll cover more ground on horseback," he told Chase.

The Bristle County Sheriff's Department continued the long tradition of patrols on horseback like many Western states. Comprised of both armed deputies and unarmed civilian volunteers, also referred to as auxiliary members, the patrol provided mounted search and rescue as well as mounted community and forest patrols.

"Get on the horn with Carole and round up as many

civilian volunteers available. Then run every license plate here. I'm going home to get Truman," Alex stated, referring to his horse. "I'll meet you back here in one half hour. Keep an alert eye out for Maya Gallo and her brother. If they come out of the forest, radio me."

"Will do." Chase walked away, already using his shoulder radio to contact the station's dispatcher.

Alex sped home and in the short time it took him to return to the trailhead, towing Truman in the horse trailer, there were three other civilian volunteers with their horses waiting.

"Riley, Trevor." Alex shook the father's hand and then the teenage son's hand. The Howard men were dedicated volunteers. "Thank you for coming." There was no mistaking the family resemblance between the father and son. They also had identical quarter horses.

Then Alex shook hands with the third volunteer, local dress shop owner, Leslie Quinn, a pretty blonde with blue eyes. Leslie stared at him warily as she stood beside her sturdy paint sporting pink bows tied to its mane. No doubt for the upcoming parade. "Deputy."

Alex didn't know the reserved woman well. She tended to keep to herself when they were on patrol. "Leslie, appreciate you joining us."

Chase hurried over. Alex gave him a questioning look.

"Two local hikers came down the trail but not the Gallo siblings."

Disappointment shot through Alex and he realized how much he had been hoping to discover Maya and her brother had already descended the trail. "Did the hikers see the Gallos?"

Chase shook his head. "Claimed not to. I took their contact info."

"All right, listen up, everyone." Alex explained the situation to the others. "Okay, there are two main paths to take from here. Riley and Trevor—" he gestured to the Howards "—take the Pine Ridge Trail. Miss Quinn and I will take Aspen Creek Trail."

Alex mounted Truman, a chestnut-colored sixteen-hand Tennessee walking horse, and headed the horse toward the trailhead, where the father and son pair peeled away while Alex and Leslie took the main trail. A half hour later, Alex held up his hand in a fist, signaling for Leslie to stop. Alex slid off Truman to inspect several broken branches on the right side of the trail. It looked as if somebody had gone crashing through the underbrush.

Before he could move farther into the forest, his radio crackled on his shoulder.

"Alex, you better get over here," Riley's voice came through the line.

Thumbing the mic attached to his radio, Alex asked, "What did you find?"

"A dead body."

TWO

Alex drew Truman to a halt alongside Riley's and Trevor's horses on the Pine Ridge Trail. Both men stood off the path, staring at something on the ground with grim expressions. In the waning light, Alex could make out the prone figure nestled among the underbrush at the base of the steep rise.

A steel band wrapped around his chest.

Please, Lord, don't let it be one of the Gallo siblings.

Taking a deep breath, he moved closer and slowly pushed back the branches.

Short hair matted with blood, a navy jacket, jeans and hiking boots. Definitely male.

Not Maya Gallo. Relief washed through him.

After confirming Riley had taken preliminary photos of the scene with his phone, Alex braced himself and slowly rolled the body over.

Definitely not Brady Gallo, either.

Alex blew out another relieved breath. He was pretty sure he knew everyone in Bristle Township and County, at least well enough for a chin nod, and this man was a stranger. He first checked for a pulse to confirm the man was indeed deceased, and then searched the man's clothing for identification. There was none.

Alex stood and stared upward at the side of the mountain. Had the man been climbing and fell or had someone bashed him over the head and stashed his body behind the bushes? Was there a killer loose in the forest?

Would Alex find one of the Gallos dead?

Dread clamped a hand around his heart. He hated to contemplate the thought.

He radioed in to let the sheriff know they needed the medical examiner, and then, turning to Trevor and Riley, he said, "Wait here for the sheriff and the ME. I'm going back to the other trail." He was sure someone had gone through the forest. Maybe Brady or Maya. He had to be thorough in his search.

From her perch on the back of her paint, Leslie took one look at the dead body and gagged. Looking away, she said, "I'll never get used to that."

"I'd be worried if you did," Alex told her. She was an accomplished horsewoman and a hard worker when on patrol but still a civilian. "You go back to the trailhead. I'm returning to the Aspen Creek Trail."

"You'll never make the summit before dark," Leslie told him with worry in her voice.

"I have to check something," he said. "Let the sheriff know."

Though concern showed on her face, she nodded. "Be careful." She turned her horse and moved back down the trail.

Alex urged Truman, as quickly as he dared in the waning light, back to the place where he'd seen evidence that someone had gone off the trail. He dismounted and dropped the reins, letting them hit the ground, a signal for Truman to stay put while Alex made his way through the bushes, following the broken branches and the faint outline of two sets of booted feet.

The dimming daylight plus the canopy of branches overhead made tracking the footsteps difficult, but he didn't want to break out his flashlight just yet and risk revealing his presence to whoever might be nearby.

A rustling in the bushes a few feet to his left sent his senses on high alert. His heart hammered in his chest. His hand went to his holstered gun. With caution and stealth, he moved slowly forward.

Fear that her attacker had returned stole Maya's breath. Praying the bright blue backpack now on her back wouldn't be a beacon to her location, she hunkered down in the bushes and tightened her fingers around the tree branch gripped between her hands. She kept her head low and prayed for protection.

After she'd hidden behind the tree trunk, she'd heard the assailant crashing about the woods, mumbling and cursing to himself. Then he moved south, back toward the trailhead, no doubt thinking she'd headed in that direction.

She'd started to make her way back to the path when she had heard heavy footsteps coming her way. She'd taken cover here in these bramble bushes.

The woods had gone silent.

Daring to peek out from behind the bushes, her gaze landed first on a pair of dark boots standing on the other side of the shrub she'd hidden behind.

"Come out with your hands up," a deep, familiar voice commanded.

Deputy Alex Trevino.

This wasn't her attacker. This was her rescuer. God had answered her prayers. Though why he'd send Alex, of all people, she couldn't fathom. Wasn't Kaitlyn available?

Shaking her head at her own idiotic thoughts—who was she to complain about how God answered her prayer—she slowly rose and stepped out from behind the bushes. "Alex."

He quickly holstered his drawn weapon, for which she was thankful.

He hurried to her side. "Maya? Are you okay?" He gripped her shoulders, visually searching her, his gaze warm and concerned.

She let go of the stick she'd expected to use as a weapon and hugged her arms around her middle as a measure of relief ebbed through her veins. She could only imagine how frightful she must look considering her trek through the woods. And why that should even matter she didn't know. The only thing that mattered was her brother. "I'm fine. But Brady…" She swallowed back the bile of fear burning her throat.

"What happened to your brother?"

"I don't know. He didn't return when he was supposed to this afternoon. I got worried so I came out here. I found his backpack." She hitched the straps higher on her shoulders. "Someone attacked me from behind, but I escaped and whoever it was chased me into the woods." She shuddered as the memory flooded her mind.

Alex cupped her elbow and started her walking back toward the trail. A sense of safety and well-being blanketed her, allowing the constriction in her chest to ease a bit.

"Did you get a look at your attacker's face?"

She shook her head with regret. "No. I think it was a man." She shrugged. "He had on a hoodie and a weird mask. But he had cold dark eyes." A shiver slid over her skin. "I'm pretty sure he went south so I waited until I thought the coast was clear. I was working my way back to the trail when I heard you." She grasped his arm. "We have to find Brady."

"We will," he assured her in a voice full of confidence.

She hoped he was right and that Brady was uninjured. What if the maniac who'd attacked her attacked Brady? Brady wouldn't know how to defend himself. Worry for her brother ate at her, making her limbs shake.

Alex helped her over a root. "We found a deceased man on Pine Ridge Trail."

She sucked in a sharp breath as panic whirled through her like a tornado. But he'd asked about Brady, so it couldn't be her brother, could it?

Her thoughts must have shown on her face because Alex threaded his fingers through hers. "It's not your brother."

"The man who attacked me?"

"Maybe." Alex's voice held a grim note. "Hard to know if you can't identify your assailant."

"But who killed him?" None of this made sense. First, she was attacked for no apparent reason and now, her assailant could be dead.

What about Brady? Where was he?

They emerged out of the thick forest onto the trail where Alex's beautiful horse, Truman, waited. Alex quickly stepped into the stirrup and hoisted himself into the saddle, then reached for her. She grasped his larger hand and let him lift her off the ground. She swung a leg over the back of the horse and settled behind Alex on the horse's back.

"Set your feet on the back of my calves," he told her.

She did but wasn't sure what to do with her hands. She lightly placed them on his waist. With sure movement, he clasped her hands and drew them forward so that her arms wrapped around his middle.

Awareness zipped along her veins. She felt secure and cared for as she hung onto him. The scent of his aftershave mingled with the earthy forest and horseflesh, and teased her senses, making her realize how long it had been since she'd allowed anyone, besides Brady, this close.

If the circumstances were different, she'd have been embarrassed by the close contact. But the situation had her stomach tied up in knots and with every step the animal took, she hurt knowing she was possibly moving farther away from her brother.

Alex kept the horse moving at a slow pace because the forest was now shrouded in darkness. With a flashlight held in one hand, he illuminated the trail. They had gone several hundred feet when Truman neighed loudly and reared back.

"Whoa, there." Alex expertly controlled the horse. Maya shifted, trying to see what had caused the animal to spook.

Someone careened out of the branches of the tree above them, slamming into her, causing her to loosen her hold on Alex and forcing her off the horse. She hit the ground hard on her shoulder, a fiery pain exploded at the point of contact and radiated down her arm.

Her assailant landed on his feet like a ninja from a

movie and grabbed her by the backpack, dragging her toward the forest. Hoping to make it more difficult for him, she went limp. The blinding light of Alex's flashlight shone on them.

"Halt," Alex yelled as he jumped off Truman with his weapon drawn and aimed at the man's chest.

Her assailant let go of her and raced into the inky woods as if snapping dogs were at his heels.

Holstering his weapon, Alex crouched down beside Maya. "Are you hurt?"

"Not sure." She tried to sit up. Agony ripped through her shoulder. She cried out.

"Don't move." Alex stared at the forest and back at her, clearly torn between chasing after the assailant and taking care of her. She wanted to tell him to go find the maniac. But she didn't want to be left here on the ground alone, either. And she desperately wanted his help finding Brady.

Clearly deciding she was the priority, to which she breathed a sigh of relief, he used his shoulder-mounted radio to call in the situation before he positioned himself behind her to ease her into a sitting position. She gritted her teeth as the movement jostled her injured shoulder. He slipped the backpack down her arms with gentle hands and put it on himself.

"I'm going to lift you and put you into the saddle," he said. "Do you think you can handle that?"

Grateful for his kindness she nodded. "Yes. I can do that." And she would bear the pain no matter how much her shoulder hurt.

Coming around to her uninjured side, he wedged one arm under her bent knees and slipped his other arm around her waist. With apparent ease, he lifted her into his arms and stood. She'd always thought he looked strong, now she knew for sure. She wasn't a tiny woman, measuring five feet seven inches with a figure that could be called curvy, but he didn't seem the least bit exerted in holding her.

She couldn't help but notice the five o'clock shadow on his strong jaw and the way his dark brown hair curled at the ends. He really was attractive. She'd noticed before but now... She met his warm brown gaze and a blush heated her cheeks. "I'm sorry you have to do this."

One corner of his mouth lifted. "I'm not."

What did that mean? She didn't have time to contemplate his words as he lifted her so she could sit in the saddle. At well over six feet tall, he had no trouble placing her on the horse. Thankfully, she could grasp the saddle horn with her right hand while keeping her left arm bent close to her middle and as immobile as possible.

This time he sat behind the saddle's cantle, mounting with easy grace. One of his arms slid around her waist holding on to her while he held on to the reins with his other hand.

"If it helps, you can lean back against me." His voice rumbled from his chest, making his invitation inviting.

When was the last time she'd ever leaned on someone else? For anything? She couldn't remember.

Slowly, she eased back until he took her weight against his chest, reducing the pressure from her bad arm and shoulder. Tiny shivers of shock and adrenaline slid through her. She took deep, calming breaths. Alex's warmth enveloped her but did nothing to ease the boulder-size fear for her brother sitting in the pit of her stomach.

They headed down the trail until they reached the trail kiosk. She squinted against the flashing lights of the ambulance and the sheriff's department vehicles.

Two paramedics rushed forward. With Alex's help, she was taken from the back of Truman and laid on a gurney. The jostling sent streaks of fiery pain through her shoulder.

As the EMTs carried her to the ambulance, Maya nodded at Riley and his son and was grateful to see her friend Leslie Quinn.

The other woman stepped close and grasped her hand. "We've all been so worried about you."

"Brady?" Maya hoped her friend would have good news.

Leslie shook her head.

Disappointment and fear clogged her chest. A crowd had gathered, and Deputy Daniel Rawlings was keeping the townsfolk back. She searched the throng, praying she'd see Brady's sweet round face. But he wasn't there.

"Stop," she told the paramedics. Biting her lip against the aching in her shoulder, she propped herself up on her good arm. "Alex!"

He stood a few feet away and turned at the sound of his name. He handed Truman's reins to Chase and strode to her side.

"We have to find Brady. I'm not leaving here until we do," she told him as she swung her legs over the side of the gurney and attempted to stand. The whole world tilted on its axis and a fresh wave of agony from her shoulder crashed through her but she gritted her teeth and rode it out.

Alex held up a hand. "No. You need to let Jake and

Gabby see to your injury," he said, pointing at the two paramedics.

Fighting through the dizziness, she protested, "It's getting dark. He'll be frantic. He doesn't do well in the dark." Hysteria bubbled within her. She fought for composure. "I'm going back out there. He's my responsibility."

She steadied her feet under her and stood. "You coming with me or not?" She turned to the paramedics. "You can put me in a sling or something but I'm going back up the trail."

The EMTs looked at Alex whose gaze shot to the sheriff before settling back on her. "I'll go. But you need to stay here."

"No, I'm going with you." Her baby brother needed her.

Alex's strong jaw set in a determined line. "We can stand here and argue about it some more. But the best thing for Brady is for you to let me do my job and let Jake and Gabby do theirs."

His chastisement stung, but she understood. If she went up the trail, she'd only slow Alex down. And if she stumbled or fell in the dark, she'd do more damage to her shoulder.

Though it grated on her nerves and her pride, she acquiesced. "Fine." She sat back on the gurney. A leaf dislodged from somewhere on her and landed in her lap. She slapped it away with her uninjured hand. "Only I'm not going anywhere until you return with Brady."

She could only hope her trust in Alex was well placed because she didn't know what she'd do if something happened to her brother.

* * *

Alex shook his head, half exasperated and half admiring. Maya was a fiercely loyal, protective and loving sister. She was also determined and stubborn and so pretty, even with sticks and leaves clinging to her long wavy dark hair and her big brown eyes a little wild with worry. He could only imagine what it would be like to have someone care about him with such devotion. A strange yearning clamored for his attention. He ignored it.

"Chase, find a couple of headlamps," he called to the other deputy while he led Truman back into the trailer. It was too dark for the horse to attempt the trail.

Within a few moments, Alex and Chase moved to the trailhead. Alex paused. "You go up Pine Ridge Trail. Keep your wits about you."

"Yes, boss." Chase saluted and hurried up the trail to the left.

Shaking his head at Chase's insistence on calling him that, Alex took the Aspen Creek Trail at a fast clip. His headlamp provided a large circle of light on the path. He swung the light into the forest on both sides of the trail, hoping Brady would see the glow and seek the source.

"Brady!" Alex called as he went. He was near the summit when the sound of pounding feet coming at him jackknifed his heart. He sent up a quick prayer that he'd found Brady as he stepped to the side of the path, keeping the glow of his headlamp focused in the direction of the person racing toward him. He rested his hand on his gun.

A man came into view, shielding his face from the light trained on him. "Help," the man said. "We have an injured hiker."

Alex moved the headlamp enough to keep the man in the glow but not blinding him. "I'm Deputy Trevino. Your name?"

The man held up his hands. "Roger. Roger Dempsey." He lowered his hands. "I'm with a group of hikers and we found an injured teenager. He'd fallen down a ravine and twisted his ankle."

It had to be Brady. Relief and worry mingled, tightening Alex's chest.

"The others are trying to make a sled or something to get him back up the hill," the man continued. "But it's not going so well. There's no cell service up here. I was going for help. What are you doing out here?"

Ignoring the question, Alex thumbed the radio's mic on his shoulder and quickly called in the situation. The sheriff promised to send up the EMTs, and Chase responded he was on his way.

"Show me where." Alex gestured for Roger to take the lead. No way would Alex turn his back on a stranger.

"Right." Roger retraced his steps.

"Do you know if the teen you found is named Brady?"

Roger drew up short, forcing Alex to step to the side. "Yeah, that's his name. How did you know?"

"We've been looking for him. He didn't return home when he was supposed to."

Roger nodded. "That makes sense, considering…"

Alex understood what the man wasn't saying about Brady's Down syndrome. It was a part of Brady, but it wasn't who he was. Alex knew Brady was smart and kind and loved his sister.

They reached the summit and started toward the trail

on the back side of the mountain when Roger stopped and called, "Sybil! Greg!"

"Here," a female voice called back.

"This way." Roger trudged into the dense forest.

Before following him, Alex relayed his location to the others. Keeping his headlamp trained on Roger, Alex descended into the steep ravine. Finally, they came to a spot near the creek where two women and two men crouched around Brady, who sat on the ground, his hands wrapped around his right ankle. As Alex and his escort arrived, the four strangers stepped back.

Thankful to have found the other Gallo sibling, Alex knelt down beside Brady. Alex positioned his headlamp so that it didn't blind the young man but rather reflected on the creek water not too far away. "Hey, Brady. I hear you hurt yourself."

Brady blinked at him, and then a slow smile curled his lips. "I know you. You come to the store."

"That's right. I'm Alex. Can you tell me what happened?"

Brady's gaze bounced away. "Maya's gonna be so mad at me."

"She's worried about you, Brady," Alex said. "She sent me to find you. What happened?" he asked again.

Brady's mouth closed, his lips pressed together tight.

A tall woman with white-blond hair and wearing a bright pink down parka touched Brady's shoulder. "I'm Sybil. I think he may have been coming down to the creek to get some water and fell."

Alex looked at Brady. "Was that what you were doing?"

Brady stared at him for a long moment before saying, "I'm thirsty, and my ankle hurts."

The other woman moved forward. This one was a brunette, shorter than the other woman and dressed in a less flashy dark jacket. "I'm Claire. We've been trying to get him up the hill, but it's just not happening."

Claire moved over to Roger. "Thanks for bringing help."

"They were already out here searching for Brady."

"You did better than I did," one of the men standing to the side said. He was just outside the circle of light so Alex couldn't make out his features. "I got lost but managed to find my way back here."

"That's because you have no sense of direction," the other man, also standing in the shadows, shot back.

Roger made a scoffing noise. "That's Greg and John."

Alex eyed the five people surrounding him. Was one of these men Maya's attacker?

Could one of these Good Samaritans also be a killer?

THREE

The combination of anticipation and restlessness made Maya antsy. Her body fairly vibrated. Maybe from the residual adrenaline of being attacked twice or from the memory of Alex's arms around her as they made their way down the mountain trail. Whatever the case, she hated being left behind, not knowing what was going on while Alex searched for her brother.

The handsome deputy had radioed in that he'd found Brady and that her brother was injured. But how bad? Injured enough that the EMTs left her in the care of Deputy Kaitlyn Lanz as they hurried up the Aspen Creek Trail with a gurney and their equipment.

A sick feeling in the pit of Maya's stomach made the worry that much worse. Had Brady broken something? Was he conscious? Terrified?

Dr. Brown had said Brady was progressing admirably, but she feared that today would blast all their hard work to smithereens. She'd been told that one day Brady would be able to live on his own. She knew his independence was possible, yet the thought filled her with anxiety. There were others with Down syndrome who made lives for themselves apart from their caretakers.

But Brady wasn't ready for a life without her. If nothing else, today proved it.

This was her fault. Her heart sank.

She should never have let him go looking for the treasure. She was such a bad parent.

A soft scoff escaped. She wasn't a parent; she was his sister, but the only maternal figure he'd known for the last ten years. A deep ache throbbed in her heart. She missed their parents so much. It wasn't fair they'd been taken from them.

The sheriff walked over to her side. "Miss Gallo, how are you doing?"

She reined in her tumultuous thoughts and said, "I'll do better once I'm able to talk to my brother and make sure he's okay."

The sheriff nodded. "I understand. It's hard when we have someone we love in jeopardy. But you also had your fair share of danger today," he replied. "Can you tell me about the attacks?"

Was he just trying to distract her? She kept her gaze on the trailhead. Where were they?

"There's not much to tell," she said. "The first one happened while I was going up to Aspen Creek Trail, calling for my brother. I noticed the edge of his backpack sticking out from under some bushes." Her breath hitched, remembering the terror of finding the bag but not Brady. "A few moments later, somebody tackled me from behind."

"You managed to escape." There was admiration in the older man's voice. "Good for you."

If her friend Leslie hadn't taught her some self-defense moves, Maya wouldn't have known what to do.

"I ran deeper into the forest and hid until he was gone. That's really all there is to tell you."

He searched her face as if he was trying to see into her memory because apparently her words just weren't getting the job done for him. "Alex said you didn't get a look at his face, only his eyes?"

"That's right. He had on a dark hoodie and a mask that had no mouth covering his face."

"Were his eyes bloodshot? Any indication he was on drugs?"

She arched an eyebrow. "I was a little too busy trying to get away from him to really notice much else. I just remember a very cold expression in his eyes. He cursed a lot."

"Do you think you'd recognize his voice?"

"I don't know. He was mumbling so probably not."

"And the man who knocked you off Truman? Could that have been the same man?"

"I would assume so, unless there are two maniacs running around attacking people." She shrugged and then regretted the movement. "It happened so fast. I am just thankful Alex was with me."

"Can you think of a reason why you would be targeted?" the sheriff asked.

A wave of fear crashed over her. "No. I have no idea why someone would want to hurt me."

Movement at the trailhead drew her gaze. Her heart fluttered with renewed anxiety.

"Here they come," Kaitlyn said.

Despite the pain in her shoulder, Maya forced herself to a sitting position. Though the paramedics had said her shoulder didn't appear broken, she would need an X-ray to confirm. It did hurt but not as bad as her heart for her brother.

Finally, she saw Brady lying on the gurney the two paramedics wheeled as best they could over the rough terrain. The panic in her chest eased.

Her gaze zeroed in on Alex, walking a few feet behind Brady. So handsome. So protective. She sent up a quick thank-You to God for sending Alex.

Then she noticed Alex and Deputy Fredrick were ushering five people out of the forest. Who were these people? Had they hurt her brother?

She tried to get off the gurney, but Kaitlyn stopped her with a hand on her good shoulder.

"Stay put," she said. "They'll bring him to you. Don't worry."

"Kait, this is just torture. I need to be with my brother."

"Patience," Kaitlyn murmured.

Maya stifled a snort. Patience wasn't always an easy virtue.

As soon as Brady was close, she reached out and grasped his hand. "I thank God you're okay. I was so worried." Terrified was more like it.

He hung his head in apparent abjection. "I'm sorry, Maya. I didn't mean to make you worry."

She squeezed his hand. "What happened?"

"I—I fell." He wouldn't meet her eyes. "I don't remember how. I just went tumbling and landed by the creek. I tried to get up but my ankle hurt."

"Looks like a bad sprain," the female EMT, Gabby, said. "But like with you, we won't know if anything is broken until an X-ray is taken. We've stabilized his ankle, though."

Jake spoke up. "We're taking you both to the hospital."

Maya winced. She hated hospitals. They brought back memories of the night her parents crashed their car coming down from Eagle Crest Mountain. The smells, the sounds… They tormented her for years afterward.

Alex stepped close and she met his gaze, grateful for his steady presence. "Thank you, Alex, I really appreciate all you've done for us."

"Just doing my job," he said, though she could see he was pleased by her appreciation, which did funny things to her insides. "I'll come check on you and Brady at the hospital."

She didn't want to admit how much she liked that idea. She felt safe with him around. "What about my Jeep?"

"Why don't you give me your keys and I'll bring it to you?" he said, holding out his hand.

"That would be great." She dug her car keys from the pocket of her jacket and handed them over to him. "Again, thank you."

He gave her a smile that made her heart flutter in a way that left her a bit tongue-tied.

"Honestly, it was my pleasure." He cleared his throat and then turned to nod to the paramedics. "Let's get them to the hospital."

As Maya and Brady were loaded into the ambulance bay, she held Brady's hand but her gaze stayed on Alex as he moved over to the group of people that had come down the trail with him.

He'd not only rescued her and then protected her, he'd also brought her brother back to her. Alex was a really good man. Her parents would have liked him.

Too bad she wasn't looking for a really good man in her life. Or any man for that matter. She had more than enough to deal with as it was with Brady and the store. Putting herself out there for more heartache wasn't an option.

Alex looked at the group around him. Since he didn't have grounds to detain them, the most he could hope for was their willing cooperation. "Okay, people. Deputy Chase Fredrick and Deputy Daniel Rawlings—" he gestured to the two deputies "—will take your information. Are you all staying here in town?"

"Yes, sir. The Bristle Hotel," the man named Greg offered.

Good. He'd know where to find them if it turned out the deceased had met with foul play. Alex searched each face, wondering if one of these people was a murderer and/or Maya's assailant. He wasn't ready to reveal more until the area where the deceased man had been found could be processed in the daylight.

Leaving Chase and Daniel in charge of the five hikers, Alex informed his boss of the plan to question the hikers once he had some more information.

Sheriff Ryder nodded his approval. "You're doing well, son."

The praise was nice to hear, even if it made him uncomfortable. He'd never received much encouragement from his own father. Which reminded him, Dad was waiting at home with dinner. He unclipped his cell phone from his utility belt and called his father to let him know he had a few more errands to run before he would make it home. He could hear the disappointment in his father's voice. It couldn't be helped. Alex's priority was the job.

"Kaitlyn," he called to the other deputy, who was now talking with Leslie Quinn and Riley and Trevor Howard.

Kaitlyn extracted herself and hurried over. "What's up?"

"Would you be willing to take my truck and Truman over to the sheriff's parking lot? I need to take Maya's car to her at the hospital and drive her and Brady home."

"Sure, no problem. But I can just take Truman home with me. I can put him in one of our empty stalls."

Kaitlyn owned a large stable where several members of the mounted patrol boarded their horses. "That would be awesome. So much better than him being cooped up in the trailer any longer than necessary."

"My thoughts exactly."

"Also, I don't think Maya and Brady should be alone tonight. Would you be willing to stay with them?" He'd do it but wasn't sure how that would go over. Better to have the female deputy stand guard over the Gallos.

"Good idea. I'll pack a bag and head over after I get the horses rubbed down and fed."

"Thanks, Kaitlyn." He handed her his keys and headed for Maya's Jeep. When he opened the door, the scent of cinnamon teased his senses. He smiled as he climbed into the driver's seat. Maya liked Red Hots. He'd seen boxes of them behind the counter at the store. She was like that spicy candy. Bold, yet not abrasive. Sweet, but not a pushover. She didn't tolerate guff from anybody and yet she was kind to everyone, if a bit standoffish.

He started up the Jeep and drove to the hospital.

Bristle Township, Colorado, was barely considered a town. More of a hamlet or a village with less than a thousand full-time residents. He could walk from one end of Main Street to the other in a matter of minutes. The "downtown area" consisted of two rows of two-story buildings that housed a variety of shops, restaurants and businesses with the Community Christian Church a focal point at the north end.

The county stretched for miles but the town itself was quaint, rustic even, in some ways. That was what had drawn him to apply for the position of deputy for Bristle County to begin with when he'd left Denver. He'd wanted a simpler life in a place where he could belong.

And he would do anything to protect its citizens.

He parked the Jeep in the designated spot for the sheriff. Inside the hospital, he stopped by the front desk to let them know not to tow the Jeep, then he was given directions to Maya and Brady's whereabouts. He entered the emergency room to find the siblings on side-by-side gurneys with a doctor and nurse hovering over them. Maya's eyes widened when she saw him, and the small smile of welcome she gave him sent his pulse skittering.

Brady was more exuberant in his greeting. "Deputy Alex!" He waved. "Come over here and see what they're doing to me."

His injured ankle had been wrapped and placed in a walking boot.

"That is some fancy footwear there, Brady."

"They shod my foot. Like a horse," Brady said with a grin.

Turning to the doctor, Alex asked, "How are these two doing? Will they be released tonight?"

After looking to Maya for permission to share details and receiving an affirmative, the doctor said, "X-rays show no fractures for either of them. Brady will have to wear the boot for a week and follow up with his primary doctor. Maya's shoulder will be sore for a while. I prescribed some PT. We will have to wait until the swelling goes down before we can do an MRI to see if there are any tears."

Alex was glad to hear no bones had been broken. The worry that had been churning in his gut lessened.

"As to your other question, yes, they are good to go," the doctor finished.

"They have both had pain medication." The nurse handed him a small bag and a large one. "There's more here. And here are their personal items."

Alex glanced inside the large bag to see Brady's backpack, shoe and Maya's jacket.

The doctor turned to Maya. "Don't let the pain get out of control, for either you or Brady. Stay on schedule at least for the first twenty-four hours."

"Yes, sir," she said.

"Your chariot awaits," Alex said.

Two nurses appeared with wheelchairs.

"I get to ride a wheelchair," Brady said, pumping his fist in the air.

Alex was glad to see Brady taking this all in stride. Alex still needed to question the boy to find out if he'd seen the deceased man and he had some questions about the Good Samaritan hikers. But that would have to wait.

After getting Maya and Brady into the Jeep, Alex drove them to their house, a cute little bungalow on a residential street behind the Community Christian Church.

He helped Maya out to the car. "You sure you can walk?"

She slanted him a chiding glance. "I hurt my shoulder." She gestured to the sling encasing her right arm. "Not my legs."

"Just checking." He kind of wished she'd said she wanted him to pick her up again. He had liked holding her far more than he should have and the memory of her in his arms would stay with him for a long time.

However, Brady needed help so Alex scooped the boy up into his arms, carried him inside the house and placed him on the couch in the living room. Alex stepped back and looked around, liking the cozy feel of the Gallo home with its leather couches, bright throw pillows, a warm colorful woolen floor rug covering cherry hardwood floors and a gas fireplace below a flat-screen television.

One wall held bookshelves and framed photographs. His gaze snagged on a picture of the Gallo family when Maya and Brady were younger. His heart ached for the siblings' loss.

The yellow-and-red-striped flag of Spain hung proudly on another wall. Off center in the wide yellow stripe was the decorative coat of arms, which reminded him of learning in grade school about Columbus and the New World.

"Alex, Alex!" Brady exclaimed. "Come sit with me." He grabbed the remote. "It's time for my show."

"Can you hold off for a moment?" Alex asked. "I need to ask you some questions."

Brady blinked at him. "Questions?"

"About what happened on the trail."

"I already told you." Brady aimed the remote at the television and turned on the device. An announcer's voice filled the house as contestants ran through obstacle courses.

Maya touched Alex's sleeve to get his attention. She gestured for him to follow her into the kitchen. Like the living room, the eating area was cozy and the counter and appliances clean.

Once they were out of earshot of Brady, Maya said, "I tried to get him to tell me what happened on the trail. But he clammed up and wouldn't look me in the eye. I've never seen him do that before. Usually he's so willing and eager to tell me every little detail of everything he does. This is unlike him. Something definitely happened, but for some reason he doesn't want to talk about it."

Alex wondered if the teen would open up if Maya weren't around. Maybe Brady was afraid he'd get in trouble with his sister. Alex would try again to talk to Brady alone. "How are *you* doing?"

"I'm okay. Other than the shoulder." She turned away to busy herself making coffee with one hand. It shook and sent coffee grinds skittering across the counter. She was trying to appear strong and in control, but she'd suffered trauma out on the trail, too.

Unable to stop himself, he grasped her hand. "Coffee is not what either of us need right now."

She stilled. He expected her to move away, but she didn't. "Right. Caffeine probably isn't a good idea."

He gave her hand a squeeze, then released her. "How are you going to get Brady to his room?"

She frowned. "I hadn't thought about that."

"Kaitlyn will be here soon to stay with you."

Worry lit her eyes. "Do you think I'm in danger?"

He wasn't sure what to think. "I'd rather be overly cautious and not risk your safety."

Her gaze softened to tenderness and he clenched his gut. "That's very thoughtful of you. You're a thoughtful man."

Her compliment arrowed straight through him. He wasn't used to things like that being said to him. "Thanks." For a moment, he held her gaze, then he cleared his throat. "What can I do to help until Kaitlyn arrives?"

"If you could carry Brady to his bed that would be great," she said. "You must be beat, as well."

He was weary, but he wouldn't let that keep him from helping Maya and Brady. "I'll rest once I'm sure you're settled for the night."

She inclined her head. "I'd appreciate that."

They went into the living room. Brady had fallen asleep on the couch.

"Let's not move him." Maya turned off the television. "There's a blanket in the trunk in the corner."

Alex retrieved the blanket, a fuzzy version of the Spanish flag, and spread it over Brady.

An awkward silence filled the space between them as they moved back into the kitchen.

"I take it your family has ties to Spain." As far as small talk went, it seemed like a safe subject.

"Yes. On both sides. My father's parents moved to the United States before my father was born. Then Dad met my mom at the University of Michigan when she was there with a study-abroad program."

"So you have relatives still in Spain?"

She nodded. "Cousins. They live in Málaga. I visited when I was a kid. Someday I'd like to go back."

"How did your parents end up here?" He sat on the stool.

A smile played at her pretty mouth, drawing his attention. "Dad had an interview in LA so they decided to take a road trip. He was offered the job but they weren't sure about living in Southern California. On their way back to Michigan, they stopped here and fell in love with the town and the people."

"It's a great place to live." He was thankful he'd taken the job with the sheriff's department.

"That's what they thought. They were staying at the Bristle Hotel and heard that people had to drive to Denver or Boulder for their hardware and feed supplies."

"Ah. They decided to fill that need."

"Yes." Her gaze was curious. "What about you? Do you know your heritage?"

"No. My mother was adopted by a single woman who died long before I was born. My dad's family lived in Alabama, but he left home at eighteen and never went back."

"You've never met your grandparents?"

He shook his head. "I tried looking them up when I was a teen, but I couldn't find the right Trevinos. No one seemed to know my dad. And he wouldn't talk about them. I decided it didn't matter."

A soft knock sounded at the front door. Alex peered through the peephole. Kaitlyn. He opened the door and held a finger to his lips while pointing to Brady on the couch.

Kaitlyn nodded. She held a duffel bag in her hand. "Where shall I put my things?" she whispered.

"The den." Maya pointed to a room off the living room. "There's a bathroom at the end of the hall."

Kaitlyn walked away, leaving Alex to say goodnight.

"I'll come back in the morning and check on you," he told her. "Maybe by then Brady will be ready to talk."

Maya opened the door and smiled at him. "I'd like that. He seems to respond well to you. Good night, Alex, and again, thank you."

It occurred to Alex he had no way to get home. "Do you mind if I use your vehicle? Kaitlyn took my truck and Truman to her place." He still had her keys in his pocket.

"Of course you can." She gave him a generous smile that made him want to linger. He'd always thought she was pretty and nice but he'd never considered...

How was it that he was seeing Maya in a whole new way?

He better get his head on straight. She was a victim of a crime. She might be a damsel in distress today, but soon life would go back to the way things had always been between them. Polite acquaintances.

The thought left him cold.

Maya leaned against the closed door. It had been strange yet thrilling to have Alex in her house. His concern and care were apparent and appreciated. Had it only been this morning she'd been embarrassed because she'd thought he would think she was flirting with him through the window of the store?

So much had happened since then. And despite the terror and the trauma of the day, she had to admit she was glad to have someone like Alex watching over them.

Brady's soft snores assured her he was still sleeping.

After Kaitlyn secured the house, making sure every door and window was locked tight, she retired to the sofa bed in the den.

Instead of going upstairs to her room, Maya grabbed another blanket from the trunk and settled herself in the recliner next to the couch. She wanted to be close in case Brady awakened. He'd be scared and in need of her.

She leaned back against the worn fabric, convinced she could still smell her father's aftershave clinging to the material. That was ridiculous, of course, but it offered her comfort at the end of a horrifying day.

She was just dozing off when a noise at the back door sent the fine hairs on her arms standing at attention.

Holding very still, she listened, trying to discern the sound over Brady's snoring.

Kaitlyn ran out of the den with her weapon in hand and waved Maya behind her.

Maya's heart jolted. There was definitely something or someone trying to get in through the kitchen door.

FOUR

"Call 911," Kaitlyn whispered to Maya.

Swallowing the lump of fear in her throat, Maya had hurried through the darkened living room toward the den, where Kaitlyn had been sleeping before they'd both heard someone trying to break in through the kitchen door.

"Maya?" Brady called out from where he lay on the couch.

"Shhhh." She put her finger to her lips, but knowing he couldn't see her, she veered toward the couch and crouched down beside him.

"Quiet," she whispered and took him by the hand. "Come with me."

She led him as quickly as his booted ankle would allow into the den and maneuvered him to a crouch between the bookcase and the edge of the pullout sofa, made up into a rumpled bed that Kaitlyn had hastily departed.

"Stay here," she told him. "You'll be safe. Don't move."

She grabbed the landline and called 911. The night-shift dispatcher at the sheriff's department, Larry

Kingly, answered. Maya quickly, and as quietly as she could, told him the situation. He promised to send help right away.

Hating the thought of Kaitlyn out there facing the unknown alone, Maya went to her father's gun safe in the corner, spun the dial of the combination lock and opened the heavy door with her uninjured hand. Not comfortable using his hunting rifle, she grabbed the airsoft gun her dad had used to scare off coyotes. It was a little trickier loading it with her other arm in a sling, but she managed to get the gun functioning.

Pausing at the open doorway of the den, she could see through the house to the kitchen door, which was closed. Cautiously, Maya made her way through the living room and to the kitchen door, where she pressed her back against the edge and peeked out into the backyard through the door window. The moon's bright glow illuminated parts of the porch and yard, but there were plenty of shadows to make the fine hairs at Maya's nape jump to attention.

She popped open the door. "Kaitlyn?" she whispered, but there was no answer.

What had happened to the deputy?

Dread that something horrible had befallen the female officer spread through Maya, but she gathered her courage and stepped out onto the porch. She held the airsoft gun awkwardly against her hip with her uninjured hand close to the trigger. It wouldn't do much damage to a human or animal, but it was better than nothing and would hopefully chase away the intruder.

To her right in her peripheral vision she saw movement in the shadows of the back porch. Heart jumping in her throat, she spun with the airsoft gun aimed into the darkness. "Who's there?"

She could faintly make out the shape of a human seconds before the person lunged at her.

Backpedalling toward the safety of the house, she shouted, "Don't come any closer. I'll shoot."

The distant sound of a siren heralded the arrival of help. She silently urged them to hurry.

In a swift movement that left her breathless, the shadowy figure leaped over the railing of the porch like he was jumping over a garden hose, landing soundlessly three feet down onto the ground below before racing away from her across the backyard. The man jumped up, grabbed the top of the fence, leaped over the fence and disappeared.

She heard a noise to her left and spun in that direction, her finger hovering over the airsoft gun's trigger. Kaitlyn ran into view, her weapon drawn.

Relieved to see the deputy, Maya set the airsoft gun on the porch and hurried down the steps. "Kaitlyn, are you hurt?"

"My pride more than anything," she grumbled, holstering her weapon. She rubbed the back of her head. "The intruder got the drop on me from behind. Hit me over the head with something. But I stayed on my feet and chased the suspect around the house to the front yard, then I lost him. I heard you shouting."

"He came around to the back again," Maya told her. She had never seen somebody so agile or quick. "It had to be the same person who attacked me in the forest earlier today."

And the person obviously knew where she lived.

* * *

Alex brought his truck to a halt next to the sheriff's cruiser. Worry for Maya and Brady ate at his gut. He'd been at home sleeping, when Larry, the dispatcher, had called per the sheriff's instructions. As the lead on the case, Alex had rushed over, afraid that something bad had happened to the Gallos. The sheriff was already talking to Deputy Kaitlyn Lanz.

Maya and Brady stood in the glow of the porch light. Both looked unharmed beyond the injuries from earlier in the day. Alex breathed easier as he vaulted up the stairs of the Gallo house. "What happened?"

Maya shook as she explained. Alex fisted one hand and turned to Kaitlyn. "You okay?"

She gave him a sheepish look. "Yeah, I'm fine. Took a hit on the back of the head but I didn't lose consciousness or anything. I chased the perp but he's a fast runner."

"And agile," Maya added. "Just like the guy on the trail today."

Dread gripped his chest. The guy had somehow learned where Maya lived. Not good.

"I'll be taking over Maya and Brady's protection from here on out," Alex announced.

Kaitlyn winced. "He got the drop on me. It won't happen again."

"No doubt it won't," the sheriff stated. "But you were clocked on the head. You need to take it easy. See the doctor and make sure you don't have any kind of concussion."

"I don't have a concussion," Kaitlyn grumbled.

"It would make us all feel better to be on the safe

side, Kait," Alex said. "I'll take over for tonight. We will regroup in the morning."

As the sheriff and Kaitlyn left, Alex urged Maya and Brady back into the house.

Brady let out a big, noisy yawn. "Maya, I'm going to my room."

"Actually, I'd like you both to pack a bag," Alex said. "You're coming home with me." He hadn't really made the decision to take them to the ranch until this moment, but it made the most sense.

"What?" Maya stared at him. "We can't stay with you."

"Why not? I've plenty of room at the ranch and it will be easier to protect you there."

"You'll have to drive us to the store in the morning."

"Not a problem," he told her. "I have your Jeep, remember?"

Though she nodded, she said, "I'm not sure about this."

"I am." He wasn't leaving here without her and Brady. "I don't suspect the perp would return tonight, but he may eventually. I'd rather have you where it would be harder to get at you."

After a heartbeat, she turned to her brother. "Brady, Alex has invited us to stay with him. Are you okay with that?"

Brady's sleepy gaze bounced between them. "Okay. We'll sleep at Alex's house. That's cool."

Maya hugged her brother with her one good arm. "Go to your room and pick out some clothes. I'll be right in to help you pack."

Brady ambled off down the hall, his booted foot making a clomping sound as he went. Once he was out of earshot, Maya said, "Thank you for this. It's beyond the call of duty."

Uncomfortable with her assessment for reasons he didn't understand, he shrugged. "Protecting you two is my job. My duty, as you put it. I can keep you safe better on the ranch than here."

"But for how long?"

"As long as it takes."

"I hate to be a burden."

"You're not. Now, go pack so we can get a move on."

She bit the bottom of her lip, drawing his gaze from her pretty, troubled eyes to her lush mouth. He forced himself to turn away before he gave in to the sharp yearning to pull her close and kiss away her worry. She had every right to be scared. Someone had tried to break into her house. She'd been attacked this afternoon. And he would do everything he could to keep her and her brother safe. His attraction to the pretty shopkeeper had no part in the equation.

Maya let out a small sigh of apparent worry—or maybe acceptance, he hoped—then turned and hurried down the hall. Alex expelled a heavy breath, then checked to make sure the kitchen door was securely locked.

Ten minutes later, they were in Maya's Jeep, with Alex driving, Maya in the passenger seat and Brady dozing in the back passenger area.

"Go through what happened again for me," Alex asked Maya as they headed out of town toward his place.

"There's not much more to tell you," she said. "I was sleeping in the recliner when I heard a noise at the kitchen door. Kaitlyn had been sleeping in the den. She came out to investigate. I got Brady into the den and called 911. I took my dad's airsoft gun out to the back porch. The guy was in the shadows. I couldn't make out his size or shape."

"You shouldn't have gone outside," Alex stated, frustrated that she'd taken such a risk.

"I was afraid for Kaitlyn," she said.

"Kaitlyn can take care of herself," he replied, hating the thought of something happening to Maya.

As Alex approached the long drive that led to his house, he kept a watch for any signs of being followed. All was dark behind him. He took the turn and drove through tall trees to the clearing where his ranch-style house sat smack-dab in the center of thirty-five acres. The house was already here when he'd purchased the land, but he'd built both the barn, where he housed Truman, and the corral. He was proud of the place and the work he'd put into it. Growing up, he and his dad had lived in a series of run-down apartments with no yards, let alone room for animals.

He brought Maya's Jeep to a halt in front of the house. Floodlights illuminated the wraparound porch and his father and his dog, Rusty, a four-year-old red tri Australian shepherd, standing in the open front door.

"Who's that?" Maya asked.

"My dad," Alex replied. His dad must have heard him leave and gotten up.

Maya eyed him curiously. "You've never mentioned your father."

No, he hadn't. Talking about his parents wasn't something he liked to do. He hadn't seen his father until six months ago when he'd shown up on Alex's doorstep, sick and in need of a place to live. "He's staying with me temporarily."

"Where's your mom?"

There was a tentative note in her voice that made his chest tight. He knew she'd lost her parents at a young age. "Mom lives in Idaho Falls with her third husband."

"Oh."

"Yeah. My parents divorced when I was a kid."

"I'm sorry."

Her sympathy grated on his nerves. "No big deal." He popped open the door. Rusty raced down the stairs to greet him with sloppy kisses and happy barking. He held out his hand in the stop formation, indicating for the dog to wait and give him space. Rusty backed up, but his backside wiggled with excitement. "I'll get your bags and then come back to carry Brady inside."

She chuckled. "As strong as you are, I don't think carrying Brady up a flight of stairs is a good idea. If you fell, then you'd both be injured. I'll wake him."

The compliment slid over him like a warm blanket.

"You think I'm strong, huh?" He reached out and tucked a lock of her dark hair behind her ear.

She seemed startled by the question or maybe it was his touch as his fingers lingered, tracing the line of her jaw.

She leaned back, out of his reach, her eyes wide.

Stung by her rejection, he tucked his thumbs into his utility belt. Clearly, he'd overstepped, which wasn't like him at all. He wasn't angling to romance Maya. He wasn't willing to go down that road. And now, realizing she didn't want his attention only solidified his vow to never suffer heartache again.

He jumped out and, with Rusty at his heels, he moved

to the back compartment of the Jeep to grab their gear while Maya woke Brady. The teenager climbed awkwardly out of the Jeep and glanced around. "Big place. Dark out here."

"It's peaceful," Alex said.

"Dog!" Brady exclaimed softly.

"He's friendly," Alex assured the younger man. "This is Rusty."

"Remember how I taught you to greet dogs?" Maya asked her brother.

Brady put his hand out for Rusty to sniff. Then the dog leaned against Brady's legs for a good scrub behind the ears. "Good dog."

The sweet sight had Alex and Maya sharing a gentle smile.

Unfamiliar with the tender emotion filling his chest, Alex quickly gestured toward the house. "Shall we?" He ushered them up the front porch stairs.

"What do we have here?" Frank Trevino asked as the trio stopped.

Alex tried to view his dad as Maya would. Frank was slight of build with a craggy face and thick salt-and-pepper hair. There wasn't much resemblance between them as far as Alex was concerned. "Dad, this is Maya Gallo and her brother, Brady. They are going to be staying with us for a while."

Dad's eyebrows shot up. "Okay. Welcome. I'm Frank Trevino."

"Hi, Frank," Brady said and stuck out his hand while hitching his backpack higher on his shoulder. "I'm Brady."

Dad shook Brady's hand. "Nice to meet you, young man." Dad stepped back. "Come in. Let's get you two settled." He gave Alex a questioning glance as he closed the door behind them.

"We'll put them in the back bedroom," Alex told his dad as he set Maya's and Brady's bags on the scarred cherry hardwood floor. Then he turned to Maya. "Do you mind sharing with Brady tonight? Tomorrow, I can get the office set up with another bed."

"That's fine. You don't need to go to any trouble on our account," she said.

Despite her words, Alex would make sure they each had some space. The house was big enough, and he actually would enjoy the diversion from his father's troubles.

"Come with me, young man," Dad instructed Brady as he grabbed the bags. "We'll get you settled in."

Dad and Brady headed down the hall. Once they were out of view, Maya said, "Thank you for taking us in. I feel bad that we're putting you and your father to so much trouble."

"No trouble at all. You and Brady need to get some rest. Morning will be here fast."

"What about you?" she asked. "You need to rest, as well."

He appreciated her concern, though he wished she'd show more concern about herself. "I will sleep. But I'm not nursing an injury. You are. And after the trauma today, you both must be exhausted."

"I am," she confessed.

"Can I get you anything?" he asked. "Bottled water?"

"I'll take one and so will Brady," she said.

He stepped into the kitchen and took two bottles of water out of the fridge. "Here you go."

"I like your home," she said, her hand caressing the

granite countertop. "I've thought about updating our kitchen counters."

The wistful tone had him moving closer. "I could help with the updates. I did most of the work here."

Her eyes widened. "You did?"

He smiled. "Cheaper than hiring someone else to do stuff I can do."

"That's very handy of you." She smiled shyly. "I might take you up on that offer someday."

"Anytime." Attraction zinged through his blood. He wanted to offer her more than just his carpentry skills. He wanted to give her comfort and support. Would she accept?

Oh, man. He'd better reel in his wayward thoughts. She was his to protect, not romance. This was so unlike him. He usually was better able to separate his personal feelings from his professional ones. But for some reason with Maya Gallo, he wanted to set aside his job and just be a man who wanted to get to know a beautiful woman. Bad idea on so many levels.

He stepped back, putting much-needed distance between them. Gesturing toward the hall, he said briskly, "The bathroom is next door to the room you'll be sleeping in. There are fresh towels and such in the cabinets. Help yourself to whatever you need."

She nodded and walked out of the kitchen. Alex waited a beat to catch his breath and calm his racing blood before checking that the doors and windows were locked.

He was confident they hadn't been followed here, but he wasn't taking any chances. He'd stay up tonight, and tomorrow he'd call to have an alarm system installed, not that Rusty wouldn't alert him if someone approached the house. But he wanted even earlier warning. He'd put sensors on the drive and motion sensors in the trees in a hundred-yard perimeter, because there was no way he was going let anyone get close to Maya and Brady again.

After settling Brady down for the night, Maya took refuge in the bathroom. The soft yellow lights over the sink revealed dark circles beneath her eyes. Her hair was a mess. Who was she kidding? She was a mess. The day, the evening had been one harrowing experience after another.

Except for Alex. He'd been a beacon of hope and light that she wanted to cling to.

And now she and Brady were ensconced in Alex's home. A place she'd never expected to be. But she was so thankful for his protection and concern. He was a nice man. Kind and giving. The type of man she could fall for if she weren't careful. Her heart rate accelerated.

She had to be careful. She had Brady to think about. Complicating her life with a crazy attraction wouldn't be smart. She had responsibilities and wouldn't allow anything or anyone to distract her from the life she'd painstakingly built for her and Brady.

Going through the mundane task of brushing her teeth and hair helped to calm her nerves. With her arm in a sling, she wasn't able to put her hair up like she normally would at night. Carefully, she changed into lounge pants and an oversize flannel shirt. Buttoning it with one hand was a challenge, but she managed to get it done. She tucked her toiletry bag out of the way under the sink before turning out the light and heading back to the room she'd share with Brady tonight.

She paused in the hall. A flickering glow drew her toward the living room. Alex sat on the raised hearth of the fireplace staring into the flames, apparently deep in contemplation, with his dog sitting at his feet. Firelight danced, lighting the dark depths of his hair and washing his face in a warm glow. He was a handsome man with strong features and broad shoulders. He was a man people relied on, a man people trusted. A man she trusted.

Rusty turned and looked toward her. She shrank back into the shadows, unwilling to disrupt Alex's thoughts. But the dog would have none of it. He left Alex's side and trotted to where she stood with her back plastered against the wall. He licked her hand.

A soft chuckle startled her. Her gaze jumped to meet Alex's. He'd followed his dog and now stood very close.

"Sorry, I didn't mean to disturb you two," she said in a voice barely above a whisper.

"No worries. Come join us." He gestured for her to follow him.

"Can't sleep?" she asked as she settled on the hearth with her back to the warm fire.

"Not yet. But you really should be sleeping." He sat beside her, leaving a safe gap between them.

"I will," she said, wishing she didn't want to scoot closer to him. "But I'm still a bit keyed up."

"Is the shoulder painful?"

"A bit. The ER doc gave me some pain meds. I took one. I have to wait for it to kick in."

"It's amazing nothing broke," he said. "You hit the ground hard."

"It's a blessing for sure. The doc said it will take a

while for the soft tissue to repair itself, but I should be good to go fairly soon."

"I believe the Lord was looking out for you today because it could've been so much worse," Alex stated. The darks of his eyes reflected the flames of the fire.

"Yes. I could've landed on my head." Or went over the edge of a cliff or been killed by some crazed maniac. She shuddered with residual fear.

Forcing herself to focus on something other than the drama of the day, she asked, "Where did you grow up?"

"I was born in Whitefish, Montana, but my parents moved to Denver not long after," he said, his gaze trained on the fire while he petted Rusty. The dog leaned against him as if sensing his master needed support. "After the divorce, Mom and Dad both stayed in Denver for a while and then Mom moved away."

"That must have been hard going back and forth for visits." She'd only ever lived in Bristle Township.

"Yes, it was tough at times. But no big deal. Lots of kids do it."

Maya knew that just because many children had to travel back and forth between their parents after a divorce, it didn't make it any less painful. She'd had friends growing up who'd had to do the trek to visit a parent. She hated to admit that at times she thought it would have been nice to live part-time somewhere other than Bristle County. But she realized how blessed she'd been to have her parents together for her childhood.

It made her sad that Brady hadn't had them. And sad for Alex because despite his assurance it was no big deal, there was a thread of hurt there. But he obviously didn't want to address it with her. "What brought you to Bristle Township?"

"I wanted a place of my own," he said. "This ranch came up for sale at the same time that Sheriff Ryder was looking for another deputy. Moving here made sense."

"A God-sequence," she said with a soft smile. It was word she'd heard her parents use often.

"Excuse me?"

"My parents taught me to believe that God is in control and when things work out in a way that seems… random or a coincidence, that really it was God orchestrating things." She tapped his knees. "He wanted you here."

Alex's gaze touched her face like a caress. "I'm glad I *was* here today."

And she was grateful God had used Alex to protect her, despite her initial reaction. "Me, too."

He held her gaze. Her breath caught in her throat. Had he leaned toward her? Her gaze dropped to his mouth. Would he kiss her? Did she want him to?

A piercing scream rent the air.

Jolted out of whatever stupor had gripped her, she jumped to her feet. "Brady!"

FIVE

Maya's heart hammered against her ribs. Brady's scream echoed through her head like a siren. Needing to get to her brother, she raced headlong down the hall with Alex and Rusty at her heels.

She burst into the room she was to share with her brother and flipped on the light. For a moment, the room appeared empty. Terror clawed at her throat.

But then she noticed the lump underneath the covers. She ran to the bed and pulled back the comforter. Brady was curled into a ball, his hands over his head and tears streaming down his cheeks. Rusty jumped onto the bed and licked Brady's face.

"Honey, what happened?" She gathered him into her arms. He came willingly and laid his head against her chest, much like he had when he'd been a little boy after they had learned of their parents' deaths. Rusty settled next to her brother, his paws on Brady's legs.

"I had a nightmare," Brady said, his voice wobbly.

Maya winced with empathy. No doubt the trauma he'd suffered out on the trail had caused the bad dream.

The bed dipped where Alex sat on the edge. He put

his hand on Brady's shoulder. "Can you tell us what the dream was about?"

Brady shook his head. "Too scary."

"You're safe, Brady," Alex assured him. "I'm not going to let anything happen to you."

Brady lifted his head and stared. "Do you promise?"

Maya's gut twisted. She'd emphasized to Brady that breaking a promise wasn't acceptable. So over the years, just as her parents had done, if she couldn't be sure she could keep her promise, she never made one.

Alex gave Brady a gentle smile. "How about we pray and ask God for protection? And I promise I will do everything in my power to make sure that you are safe."

She would have hugged Alex for his response if she hadn't already had Brady in her arms.

Brady shook his head. "No. Promises can be broken. God sometimes breaks His promises."

Maya leaned back to look at Brady in surprise. "Why would you say that?"

"I prayed for Mommy and Daddy to come home and they never came home. God never answered me. He never brought them home."

Maya's heart hurt for her brother. He'd been so young when they died. For months after their deaths, he'd sit staring out the front window as if waiting for them to return. Under the advice of his medical doctor, she'd taken him to see a grief counselor. After several sessions, he'd seemed to accept their parents were gone. But apparently he held resentment toward God for not bringing them back.

Alex met Maya's gaze. She could see the uncertainty in his eyes. She was at a loss how to explain to Brady the finality of death.

"What happened to your parents hurt God as much as it did you." Alex's tone was gentle. "God loved your parents. He loves you. And Maya. Your mom and dad are with God now."

Heart melting, Maya mouthed, *Thank you*, to Alex.

Brady nodded. "That's what Maya says. But I want them back."

"I know you do, sweetie." Maya fought back tears. "One day we'll see them again. But for now, you have me."

"And Alex," Brady stated.

Surprise flashed in Alex's chocolate eyes, and then his expression filled with tenderness. "Yes, Brady. You have me, too."

Maya wanted to tell Alex not to make an implied promise when there was no way he could keep it. Yes, Alex was a part of their lives now but there would be a day when Alex wouldn't have time for them. He'd go back to his job and they'd resume their uneventful lives, which seemed so far away at the moment.

Alex touched her hand. Her pulse jumped as their gazes locked. She couldn't do this. She couldn't form some sort of attachment to this man. She had enough to deal with and she couldn't put any energy into a romantic relationship.

She both broke the eye contact and eased away from Alex. "Brady, it's time for you to try to go back to sleep."

Brady held on tighter. "Don't leave me."

"Never. It's time for me to sleep, as well. I'll be right here with you."

Standing, Alex motioned for Rusty to follow him as he headed to the door. The dog seemed reluctant to leave

Brady but Rusty slowly climbed off the bed and went to Alex. "I'll see you both in the morning."

Alex and Rusty walked out of the room, shutting the door behind them. Maya climbed under the covers next to Brady. He turned his back to her and within seconds was softly snoring. She lay there for the longest time staring up at the ceiling before turning out the light.

"Please, God," she whispered. "I don't know what purpose this all serves but I'm trusting You. And I'm trusting Alex. Please, don't let me be making a mistake."

After letting Rusty outside, Alex sat on the hearth and dropped his head into his hands. Being responsible for people's lives was one thing but trying to answer questions about God… That was so far out of his comfort zone. His relationship with God had been tenuous at best most of his life. His mother's parents had taken him to Sunday school when he was a kid. But they'd passed on when he was teen and his mom and dad hadn't thought church was necessary.

He knew some people looked at God as a father and then equated God to their earthly fathers. And when their earthly fathers failed, the blame shifted to God.

On some level that had been how Alex had felt until he'd moved to Bristle Township and started attending church regularly. Through hearing of the word and reading his Bible, he'd been able to distinguish the difference between the heavenly Father and his earthly father. Maybe the realization had been why Alex had allowed his father back into his life. He let out a scoff. Probably why God had brought Frank back into Alex's life. A lesson to learn?

He glanced toward the ceiling. "Okay, God. What do I do here? How do I navigate this quagmire of self-doubt and danger? How do I be a good role model for Brady?"

And the man Maya needs?

He quickly scrambled away from that thought like a burning ember had hit him on the head. No. He was not the man Maya needed. Maybe she needed him now, in this situation. But she didn't need him long-term, just as he didn't need her. He was happy being a bachelor. He wasn't ready to trust another woman with his heart after his ex-girlfriend Evie's unfaithfulness. It didn't matter how much time had passed; her betrayal had cut deep, leaving a raw wound he feared would never completely heal.

He needed to stay focused on his job. Protect the Gallo siblings. Protect himself. And find a killer. That was the primary goal. Letting himself get sidetracked by his unwarranted attraction to Maya Gallo served no purpose and would only lead to heartache.

The next morning, Alex put on a pot of coffee and made breakfast. He'd finally dozed in the recliner but as soon as the sun had come up Rusty had nudged him, wanting to go outside again. After a shower and shave, he changed into a fresh uniform. He was ready to start the day and resolved to keep his emotions under wraps. He needed a clear head. Though he suspected as long as Maya was nearby that would prove difficult.

He went down the hall and knocked on his father's bedroom door. "Breakfast," Alex said shortly.

"Just a sec" came his father's muffled reply.

Alex shook his head in wry amusement as he thought about his teen years when he lived with his father. Dad had been an early riser then and the one who would make breakfast. But that was before he'd lost his job due to his alcoholism.

Interesting how times changed and their roles reversed. He went to Maya and Brady's room and knocked on the door.

Brady opened it with a wide grin on his face. "Deputy Alex. I smell bacon."

"Brady, your manners," Maya said from the doorway of the bathroom.

Startled, Alex spun to face her. "Good morning. Breakfast is ready."

"We'll be right there."

She looked lovely. She'd changed into formfitting jeans and another plaid shirt, probably because it was easier to get on with her bum shoulder than something she'd have to yank over her head. Though today's shirt wasn't oversize like the one she'd had on last night. This one showed off her curves. Her long hair gleamed as if recently brushed. Normally, she wore a single braid, but he figured she probably couldn't manage the braid with her injured arm.

"If you'd like, I can braid your hair for you after breakfast."

Her eyes widened. "You know how to braid hair?"

He grinned. "I've done my share of braiding horse manes for the parade. Your hair can't be much different."

Amusement danced in her eyes. "Wow, thanks. Being compared to a horse really builds up a girl's confidence."

He flushed with embarrassment. "I didn't mean it that way."

She laughed, the sound lodging in his chest and spreading out like a burst of sunshine.

"Of course, you didn't, silly. I'm teasing you."

Her intimate smile had his heart thudding in his chest and his blood racing. "Okay. Well, hurry up before it gets cold," he said briskly before striding back to the kitchen. With each step, he willed his emotions under control.

His father was already in the kitchen, pouring himself a cup of coffee. His hands shook. He looked haggard as if he'd had a bad night's sleep. Concern arced through Alex.

"You okay?"

Frank glanced at him. "I'm good."

They both knew he was lying, but Alex wasn't going to call him on it. If his dad wanted to pretend he wasn't sick, then Alex would let him. He didn't know how to help his dad, anyway. Giving him a place to live was more than enough as far as Alex was concerned.

Once everyone was seated at the table and eating, Alex said, "It would be best if you don't open the store today, Maya."

She set her fork down in a slow movement before giving him a measured look. "That is not your call. I have never closed the store for anything other than a holiday. The only time the store has closed unexpectedly was when—" She glanced at Brady, then back to Alex. "It's been a long time."

"Surely you have someone who can work for you?" *Did the woman never take a vacation?*

She sipped from her orange juice, then set the glass down. "Trevor Howard fills in for me when I need to be away from the store."

The teenager was a solid citizen and rode as a volunteer for the mounted patrol. "Then call him and see if he can take over for a while."

"He's already scheduled to work during the Harvest Parade this weekend," she said. "Besides, he's in school today. I can ask him to fill in this afternoon and evening."

He'd take the concession.

"I have school, too." Brady said.

Alex and Maya looked at each other.

Maya reached over to take Brady's hand. "I think you'll come with me to the store today."

"If you'd like, Brady can stay here with me," Frank said. "I could show him around the ranch. And he can help with the chores."

Brady bounced in his seat. "Yes, yes. Please, Maya, yes?"

"That's okay, Dad," Alex said, cutting Maya off from speaking. He wasn't sure his father would be a good influence on the kid. He noticed his father's flinch so he added, "I'm sure Maya would prefer to have Brady by her side."

Frank stared at him with determination in his gaze. "I won't let anything happen to Brady."

Maya's gaze searched Alex's face before focusing on Frank. "I think that's a splendid idea. Nobody knows Brady's here, so he'll be safe. I'll call his teacher and let her know he won't be there today."

"Yay!" Brady exclaimed. "Do I still have to do my schoolwork?"

"Yes," Maya said. "I'll bring your computer back with me when I return, along with today's assignment."

Alex clenched his jaw. He didn't like relying on his

father for anything. But he had to admit Brady would be safer here out of the public eye. He only wished Maya would stay, too. "He could use my computer to do his schoolwork."

"Really? That would be great." Maya turned to Brady. "Did you hear that? Alex will let you use his computer, but you have to be careful with it."

"I will be."

Brady's joy was contagious. Alex found himself smiling. After a moment, he turned his focus to something less delightful. "I'm going to have a security system installed today," he announced. He'd never felt the need before but now, with Maya and Brady staying here, he wanted to use every resource available to protect them.

For a moment everyone was silent, then his father nodded. "Good idea, son."

His father's praise seared through Alex. He couldn't remember him ever saying, "Good idea, good job, well done." And it made Alex mad that Frank was putting on the show now for Maya and Brady when Alex knew the real Frank Trevino was a drunk who yelled and screamed and threw things.

Alex gathered up the dirty dishes and took them to the sink without comment.

Maya joined him at the sink as he rinsed the dishes and set them in the dishwasher.

Curiosity radiated from her in tangible waves. "What's going on with you and your dad? I noticed tension last night and now even more this morning."

Alex glanced to where Brady and Frank had left the table and had started pulling out some board games from the hall closet. Alex knew she wouldn't understand. She'd adored her parents and had good memories of them. He had no good memories of his dad. Or his mom, for that matter. The two had fought constantly until the divorce. Then Dad had proceeded to drown his sorrows in a bottle.

"We're trying to get used to each other again," he hedged.

"Has your dad been sick?"

Alex was startled by her observation. The jaundice that had startled Alex when his dad first showed up had decreased and Frank had gained back a little of the weight he'd lost. But he did look haggard and ill.

Alex clenched the dishrag in his hands and he breathed in deep before replying, "His liver is damaged. The doctors told him he wouldn't live much longer if he continued to drink. He came here to dry out."

Sympathy softened Maya's expression. She put her good hand on his arm and gave a gentle squeeze. "I'm so sorry. That must be hard."

She had no idea. "He did it to himself." Before she could respond to his less-than-gracious statement, he said, "We better get you to the store if you are going to open on time."

She nodded and stepped back. "I'll go get ready."

He watched her walk away. What was it about this woman that burrowed under his skin? He had to find a way to thicken his armor, because he had a feeling if he weren't careful she would unintentionally tunnel her way into his heart.

And that was the last thing he or she needed.

SIX

Maya's heart ached for Alex and his dad. There was obviously a great deal of unresolved resentment and pain between the two men. She wished she knew how to soothe the hurt, but she had no clue. She lifted up a silent prayer that God would soften the hard edges of anger she had sensed in Alex toward his father and bring healing to Frank.

She was halfway down the hall when Alex called to her, "Wait! Your hair."

She paused, remembering his offer to braid her hair. "It's fine. I'll just leave it loose today."

He walked toward her, his gaze intent. "As lovely as it is down, I have a feeling you usually put it up because it bothers you at work. Am I right?"

His compliment and his perceptiveness both pleased and confused her. She had to admit he was right. Having her hair down while at work could be a nuisance. She'd rather not have to deal with the mass of curls. She walked back to him. "Are you sure? I hate putting you out like this."

"You're not putting me out. Come. You'll get an apple-and-oat treat if you hold still," he joked over his shoulder as he moved to the dining table and pulled out a kitchen chair for her.

She gave him her best horse whinny in response, but still took the seat he offered with trepidation. He immediately buried his hands in her hair, gently working out the knots from the curls.

Having his big strong hands running through her hair caused goose bumps to rise on her skin. Her breath hitched, and she tried not to purr like a cat. She didn't want him to know how much his touch affected her. She never experienced this sort of overwhelming sensation when her hairdresser, Janie at Honey Curl beauty salon, washed and cut her hair.

Under Alex's gentle but methodical machinations, she could feel her body relaxing even as her heart raced. He braided her hair into one long braid down her back. From the pocket of her jeans, she produced a hair tie. He secured it around the end and gently placed the heavy braid over her shoulder.

"There you go," he said, his voice oddly thick.

Standing, she smoothed her fingers over the braid in wonder and she murmured, "Thank you, Alex. You're a good man."

He swallowed and stepped back, shoving his hands into the pockets of his uniform pants. "It's really not anything to brag about. I'm going to warm up the Jeep." He turned on his heels and headed toward the front door.

"When can we expect you back?" Frank called from where he sat with Brady in the living room. "I'll fix dinner."

Alex's jaw firmed. "I don't know." He stepped outside with Rusty in his wake.

The dog stopped in the open doorway and looked back at her, cocking his head as if waiting for her.

She felt compelled to say, "I'll be right there."

Seemingly satisfied, the dog trotted out.

Feeling a bit shaky by her reaction to Alex and the dog's uncanny behavior, Maya went into the bathroom and checked the braid. It looked perfect. He'd done a great job. Bemused by his act of thoughtfulness, she quickly stowed her things away and made the bed. She hurried out to the living room, where Brady and Frank were playing Settlers of Catan.

"Are you sure about this, Frank?" she questioned again. It was kind and thoughtful of him to take on the responsibility of caring for her brother, even if only for a few hours.

"Of course. We'll be fine. Don't worry," he said.

She hugged Brady. He shrugged her off. "I'm playing here." His face was a study in concentration as he looked at the board and plotted his next move.

Heart aching just a little to think, in this moment, he didn't need her, Maya kissed the top of his head. She met Frank's gaze. "I'll let you know when we're heading back."

He rose and walked her to the front door. "I'd appreciate it." He gave her the house number to input into her cell phone.

Rusty slipped past her and entered the house as she left. She liked the idea of the dog standing guard. Maybe she should consider getting one. She climbed into the passenger seat of the Jeep.

"Were you serious about getting an alarm system?" she asked Alex.

"Yes. I called the alarm company, but they weren't open yet."

"I think I should have an alarm installed on the house," she said. "And the store." She'd never felt unsafe before. Nor had she worried about anyone breaking into the store at night. Stuff like that didn't happen in Bristle Township.

Alex glanced at her. "There usually isn't much crime in the county. Maybe a few rowdy teens or drunk tourists, but not much more than that."

"The treasure hunt has caused lots of problems," she said. "So many people flooding the Rockies. I think the whole thing is a bit nuts."

"It's a pain, that's for sure," he agreed.

"I wish somebody would just find the treasure, already. Then everything could go back to normal." And Brady would find something else to keep him occupied. The idea of a dog for him to take care of sounded more and more like a good idea.

"That would be nice."

When they arrived at the hardware store, Alex parked next to the back entrance. Maya unlocked and opened the door, but Alex stopped her with a hand on her arm. "Wait here while I check out the interior and make sure there's nobody waiting inside."

Unease slithered down her spine and she nodded. She let the back entrance door shut behind them but she remained near the exit. Alex stepped into the dim interior of the store. Though sunlight filtered through the glass front windows, there were still shadows that mocked her and caused her pulse to spike.

Frustrated by the fear taking hold, she decided Alex needed some light, so she went to the wall panel and flipped on the switches until the place was lit up like a Christmas tree.

A few seconds later, Alex returned to her side. "All clear."

Determined to not be afraid in her own store, she strode forward and started prepping for the day. She made sure all the shelves were adequately stocked and there was cash in the register. Alex trailed behind her, making her already-taut nerves stretch even more.

As she unlocked the front door, she heard him on the phone talking to the sheriff. When he was done, she said, "You should probably get to the sheriff's station. I'm sure you have more important things to do besides babysit me."

His gaze narrowed. "The sheriff knows I'm here. If he needs me, he'll call. If I have to leave, then I'll see who's available to stand guard."

"You don't need to do that," she insisted as she went back to the register. "I'll be fine. I'm sure you all are busy."

"I'm not leaving you unattended," he said.

Using her uninjured hand, she straightened the front counter with nervous energy. "Why are you doing this?"

His eyebrows drew together. "What do you mean?"

"First, you take us into your home and now, you won't leave my side."

"You're in danger, Maya. For whatever reason, someone is after you, and I'm not going leave you alone."

Flutters of anxiety hit her tummy. "I understand and appreciate your diligence but surely I'm safe in the store."

"I'm not willing to take any chances."

She wasn't sure how to respond to that. His insistence on sticking close was sweet and scary at the same time. Would her attacker risk striking in broad daylight? But, more important, could she withstand the onslaught of attraction that zinged through her blood every time Alex was near?

The bell over the front door dinged, and she jumped. Okay, so she was more freaked out than she wanted to admit.

"Maya?" Ethan Johnson called out.

"Here." Glad for the distraction, she hurried toward the front of the store. The older gentleman wore a chambray shirt tucked into belted jeans. His wispy gray hair was hidden beneath a baseball hat sporting the logo of a tractor company. "Hello, Ethan. You're here early today."

"Maya, I was so worried about you," Ethan said, coming forward to take her uninjured hand in his rough and calloused ones. He nodded a greeting to Alex. "Deputy Trevino."

"Ethan." Alex returned the nod.

Turning his attention back to Maya, Ethan asked, "What happened to you? Is everything okay?"

Maya wasn't sure how much to tell him. Her gaze went to Alex for help.

Alex spoke, saving her from having to answer. "Maya, Ethan is the one who alerted us to the fact that you and Brady were missing."

Her heart swelling with gratitude, she said, "Thank you for looking out for us."

"Of course, my dear. You and Brady are like family."

Touched by the sentiment, she hugged him with her good arm while fighting back a sudden wave of tears. She wasn't sure why she was so emotional. It had to be the circumstances in which she found herself. Someone had attacked her twice and tried a third time last night. And here was Ethan being so kind and making her realize how alone she'd felt for so long. Now she had two people showing concern for her and Brady's welfare. It was a bit overwhelming.

"We found them both on Eagle Crest Mountain," Alex said. "Brady had fallen and twisted his ankle. And Maya took a fall as well and hurt her shoulder."

Clearly, Alex felt the need to keep her attacker out of the conversation. She figured it was to prevent upsetting Ethan any more than necessary.

"That's horrible." Ethan's voice held sympathy. "What can Bess and I do to help?"

Maya smiled. "Honestly, Alex is taking good care of us. Helping out here and…such."

Ethan nodded, but there was speculation in his eyes that had alarm bells sounding in Maya's head. Oh, no. She hoped the older man didn't think there was something personal going on between her and Alex.

"That is good to know." Ethan focused on Alex. "I heard there was a dead body found on the mountain."

So much for not worrying Ethan.

Alex sighed and hitched his thumbs in his utility belt. "News does travel fast in a small town."

Ethan gave him a pointed look. "Hard to keep a thing like that quiet. Everybody's talking about it."

"Just what we need." Alex shook his head.

Maya grimaced. She hated being the subject of gossip around town. But then again, maybe if people were aware of the danger, her attacker would leave her alone. One could hope.

Alex's phone rang. He stepped aside to answer.

"Was there something I could get for you, Ethan?" Maya asked.

He shook his head. "I'm done with my shopping for the week. I just wanted to see how you were doing and make sure you were all right."

His concern warmed her heart.

Alex returned and said, "I need to run to the station for a bit. Daniel will be here in a moment."

Concern darkened Ethan's eyes. "I'm happy to stay and keep Maya company. Where's Brady?"

"He's safe," Alex said quickly. He looked out the front window. "Here's Daniel. I'll be right back." He headed out the front door, pausing to talk a moment to the other deputy.

Maya watched Alex through the front window, liking the way Alex's dark hair gleamed in the morning sunshine. She admired his wide shoulders beneath his uniform. She knew he took on the burdens of the town without any hesitation, just as he'd taken on her and Brady.

Alex nodded at Daniel, then glanced toward the store. This time she had no qualms about raising her hand in a wave. Not as a means to flirt with him, but to assure him she'd be okay while he was gone. He lifted his hand in acknowledgment before striding across the street and entering the sheriff's station.

Slipping sunglasses over his eyes, Daniel stayed outside near the front door.

Ethan chuckled. "Alex is a nice young man. A good catch as Bess would say."

She murmured her agreement, then flushed with embarrassment. Aware of Ethan's gaze, she plastered on a calm smile. "How is Bess? And Mary?" Referring to his wife and his adult daughter.

Ethan met her gaze. His blue eyes were gentle and amused. "Bess and Mary are both well, thank you. You know your parents were friends of mine and Bess's."

Good friends, if she remembered correctly. Her parents had known everyone in town. She nodded, unsure where he was going with this.

"I'm sure your parents would like for you to find someone special," he stated with a gleam in his eyes. "You know Brady is always welcome to visit if you have a date."

A wry laugh escaped Maya. "That's a kind offer. But dating is the last thing on my mind."

How did she dispel him of any matchmaking notions without revealing how much danger she and Brady were in?

Sheriff James Ryder sat at his desk and looked up as Alex entered his office. "Alex, glad you're here. How are the Gallos?"

"Brady is at my place with my father, and Ethan Johnson is with Maya at the store." Alex took a seat opposite the sheriff. "I have Daniel posted out front. You said you have news on our victim?"

James handed him a sheet of paper. "His name was Ned Weber, a dentist from Steamboat Springs."

Alex looked at the photocopy of Ned Weber's driver's license. Definitely the man they'd found dead on the trail.

"He didn't have a rap sheet," James said. "Unmarried. I put a call in to his practice, but the call went to voice mail. I'm not sure what he was doing up on that trail."

Alex suspected he knew. Treasure hunting. "Has the ME found the cause of death?"

"Blunt force trauma to the skull mixed with multiple lacerations from tumbling down the side of the mountain."

"He could have sustained the head injury during the fall."

"According to the ME, it could have been an accident or it could be murder. Unless we can place someone else up on the side of the mountain, we won't know for sure," James said.

"I'd like Hannah to blow up this photo," Alex said, referring to the county's resident crime scene tech. "I'll take it to the group of hikers we ran into yesterday and see if they knew him."

"Good thinking. You better hurry if you want to catch her. She and Chase are heading up the mountain trail in search of evidence."

"Thanks." Alex stood and walked toward the door.

"Have her make copies for the others, as well," Sheriff Ryder said to his retreating back. "They can ask around town, see if anyone remembers seeing him before he hiked up the mountain."

"Will do," Alex called over his shoulder before he headed to the back of the department building where the crime scene lab and evidence locker room were housed. He found Hannah at her desk. She made quick work of the task.

"Thank you, Hannah," Alex said, taking the photos from her. "You're the best."

Her freckled face broke out in a grin. "Don't you know it."

Chuckling, he shook his head. "I hear you and Chase are going up Pine Ridge Trail, where the deceased was found."

"Yes, sir." She saluted him. "If there is something to find, we'll find it. Chase should be here any minute. I let him drive. Makes him think he's in charge."

"You do that. Also, can you give the others copies of the photo?"

"Sure thing."

Deciding to tackle the hikers first, Alex left the station and headed to the Bristle Hotel with the photo in hand. At the front desk, he asked the concierge to ring the rooms of the five hikers and request they come to the lobby. Within a few minutes, three of the five friends arrived. Alex studied each one for a moment, taking stock.

The two women were exact opposites. The blonde Sybil Kelso was a big-boned woman with a small gap between her front teeth, reminiscent of Lauren Bacall. She wore a pink shirt with jeans tucked into knee-high boots and held a small clutch purse in her manicured hands. Not a hair was out of place.

While the petite Claire Owens had her brunette hair pulled back into a messy ponytail and wore unstructured pants and a sweatshirt with the Colorado Rockies baseball team's emblem. She sported a cross-body backpack in lime green.

Roger Dempsey, the man who'd led Alex to Brady, had a clean-shaven face, his sandy hair slicked back. He looked ready for the office in khakis, a white button-down shirt with a red tie and expensive leather shoes.

"Good morning, Deputy Trevino," Roger greeted him. "I assume you're the reason we were summoned."

Alex inclined his head. "I am. Where are the other two? Greg and John Smith?" Yesterday, Alex hadn't been able to see the men's faces due to the darkness of the trail.

"They'll be along," Sybil answered. "Those two are as slow as molasses."

He held up the photo of Ned Weber. "Do you know this man?"

"Hey, that's Ned," Sybil said. "Is he in some kind of trouble?"

"Why would you ask that?" Alex searched the faces of the man and women.

"He didn't show up yesterday for our excursion," Claire said. "We tried texting him, but he never responded."

"So he was supposed to go hiking with your group?" Alex confirmed.

"Yes," Sybil said. "We all met in an online chat. We've teamed up the past few weeks."

"Teamed up?"

Claire shrugged. "It's better to hunt for treasure in a group than alone. We'll split the bounty when we find it."

Treasure hunters. He'd have to chew on that for a bit to see how the information changed the dynamics.

"What's going on, Deputy?" Roger asked. "Has something happened to Ned?"

"I'm sorry to inform you that Mr. Weber's body was found yesterday on one of the trails of Eagle Crest Mountain."

"Oh, poor Ned." Tears gathered in Sybil's blue eyes.

Claire blinked, looking stunned. "He's really dead? How did… Where was he?"

"That scoundrel! He went out hunting without us," Roger exclaimed.

"Roger," Sybil chided. "Don't speak ill of the dead."

Roger rubbed a hand over his jaw. "Sorry. This is so shocking. How did he die?"

"It appears that he was climbing above one of the trails and fell," Alex told them as he watched each face for some hint of guilt.

"Why was he there?" Claire asked. "The latest clue for the Delaney treasure clearly leads up the Aspen Creek Trail, where we were."

"Unless he knew something we didn't," Roger said.

"Here's John and Greg," Sybil said. She sniffed as a fresh tear rolled down her cheek. "Does anyone have a tissue?"

Claire dug one out of her bag and handed it to the other woman.

Alex focused his attention on the two men who'd joined them. They were nearly identical with the same hooded light brown eyes, dark hair parted on the right. But one was a few inches taller than the other.

Roger informed the latecomers of the tragic news of Weber's death.

"We talked to him yesterday," the taller one, John, said. "He claimed he couldn't make it. He had too many clients lined up."

"Apparently he lied to us," Greg said.

"It's so heartbreaking," Claire stated.

Alex made a mental note to check into Weber's phone calls to verify their stories. Hopefully, Chase and Hannah would find the victim's cell phone. "How long will you all be staying in town?"

"We're planning on staying through the weekend," Roger said. "But now I don't know."

"Can you tell me what kind of vehicle Mr. Weber drove?"

"Usually he got a ride with us," Claire told him as she gestured to herself and Sybil. "I don't know what kind of car he drives."

"I think it's a truck," John said. "Silver, maybe. Or light blue. That's what he drove the last time we all met."

"If any of you think of anything that might help us figure out what happened to your friend, please call the sheriff's department," Alex said.

"Did you find his notebook?" Roger asked.

This could be interesting. "What notebook?" Alex asked.

"Ned was meticulous in his quest to find the treasure. He maintained notes in a black leather-bound journal," Sybil said. "He kept tabs on other treasure seekers and recorded their progress."

"He wrote down every theory and speculation on the treasure he could find," Claire added. "He was determined to discover the hidden fortune before anyone else."

Alex's mind whirled with possibilities. Had Ned Weber uncovered something he hadn't wanted to share with his friends? Where was this notebook?

SEVEN

Alex left the Bristle Hotel with his thoughts churning. The deceased dentist had gone off seeking the fortune alone. Had he suffered a tragic accident or foul play? How had he ended up on the trail so banged up? Was one of the five treasure hunters involved?

And where was the victim's notebook?

But, more important, why had Maya been attacked?

He radioed Chase, telling him to keep an eye out for a cell phone and leather-bound journal.

Returning to the station, Alex sought out the sheriff again. "Sir, you need to talk to Mr. Delaney again," Alex said to his boss. "We need to know if this treasure is for real. And if it is, he needs to reveal the location so we can end this chaos. A person is dead and one of our citizens has been attacked."

"You're in charge of this investigation, Alex." The sheriff smiled that patient, teaching smile that Alex had come to dread. "If you feel it's necessary to take a run at Patrick, I'm in full support."

Alex rubbed a hand over the back of his neck. "Are you sure? You have a relationship with him. I've never met the man or his sons." The Delaneys were reclusive, though Alex had read in the tabloids about the two adult sons and their exploits around the globe. Apparently, the small-town life of Bristle Township wasn't their speed.

"That is true. But it would be good for you to do this. When I retire, somebody has to be willing to stand up to Patrick Delaney."

Alex frowned. "You're not retiring anytime soon, right?"

The sheriff shrugged. "Lucille's been getting on me about wanting to travel. We're approaching our fortieth wedding anniversary this winter."

"That long? Wow. That's incredible." Alex's longest relationship had lasted eight months. He'd realized quickly that Evie hadn't been one to let commitment get in the way of her fun with other men. He hadn't felt the need to seek out a new romantic relationship since moving to Bristle Township. Romance was complicated and took too much energy. Plus, he really had no desire to end up like his parents.

Sheriff Ryder grinned. "Yep. I know it's crazy, I don't look old enough, but we married young."

"You are a blessed man." Alex felt a familiar spurt of envy gush through his chest. There was a time when he would have given anything to be a part of a couple, to belong to someone. But somewhere along the way he'd lost hope of ever finding "the right one." Instead, he had found a place to belong to here in Bristle Township.

"I am. Lucille's a wonderful woman. And I'm not an easy man to live with, but she loves me. It hasn't all been sunshine and unicorns. We've had tough times and our share of sorrow," the older man said with a touch of sadness in his eyes. Though the sheriff had never mentioned it, Alex had heard that the Ryders had lost their only son to a drug overdose when he was a teen.

Giving his head a shake as if to loosen the past's hold on him, the sheriff said, "Now, about Patrick. He's our wealthiest citizen. And he and his sons financially back most everything this town does. I'll call and let him know you're coming. You will need to proceed with caution. This will take some finesse." He paused. "Take Maya Gallo with you. She'll charm old Patrick for sure."

"Take a civilian with me?" Alex wasn't sure Maya would agree to go.

"He can see firsthand what his treasure hunt has done," Sheriff Ryder stated in a grim tone.

Alex needed all the leverage he could get. "I'll ask her if she'd be willing."

He left the station. Daniel was standing out front, talking to a couple who looked like tourists in for the festival. Instead of approaching the store directly, Alex walked up the street, keeping an eye out for anything out of place. He loved this town and the people. As he passed the bookstore, the owner, Milly Reeves, paused in arranging a display to wave. Alex returned the friendly greeting before stepping to the corner to cross at the light with several teenagers. The group lowered their voices and jostled each other, clearly self-conscious as teens sometimes were around authority figures.

"Stay safe, kids," he said to the teens after they crossed Main Street and the kids headed in the opposite direction from him.

"Yes, sir," a couple of the teens called out.

Smiling, Alex veered around to the back alley be-

302   **Buried Mountain Secrets**

hind the hardware store, intending to circle the building before joining Daniel in front.

The back entrance door was cracked open.

He frowned with unease. Had Maya or Ethan gone out the back door to dump some trash in the nearby bin and forgotten to close the door behind them? He doubted either one would be so careless.

Caution tripped down Alex's spine as he skirted around Maya's Jeep to approach the open door. With his hand on his weapon, he slipped inside the back door and looked down the hall. He could hear Maya and Ethan talking near the front counter. Closing the door silently behind him, he took a step then hesitated as his gut tightened with anxiety. Something wasn't right. He couldn't put his finger on what had him spooked, but he knew to listen to his instincts.

Slowly, he made his way down the hall and paused outside the open door of what appeared to be Maya's office. There were two desks set up, one obviously Maya's with a desktop computer and a stack of ledgers sitting on top, while the other desk had to be Brady's. A laptop covered in stickers was surrounded by action figures. The room appeared empty.

Yet the fine hairs on Alex's arm rose in apprehension. He wasn't alone.

Was there someone behind the door?

Using his shoulder, he slammed into the door. He heard a muttered curse and then the door was flung back at him. He used his booted foot to stop the door before it hit him in the face. A man wearing black coveralls, a black hoodie and a plain silver mask with no mouth covering his face darted out from behind the door swinging what looked like a tire iron.

Alex ducked, and the weapon rammed into the door-jamb, taking out a chunk of the wood. Alex made a grab for the intruder, but the assailant jumped onto the desk, evading Alex's grasp.

Blocking the only way out, the intruder was trapped in the office, Alex drew his weapon. "Come down and put your hands up."

Slowly, the intruder raised his hands.

Alex moved closer. "Step off the desk."

The perp rocked back on his heels, then sprang up, somersaulting over Alex's head, easily landing on the floor and racing out of the office.

"What in the world?" Alex chased after the assailant, but by the time Alex burst through the back exit, the intruder was nowhere to be seen.

Alex ran around to the front of the building, thinking maybe he could catch a glimpse of the intruder, but there was no sign of him anywhere.

Daniel jogged to his side. "Hey, what's up?"

"Did you see a guy dressed in black run this way?"

"No. No one has run by."

"Alex, are you okay?" Maya's concerned voice halted him in his tracks. He turned around to find Maya and Ethan had come out the front door.

"Someone was in your office."

Maya sucked in a breath. "What? When?"

"Just now." Alex replied. "But the guy managed to evade me."

"We didn't hear a thing," Ethan told him in a gruff, concerned tone. "We only saw you running past the window."

"Man, I'm sorry." Self-recrimination echoed in Daniel's voice.

Alex held up a hand. "He went through the back door. There's no way you could have seen him."

"Still…" Daniel ran a hand through his hair.

Alex understood the pain of feeling like he'd failed at his job. One of his first assignments out of the police academy had been patrolling downtown Denver. One night, he'd walked right past a convenience store being robbed. When the call came, he'd doubled back but was too late to be of help. "Seriously, don't beat yourself up. Everyone is safe. I'll take it from here."

Alex ushered Maya and Ethan back inside.

Worry pinched her dark eyebrows together. "Why would someone break into my office? Other than the desktop computer and Brady's laptop, I don't keep anything of value in there. All the money is here." She gestured to the small safe bolted beneath the counter. She frowned. "Do you think this was the same person who broke into my house?"

"Broke into your house?" Ethan exclaimed. "What is going on?"

Alex explained to Ethan about the attacks on Maya. "I believe the person is searching for a leather-bound journal," Alex said. He caught Maya's frightened gaze. "You sure you didn't come across a notebook or a cell phone in the woods?"

Frustration crossed her face. "No. I told you I only found Brady's backpack and then you."

"Are we safe, Deputy?" Ethan's agitation was palpable. "What's happening to our town?"

The last thing they needed was panic. "The sheriff's department is doing all it can to protect the town and Maya and Brady. There's no reason to believe you or anyone else in town are in danger."

"Sure, you say that now," Ethan said dramatically. "I need to go home. Bess will worry if I'm gone too long." He turned to Maya. "You and Brady can stay with us. We're off the beaten path and have an alarm system. Bess thought I was crazy to put one in, but I told her it was better to do it now and not wait until after something happened."

Maya took the older man's hand. "You are a wise man. Please give Bess a kiss from me. Brady and I will be fine with Alex."

Ethan narrowed his gaze on Alex. "You better keep her safe, young man."

"I will, sir."

After Ethan left, Alex said to Maya, "You should close the store today. I know you don't like the idea, but—"

She cut him off. "You're right. The safety of the customers comes first." She squared her shoulders, then flipped the sign hanging on the front door and turned the lock.

Admiring her strength, Alex helped her close up the store. Then he got on the phone and arranged for an alarm system to be installed at his house, Maya's house and the store. The company worked out of Boulder and promised they would have it done by Monday evening. That meant they would have to get through the weekend without the added security measure.

Alex showed Maya the driver's license photo of the deceased dentist. "Do you recognize this man?"

Maya shook her head. "No, I've never seen him. Is he from around here?"

"Steamboat Springs."

"Who is he?"

Putting the picture away, Alex said, "A treasure hunter."

"Is he the man who was found dead?"

Alex nodded, his expression grim.

Maya shivered with unease. "That could have been Brady." She put the cash from the register into the safe and tried to keep her hands from shaking too much, but her effort was unsuccessful.

Taking her hands in his, Alex said, "But it wasn't. He's okay. You're okay. I'm not going to let anything happen to you."

She stared at him for a moment, seeing the earnestness in his eyes. His confidence calmed her nerves. "I know."

"I need to ask a huge favor from you," he said.

Naturally wary when anyone said that, she replied, "Okay."

"I need to run out to the Delaney estate. I hope to talk Patrick Delaney into giving up the location of the treasure so we can end this fiasco."

That sounded like a good plan to her. "How can I help?"

"Come with me. Maybe if we give a face to someone his game has hurt, he'll be more inclined to bring the hunt to an end."

Without hesitation, she said, "Let's do it."

When they were outside, she locked the back entrance and headed to her Jeep, but stopped midstride and pointed to an indentation where someone had stomped on the hood. Indignation that someone could be so destructive echoed in her voice. "Why would anybody do that?"

Alex inspected the footprint and then he turned to look up at the top of the building. "Parkour."

"What?"

"The intruder in the store, I'd say he's a freerunner."

"You mean like people who compete in that reality-TV show that Brady likes to watch? Where they have to go through the crazy obstacle courses?"

"Similar. Freerunning, or parkour as it was originally termed, is more of a martial arts–type thing. I learned about the discipline while on duty with the Denver PD. The practice is very popular with the young-adult crowd. It would explain the guy's agility."

She looked up to the roofline of the building. "So you think this freerunner jumped from the hood of my Jeep to the roof?" It had to be at least ten feet high.

"He most likely used the hood as a launching point to jump up to grab the lip of the roof and pull himself up. Which is why I was running around like a chicken with my head cut off, looking up and down the street for him, and couldn't find him. He was up there laughing at me."

She could hear the frustration in his voice. "Do you think he's still there?"

Alex shook his head. "No. I'm sure he's long gone by now. But I don't like driving around in your Jeep. He probably knows that this is your vehicle."

A bubble of fear pressed against her heart. "Brady. I have to see that he is all right."

"I'll call the ranch." He took out his cell phone. "I'm also going to call Kaitlyn to pick us up at your house. We'll leave the Jeep there. She can drive us to Delaney's, then out to her place so I can get my truck and Truman."

Sending up a quick prayer, Maya waited as Alex called the ranch's landline. After a moment, he frowned. "No answer." He hung up. "I'll ask Kaitlyn to swing by there since she's closer. After, she can meet us at your place."

With no other choice but to wait, Maya kept an eye on the rooftops as they headed toward her family home. But there was no sign of anyone lurking on the roofs. They arrived at the house before Kaitlyn.

Needing to burn off the nervous energy coursing through her veins, she couldn't relax until she knew Brady was safe, she said, "I'm going to run in and get a few more things. I only packed enough for one night."

"Let me check out the house first," Alex said, stopping her before she could go inside. "You stay here."

Maya waited on the porch with a rising sense of panic. She didn't like the vulnerable, exposed sensation coiling around her. Or the fear of losing her brother. She studied the residential street, looking for any signs of danger but all she saw were her neighbors' homes with their neat yards and pretty houses. All appeared quiet and serene. Normal.

But things weren't normal.

Someone had broken into the store. What had they wanted? She shuddered to think what would have happened if Alex hadn't returned when he had. She and Ethan could have been hurt. The idea of something happening to the dear older gentleman made her insides twist.

Alex stepped out of the house. "All clear. Kaitlyn called back and should be here any minute. She said all was well at the house."

Letting out a thankful breath, she said, "I'll hurry."

She rushed inside and grabbed a few more items for her and Brady, enough to get them through the weekend. Monday, the alarm system would be put in and then she could return home… She hoped.

Kaitlyn arrived in an official sheriff's vehicle, along with Brady. He awkwardly climbed out of the passenger side, sporting his backpack and carrying his music player. He rushed as best he could with his booted foot to Maya's side.

"He insisted on coming," the deputy told them. "Neither Frank nor I could dissuade him." She shrugged.

"I won't be any trouble," Brady told her. "I just want to see what the man who made the treasure hunt looks like and see where he lives. I promise I won't ask him any questions. I'll keep my music in my ears so I don't hear anything about the treasure. I'm not a cheater."

Relieved to see him, Maya pulled her brother into a hug. "Okay, sweetie. It will be fine."

Alex put his hand on her shoulder. "We should go."

Kaitlyn handed the keys to Alex before hopping into the back passenger compartment with Brady, leaving Maya to sit up front with Alex.

Now that she was sure that Brady was safe, anticipation made her antsy. Would Mr. Delaney cooperate? Surely, once he learned that someone had died because of the buried treasure, he'd have to put an end to the hunt.

At least, Maya prayed so.

EIGHT

The country road gave way to a large gate. Alex sent Maya a quick glance as he pulled the sheriff's cruiser to a stop next to an electronic keypad on a post sticking out of the ground. Her determined nod was all the confirmation he needed that she was ready to meet the man behind her little brother's obsession and possibly the threats to her life. He pressed the intercom button. A moment later a tinny voice said, "How can we help you today?"

"Deputy Alex Trevino to see Patrick Delaney. I believe Sheriff Ryder called to let you know I was coming."

There was no answer. But the big wrought iron gate clanked once—probably a lock being released—then slowly rambled open inward.

Kaitlyn snorted from the back seat. "Paranoid much?"

Beside her, Brady was oblivious to the sarcasm. He had earbuds in and his head bobbed to a downloaded tune only he could hear playing on his small music device.

As soon as there was enough clearance, Alex drove

through the gap and followed the private road flanked by well-maintained landscaping up to a circular drive in front of the large limestone mansion. Sunlight danced off a myriad of windows. Turrets rose out of the roofline, giving the estate a castle-like feel.

"Wow," Maya breathed out. "Spectacular."

"A castle!" Brady exclaimed overly loud.

The place looked more like something out of a movie about modern-day royalty. Though, to some degree, the Delaneys were this part of Colorado's version of royalty.

Kaitlyn whistled. "This is some spread," she said. "I've never been here. Have you?"

He shook his head. "No. I feel underdressed."

Shooting him a grin in the rearview mirror, Kaitlyn said, "We should shine our badges before we go in."

"I should have changed into a dress," Maya whispered. "I don't think Brady and I should be here."

Alex took her hand and squeezed. He liked her in her jeans and plaid button-down shirt. Her injured arm was still tucked in the sling the ER doctor had given her. "You are beautiful. Don't let all this intimidate you." Though he had to admit, he needed the reminder, as well.

She blinked up at him. "Thank you."

He let go of her hand. "I'll come around." He climbed out and closed the door.

Kaitlyn exited at the same time and playfully socked him in the biceps. "Good for you."

He scowled at her over his shoulder. "What?"

Kaitlyn's laugh followed him around the vehicle. He helped Maya out first, then Brady.

In tandem, they climbed the stone steps to the massive front door. He could barely reach the knocker.

Kaitlyn leaned on the doorbell to the right side of the door. "For us shorter folk."

He laughed. His coworker wasn't short by any measure.

The huge door opened to a well-dressed man with graying hair.

"Mr. Delaney?" Alex compared this man against the pictures he'd seen of Patrick as a young man. The reclusive billionaire didn't do photo ops.

An amused smile split the older gentleman's face. "No, I'm Collin. Mr. Delaney's valet." He gestured for them to enter.

Alex and Maya exchanged a glance.

"Swanky." Brash as always, Kaitlyn had no filter. "I thought those were only in England," she commented as they followed Collin through the massive entryway. Maya guided Brady with her good arm. His booted foot made a soft clicking noise on the marble floor.

Over his shoulder, Collin said, "Mr. Delaney likes things just so. If you'll wait here, please."

"Apparently," Alex muttered, taking in the marble floors, sweeping view windows—at least twenty feet tall—and a wide staircase leading upward to a second floor with a wrought iron railing. Impressive paintings, which he would imagine were not fakes, adorned the walls. There was a museum-like quality to the home.

A few moments later, a tall dark-haired man, probably in his early to midthirties, walked into the room from the arched opening to the right of the staircase. He wore black slacks, a black turtleneck and shiny black shoes that made no noise as he strode forward. His vivid blue eyes assessed them with curiosity.

Kaitlyn made a small noise in her throat. A slight

pink stained her cheeks. Alex nearly snorted. His gaze shot to Maya to gauge her reaction to the man. No flush to her cheeks. Good. She studied the newcomer politely but didn't seem overly interested, which made Alex happy. Though why, he didn't want to contemplate. Brady, with earbuds still in place, ignored the newcomer to inspect a large vase filled with exotic flowers.

"Ah, two deputies and guests."

The man's smooth voice grated along Alex's nerves.

"The sheriff said you were coming, Deputy Trevino, but he failed to mention your lovely companions and a teenager."

"You have me at a loss," Alex said. "You are?"

"Forgive my lack of manners." He held out his hand. "Ian Delaney."

Alex shook Ian's hand and was surprised by the roughness of the man's palm. As rich as this family was, he'd expected smooth and soft. Maybe there was more to the man than met the eye. "Alex."

Ian shifted his attention to Kaitlyn. "Deputy…?"

Kaitlyn pumped his hand. "Lanz. Deputy Lanz."

His gaze narrowed slightly. "Charmed." He extracted his hand and focused on Maya. "And you are?"

"Maya Gallo," she said, taking his offered hand. "This is my brother, Brady." She tipped her chin toward Brady.

"Miss Gallo. And Brady." His gaze flicked to her sling. "I had heard you both were injured." Sympathy oozed from his tone. "I hope you will recover quickly."

Retracting her hand, she inclined her head. "Thank you."

"How did you hear of their injuries?" Alex asked.

Had the sheriff told him of the attack on Maya? Or Brady getting lost in the woods?

Ian smiled in a way that made Alex wary. "We make it our business to keep abreast of the activities in town."

Really? Alex wasn't sure why that bothered him.

Another man emerged from a different arched opening. This one younger, midtwenties, wearing an outfit nearly matching his brother's.

Annoyance flashed in Ian's eyes, then quickly receded. "My younger brother, Nick."

Nick went straight to Kaitlyn. Taking her hand, he murmured, "You are beautiful. What are you doing working such a menial job?"

Kaitlyn extracted her hand just as Nick lifted it to kiss her knuckles. Tucking her hands behind her, she rocked back on her heels. "I have a very important job."

There was no mistaking the defensiveness in her voice.

"Excuse my brother." Ian's tone held a tight note of chastisement. "He still hasn't learned his manners."

Ignoring Ian, Nick smiled at Maya and tugged on her braid. "You should wear your hair loose."

Alex's fingers curled. Only the badge on his chest kept him from pushing the younger Delaney out the front door.

Maya plucked her braid back from the man. "And you should not touch unless given permission."

Alex silently applauded her.

Nick, however, only laughed. He looked at Brady, then away as if he didn't find anything interesting there. He refocused on Kaitlyn.

Taking control of the situation, Alex said, "I need to speak with your father. Now."

Ian gave a gracious nod. "Of course, Deputy Trevino. My apologies." He spun on his heels. "This way."

Holding out his arm to Kaitlyn, Nick said, "Shall we?"

"No." She strode forward, leaving Nick a few paces behind. She paused. "Is there a restroom available?"

Eager to please, Nick said, "I'll show you."

Kaitlyn rolled her eyes but followed the younger Delaney down a hallway to the left.

Alex shook his head at his colleague's retreating back. When Maya tucked her fingers in the crook of his arm, he stood taller. Ian led them into a large dining room where Collin, the *valet*, had taken a position near a side door and stood at attention.

The opulence of the room was overwhelming. A bank of windows with a stunning view of the Rocky Mountains provided an impressive backdrop to the elderly man sitting at the head of a large oval table, dominating the center of the space. Alex hadn't expected such frailty. Obviously, Patrick Delaney had had his sons late in life. A colorful afghan surrounded his thin shoulders and wispy tufts of hair sticking straight up off his head gave him a mad-scientist kind of vibe. Round spectacles covered blue eyes rummy with age. His pale skin made Alex question his health. He held out a spindly hand.

"The detective," Patrick Delaney said, his voice shaky. "Please join me."

Alex stepped up to the table beside him and took the frail limb for a brief moment. "Sir, I'm not a detective. I'm Deputy Trevino of the Bristle County Sheriff's Department. And this is Maya and Brady Gallo." He gestured to Brady, who had wandered to a window and stood swaying to the music in his ears. He kept his back to the adults.

Patrick's gaze swept over them before once again landing on Alex. "Ah. Yes. How is Sheriff Ryder? I'm surprised he did not come to see me. Why is that?"

Alex wasn't about to explain the sheriff's reason for not coming. Just then, Kaitlyn and Nick returned. Taking the distraction of their arrival as a way to avoid Patrick's question, Alex said. "I'm leading the investigation into the recent death on Eagle Crest Mountain."

"And that concerns me how?" Patrick countered.

"Father." Ian's voice was low and held censure.

Patrick waved a hand. "Sit. All of you. I don't like craning my neck to see you."

Out of respect, Alex pulled the chair in front of him out for Maya to sit, then he took the seat beside her. If the old man wanted to orchestrate this meeting by ordering them to sit, so be it. Alex was determined to convince Patrick to cease the treasure hunt.

Nick rushed to pull out a chair for Kaitlyn. She slid him a sharp glance but politely mumbled, "Thank you."

Nick plopped down in the seat next to her.

Ian, however, remained standing at his father's elbow. To guard him or to keep him in line?

It occurred to Alex that the two brothers might be allies in convincing Patrick to end the treasure hunt. The prize would come out of their inheritance. Would that be motive to find the treasure themselves? Or to kill for it?

Tucking the questions away for further examination, Alex said, "Mr. Delaney, this treasure hunt you've instigated has caused a death and numerous injuries all along the Rockies."

Patrick rubbed his hands together. "So much fuss! Isn't it glorious?"

"No, sir, it's not." Kaitlyn piped up. "It's a royal pain in the neck."

"I could help you with that," Nick said.

Kaitlyn clamped her lips together with a shake of her head.

Ian nodded. "I've been telling my father this wasn't a good idea from the beginning. Maybe he will listen to you."

From the glee on the older man's face, Alex doubted that Patrick would listen to anyone. "Sir, I need the location of the treasure so we can put an end to this chaos."

"Tsk, tsk. I'll be releasing a new clue on Monday. You'll have to wait like everyone else."

"I don't want your treasure." Alex couldn't keep the frustration from his voice.

The elder Delaney's expression hardened and his blue eyes turned ice-cold. Alex ground his teeth together. He heard the sheriff's words about *finesse* echo in his head.

Alex turned his palms up in a gesture of entreaty. "Sir, please, people are getting hurt." He put a hand on the table in front of Maya. "As you can see, Miss Gallo has been injured due to this treasure business. She and her brother have been threatened."

He frowned and peered at Maya. "We'd heard you were injured, my dear. No one said it had to do with my hunt. And I didn't know about any threats." He sent a sharp glance at his eldest son before refocusing on Alex. "What does any of this have to do with my treasure?"

"My brother, Brady, is a big follower of the hunt for the buried prize," Maya said, drawing Patrick's attention back to her. "He loves the challenge. And he is good at it."

Patrick glanced to Brady and nodded. "It's supposed to be fun."

"Sir, there are desperate people who will do anything to win," she replied softly.

Attention snapping back to her, Patrick groused, "That's not my fault. If you feel threatened, then we will get you a bodyguard."

Ian arched an eyebrow but didn't comment.

Anger simmered low in Alex's belly. He held on to his temper. "Are you prepared to provide protection for every person who is being threatened or hurt by this treasure hunt?"

"Certainly not," Patrick declared. "The Gallos are family. This town is my family."

The younger brother snorted. "Dad, you don't know anyone down there. You never even visited the town except once when you first bought this property."

Patrick waved his hand at him. "Doesn't matter. I know who each and every one is in this county. I know what they have and what they need."

Alex was sure right then and there that several laws had been broken. But that was a fight for another day. Right now, he just needed to know the treasure was buried in the Eagle Crest Mountain. "Sir, I'm pleading with you. I need to know where the treasure is so I can end the threat to our town and its citizens."

Patrick put his hands on the table and hefted his frail body to his feet. "This interview is over. Monday, the new clue will be uploaded to the website. Good day, Deputies. Miss Gallo."

Collin rushed forward to help the old man out of the

room. With effort, Alex contained his frustration as he watched the man leave.

Once his father had exited the room, Ian shook his head. "I'm sorry that you have to deal with this. My father has become very eccentric. For some reason this treasure hunt has brought him immense pleasure. I will do my best to convince him to put it to an end."

"I would think you'd want it ended," Kaitlyn stated, echoing Alex's earlier thought.

Ian focused on her. "And why would that be?"

Tilting her chin up, Kaitlyn replied, "When your father is gone, all this—" she swept a hand to indicate their surroundings "—becomes yours, right?"

"Ours," Nick corrected her.

A small smile tipped the corners of Ian's lips, but there was no smile in his cold blue eyes. "My brother and I do have a vested interest in putting an end to our father's shenanigans. But there is no controlling our father." Ian slanted his gaze to Alex and Maya. "We can provide protection if you require it."

"I've got that handled," Alex said. "But I would appreciate if you could persuade your father to not put up the next clue and tell you where the treasure is buried, so you can relay the information to us."

"Don't count on it," Nick said. "Once Dad gets his mind set on something, there's no turning back."

"Don't mind my brother. He's just chafing under our father's strict rules."

"*Strict* doesn't even begin to cover it," the younger man griped.

Ian gestured toward the arched doorway they'd entered through. "I'll show you out."

Alex helped Maya to her feet. She corralled Brady, drawing him away from the view.

Kaitlyn rose and skirted around the table to walk beside Ian as they left the room and headed for the entryway. "What do you do?" she asked.

"I manage the estate," he replied curtly as he stepped in front of her to open the massive front door.

Kaitlyn wrinkled her nose at his back. Alex pressed his lips together to keep from barking out a laugh. He noted Maya's lips twitching, as well.

"I appreciate you coming and trying to talk my father out of this ridiculous game," Ian said. "Anything you need that we can provide you, just let me know."

Kaitlyn walked past him and out the door. "We'll do that."

Nick rushed out after Kaitlyn. "Hey, I didn't catch your first name."

Kaitlyn didn't break her stride. "That's because I didn't say it." She climbed into the back passenger compartment of the vehicle and shut the door.

Alex shook hands once again with Ian. "Thank you for your time."

"A pleasure," Ian said. To Maya, he said, "I do hope you recover quickly."

"Thank you," she murmured and guided Brady out of the house.

Alex followed them to the vehicle and helped her into the front passenger seat and Brady in the back, then jogged around to the driver's side. Once he was settled in his seat, he asked, "So what do you think?"

"I think Patrick Delaney has lost his mind," Kaitlyn said from the back seat.

"The brothers are interesting," Maya said. "Not sure what to make of them."

"The younger one is a total playboy. He needs to grow up. You know they have a gymnasium in the basement. Nick was gushing about how fit he is." Kaitlyn leaned forward so that she was between Alex and Maya. "It's that older brother we have to worry about."

Alex glanced at the man, who remained standing at the open door, watching them. "He's certainly smooth." And obviously had Kaitlyn's hackles up.

"We should do background checks on both of them," Kaitlyn said as she sat back and buckled up. Then she helped Brady to buckle his seatbelt. "I think Ian is in more control than he'd like us to believe."

"You could be right." They hadn't accomplished what they'd set out to do. Patrick Delaney wasn't going to cooperate.

They left the estate and headed down the winding mountain road. From the corner of Alex's eye, he saw a flash of movement that raised the fine hairs at the nape of his neck. A car shot out from a side road, aiming straight for back end of the SUV.

Alex swerved, barely avoiding a collision.

The beat-up sedan braked, tires squealing as the car veered away from the guardrail with seconds to spare. The smaller car roared up behind them.

"Maniac is going to try a PIT maneuver," Kaitlyn shouted.

Not if Alex had anything to say about it. He floored the gas pedal, making the big engine of the vehicle hum as they picked up speed, quickly outdistancing the less powerful sedan.

"Can you get a plate number?" Alex threw over his shoulder to Kaitlyn.

"Plates removed," she replied. "I'm calling it in."

Alex drove as fast as he dared until they hit a T in the road. He turned toward town. The sedan turned the opposite direction and zoomed out of sight.

Slowing down, Alex glanced at Maya. She'd paled, her eyes were closed and her good hand clutched the dashboard. In the back seat, Brady's eyes were wide and he was grinning as if he'd just ridden his favorite roller coaster.

Alex reached over to touch Maya's arm. "We're okay."

She opened her eyes and blinked at him. "What was that?"

"I don't know." The grim possibility that whoever had been in the car had intended to ram them into the guardrail and potentially off the side of the mountain had his gut twisting.

He sent up a grateful prayer to God they'd survived. Obviously, someone had been watching Maya's house and had followed them up the mountain to the Delaney estate.

Clearly, Maya's attacker was out for blood.

But why?

Determination solidified in Alex. He intended to find the answer before the villain succeeded in his quest to harm the Gallos.

"Hey, boss," Chase greeted Alex as he, Maya and Kaitlyn returned to the sheriff's department. Alex tried not to grimace at the moniker. Obviously, Chase had recently returned from the mountain trail. His blond hair was matted with sweat and his uniform dirty with bits of brush stuck to it.

Alex glanced toward the sheriff standing in the doorway of his office. Was that a nod of approval?

Maya steered Brady toward the empty conference room. "We'll wait in here."

The shaky tenor of her voice made Alex want to take her into his arms, but he kept his hands at his sides. "I won't be long. Then we can head to the ranch."

Kaitlyn filled the sheriff in on the incident with the sedan. She put out a BOLO on the car.

After assuring the sheriff and Chase they were all well and uninjured, Alex went to his desk. To Chase, he asked, "How did it go for you?"

"We searched the whole area around where the victim was found. Hannah collected a lot of broken branches, rocks and dirt samples. It appears Weber was climbing the side of the mountain."

"Did you find a cell phone or notebook?" Alex asked.

"No, nothing like that. We did find several sets of footprints on the path and near the body, but there's no way to determine how long they'd been there or who they belong to. We took photographs and will compare them to our victim's shoe prints."

So, in other words, they still had no clue how or why the man died. He told Chase about the incident at the store that morning. "We need to know if our five friends are into freerunning."

"I did a preliminary search last night with the contact info they provided," Chase informed him. "Nothing popped up. I'll do a more thorough search over the next few days."

Appreciating Chase's efforts, Alex said, "Great. Also

do a check into Ned Weber. His friends said he was determined to find the treasure. If he was out hunting alone, maybe he had no intention of sharing it. I wonder why. Deep in debt? Or just greedy?"

"Will do."

"Also, see what you can find out about Ian and Nick Delaney," Alex added. "Where do they spend their time? I can't say I've seen either man around town."

Sheriff Ryder strode forward. "What's this about?"

"Those Delaney men are psychotic," Kaitlyn groused, plopping into her seat at her desk.

The sheriff arched an eyebrow.

She made a face. "Okay, maybe not, but the old man is certainly crazy. He's getting a kick out of this whole treasure thing. He doesn't care how dangerous it's become."

"And the sons? You think they are involved in Weber's death?" the sheriff asked.

Alex shrugged. "Not really sure. We think, maybe, Ian Delaney is in more control than he lets on. The younger one... I'm not sure what to make of him."

"Tread lightly, people," Sheriff Ryder told them.

"*Ugh.* Nick." She shuddered. "Pretty and harmless."

"So you thought this Nick character was *pretty*?" Chase teased.

Kaitlyn shook her head. "No, but he thinks he's pretty. The older one now... He's one to keep an eye on."

Alex had the feeling her interest in Ian Delaney went beyond just duty to the county.

"Ohhh. He got to you," Chase crooned.

She scoffed and popped up from her chair. "Hardly. I know that type. Cool, charming and controlling. I don't want anything to do with him."

Alex and Chase exchanged an amused glance as she stalked out of the station. Kaitlyn rarely let anyone get under her skin. And that it had happened so fast with Ian Delaney was interesting but wasn't Alex's concern. Right now, he had to think about finding a murderer. And protecting Maya and Brady.

He rose from his desk. "Let me know if you find out anything of interest." He headed toward the conference room to check on Maya and Brady.

NINE

Maya settled into the back passenger seat and closed her eyes, allowing her tension to drain into the floorboards. Kaitlyn was driving her, Alex and Brady to Kaitlyn's ranch so they could pick up Truman.

The adrenaline rush from the car chase was finally ebbing, allowing Maya to breathe easier. Her mind wandered all over the place. The break-in at the store, a car trying to run them off the road and visiting the Delaney estate. So much in such a short time.

She focused her thoughts on the Delaneys. Maya had never seen anything so grand or met someone so… She wasn't sure what word to use for Patrick Delaney. She couldn't believe how callous he'd been regarding the treasure hunt. The sons were an interesting pair. Ian had kinetic energy about him, like a tiger on a short leash. Nick was all fun and games. She doubted the youngest Delaney took much seriously, while Ian was all business.

"Maya, we're here."

Maya's eyelids popped open. Embarrassment flooded her. She must have dozed off. They were at the Lanz ranch. It was larger than Alex's with several barns and many horses of different sizes and colors grazing in the pasture. Kaitlyn's family ran a horse boarding and training facility, as well as a rescue.

Maya and Brady climbed out of the SUV.

"Chickens!" Brady hurried over to a large chicken coop where Mr. Lanz was working.

Maya thought about calling her brother back but then decided to let him enjoy the animals as she followed Alex to the corral. Alex whistled, and a large horse came at a gallop. The horse was a beautiful, rich chestnut color with a black mane.

"You remember Truman, here. He remembers you." The horse made a deep rumbly sound in his throat as he attempted to nuzzle her hair, tickling her.

She laughed and stepped back. "Of course, I remember."

"Here." Alex handed her a bag of carrots. "He'll be your friend for life if you give him a few."

Tentatively, she took the bag, but stared at the horse. It had been so long since she'd interacted with an equine that she debated the best way to feed the animal. Did she hold a carrot upright and let the beast chomp on it?

Alex must have sensed her uncertainty because he took a carrot and placed it on the palm of his hand. "Keep your hand flat with your fingers straight," he instructed and held the carrot beneath Truman's nose and then said, "Gentle."

The horse nibbled the carrot right off his hand without taking a finger with it.

"Your turn," he said with a smile before striding away to prep the trailer to take Truman home.

When Alex was out of earshot, Maya murmured, "Please be nice." And she followed Alex's example, feeding the horse a couple of carrots. The horse barely grazed her hand taking the treats. "Good boy."

After three carrots, she said, "I'm not sure how many I should feed you. I don't want you to have a tummy ache."

Cautiously, she stroked the animal's cheek. "You're a beautiful guy, you know that? Just like your owner."

She glanced over her shoulder to make sure Alex couldn't hear her. "He is really something. I don't know that I've ever met anyone so competent and protective."

Actually, she hadn't allowed anyone close enough to know if they were kind and thoughtful in the way that Alex was. But he was just doing his job. It was not because she was his girlfriend. She didn't want a boyfriend. She wanted… She didn't know what she wanted anymore.

No, that wasn't true. Her heart thumped in her chest, making her aware that deep inside she was lonely and longed for a romantic companion. But as soon as the thought came, so did the specter of fear that haunted her. It was hard enough loving Brady and not letting the fear of losing him take hold of her. How could she ever love someone like Alex?

Just the thought of letting him into her heart made her mouth go dry. He had a career that put him in danger more often than not. Granted, this was Bristle County, and as Alex already pointed out, crime here usually wasn't more than a few unruly teens or tourists. But somebody had died—had been murdered, recently—and who knew what other kinds of horrors could come their way? Alex would be right in the middle of it. Because he was that kind of guy. The kind who ran toward danger instead of from it.

She didn't know that she could live with the constant dread of wondering if he'd come home at night. The dilemma of everyone who loved a real-life hero.

The horse nickered, and awareness zipped along her limbs. She glanced sideways. Alex strode toward her with purpose in each step. He carried a halter in his strong, capable hands.

She moved aside to allow him access to his horse.

"The trailer is all set. And Brady's already inside the cab." He looped the lead rope over Truman's neck, then slipped the halter over the gelding's nose and ears before buckling the strap on the side. "Are you ready to go?"

Guessing he was talking to her, she said, "Of course. I only fed him three carrots. I didn't know if he should have very many more."

"That's perfect. He'll have his regular meal when he gets home." He steered Truman to the gate.

She hurried past Alex to release the latch.

Alex inclined his head as he led Truman out of the corral. "Thanks."

"Sure." She closed the gate behind the horse.

After securing Truman in the trailer, they both climbed into the front cab of the truck. Brady was fast asleep in the small back seat. She smiled with tenderness flowing over her. He had no idea how close they'd come to harm today. She hoped he never had to experience anything bad.

"This is a nice rig," she commented as she ran her hand over the leather seats and eyed the latest gadgets on the dashboard.

"I splurged. But I figure I'll drive this baby into the ground. I needed something reliable to cart Truman around." He drove them away from the Lanz ranch.

"Have you always been a horse guy?"

His mouth turned up at the corner. "No, growing up in the city there wasn't much opportunity to be around horses." He let out a wry laugh. "Or animals of any kind really, besides dogs and cats. But we didn't have any of those, either."

"Brady has always wanted a dog. After seeing him with yours, I'm thinking maybe we'll get one."

"Not a bad idea. He's good with Rusty."

She liked that he approved. Then she turned away to roll her eyes at her own silliness. "How long have you been in town?" She tried to recall the first time he'd come into the feed and hardware store.

"Three years."

She turned to stare. Only three? She would have guessed longer. He seemed such an integral piece of the town.

"Part of what drew me to the job was I wanted to be a member of the mounted patrol," he said. "When I asked the sheriff, he taught me how to ride. I got the hang of it pretty quickly. James said I was a natural." Alex shrugged, his broad shoulders lifting beneath his uniform shirt. "I don't know if that's true so much as I was determined. And then, of course, I had to buy Truman and all the gear that went with having a horse. Including the ranch," he laughed ruefully.

"The sheriff's department doesn't provide anything?"

"No. Every member of the mounted patrol, both law enforcement and civilian, has to own their horse and trailer, as well as house and feed their animals. And keep them in good health. Plus, we pay for our own training, which is extensive, and the certifications."

"What kind of training?" She had no idea the level of commitment participating in a mounted patrol entailed.

"Everything. Personal safety, general search-and-rescue procedures, event management, map and compass navigation as well as tracking," he laughed. "It's a lot. The certification process is rigorous, and each rider must demonstrate that the horse and rider are able to work under a variety of potentially distracting or stressful conditions. Like the upcoming parade."

Thinking how rowdy the crowds could get during the festivals in town, she was in awe. "But how does it work for the volunteer members?" She thought of her friend Leslie, who rode for the mounted patrol.

"The auxiliary members don't carry weapons, so we utilize them mostly for search and rescue or pair them with a deputy if the situation warrants."

"I'm impressed."

His grin made her heart thump in her chest. "Being part of the mounted patrol is worth all the expense and time."

"That's great you can afford everything on a deputy's salary."

He laughed, "The pay is about average. Most people around here already owned their horses and stuff. I taught myself how to do day-trading and have built up a healthy portfolio."

Her interest piqued, she asked, "Do you still trade?"

"I dabble. On my off time."

"Would you be willing to show me how? The store does well, but I'd like to build up our savings account."

He slanted her a quick glance as he turned onto his property. "Of course. I can teach you."

She thought about Brady's desire to go to college

one day. The thought terrified her. She wasn't sure she could handle him leaving Bristle County. She couldn't even bring herself to let him go off to camp for a week. She'd be all alone.

Who would she be if she didn't have Brady to take care of?

When they arrived at the house, Brady woke and hobbled out of the truck in search of Frank. Rusty yipped at his heels, but Brady didn't seem to mind.

For a long moment, she stood there, unsure what to do with herself. Alex was seeing to Truman and she didn't want to be in the way, so she decided to take some time with God. She sat on the porch and allowed herself a few quiet moments of prayer, thanking God for their safety.

As the sun began to set, she went into the house, but Brady and Frank were not inside. Through the kitchen window, she saw them in the backyard planting bulbs in planters. Brady sat on the ground with his booted foot straight out. He had dirt all over him. But he looked so happy chatting away with Mr. Trevino. Maya's heart swelled.

Brady had missed out on so much when their parents passed away. She was thankful to the two Trevino men for taking her and her brother in for this short period of time. Yes, it was to keep them safe. But it was nice to see Brady having a good time, totally unaware that someone had broken into the store. She wished she understood what the intruder wanted.

Brady saw her and waved.

She went out the back door and hurried down the porch steps to her brother's side.

"Maya, come look at what we're doing. Planting

flowers," Brady said, then shook his head. "They're not flowers now, but they will come up in the spring. Kind of like the ones you planted in our yard."

"Wonderful." Maya looked at the older man. "Thank you, Mr. Trevino."

"My pleasure," he replied with a kind smile. "Call me Frank."

"I like gardening." Brady held out a trowel. "Do you want to plant a bulb?"

"Not right now, sweetie." She squatted next to him. "Did you finish today's school assignment?" She'd forgotten to ask Brady in the excitement of the day.

"I did. I even got all my homework done after we played our game," Brady responded proudly.

"He's a hard worker," Frank said. "He beat the socks off me in our board game."

Brady looked up at Maya. "That's a saying. His socks didn't really come off."

Maya ruffled his hair. "I would hope not. Then his feet would be cold."

Brady laughed as he dug the trowel into the planter with abandon.

For a moment, Maya was content to watch until he accidentally flung dirt in her direction. She stood and moved back, brushing off the dirt from her clothes. "When you're finished, you're going to need a shower," she said. "You've got dirt in your hair."

Brady touched his hair. "Maybe a little flower will grow." He laughed at his own joke. "I know that won't happen. I'll take a shower later."

Her brother never failed to lift her spirits. "Okay. I'll see you inside, then. I brought more clothes from the house."

Maya left the two gardeners and reentered Alex's home. She took a moment to just take a breath. The way the house was decorated appealed to her. Not overly cluttered with knickknacks or personal items but the place still had some personality with a framed oil painting of horses running wild over the mantel and books filling the bookshelves. She liked the comfy worn leather couch, wood paneling and the wagon wheel chandelier with downlights and amber shades hanging over the dining room table.

The effect was… She thought for a moment, trying to come up with the word. *Rustic* wasn't quite right, and *quaint* didn't accurately describe the motif, either.

Homey. Masculine. Very much like Alex.

She went to the back bedroom and unpacked the duffel bag she'd brought to the ranch house. A few minutes later, she heard Alex come inside, and she joined him in the kitchen. He took four steaks out of the freezer. "I'll barbecue these."

Her mouth watered. She had never mastered the art of barbecuing. "That would be wonderful. I could make a marinade?"

"Not sure what we have for ingredients but go for it," he replied as he pulled fresh ears of corn out of a bag along with four large russet potatoes.

"Brady will be so happy. He loves corn on the cob."

"Me, too. A little butter and salt and pepper." He kissed his fingertips. "Yum."

With a laugh, Maya went to work making the marinade. She found several useful ingredients in the cupboards and the refrigerator. She whipped together olive oil, balsamic vinegar and herbs, and chopped a small onion and pressed garlic. Alex set the steaks in the mixture to soak.

As they worked side by side, skirting around each other in search of supplies or ingredients, accidently bumping into each other with a laugh. Unbidden, a longing welled up inside Maya, surprising her with its intensity. She liked this, being here with Alex, acting like a couple who cooked together often. It was foreign and yet comfortable and, oh, so thrilling.

Her skin heated, not from the water boiling on the stove but from the very real desire for home and hearth. For a man to share her life with.

She stilled for a moment, then hurried to the refrigerator for a stick of butter to melt and to give herself time to push such nonsense from her mind.

Okay, maybe she was lonely. But she'd already decided Alex wasn't the man for her no matter what her traitorous heart decided.

Brady and Frank came noisily into the house, providing a welcome distraction. Her little brother was covered in streaks of mud from the top of his head to his feet.

"Ack!" Maya exclaimed. "Brady, your shoes!"

"It's fine," Alex said, laughing.

Not to Maya. She had her brother take off the one dirt-caked tennis shoe and set it on the porch while she took possession of his orthopedic boot. "Grab my good arm," she told him. "You'll have to hop to the shower."

She hustled Brady down the hall for a shower.

He balked at the door to the bathroom, barring her from entering with him. "I can do it myself, Maya. I'm not a baby."

His sharp tone surprised her. "I know you're not.

This is a strange shower for you. I just want to show you how the knobs work. Plus, you have an injured foot."

"I can figure it out. I'm smart." He put weight on his foot. "I can stand on it. It doesn't hurt."

She searched his face for a wince and saw none. "Yes, you are smart. Even if it doesn't hurt, you shouldn't put too much weight on it yet." He opened his mouth to argue more, so she held up her hands in surrender. "Be careful you don't burn yourself with the hot water."

He rolled his eyes. "Maya."

She chuckled. "You are such a teenager."

"I'll be sixteen soon."

Time was flying by too fast. His birthday was the week before Christmas, just three months away. "I know. We'll celebrate."

"Can Frank and Alex join our celebration?"

Her stomach knotted. He was growing attached to the two men. But truth be told, so was she. "Of course they can. We can invite the whole town if you want."

"I don't need the whole town. Just Frank and Alex, and maybe Aunt Leslie and Mr. and Mrs. Johnson."

Leslie Quinn was Maya's childhood friend. She'd been a big part of her and Brady's lives before Leslie left home at eighteen to pursue an art career. She'd lived in Paris and London and had sent postcards regularly. Maya had been happy for her friend but she'd also missed her.

And if Maya were honest, she'd envied Leslie. Not that Maya begrudged her friend the freedom to pursue her dreams.

Life hadn't work out that way for Maya.

So she'd lived vicariously through Leslie's adventures before Leslie returned to Bristle County last year to take over her mother's dress shop while her father battled prostate cancer. He'd beat it, and Lorraine and Henry Quinn had decided to explore the world to celebrate. Leslie had remained in town, running the shop and volunteering for the mounted patrol. Now that Maya knew more about how the patrol worked, she admired her friend's commitment even more.

"Of course, we can invite Leslie and Mr. and Mrs. Johnson."

"Yay."

"There are towels and a washcloth in the cupboard under the sink," she told him. "And shampoo and conditioner on the counter."

"Okay, I got it."

"I'll be out here if you need me."

"I won't need you." He waved her away as he shut the door and locked it.

Shaking her head, she stood there, uncertain if she should wait or trust that he would be okay. This parenting thing was so stressful.

Alex joined her in the hall. He brought with him the scent of hickory that had her mouth watering.

"Dad cleaned up the office so you can have that room, if you like," he said. "There's a Murphy bed in the wall."

He took her hand and tugged her to the office. Her fingers easily curled around his and she told herself it was no big deal that they were holding hands. Her brain was hearing the message, but the rest of her? Not so much. By the time they reached the office door, she felt as if she'd trekked across the Sahara.

The office had a dark wood desk and a beautiful armoire. Alex released her hand and moved to the armoire. "This is the Murphy bed." He showed her how it worked.

"This will be lovely. I'll have to see how Brady is doing. If he has another nightmare, it might be best if I'm there with him."

Alex nodded and tucked the bed back into place. "Okay. Whatever you think is best. Just know this is an option."

"Thank you."

"Do you want your first investment lesson? We have time before dinner."

"Sure."

He moved to the desk and turned on his desktop computer. He pulled up a trunk for Maya to sit on. He sat in the desk chair.

Twenty minutes later, Maya's head was spinning with all the information Alex had given her about investments, market shares and the difference between day-trading and long-term trading. He knew his stuff. Her admiration of the handsome deputy tripled.

"Dinner's ready."

Brady's call drew them out of the office and into the dining area, where Frank was bringing in the steaks and Brady setting the table. Brady's hair was still damp, but he looked clean and had put on fresh sweat bottoms and a T-shirt. His ankle was purple and swollen but he didn't seem to be in discomfort as he hobbled about. Maya was proud of him. He was growing up so fast.

"Look, Maya, corn on the cob!" Brady clapped his hands.

"I see that." Maya took a seat. "Sit down, buddy. Let's put your boot back on." She'd wiped the mud off it.

Brady plopped down on Maya's right. He held out his

foot for her to slip it over his injured appendage. Once done, he picked up his fork. "I'm hungry."

Frank laughed, "That's good to hear."

Alex took the seat on Maya's left. "Do you mind if I say grace?"

"Please do."

He held out his hand. She slipped her hand into his and then took her brother's. Alex and Brady both held on to Frank's. Tears bubbled to the surface and Maya squeezed her eyes tight as Alex asked God to bless their food. She missed family dinners. For so long it had only been her and Brady. She'd forgotten how nice it was to be a part of a unit of more than two. Best not to get used to it. Come Monday, she and Brady would go home and this would be a wonderful memory.

After dinner, Alex touched her arm as she cleared the table. "I need to talk to Brady in the living room."

"What about?"

He slipped the photo of the deceased hiker from his pocket. Her stomach knotted. She wanted to protect Brady. It was her first instinct. Always was, always would be. "Do you have to?"

"Yes."

She sighed. Brady and Frank were washing and drying the dishes. "Can it wait a bit?"

Alex watched Brady and his father for a moment, a muscle working in his jaw, then nodded.

When the dishes were put away, Maya tucked her arm through Brady's. "Come into the living room with me."

She led Brady to the couch and gathered his hands in hers. Alex sat on the couch next to Maya.

"Alex has a picture he wants to show you."

"Have you seen this person?" Alex held up the photo of the dentist, Ned Weber.

Brady stiffened. He squeezed Maya's hands and his breathing became rapid. He shook his head but he didn't say anything.

"Brady, have you seen this man?" Maya pressed, concerned by his behavior.

He continued to vigorously shake his head.

Alex and Maya exchanged glances. She wasn't buying his denial. He was scared. "Brady, this man took a tumble down the side of the mountain."

Brady's gaze shot to hers. But his lips were pressed tight together.

Heart hammering in her chest, she said, "Did you see him fall?"

"No. No, I didn't see that man. No, no, no." Brady jumped to his feet. "I'm going to go find Frank." He hobbled out the back door as fast as his booted foot would allow.

Anxious, Maya hurried after him.

Alex stalled her with a hand on her arm before she could leave the house. "Let me go talk to him."

"Not without me," she said. "He's my brother."

"He might open up to me if you're not there. Maybe he's afraid of getting in trouble. I could talk to him, guy to guy."

She gestured toward his uniform. "Really? You think he's afraid of getting in trouble with me? You're the cop. He knows what you do."

Alex's lips firmed. "Then we talk to him together."

"Fine." She shook off his hand and hurried after her brother.

Brady had made it to the corral and he was standing at the railing. Truman had come over and he had one hand on the animal, scratching his nose. Animals always seem to like Brady. She guessed it was because animals didn't see him as a threat.

Truman nickered as she and Alex approached.

"Brady, talk to us."

He shook his head and wouldn't look at her.

"You're not to going to get in trouble if you tell me the truth. You know that."

He glanced at her. "I know you won't be mad at me. But—"

"But?" she prompted.

Brady lifted his gaze. Worry radiated off him in waves. She wanted to take him into her arms and chase away whatever had him so scared.

"You're safe, Brady," Alex said softly. "I'm not going to let anyone hurt you or Maya."

Grateful for Alex's steady presence, she said, "Let's go back inside, Brady, and you can tell us what's going on."

TEN

Alex followed in Maya and Brady's wake back inside the house. She was so good with her brother. Respect and admiration filled his chest. She'd been so young when she'd had to take on the role of parent.

He wondered, what were her dreams? What had she planned for her life before the tragedy that had taken her parents and put her on a new path? He wished there was something he could do to help her and Brady.

Something more than just protection. Though what, he didn't have a clue.

He liked this woman. He liked the way she pitched in when she saw the need. He liked the way she was so calm and gentle with her brother and with Mr. Johnson. With his dad.

He'd told her the unvarnished truth of his childhood and she hadn't judged him or his dad. He appreciated her acceptance. And admired her for her dedication to her brother and to the legacy that her parents had left behind in the store and in the town.

Maya directed Brady to the dining room table. Alex sat and folded his hands on the table. He should've changed out of his uniform but there was no helping it now.

Alex waited, letting Maya take the lead.

With her arm around his shoulders, Maya said, "Okay, Brady. Tell us about that man in the photo."

Brady's gaze was filled with anxiety. "You sure he can't get me?"

Alex clenched his fingers. "I'm sure."

Brady nodded. "I saw him on the trail. But he got mad at me because he didn't want me to see him. He told me not to tell anybody I saw him or he would get me. He yelled at me and made me very scared, so I ran and I ran and then I tumbled and hurt my ankle. And then the nice people found me."

"That must have been very scary," Maya said.

"Thank you for telling me, Brady." Alex glanced at the large watch Brady always wore. "Do you remember what time you saw the man?"

Brady frowned and looked at the watch on his hand. "It was time for me to turn back." He made a face. "But I ran in the wrong direction."

Alex met Maya's gaze. "Any idea when that would have been?"

"Brady left the store at nine. He should've headed back around ten thirty."

That narrowed down the window of when the man had died. Alex rose. "I need to talk to the sheriff."

The next morning, Alex dressed in his parade uniform. He and Truman were slated to ride with the other mounted patrol officers in the Harvest Festival parade. The plan was Brad, Maya and Frank would come to the parade and watch from the announcers' podium. Since

Sheriff Ryder and Mayor Olivia Yardlee would both be doing the announcing, Alex figured Maya and her brother would be safe in the box. Plus, it had the best seat in the house to see the floats.

He told Maya and Brady the plan.

"That would be good for us," Maya said, clearly pleased by the arrangement.

"No!" Brady protested, his face scrunching up. "I'm riding on the church youth group float."

Maya grimaced. "Honey, you're going to have to skip the float this time."

"I always ride on the float. That's my thing. I get to ride on the float."

From the stubborn jut of Brady's chin and the mutinous expression in his dark eyes, Alex could see the kid was not going to bend about riding on the church youth group's float.

Maya sent Alex a pleading look. "Is there any way to make that happen?"

If Maya wouldn't forbid her brother from the float, then Alex had to figure out a way to keep them both safe. "How about this? Maya, you'll sit in the announcers' booth with Dad, the mayor and the sheriff. I'll ride as an escort for Brady on the float instead of with the other mounted patrol officers."

"Yes!" Brady pumped his fist in the air.

Maya gave him a very warm smile that made his heart pound. "You'd do that for us?"

"It's not ideal but we'll make it work. Truman and I will stick close to Brady. If anybody tries anything, they will have us to deal with."

There was affection in Maya's gaze and Alex wanted to lap it up like a cat drinking milk.

"I appreciate everything you're doing for us, Alex. Brady looks forward to the float every parade. And the church kids are so accepting of him."

Alex chuckled. "This town does love its parades and festivals." Every month there was a reason to celebrate.

Brady grinned. "I like the floats. I get to be up front and throw candy. People like me then." His expression changed into sadness as his smile faded. "The rest of the time nobody really likes me."

Anguish crossed Maya's face. She put her good arm around Brady. "That's not true. You have plenty of friends."

Brady sighed. "I have a few. But there's nobody like me here. But if I went to the camp that Doctor Brown told us about…"

Maya made a pained expression. "Brady, we've talked about this. It's not an option."

"If I found the treasure, then we could afford it," he insisted.

Alex gave Maya a curious look. She shook her head, apparently not wanting to explain.

"We need to finish getting ready if you want to be on the float when it takes off from the high school," Alex said, hoping to distract Brady from the subject.

"Yay!" Brady beamed, quickly switching from his momentary blue mood. "I'm ready."

"Did you brush your teeth?" Maya questioned.

Brady wrinkled his nose. "I will." He raced down the hall to the bathroom and disappeared inside.

"What camp?" Alex asked.

Maya pinched the bridge of her nose with her good hand. "Camp PALS. It's an organization that provides a camp experience for individuals with learning disabilities. Doctor Brown thinks it would be good for Brady to attend."

"Brady sounds game."

She turned an anguished gaze his way. "It's too expensive. I hadn't realized paying for the camp was why Brady was so determined to find the Delaney treasure."

His heart folded in half, and before he realized what he was doing he offered, "I could help pay for it."

Maya shot him an incredulous stare. "No. Besides, it's in Denver. That's too far away."

Ah. Alex figured she'd just admitted the real reason she was loath to let Brady go to camp. Maya wanted to keep her brother close. He wasn't sure he agreed with her but it was none of his business. "I'll get Truman in the trailer while you finish getting ready and meet both of you at the truck."

"We'll be right out."

Alex went outside and found his father had already trailered Truman and loaded a packed ice chest in the back of the truck.

At Alex's raised eyebrow, Frank shrugged. "I needed something to do."

"Thanks, Dad." Alex wasn't sure what to make of his father. His dad had changed but Alex kept expecting the man he'd known growing up to reappear. The man who'd been drunk more often than not, who had a hair-trigger temper and wouldn't lift a finger to help anyone. Not even his family. This new version of Frank Trevino was unsettling.

A few minutes later, Maya and Brady joined them and they left the ranch. They arrived at the high school football field. The floats were lined up and preparing for the start of the parade. Alex parked off to the far side of the field. Brady and Maya headed toward the float area while Alex led Truman out of the trailer. Dad hung back with the truck.

The theme of the Bristle Community Church's youth group float was of the Bible story "Daniel in the Lions' Den" with a crouching papier-mâché lion painted yellow and brown. A dozen or more kids were on the float and they all cheered when they saw Brady. He hopped up and took a seat at the front of the trailer. Someone handed him a large plastic bag filled with candy.

Alex could see how the warmth and acceptance of the teens and children on the float touched Maya. Her eyes grew teary.

"Wait! Brady, your backpack," Maya called and rushed to the front of the float. "You don't need it. Let me hang on to it."

Brady relinquished the blue backpack to Maya. She walked back to Alex's side. "You'll keep an eye on him?"

"Of course." Alex wished he could alleviate her fears. "Nothing is going to happen to Brady."

"Okay. Okay," she said as if she was convincing herself that her little brother would indeed be okay.

Alex flagged down Deputy Chase Fredrick atop his own mount, a beautiful Arabian named Sanchez. "Hey, can you hang here for just a bit? Keep an eye on Brady while I get Maya and my dad settled in the announcers' booth?"

Chase gave a slight tug at the brim of his Stetson. "Sure."

"Thanks, man." Alex handed Truman's reins to Chase. "I'll be right back."

Alex drove Maya and his dad closer to the town center, where the announcers' booth had been erected in the green space between the library and the pharmacy. They climbed the ladder to the raised platform. Sheriff Ryder and Mayor Yardlee were already in their chairs beneath the attached awning.

Alex introduced Frank to the sheriff and the mayor. Mayor Olivia Yardlee was a descendant of the founding family of Bristle Township. She was in her late sixties and was an attractive woman with silver hair held back at her nape by a fancy clip. She wore pearls around her neck and at her earlobes. She had sparkling green eyes and tan skin, which was a testament to her time spent outdoors.

She was no delicate flower. Olivia Yardlee was a woman who got things done. From what Alex had heard, since she'd come into office nearly twenty years earlier, she'd implemented the various festivals as a means to draw in more tourist trade. Her efforts had brought Bristle Township from the brink of bankruptcy to the thriving town it was today.

"I better head back," Alex told Maya.

Sheriff Ryder pushed himself out of his chair and settled a big hand on Alex's shoulder. "We'll keep her safe, deputy."

Clearly, the sheriff meant he would keep her safe so Alex could focus on Brady. He released the breath he'd been holding. Sheriff Ryder nodded in approval.

Maya stopped him with a touch on his sleeve. "Be careful."

Her concern was nice, though not warranted. "It's going to be a good day." He winked at her before slipping down the ladder.

Secure in the knowledge that Maya and his father

were safe in the sheriff's care, he hustled back to the high school. He took the reins from Chase. After checking Truman's saddle, he put his foot in the stirrup and pulled himself onto the seat.

He moved Truman into position alongside the church float. Brady waved, grinning from ear to ear.

The high school marching band began to play, indicating the start of the parade.

Alex smoothed a hand over the horse's neck. "We've got this," he murmured. And sent up a silent prayer that the dread gripping his gut wasn't worth worrying about.

From the vantage point of the announcers' booth, Maya could see all of downtown Bristle Township. Down at the far end of Main Street, the first of the floats were just starting to turn the corner as the parade began. Mayor Olivia Yardlee and Sheriff James Ryder began talking into the mic. Their voices boomed out of large speakers set up at strategic places along the parade route and the local radio station would broadcast their parade commentary.

A large crowd gathered along both sides of the main thoroughfare. Maya had heard that the Bristle Hotel and the many bed-and-breakfast inns around town were filled with people wanting to be a part of the Harvest Festival.

The coffee shop was operating a portable booth, and serving lattes and hot chocolate. The rotary club was selling helium balloons in fall colors. After the parade, the stores would open, welcoming the tourists and the locals in for special deals and sales.

She should have the hardware store open but had decided to close for the weekend. She wasn't sure what the loss of income would be, but after the scare of yesterday, she wasn't in a mood to put money over safety.

Later today, there would be a mini rodeo at the fairgrounds and other activities for young and old. Usually, she and Brady would attend. Leslie would be riding along with many other local favorites and out-of-town riders, as well.

Tomorrow, after church let out, there would be a huge pancake breakfast with more activities, like a pumpkin toss on Main Street and hayrides around the county to various farms and ranches for more merriment. All in an effort to boost the economy of the town.

Alex hadn't mentioned if his ranch would be participating. She glanced at Frank. "Is this your first time at one of our parades?"

"Yep. I don't think I've actually ever been to a parade." A pained look crossed over his face. "One of many regrets I have from Alex's childhood. I was too caught up in my own stuff to make good memories with him."

Maya touched his arm as empathy bubbled within her chest. "You can't live in the past. You have to look forward. You can make new memories with Alex and forge a new relationship."

"That is my hope," he said in a voice that broke. "I just don't know how to break down the walls he's put up. I don't blame him. His mother and I were too young and too dysfunctional to be a couple." There was shame in Frank's tone. "Let alone good parents."

"Alex is resilient." She touched his arm, empathy flooding her. "He'll come around. He just needs time."

Frank smiled at her, his gaze warm and contemplative. "Maya, I appreciate your words of encouragement. Pastor Foster has said something along the same lines."

"Pastor Foster is certainly a wise man. He's counseled me much over the years as I've tried to raise Brady."

"I'm amazed and in awe that you took on the challenge of your brother at such a young age. And the store on top of that." He regarded her for a moment and then said, "I'm really glad Alex brought you and Brady home. I think you are good for him. He's different when you're around. Not so withdrawn. More open."

His words both delighted and confused her. "We're only there for the time being," she said, careful to keep her voice low so that it wouldn't be picked up by the announcers' microphones.

"Is that what you want?" he asked.

That was a good question—one she didn't have an answer for. Yes, she wanted things to be calm, she wanted to be able to move around freely and not worry that somebody was going to attack her or Brady. She wanted to not feel the need to look over her shoulder every time she went somewhere.

And to be honest, she liked being so close to Alex.

But once the danger was resolved, life would go back to normal.

Maybe they could be friends now, though? Friends who spent nonromantic time together. Like his teaching her about stock and bonds, and all that. Her gaze went to the street as the church's youth group float rolled toward them. She stood up to wave. "Here come Brady and Alex."

Brady grinned and waved.

Alex nodded at her and Frank, a very serious look

on his handsome face as he and Truman trotted alongside the float.

The fine hairs on the back of her neck rose, sending a shiver of unease sliding down her spine. She wasn't sure why. She scanned the crowd. Was her attacker out there somewhere? Watching her? Waiting?

For that brief moment of talking to Frank, she'd let her guard down. Now, standing up, waving to her brother, she realized she was also making herself a target. Abruptly, she sat down and watched as the church float rolled farther down the street, taking her brother and Alex with it.

A whisper of noise grabbed her attention. She swiveled in her seat to look at the back of the booth. A person dressed in black jeans, a black hoodie with a strange-looking silver mask covering his face appeared over the top of the ladder. The same type of mask she'd seen on the guy who'd attacked her in the woods.

She took in a sharp breath and prepared to scream. The person put a gloved finger to the mask where lips should have been but weren't, while making a grab for Brady's backpack.

"Oh, no, you don't!" she yelled. "Sheriff!"

The intruder snagged the strap of Brady's backpack and raced down the ladder to the ground below.

The sheriff scrambled out of his chair to follow. Maya beat him to the ladder. She raced down the ladder rungs with the sheriff close behind her, talking into the radio at his shoulder. Maya chased after the masked thief along the back street behind the businesses of downtown Bristle Township. Why would he want Brady's old and beat-up backpack?

The thief easily dodged the large metal garbage can

and vaulted over a stack of empty pallets. This had to be the same person who'd attacked her on the trail, confronted her at her home and broken into the store.

When the thief reached the bank building, Maya skidded to a stop to watch the person shimmy up the downspout.

The thunder of a horse's hooves alerted Maya seconds before Alex brought Truman to a halt beside her. "Where did he go?"

"Up." She pointed to the roofline.

Alex spurred Truman forward. Maya raced behind them, keeping an eye on the masked thief. He had to come down at some point.

Her breath caught as the thief leaped from building to building. When he reached the end of the block, there was nowhere for the masked person to go. Maya paused to catch her breath. She saw the sheriff and other deputies filling the end of the street.

Unbelievably, the thief did an about-face and ran back the way he'd come. Did this maniac never tire out?

Alex pulled on the reins, turning Truman into a ninety-degree turn. Maya jumped out of the way as the horse raced past. Pushing her quivering legs to move, she ran in Truman's wake, but stumbled to a stop as her attention snagged on the masked thief as he swung over the side of the brick building of the bakery and used the fire escape like a slide until his feet hit the ground.

"Alex!" Maya yelled, pointing down the alley between the bakery and the real estate office.

Truman and Alex galloped to the alley entrance.

The thief raced out onto the main street. People scattered as Alex and Truman gave chase. Though Maya couldn't hope to catch up with Alex and his horse, she managed to keep an eye on the thief as he darted across the street in the middle of the junior high school marching band.

"He's going into the park!" Maya called out to Alex, though she wasn't sure he could hear her. She bolted across the street, nearly taking a tuba player down. "Sorry!"

The intruder veered toward the restrooms. A crowd of teens slowed the crook's progress, allowing Maya to gain on him. She managed to grab the backpack, her fingers curling around the thick material. "Let go!"

The masked bandit spun toward her and growled. He must have seen Alex on Truman bearing down on them because in a quick movement, he shimmied out of Brady's backpack before racing away, disappearing into the restrooms.

Alex brought Truman to a skidding halt, the horse's hooves digging into the grass. Alex jumped off, dropped the reins and ran for the restrooms after the perp. Maya hugged Brady's backpack to her chest. Truman snorted loudly. One look at the horse made the hairs on her arms raise. His head and his tail were held high and his feet pawed at the ground.

Then Truman let out a mighty bellow that sent a shiver down her spine. She turned away from Truman to see the masked thief coming straight at her. Confusion momentarily held her in place. How could…?

Truman shoved his way in front of her, lowering his head as he snorted and stamped his foot, clearly not about to let the oncoming threat near Maya. The masked man spun and raced away.

"Alex!" Maya screamed. They couldn't let him get away.

Alex ran out of the restroom building holding a dark hoodie and a silver mask.

Maya's breath caught in her throat.

"Are you okay?" he asked.

Maya's gaze bounced between the items in his hands and the direction her would-be attacker had disappeared. A terrifying realization washed over her. She lifted her gaze to Alex. "There's two of them."

ELEVEN

Alex's chest tightened. While he'd been chasing the masked assailant into the men's restroom, another man in black had come after Maya. "I never considered partners in crime."

He'd thought he'd had the assailant trapped in the restroom, but not so. His quarry had escaped through the high window and disappeared before Alex could identify him. A simmering anger made Alex's hands tremble as he pulled an evidence bag from a pouch on his utility belt and slipped the discarded mask he'd found on the restroom floor inside it.

"I can't believe Truman protected me," Maya said, her gaze soft on the horse.

"All those hours of training," Alex told her. "Plus, he likes you." He would give the horse some extra carrots for a job well-done.

"Apparently, they wanted Brady's backpack." Still clutching the backpack to her chest, Maya dropped to her knees in the grass and unzipped the front pouch. A set of keys tumbled out with a small square tracking device. She held it up. "I hadn't thought of this before, but do you think you could track Brady's movement and see where he actually went on the trail through this?"

"That's a smart question." *From a smart lady.* "I'll give it to Hannah Nelson. If it can be done, she'll figure it out."

Maya opened up the main part of the backpack and pulled out a safety blanket, a lunch bag and a small emergency kit containing Band-Aids and antibacterial ointment. She froze. "Oh, no."

Alex squatted next to her. Anticipation revved through his veins. "What is it?"

Truman shifted his feet as if he, too, sensed the tension radiating off Maya.

Slowly, she withdrew a black leather-bound journal, the edges of the pages smeared in dried blood. It had to be the same journal the treasure hunters had described the deceased dentist keeping his notes in. Her hands trembled. "Why would Brady have this?"

Stunned for a moment by the unexpected find, Alex struggled to believe what he was seeing. Could sweet Brady be a murderer?

Forcing himself to push aside his reaction, Alex said, "Lay that on the grass." He dug through the pouch on his utility belt for another evidence bag.

Tears gathered in her eyes as she did as he instructed. "You can't think… Brady wouldn't have hurt anyone."

A knot formed in Alex's gut. He carefully slid the notebook into the bag and stood. "Maya, we need to get you back to the podium, where you'll be safe with my dad. And then I need to find Brady."

She rose to her feet and put her hand on his arm. "What are you going to do?"

"I have to bring Brady in for questioning." As much

as he didn't like the idea of detaining Brady as a suspect, his job required him to be impartial and follow procedure.

"He didn't do anything," she pleaded with Alex. "Brady did not kill that man. You heard him. He ran away when the man yelled at him."

"Then how did the dentist's notebook end up in Brady's backpack?"

Maya dropped her hand and stepped back. The devastation in her pretty eyes punched him in the midsection. "I don't know. There has to be a logical explanation."

Alex prayed she was right. "I have no choice, Maya. I have to take your brother into custody."

Maya couldn't believe this. Brady was a suspect in a murder. It just didn't make any sense.

She paced the length of the outer reception area inside the station. Brady would never hurt anyone. And no matter how much she had tried to convince Alex, he insisted on bringing Brady to the sheriff's station and putting him in an interrogation room. They wouldn't even let her see him.

She didn't know how the dead man's notebook had found its way into her brother's backpack, but she was going to find out.

Brady hadn't been the only one on the hiking trails that day. There were five people who had known the victim. Though Alex had told her the five treasure hunters claimed to have not seen the victim, that didn't mean they weren't lying. An image of the masked ninja-like thief—make that *thieves*—appeared in her mind and she shuddered.

But right now, her focus had to be on Brady. As soon as Alex and the sheriff stepped out of the sheriff's office, she rushed forward and blocked their path. "Let me talk to my brother," she said, her voice thick with frustration. "He's scared. He doesn't understand what is happening."

The compassion on Alex's face scraped her emotions raw. "Maya, he's safe. No one can hurt him while he's in our custody. You need to stay here. I can't have you interfering."

Desperation clamped a steely hand around her heart. Anxiety twisted in her tummy. How could they possibly believe Brady was capable of such a horrendous crime? "I watch enough crime dramas to know he needs a lawyer."

"That is certainly your choice, Maya," Sheriff Ryder stated.

"It is my choice." She glared at Alex. "You know he didn't hurt that man."

Alex's expression held empathy and sorrow. "Maya, maybe he didn't mean to."

"No," she insisted. "He wouldn't do anything that would hurt someone else. You said you don't even know how that man died."

"We do know the cause of death." Alex glanced at the sheriff, as if asking permission to proceed. The sheriff nodded.

"Blunt force trauma to the back of the head."

She frowned. His explanation didn't prove anything. "How tall was the deceased?"

"Five feet nine inches."

"Brady's only five-six. How could he have reached

the back of that man's head *and* hit him hard enough to kill him?"

Alex rubbed his jaw, his gaze troubled. "Maya, we don't know enough at this point to hypothesize. We need to talk to Brady. If he is innocent, then he may know more than he realizes."

She knew her brother was innocent. There was no *if*. But maybe Alex was right, perhaps Brady had seen something or heard something that would lead them to the real killer.

A thought slammed into her. How had he become separated from his backpack? And why was it hidden beneath the bushes? Something else had happened on the trail. But what? "I'm calling our family lawyer."

Alex nodded. "I think that is a good idea."

She turned on her heels and stalked to the reception desk. "Carole, may I use your phone?"

Carole glanced toward Alex, who had followed Maya.

"That's fine," Alex told the older woman.

Without comment, Carole turned the landline phone to face Maya.

In the days, weeks and months after her parents' death, she'd had to call Grayson and Sons law firm so often she had the number ingrained in her brain.

When the firm's answering machine kicked in, Maya's stomach sank. Most likely the Graysons' were at the parade like the rest of the town. The message gave an alternate number to call in case of emergency. Maya declared the situation an emergency. She dialed the number.

A man answered. "Grayson here."

She recognized the voice as that of the younger Grayson, Donald. He'd been two grades behind her in school. Over the past few years, ever since he'd returned to Bristle Township to practice law in his father's firm alongside his two siblings, he'd attempted to entice her out on a date. Even going so far as to buy her picnic basket during last July's rodeo days auction. She gritted her teeth. "I'm trying to reach Oscar Grayson." She wanted his father to handle Brady's case.

"My father's unavailable. How can I help you?" came the clipped reply.

She sighed. There was no help for it. "Donald, this is Maya Gallo."

"Maya!" His voice warmed. "Have you reconsidered my offer of going to the Harvest Festival dance with me tonight?"

She'd completely forgotten he'd asked her last week. She'd declined with the excuse that she already had plans. She hadn't explained those plans were to hang out at home with Brady. But now she wouldn't be doing that. He was sitting in an interrogation room.

"No. I need your help. Brady has been taken into custody. We need a lawyer."

"What's happened?" His voice changed from would-be suitor, which she usually heard from him, to a professional lawyer. That gave her hope. She quickly explained the situation, leaving out no details.

"I'll be right there. Don't let him talk to anyone," he said. "Maya, you did the right thing by calling."

"Thank you, Donald." Maybe she needed to rethink her feelings for the youngest of the Grayson clan. But right now she wasn't ready for romance, whether with him or anyone else. Her gaze strayed to Alex standing at his desk with a file in his hand. He wasn't reading the file, though. His attention was aimed directly at her.

Right now, her priority had to be her brother.

She hung up. "Our lawyer is on his way. Brady isn't to talk to anyone until Donald arrives."

"Of course not." He reached out as if to comfort her but then dropped his hand to his side. "I'm sorry about this. You have to understand, I have to follow protocol. I can't show any favoritism."

She gathered every ounce of patience she possessed. Of course, he would want to proceed in a professional manner. But that didn't mean she had to like the situation even if she appreciated his integrity. She moved to sit on the bench beneath the window and tapped her foot against the hardwood floor. How had life gone from mundane and normal to chaos in such short order?

The masked assailants had been after Brady's backpack. But how had the thieves known the leather-bound journal was inside? Had the dentist somehow come across Brady's backpack, hidden his journal inside, then told the assailants before succumbing to his injuries? Maya rubbed her temples in dismay. How could she protect her brother from this?

The door to the sheriff's office opened and Donald Grayson strode inside wearing pressed khaki pants and a light blue button-down shirt. His blond highlighted hair was perfectly combed and his bright blue eyes filled with concern. Maya wondered why she wasn't interested in him. He was single, good-looking and successful. But he didn't make her heart leap or her pulse pound. Not the way Alex did.

She mentally rolled her eyes. *Stop it*, she commanded

herself. Now was not the time to contemplate her attraction to the sheriff's deputy.

Donald strode to Maya's side. She slowly rose to her feet, still wishing the elder Grayson had been available. She trusted him. "Thank you for coming, Donald."

"I'm here now," he said as he took her hand. "Everything will be okay now that I'm here."

The platitude abraded her nerves. She swallowed back her annoyance and managed to say with conviction, "I appreciate your confidence."

Grayson gave Alex a nod of acknowledgment and straightened to his full height of six feet. Not quite as tall as Alex but close. "Deputy, I'd liked to speak to my client."

Alex's gaze slid to Maya and back to Grayson. With a tilt of his head, he said, "This way."

Maya hurried after Grayson and Alex. At the door to the interrogation room, Alex paused before opening the door. "We'd like to ask him some questions."

"And we will allow it after I have a moment to understand the situation."

Inclining his head in agreement, Alex opened the door.

Maya rushed inside and straight to her brother's arms. He clung to her. "Maya, what's going on? Why am I here?"

The contrition on Alex's handsome face had Maya looking away. She wanted to be angry with Alex, but he was only doing his job.

Alex withdrew, closing the door behind him.

"Brady, this is Donald. He's a lawyer and he is going

to help us." Maya sat in the chair next to her brother while Donald took the seat across the table. He took out a notepad and pen.

"Help us do what?" Brady asked.

"Get you home tonight," Donald said. "How about you tell me what's going on?"

Maya opened her mouth to reiterate what she'd already explained, but Donald held up a hand. "I need Brady to tell me he understands what is happening."

Brady frowned, his gaze bouncing from Donald to Maya and back again.

"Brady, do you understand that you're a suspect in a murder?" Donald asked.

For a long moment, Brady didn't say anything. He turned to Maya. "I don't understand."

Maya gathered his hands in hers. "Brady, remember the man who yelled at you when you were on the hiking trail the other day?"

Brady made a mean face. "I didn't like being yelled at."

Donald held up a hand. "Let me stop you right there. I don't want to hear you say that again."

Maya's gaze jerked to Donald. "What?"

"We don't want anyone to think he had a motive for killing this man. If being yelled at made him angry, a conclusion could be formed that Brady lashed out at the man in anger."

His words struck a fire within her chest. It infuriated her that anyone would consider her brother capable of this horrendous deed. Keeping her emotions in check, she gently squeezed Brady's hands. "When the man yelled at you, what did you do?"

Though she knew the answer, he had already told her and Alex about his encounter with Ned Weber, she wanted Donald to hear Brady's story.

"I turned and ran. I ran and ran as fast as I could go. And then I tripped and then I tumbled and then I landed and my ankle hurt." He lifted his leg to show Donald his booted foot.

"I see. So you were scared and ran away." Donald made a note. "Did you see anyone else on the hike before you saw the man who yelled at you?"

Brady shook his head. "Not before."

"But after?"

Head nodding, Brady said, "These really nice people found me and helped me. They brought Alex."

Donald made more notes. "We'll get back to them. Now, think hard. Before you saw the man who yelled at you, did you hear or see anyone else?"

Again, Brady shook his head.

Donald asked, "When the man yelled at you, what did he say to you? What was he angry about?"

Brady pulled at his ear, something he did when he was deeply upset. "He thought I was following him. That I was cheating. But I wasn't. I'm not a cheater."

"Brady," Maya said, reaching for his hand. "It's okay. You're not." Hoping to distract him, she asked, "What happened to your backpack?"

"When I was running, I got caught on some bushes. I dropped the backpack." He ducked his head. "I'm sorry, Maya. I know I'm not supposed to take it off when I'm hiking."

"It's okay, Brady," she told him. Maybe whoever had killed the dentist found Brady's backpack and stowed the journal there. But why hadn't the man or woman left with the notebook? Why hide it in the backpack?

Donald spoke. "What can you tell me about the notebook?"

Brady cocked his head. "I write in my journal every night just as my teacher tells me to."

Tenderness filled Maya. "Not your school journal, honey." Referring to the one he kept on his bedside table that he turned in at the end of every month. "We found a black leather-bound notebook in your backpack today."

Brady frowned. "I didn't see any black leather notebook."

Donald tucked his pen into his breast pocket. "That's okay, Brady. We'll be sure to tell the sheriff that."

"What will happen now?" Maya asked.

"Deputy Trevino will come in to ask his questions."

"Then we can go home?" Her stomach knotted. They would be going to Alex's ranch. She didn't know if she could go with him now that he thought Brady was a murderer.

"Best-case scenario, yes, you'll both be free to leave. Worst-case scenario—the case will have to go before Judge Turpin. If the judge feels that Brady is not a flight risk, he may remand him into your custody. That's what I'll ask for. Or he might hold him on bail."

"Bail? You mean they will charge him?" Maya's voice rose with her agitation.

"Not if I can help it," Donald stated. "But we do need to let Deputy Trevino have access to Brady." He rose and went to the door.

Heartsick, Maya lifted a silent prayer heavenward. *Lord, how do I deal with the situation?* A man was dead and Brady was a suspect in the crime. *I trust You, Jesus. I trust that You will let the truth win out.*

Because she couldn't survive it if her brother were taken away from her.

Alex stepped into the interrogation room. He hated seeing fear in Maya's eyes and knowing he'd put it there. But Alex hated even more seeing Donald Grayson sitting beside her, acting protective of both Maya and Brady, as if he had some claim on them.

The burn of jealousy tightened his jaw. He forced his personal feelings aside as he sat down. He trained his gaze on Brady. The kid appeared scared. His fear seemed genuine.

Alex's mind turned back to what Brady had said about how finding the treasure would allow him to go to a special summer camp.

Was the treasure motive for killing the dentist? Had Brady thought the dentist had found the fortune and wanted it for himself?

The speculations only confused the situation.

Innocent until proven guilty, Alex reminded himself. The notebook found in Brady's backpack was incriminating. And knowing how much Brady wanted to find the treasure wasn't something Alex could ignore. He sat down in the chair across from Brady. It didn't seem right to be sitting there with Brady and Maya in the cold, impersonal room. But Alex had a job to do and he would get to the truth one way or another.

TWELVE

The single bank of fluorescent overhead lights in the small interrogation room glared down on the table and glinted in Brady's hair, a shade darker than his sister's.

Maya shifted in her seat, drawing Alex's gaze. Her long wavy brunette hair fell over her green sweater-clad shoulders. Her eyes were troubled as she watched her brother answer Alex's questions. So far, Brady had kept to his original story of seeing Ned Weber. After accusing Brady of cheating in the treasure hunt by following him, Mr. Weber had yelled at Brady to go away and not to tell anyone Brady had seen him.

Focusing back on Brady, Alex maintained a gentle tone to keep the kid at ease. "Where exactly did you see Ned Weber? Was he coming down the trail or up?"

Brady tilted his head and seemed to contemplate his answer. "No. He was climbing the side of the mountain."

"Did you climb up, too?"

Giving a vigorous shake of his head, Brady said, "No. I'm not supposed to go off the trail."

"Was he alone?"

With a shrug, Brady answered, "I didn't see anyone else until later, after I hurt my foot."

"Did you see what the man was doing?"

"He was standing there looking down at me."

Figuring Brady must have startled Weber, Alex asked, "And he yelled at you and you ran away."

"He was scared," Donald interjected.

Glancing at the lawyer, Alex inclined his head. "Yes. He was scared." Focusing back on Brady, Alex asked, "When you were running up the hill, did the man chase after you?"

Brady shrugged. The pupils in his eyes were huge. "I don't know."

"Did you hear any noises?"

Brady's eyebrows drew together in concentration. He closed his eyes for a moment. "Yes." His eyelids popped open. "I heard birds." His eyebrows shot up. "But they stopped talking when I was running. I scared them."

Or someone else did. "Tell me about the notebook."

"I never saw a notebook," Brady replied. "Maya found one in my backpack but I didn't put it there." His round face was completely guileless.

"Did you look in your pack at all over the past few days?" Alex asked.

Brady's nose scrunched up. "No. I didn't need it. Maya wouldn't let me go back up the mountain."

Alex believed him. He'd been around Brady enough to realize the kid was innocent in nature, as well as innocent of this crime. But the fact remained that Brady had been in possession of the deceased man's property. Alex couldn't ignore such an incriminating fact. Plus, there was nowhere Brady would be safer than right here, within the walls of the Bristle County Sheriff's Department headquarters.

"Deputy Trevino," Donald Grayson interjected. "Unless you're going to arrest and charge my client, I'd like him released right away."

Alex met the other man's gaze. "We have probable cause to keep him overnight." He tapped his pen once on the table for emphasis. "The notebook."

"What?"

Maya's stunned voice tugged at Alex, but he kept his gaze on the lawyer.

"Obtained illegally," Donald shot back.

"Miss Gallo searched her brother's backpack and revealed the evidence," Alex stated. He didn't like using Maya against her brother, but his duty was to see justice done. And for now, Brady was their prime suspect. And Alex would do what he needed to in order to keep Brady and Maya safe.

Maya gasped. "I didn't know. I shouldn't have…" Her gaze pleaded with Alex. "You can't put Brady in jail!"

Maya bit her bottom lip as tears gathered in her eyes. Alex clenched his heart. It tore him up inside to see Maya so devastated. He wanted to soothe away her upset. He'd already arranged with the sheriff to keep Brady tucked away in the office. At least until the end of the day. "I'm sorry, Maya. We have to hold Brady for now."

"Alex." Maya's anguished voice scored him to the core.

Unable to stop himself, Alex reached across the table and took Maya's hand. "I'll do everything in my power to prove his innocence."

She nodded, and a tear rolled down her cheek.

Donald stood abruptly. "I'd like to talk to the sheriff."

Alex released Maya's hand and rose to his feet.

"You're welcome to." Turning to Brady, Alex said, "Brady, you'll need to come with me."

She wrapped her good arm around her brother. "Can I stay with him?"

Heart hurting, Alex stared at her. "He will be fine, Maya. He'll be safe here."

Maya held his gaze for a long moment. "I guess that's a blessing." She helped Brady to his feet. "You have to go with Deputy Trevino."

Brady beamed. "I get to go with Alex? Cool. I like Alex."

Alex inwardly winced. The kid wouldn't like him much after today. But there was no help for it. Keeping him here was for the best. Taking Brady by the arm, Alex led him out of the room, but instead of taking him to the cell where he would have been housed with the few rabble-rousers rounded up during the day, Alex took him to the sheriff's office.

Maya stayed close on their heels.

Donald Grayson made a beeline for the sheriff, who'd joined them. "Sir, I need to speak to you."

"I'll walk you out," the sheriff said but made no move to go.

Maya touched Alex's sleeve. Confusion clouded her pretty brown eyes. "Alex?"

"There are puzzles he can work on," Alex told her and was gratified to see the understanding and warmth spreading across her lovely face.

Brady looked at Alex with a frown. "What's happening? Am I in trouble?"

Covering Maya's hand, Alex said, "Brady, you're going to stay here, in the office, for the rest of the day."

And despite what he'd said to Grayson, Alex had

no intention of keeping Brady overnight in the office. Alex would take the kid and Maya home to the ranch because Alex knew Brady hadn't committed this crime.

However, proving so might be difficult.

After making sure Brady was as comfortable as possible with a jigsaw puzzle that Alex had found in a supply closet, Maya bolted. She needed air. Gulping large lungs full, she blindly headed down the sidewalk, pushing past the dispersing crowds now that the parade was over. Brady was safe in the sheriff's office. Not in a cell. Thanks to Alex.

I don't understand, Lord, how can this be happening?

There was too much turmoil going on. So much chaos. Her head spun. How could anybody believe her brother could be capable of murder? She just didn't understand. There had to be a way to prove that he was innocent.

"Maya, wait!" Alex's voice punctuated the air.

She halted in front of the Java Bean coffee shop and attempted to cross her arms but her injured shoulder protested, so she settled for holding her fisted hands at her sides.

"You can't go walking around by yourself," he stated as he stopped beside her. Concern etched in the creases at the corners of his eyes. "It's not safe."

Irritation shimmied down her spine. "Why not? You have the backpack. You have the notebook. There's no reason anybody would want to hurt me or Brady now."

"We don't know that for sure," he said. "They may think you know how to interpret the notebook. Or made copies. They've already made it clear they are determined."

A sharp shiver of fear jolted through her. She had glanced in the journal, but it was full of undecipherable markings. "Then we need to tell everybody that the sheriff's department has the notebook."

"No. We need to lie low and let our forensic analyst process the notebook and the backpack. We will find evidence that will exonerate Brady."

"But what if there isn't? What if the evidence points to Brady? What if the masked men return?" Her voice hinged on hysteria. She could feel it bubbling up into her throat and she struggled to contain all the fear and dread threatening to drown her.

After a few calming breaths, she said, "Sorry. I'm just so scared."

He drew her to him, his arms encircling her like a protective blanket. For a moment, the overriding need to melt into his embrace scattered her thoughts. She wanted to snuggle in, stay wrapped in his embrace and forget all the terror of the past few days. She felt safe within Alex's arms. He was solid and steady, an anchor in an otherwise turbulent world.

But her brother needed her to be strong. Brady was relying on her. And as much as she admired and respected, and even cared for Alex, letting down her walls for him wasn't something she could allow. His offer of comfort wouldn't solve the problems she and Brady faced.

Disengaging from him, she stepped back.

Hurt flashed in Alex's eyes. "Maya?"

Flustered, she gestured to the coffee shop. "Latte?"

Though his dark eyes remained troubled, his mouth curved at the corners. "Sounds good."

They entered Java Bean and the scent of rich coffee

and chocolate teased her senses. The dark wood paneling of the coffeehouse was in sharp contrast to the light-colored granite countertops. Small round tables with occupied chairs created a cozy atmosphere full of lively conversation. The sounds of grinding coffee and steaming milk filled the space between Maya and Alex while they waited in line to order.

The platinum blonde barista behind the counter gave Maya a friendly welcome. "Hello, Maya, what can I get you?"

Maya liked the newcomer to town and smiled warmly. Jane had appeared behind the counter six months ago and Maya had immediately struck a rapport with the younger woman. "Hi, Jane. How are you today?"

"Busy, which is good," Jane said cheerily.

"I can imagine. I'll have a caramel almond milk decaf latte and a hot chocolate for Brady." Maya stepped aside so Alex could order.

"Deputy, what can I get you?"

"I'll take a hot chocolate, as well."

With a nod, Jane went to make their order.

Maya allowed Alex to pay for the bill. With drinks in hand, they walked back toward the sheriff's station. There were still many people on the sidewalks and in the stores along the main street. Maya was glad to see the shops doing good business and tried not to fret over the loss of profits she might have made today.

"Miss Gallo." A dark-haired woman stepped into their path.

Maya recognized the short female from the night they brought Brady down from Eagle Crest Mountain. "Oh, hello."

"Deputy," the woman nodded to Alex.

Alex returned the nod. "Miss Owens."

"Call me Claire." She turned her attention back to Maya. "How's Brady?"

"My brother…" Maya hesitated. What could she say?

"Brady is well," Alex answered for her, saving Maya from having to decide.

Grateful, Maya smiled at him.

"Wonderful news," Miss Owens said. "We'd love to see him."

"How long are you and your friends staying in town?" Alex asked.

"Oh, we're leaving tomorrow or Monday," she replied.

"Good to know. If you'll excuse us." Alex nudged Maya forward.

Giving Alex a curious look, Maya kept pace with him, but she could feel Miss Owens's gaze tracking them. When they reached the doors of the sheriff's station, she glanced back but the treasure hunter was nowhere in sight, yet she couldn't shake off the strange feeling of being watched.

Alex cleared away the remnants of their dinner from the top of the sheriff's desk. Apparently, cheeseburgers from Max's Diner was one of the Gallo siblings' favorite treats. The town was still filled with people celebrating Harvest Festival, so they were waiting until the crowds thinned out before heading back to the ranch for the night. The sheriff had agreed to remand Brady to Alex's custody.

Maya sat across from the desk, smiling indulgently at her brother. Brady, seated in the sheriff's captain's chair, twirled around and around, chatting away about the parade and how much fun he'd had throwing candy and how happy it made everyone.

Alex's heart swelled. He was grateful for the community of Bristle Township and the acceptance Brady had found among the townspeople.

But Alex also felt for the kid. He remembered the way Brady had lamented that there was nobody in town like him. Alex could imagine how hard it was for Brady to fit in with the other kids in school. Growing up, Alex had bounced back and forth between two households, never feeling like he belonged in either one.

When all this was over, Alex decided he would try to find a way to convince Maya to let Brady go to that camp next summer. Alex knew it was none of his business but he'd grown fond of Brady and his sister.

He met Maya's gaze across the room. She smiled and his heart thumped, kicking him in the chest.

What he felt for Maya was more than fondness.

If he were being honest with himself, he'd admit that fondness couldn't begin to describe the affection, admiration and respect welling up inside him. Not to mention attraction.

Yes, she was pretty on the outside, but her beauty was deeper, elemental to the person within. A person he wanted to be around, to cherish and...

He quickly tamped down the soft emotions crowding his heart. It wasn't professional. He needed to keep his head and his emotions in check. Maya deserved his best and he couldn't give her what she needed, what she deserved, if he let himself become emotionally involved.

Ha! Like you already haven't become emotionally involved.

Brady stopped chatting midsentence. "Something stinks." He wrinkled his nose. Then he pointed. "Who's that?" He pointed to the window behind Alex.

Alex spun around and caught a glimpse of a masked face, the same type of mask he'd found in the restroom of the park earlier that day. The man quickly disappeared from view.

"Hey!" Alex ran toward the door. The acrid scent of smoke grabbed Alex's attention and his senses went on the alert. His steps faltered.

"Alex?" Maya was on her feet moving toward him.

Pulse pounding, he held up a hand. "You two stay here." He opened the office door and a gray cloud of smoke hung in the air, growing thicker by the second. A moment later, the fire alarms sounded a shrill noise that reverberated off the walls.

Brady grabbed his ears. "Make it stop!"

"The station is on fire!" Alex yelled and slammed the door shut. The fire was coming from one of the other rooms in the building. He had to get Maya and Brady out so he could help the others inside the department. "The window."

He hustled Maya and Brady to the window. He grabbed the edge of the pane and lifted, but it wouldn't budge. They were trapped.

Why would the masked man want them dead?

Revenge for thwarting their attempts to gain possession of the notebook was the only reason Alex could come up with.

Smoke curled under the door to the sheriff's office, filling the room. Brady and Maya began coughing.

"Cover your nose and mouth with your shirt," Alex instructed. "And stay low."

Alex grabbed the office chair. "Turn away!"

He raised the chair and threw it at the window. Glass splintered, and the sound of it echoed through his ears. Cool air rushed into the room. Using the stapler from the desk, he knocked out the jagged pieces of glass sticking out of the window frame. "Hurry! This way."

He helped Maya and Brady through the window and followed them out, urging them away from the building. Flames danced at the broken window.

Torn between leaving Maya and Brady unguarded and rushing back inside to help, he sent a prayer heavenward that everyone else inside had made it out alive and unscathed.

Needing to do something, he said to Maya, "I'll be right back."

Maya grabbed his arm. "No. You can't go back in."

"I have to." He shook off her hand and hurried toward the front door.

A fire engine roared to a stop a few feet away and firefighters disembarked. One pushed him back, saying, "We've got this."

Reluctantly, he moved away to allow the men and women of the Bristle County Fire Department to do their job. He returned to Maya and Brady. Together, they watched the fire department work to put out the blaze.

Maya's friend Leslie arrived, taking charge of Maya and Brady.

"I'm going to get these two seen by the paramedics," Leslie said.

Maya touched his hand. "You better come, too," Maya said, her brown eyes worried. "You inhaled just as much smoke or more than we did."

Alex nodded and coughed. "I will. I just have to make sure I'm not needed here."

The sheriff approached and clapped him on the shoulder. "Alex, get yourself checked out. If the medical guys say you are okay, then you can come back."

"Did everyone get out okay?" He held his breath waiting for the answer.

"Yes, thankfully. Now, off with you."

Relieved by the news and seeing the look of concern on Maya's face, he relented. His job was to keep her and Brady safe. They were his priority at the moment. "Let's go."

Leslie linked her arm through Maya's and led her to the ambulance, leaving Alex and Brady to trail after them.

After Jake, the EMT, cleared Maya, Brady and Alex with mild smoke inhalation, Alex ruffled Brady's hair. "You have a good sniffer. You smelled the smoke before we did."

Brady grinned. "Yep. That's my superpower."

"What happens now?" asked Maya.

"After I check in with the sheriff, we'll head home to the ranch."

Leaving Maya and Brady safe inside his vehicle with Leslie, Alex hustled over to where the sheriff was conversing with the fire department chief, Victor Watson. The chief held a fireman's jacket in one hand and a helmet in the other. Since he had on his own jacket and helmet, Alex wasn't sure why he had ahold of another set.

"The blaze is out," Chief Watson said. "The structure has suffered some damage from the flames and the water."

Alex hated hearing that. "Chief, any idea where the fire started?"

"There will be a full investigation so I can't give an official answer, but between us, we found traces of accelerant near the back entrance close to the evidence room."

Sucking in a sharp breath, Alex, said, "This was arson."

"It was a huge blessing that no one was hurt," Sheriff Ryder said in a tone of grim anger. "Hannah Nelson was in the evidence locker running tests. Thankfully, she got out. With the help of a fireman."

"That's great." Alex respected and liked the department's tech.

"Yes." Chief Watson held up the items in his hands. "Except we found this discarded fireman's jacket and helmet in the dumpster behind the next building. They aren't even from our firehouse."

"We think the firefighter who helped Hannah out was the one who started the fire," Sheriff Ryder added.

Reeling from this news, Alex asked, "Was anything taken?"

"Yes. The black leather-bound notebook."

Alex's fingers curled into fists. The killer had wanted that book and had started the fire. Thankfully, that person had shown Hannah mercy.

His gaze going to the window of the sheriff's office, a horrifying thought filled him. He turned to the sheriff. "Sir, just prior to the fire a masked person was at the window. I believe he nailed the pane shut. I had to throw your chair through the glass for us to escape."

Chief Watson spoke up. "I'll have the arson investigators check out that window."

There was no doubt in Alex's mind—the arsonist might have shown Hannah mercy, but he had meant to trap Maya and Brady inside with the fire.

THIRTEEN

"Here's Hannah." Sheriff Ryder gestured toward the tall red-haired woman approaching where they had gathered. Alex assumed she had already been checked by the EMTs. Her white lab coat was smeared with ashes. Her freckled face had smears of soot from the fire she'd clearly been closer to than the rest them.

Behind her stylish framed glasses, her green eyes sparkled with anger. She stopped, put her hands on her hips and surveyed the men. "Do you have any idea who did this?"

"Hannah, the fire investigators will do what they can to find the culprit," the fire chief assured her.

"Could you identify the fireman who helped you out?" asked Alex.

She shook her head, her long braid swinging with the effort. "No, I couldn't see his face. He had on a respirator. As soon the alarm went off, he appeared and hustled me out the door. He said he was going back in to look for others." She clenched her fists at her sides. "Apparently, that was a lie from what I gather. You and the Gallo siblings could have been killed. As well as Daniel and Chase."

"Where are Daniel and Chase?" The sheriff glanced around.

"They're doing crowd control," replied the fire chief.

"The leather-bound notebook?" Alex had already been told that the notebook had been stolen in the chaos. But he needed it confirmed. The journal was their only lead in the case. If they lost that, they'd have a hard time figuring out who was so bent on finding the treasure that they'd kill for it, burn down the sheriff's station and attempt to kill Maya and Brady.

Hannah smirked. "Whoever it was thought they were smart by creating a diversion, breaking in and taking my evidence. But little do they know, I photographed every page of that notebook and backed it up to the cloud. Not so smart after all."

The thought that there was still a copy of the journal available sent a burst of reinvigorating energy through Alex. He asked, "Can you email me a copy?"

"Of course. I also dusted the notebook for prints. I found several."

Remembering the moment Maya had dug out the notebook from the backpack, Alex hoped that her prints weren't the only ones found on the cover and in the pages. But he also hoped Brady's fingerprints would not be found.

"Maya Gallo's prints would have been on the journal."

"That's good to know," Hannah said. "The prints are running through AFIS."

Alex could only hope the perpetrator's prints would be found in the country's automated fingerprint identification system.

"Wasn't your computer damaged in the fire?" the sheriff asked.

"Yes, the one here at work was destroyed. But again, I upload everything to the cloud and even though this computer was running the prints, my computer at home can also access the data and run the prints."

"You are a genius," Alex exclaimed. He'd always respected the woman. She had to be smart to do all she did for the sheriff's department.

Hannah grinned. She blew on her knuckles and then rubbed them on her coat, smearing the ash onto the fabric. "You know it."

Chuckling at her antics, Alex said, "I look forward to getting that email."

"You'll have it within the hour," Hannah said. Her expression sobered. "Alex, you have to get this guy."

He wasn't sure why Hannah was addressing him with her directive and not the sheriff. Alex sneaked a glance at Sheriff Ryder. Ryder arched an eyebrow and gestured with his chin for Alex to answer. "We will, Hannah."

"Good. Now, if you'll excuse me, I'm going home to clean up. And get back to work." She strode away with purpose in each step.

Alex turned to the sheriff. "We know Brady didn't set this fire. In fact, I believe this fire was set, in part, to eliminate Brady as a threat to whoever is after the treasure, as well as to allow for an opportunity to steal the journal."

"I agree," the sheriff said. "You need to take the Gallo siblings somewhere safe."

"I'm taking them back to the ranch."

"You need backup." The sheriff got on the radio and asked for Chase and Daniel to join them.

Alex didn't argue. Having backup seemed the best option since they had to wait until Monday for a security system.

A few moments later, the two deputies hurried over. Alex nodded in greeting to the two men.

Chase and Daniel both had black ash smeared on their uniforms and faces. Their eyes were red-rimmed from the acrid smoke.

"We barely got out through the break room window," Chase announced to Alex.

Alex's clenched his jaw. "Same here, through the office window."

"Trying to get two inebriated men and a nearly hysterical Carole to jump the few feet to the ground was no picnic," Daniel added.

"Where are our evening's guests?" the sheriff inquired.

"Locked up tight and sleeping off their stupor in the back of a department vehicle," Daniel replied.

Concerned for the department's receptionist lanced Alex. "And Carole?"

"Safe in her husband's arms," Chase replied.

"Good," Sheriff Ryder said. "Well, I don't suppose we can leave two detainees unattended, and I'm probably going to need help before this night is over. Those masked men might have a bigger agenda." He sighed, his weary gaze traveling over the smoldering sheriff's station Alex knew he loved. "Kaitlyn's over at the church helping dismantle the float and keeping the teens in check." He looked at Alex. "I'll have Kaitlyn head over when she's done at the church."

"Thank you, sir. If you don't need me…" Alex gestured.

"No. Take your charges home."

Alex turned to Chase and Daniel. "Check on the treasure hunters. We ran into one earlier today. I want to know they are accounted for and where they've been this evening."

"Will do." Chase hurried off to take care of the task.

Daniel snorted. "Always so eager."

Alex laughed and clapped Daniel on the back. "Remember when we were that gung ho?"

"A long time ago," Daniel groused as he walked with Alex to where Maya, Brady and Leslie waited.

"You make it sound like we're over-the-hill," Alex shot back. "It wasn't that long ago."

Daniel shrugged but his gaze was on Leslie. She stood beside the open door of Alex's truck with Maya. Both women turned as they approached.

Maya took Alex's hand when he stopped at her side. The contact surprised him. He curled his fingers around hers, relishing having her so close.

"Any news?" she asked. Her voice wavered.

He didn't want to frighten her more by telling her that the blaze was arson with a deadly intent. "The fire investigation will take a few days."

Her gaze narrowed. "What aren't you saying?"

How could she read him so well? So smart and intuitive. Better to honor her with the truth than lie by omission. "It's pretty clear the fire was arson."

Maya grimaced. "I was afraid that was the case."

"Was anyone seriously hurt?" Leslie asked.

"No," Daniel replied. "We all survived."

"That's a blessing," Leslie murmured, her gaze darting from Daniel to Maya. "Brady's falling asleep. You're welcome to come to my house."

"They are staying with me," Alex said before Maya could respond.

"All right." Leslie smiled at their joined hands, then touched Maya's arm. "Call me. Let me know if I can help in any way."

"I will."

"I'll walk you to your car," Daniel said to Leslie.

Leslie slanted him a glance. "No need." She hurried to her 4x4 parked at the end of the lot.

Daniel clenched his jaw and he shook his head. "Stubborn woman," he muttered as he watched her.

Alex helped Maya climb into the truck, then he walked back to Daniel. "What is it with you and Leslie Quinn?"

"Nothing worth talking about." Daniel gave a chin nod toward the truck. "You want me to follow you?"

Alex knew Leslie and Daniel had grown up in Bristle Township along with Maya. There was history between them. But since the man apparently didn't want to discuss his relationship with the pretty blonde, Alex decided to not pry. "Yes. And stay until Kaitlyn arrives, if you don't mind."

"Not a problem. I've got your back." Daniel strode away to climb into his vehicle.

Alex gave him a two-fingered salute of gratitude before he joined Maya and Brady in the truck.

The drive to the ranch didn't take long and the only headlights in Alex's rearview mirror were Daniel's. When Alex turned into the drive to his ranch, the other deputy flashed his lights, made a U-turn and parked at the entrance to the ranch's driveway.

Alex brought his truck to a halt and watched his dad and his dog rush down the porch stairs to the other side of the truck to help Maya and Brady out. Rusty was all wiggles and happy barking. In the distance, Truman's whinny of greeting floated in on the breeze.

Frank gave Brady a big hug. "I was worried about you."

Rusty let out a happy yip and circled them.

Seeing his father's affection for Brady, Alex clenched his gut. He didn't begrudge the kid the attention, but there was a part of Alex that still yearned for his father's love. With practiced ease, he shoved the longing to a back corner. No sense in ruminating over the past when there was no way to undo the damage done.

"Let's get everybody inside," Alex said briskly. "We're all grimy and tired."

"I'm sure hot cocoa and marshmallows will make everyone feel better," Maya stated with a soft smile, her eyes on Alex. He swallowed, wondering if she'd seen his thoughts on his face.

"That sounds like a perfect prescription," said Frank.

"Can I help?" Brady asked, all traces of sleepiness gone.

"After your shower," Maya said.

"Okay!" Brady bolted up the stairs ahead of Frank with Rusty at his heels. The kid stopped and turned to the older man. "Don't start without me."

"Never," Frank said, placing his hand over his heart.

Grinning, Brady and Rusty raced inside.

Frank chuckled. "The boy is resilient."

"He really is," Alex agreed. He met his father's gaze. There was a flash of some emotion in his dad's eyes that left Alex confused. Anguish? Regret?

Frank's gaze bounced between Maya and Alex, then he said, "I'll get everything ready and wait for Brady in the kitchen."

His dad ascended the stairs much slower than he had descended them. Alex wondered if his dad was hurting.

Maya's gait was a bit stiff as she started toward the stairs.

Stepping closer, he slid an arm around her waist. "Lean on me."

For a moment, she tilted her head to stare at him with her pretty brown eyes. He wondered what she saw and if he was lacking. Then she nodded and she wrapped her good arm around his waist. Snuggled against his side, he guided her up the stairs.

"What a trying day. A trying few days," she murmured. "I ache all over."

He tightened his hold. The need to reassure her, protect her, flooded his system. "It's going to get better."

And he sent up a silent prayer to God that he would be able to keep that promise.

After everyone showered and changed into fresh clothes, they congregated in the kitchen. Maya started a load of laundry, though she doubted their clothes would ever be rid of the acrid stench of the fire. Frank and Brady had made hot chocolate and now sat at the dining table with their mugs. Alex was in his office on his computer. Kaitlyn had arrived, popped in to say hello, then left and was now sitting in her vehicle at the end of the driveway near the main road to ensure no one approached the house.

Maya barely touched the sweet confection in her own cup. She was dead tired, but her mind was wired. Fear lay in the pit of her belly like a heavy stone. Though she and Brady were safe now, that didn't mean something couldn't happen. After all, someone had burned down the sheriff's station with them inside. If not for Alex's quick thinking, they all could have died. She shuddered.

She felt helpless and vulnerable. The only thing keeping her sane was Alex. And her trust in God.

She had to believe between the two of them that she and Brady would be okay. The bad guys would be caught, and everything would settle down. Though, unaccountably, she wasn't looking forward to return- ing to the house she and Brady had grown up in. The thought of leaving the ranch caused a ripple of anxiety down her spine and made her pulse pound. Would she feel safe ever again?

Alex returned to the dining room and set a laptop on the table in front of her brother. "Brady, could you look at these for me?" He opened the laptop and angled the screen toward her brother. "Do you think you can figure out what this all means?"

Brady set his mug down. "I'll try."

Maya gave Alex a questioning look. He shrugged. "He's good with puzzles. Maybe he can decipher Ned Weber's notes."

She blinked in surprise. "Wasn't it destroyed in the fire?"

"Actually, it was stolen."

She absorbed that news. "But you have a copy of the notebook?"

"Hannah uploaded photos to the cloud and sent them to me."

Maya wasn't sure she wanted Brady further involved in the hunt for the treasure, even if it was to help Alex.

There was such a look of concentration on Brady's sweet face as he studied the images on the screen, her heart contracted. She wanted to reach out and push back the fall of dark hair from his forehead, but she hesitated. Maybe if he could make heads or tails out of the notebook pages, then they could find the person terrorizing them.

She knew she wouldn't be able to rest until they were no longer in danger. She was so grateful to Alex and his father for letting them stay here at their house. And so thankful that the sheriff had agreed to let Brady come home.

Strange how Maya thought of the ranch as home. She was comfortable here. Content. Her gaze lingered on Alex. He made her feel special, protected, wanted…

She stifled a gasp. She knew he didn't love her, he'd done nothing to indicate his feelings for her went deeper than keeping her safe, but the way her heart was knocking against her ribs made her keenly aware of the fact that she was falling for him.

Despite her best intentions, Alex had breached the barricades around her heart. He made her see that her life with Brady could include more. But fear poked through the bubbles of rising hope.

She couldn't go through another loss.

Not like she had with her parents. How could she let Alex fully into her heart knowing that he had a job where there were no guarantees he'd come home at the end of the day?

A niggling voice in the back of her mind whispered there were no guarantees that anyone would come at the end of the day. Her parents hadn't been in law enforcement. They'd been returning from a day of fun on the mountain. Life was precarious and scary. Better to guard herself from more hurt.

"I'll head off to bed now," Frank said after taking his mug to the sink and rinsing it out.

The older man looked worn-out. Concern filled her. She was glad he wasn't pushing himself to stay up with them. "Thank you for the hot chocolate."

Frank's eyes crinkled at the corners. "Of course. My pleasure."

Maya nudged Brady. His eyes flicked from the computer to the older gentleman. "Thank you and good night."

Frank chuckled and ruffled Brady's hair before heading down the hall. Maya met Alex's gaze. She lifted an eyebrow.

His mouth with twisted with a rueful smile. "Good night, Dad."

Frank stopped midstride. From Maya's vantage point, she could see him swallow. "'Night, son," he called and continued on.

Alex sipped from his mug, dark eyes on her.

Maya wrapped her hands around her cup, the warmth of the hot chocolate fading. She tried to hold his gaze but grew uncomfortable after a moment. Did he see her feelings for him? And how afraid she was?

"Did you go to school with Daniel and Leslie?"

A safe subject. "Yes. We were in the same grade all the way through to high school. Then Daniel joined the military. Leslie went off to college and traveled the world." She heard the wistful tone in her voice and hoped he hadn't noticed.

"They don't seem to like each other much," he commented.

"*Quinn* and *Rawlings* for last names put them next to each other all through school," she returned. "Growing up in a small town, there's no getting away from each other."

"Shhhh," Brady said. His gaze never left the computer screen. "I'm trying to..."

She could see him mentally searching for the word. "Concentrate."

"Yes."

Alex's lips pressed together and amusement danced in his eyes. "How about we take our drinks to the porch?"

Maya nodded and gingerly rose from the dining room chair. Taking her mug with her, she followed Alex outside to the back porch. He sat on the swing, holding it steady as he lowered himself into it. He patted the seat next to him. "Come sit with me."

She wasn't sure that being so close to him was a good idea. She remembered what it was like to be snuggled up against him. Smelling the scent of his aftershave. The warmth of him chasing away shadows haunting her. The ache to experience it again tugged at her with an almost physical pull. Not a smart idea. Better to stand and keep a distance between them so her heart wouldn't get any more attached.

FOURTEEN

"There's nowhere to put the mug." The excuse sounded lame to Maya's ears and she winced. Would Alex see right through her?

Alex rose from the porch swing and walked to the other side of the porch, where there were two chairs and a little table. He picked up the table and brought it over and placed it on the side of the porch swing. He set his mug down, smiled at her and said, "There you go."

Okay, he'd made it hard for her to not acquiesce. It would be rude to move all the way across the porch to the set of chairs, especially now that he'd gone to the trouble to move the table. Besides, there was a part of her that really did want to sit next to him, to lean into him, to let him be strong for her and for Brady. Maybe she could absorb some of that strength.

When he resumed his seat on the swing, she carefully sat down. She held her mug in both hands. She heard his soft chuckle. She glanced up at him.

"Now, that wasn't so hard," he said. She shifted and put her mug on the little table. Sitting back, she tried to relax. His arm came across the back of the swing and his fingers gently touched the top of her biceps.

For a moment, she held herself still, then gave in to the overwhelming need to melt against him. She liked this. It seemed natural and right. Comfortable, yet thrilling. With the toe of his cowboy boot, he sent the swing gently rocking back and forth.

They were content to sit there, the quiet of the Colorado night wrapping around them with the stars twinkling in the heavens like little diamonds against black velvet. The air had turned crisp and cool, indicators that winter was fast approaching.

"Are you cold?" he asked.

She should have been. But she wasn't. The hot chocolate had warmed her from the inside and being this close to Alex was warming her from the outside. She was content. At peace for the moment. She lifted her face to his. "No, I'm fine. This is nice. It's been such a crazy, stressful day."

Moonlight crossed his face, adding strong lines and shadows to the angles of his cheekbones and jaw. The moon's glow softened the harshness of his dark hair and illuminated the depths of his eyes. Emotion welled within her, clogging her throat. She tried to sift through all that she was feeling, hoping to grab onto one that she could express without putting her heart at risk. She wanted to express to him her gratitude, her affection, her respect and admiration. "I know I've said this before, but thank you. I'm so grateful you brought Brady and me to your home. You've been so welcoming. I feel safe here."

"I'm glad you're here and that you feel safe." He brushed back hair from her forehead. And tucked it behind her ears. She shivered under his touch. "I'm here for you, Maya. Whatever you need. Whenever."

It wasn't a declaration. She shouldn't feel so giddy. She wasn't quite sure what his words meant. Her heart heard a promise. She wanted to grab hold with both hands and hang on. But she couldn't. She wasn't brave enough. "I'm so grateful for your friendship." Her voice sounded strangled. She cleared her throat.

The intensity in his gaze unnerved her. "I'm glad to hear that. Because I care deeply about you, Maya."

And here she thought he had no feelings for her. Apparently, she'd been wrong. Her heart fluttered in her chest. To cover her reaction, she reached for her cocoa. Though it was cool, the sweetness burst on her tongue, heightening her already tightly strung nerves. He cared about her. Deeply. She wanted to pump a fist in the air, dance a jig and laugh with joy. Instead, she tamped down the crazy delight. Caring was a long way from loving, right?

He made little circles on her shoulder with the tips of his fingers. "You know when this is all over and life goes back to the way it should be, I'd really like to get to know you better. Maybe move out of the friendship zone. Go on a date or two or a million."

She choked a little on the cocoa. She sat the mug down. "You would?"

She bit her bottom lip. She wanted that also. To get to know him, to explore these feelings that were crowding her chest and making her heart race. She wanted more. She wanted love and family. But she'd already decided those things weren't going to be a part of her future.

She shook her head. "I just… I just can't face any more loss."

His eyebrows dipped together. "Maya—"

She placed two fingers against his lips, stopping his

words. She had to tell him. Explain where she was coming from. She couldn't handle it if he said anything more that would make this harder. "If I let myself fall for you, really fall for you, then I'm opening myself up to pain. I just can't risk it. I don't have that kind of courage."

For a long moment, Alex didn't say anything. Gently, he traced the line of her jaw. "I understand, Maya. There are no guarantees in life."

Surprise washed over her that he would voice what she'd been thinking. She'd never been so in tune with anyone before.

"Life can change in an instant," he continued, his voice low and drawing her in so that all she could see, hear and feel was him. "We have to grab a hold of the joy and the love that we can, now, before it's too late."

His words echoed her earlier thoughts. Such a strange sensation. Intellectually, she agreed with him, but emotionally, deep in her heart, fear dug its sharp talons into her. "Is that what you're doing with your father?"

Alex drew back. His expression closed to her. "That's different."

She hadn't meant to ask the question or to send him emotionally retreating, but now that she had, she pressed forward. "Why? In what way?"

"Your parents loved you. Their deaths were a horrible tragedy. But it wasn't their choice to leave you." There was a sharp edge to his tone.

"You're right, it wasn't their choice to leave me. It was an accident. No one's fault." She repeated the mantra she'd relied on to get her through the worst of her grief. "God was with them. Just as He was with me and Brady. Just as He is now." It had taken her a long time to get to a place where she could see the truth. And to feel God's presence. "It would have been so easy to be angry at Him for taking them away from us."

"It's really good you can see that."

There was a tone of respect and admiration in his voice that made her want to cry. Because she also heard the hurt that he carried in his heart. She'd glimpsed his wound before and it tore her up inside.

She placed a hand on his chest. All his strength, warmth and resilience was right there, beating steadily beneath her palm. "I know your father wasn't there for you when you were young and you resent him. Resent his lack of parenting. I can only imagine how that made you feel. But you have a second chance with him now. A chance most people don't get."

He closed his eyes for a moment as if shielding himself from her words. "You don't understand."

Thinking about his earlier statement that her parents had loved her, she realized that at the core of Alex's pain was the belief he had not been loved. "You're right, I may not understand what you are feeling. It must have hurt horribly when your parents' marriage broke up. I know you said you never felt like you belonged in either of their homes. I would imagine you questioned their love for you. But, Alex, you did belong and you do. You belong to this town. You belong to the people of this town. You *are* loved. And now your dad is back in your life. I can see that he is wanting to forge a bond, a relationship with you."

"I'm trying." The defensiveness in his voice made her heart ache.

"You're still so angry. You won't heal until you let that go."

He ran a hand through his hair. "That's easy for you to say. I just don't know how—"

Brady burst out the back door. "I think I decoded the map. I know where the treasure is."

Maya's heart leaped into her throat. Finding the treasure would put an end to this masked-men nightmare once and for all.

She met Alex's gaze. Would it also mean the end of them?

Seeing Brady's excitement revved Alex's blood and chased away the angst of where the conversation with Maya had veered. Talking about his father and the past wasn't productive. He couldn't change what was or how he felt toward his dad. Alex knew Maya meant well and maybe shifting the direction of their conversation away from them had been her way of telling him she wasn't interested in more than friendship.

Because she was afraid to risk her heart.

A sentiment he completely understood. He'd never thought he'd come to a place where he was willing to let someone in again but that was before a certain dark-haired beauty had entered his life.

Unsure what he could do to change her mind, he instead focused on the matter at hand. "That's great, Brady. What did you find?"

"You have to come see," Brady said, disappearing back inside the house.

Alex rose from the swing with anticipation making the small hairs on his arms rise. This could be the end of the whole treasure-hunting fiasco. If Brady had found the treasure, they could look for it tomorrow. And hopefully solve the mystery of the masked men.

Alex stretched out his hand to Maya, who still sat on the porch swing. "Are you coming inside?"

She gripped his hand with icy fingers. He frowned. "Why didn't you tell me you had a chill?"

She gave him a weary smile. "I'm warm enough. Let's go and see what Brady has discovered."

Inside the house, they found Brady and Frank sitting at the dining room table. A pile of papers sat next to the computer.

Surprised to find his father still up, Alex said, "Dad, I thought you went to bed."

"I was getting ready when Brady needed help with the printer."

Brady fanned the pile of papers. They were printed copies of the pages from inside Ned Weber's notebook.

"The kid's amazing," Frank said. "So smart."

Alex had no doubt. Brady had Down syndrome, but the kid had a keen intellect and needed to spread his wings. Focusing on the pages and still unable to decipher them, Alex said, "Show me what you have."

Brady put his hands on the table like he was holding court. "Okay, here's where it gets really interesting." He gestured to the pages on his left. "These notes are from all the places where he'd been hunting and not found the treasure." Brady gestured to the notes to the right. "These are the places he has yet to explore. He made notes about the different locations and the possibilities of where the treasure might be buried."

Alex stared at the pages. It was all gobbledygook to him.

Brady picked up the pages in the middle. "This part talks about his search on Eagle Crest Mountain."

"But he didn't find the treasure," Alex stated. At least

they hadn't found any sign of the treasure, so whoever killed him and burned down the sheriff's station to acquire the notebook hadn't found it on Weber.

"I think he might have found it," Brady's voice rose with enthusiasm. "And I know where to look for it."

Maya gave a sharp intake of breath. "You are done treasure hunting. It's Alex's turn."

Brady's face scrunched up. "But he doesn't need the treasure. I need the treasure."

A pained look spread across Maya's face. "Brady, no amount of treasure is going to convince me to let you go to that camp. Honestly, you need to let that go. You're too young."

Brady jumped to his feet, the chair tipping over behind him and the pages he held fluttering to the floor. "I'm not too young. I'll be sixteen soon. Sally Mortensen down the road is only ten and she went to summer camp *this* summer."

Maya reached out a hand to her brother. "Brady, you have to understand—"

"No, I don't understand." He turned and raced down the hall to his room, slamming the door behind him.

Maya's shoulders slumped.

Compassion filled Alex. He knew how much the camp meant to Brady and he also understood that Maya wanted to protect him by keeping him close. "Maya," he said gently. "He would be going to a safe place where there would be people he could relate to and who would relate to him."

She stood, her dark hair swinging with the movement and her dark eyes sparking. "You don't know anything about it. Stay out of it." She stalked off and went into the bathroom, closing the door with a sharp *click*.

Alex heaved a sigh. He hoped he hadn't just blown his chance to convince her to let Brady attend the camp.

"She's struggling to come to terms with the fact that her little brother doesn't need her in the same way that he always had," Frank stated.

Alex sent his father a sharp glance. "I know that. She raised him and he wants to fly the coop, even for a short time. I get that it's scary for her."

"It's scary for every parent when their child no longer needs or wants them," Frank stated softly.

Anger ignited deep inside of Alex. "What would you know about it? There wasn't a lot of parenting going on from you."

Sadness filled Frank's eyes. "I know I wasn't a good father to you. And I regret that more than I can even begin to explain. But I did love you. I do love you. You are my son and I have only wanted the best for you."

Alex didn't want to hear this, didn't want to feel the cascade of emotions marching through him at his father's words. Loved him? Alex felt anything but loved by his father.

Focusing his gaze on the papers now lying on the floor, Alex reminded himself that those pages contained the location of the treasure. That was what he needed to be thinking about, not dredging up old pain with his father.

"I was a drunk. And I was angry." Frank's tone held no self-pity. "Honestly, I was afraid that I would take out my problems on you."

Alex jerked his gaze to his father. He'd never heard him own up to his drinking. Not even when he'd arrived on Alex's doorstep, telling him he was sick and needed a place to recuperate. It had taken Alex some digging to discover that his father had liver damage. Cirrhosis, the doctor had said.

"You could've made a different choice," Alex said.

"I wish I had made a different choice. But I was weak and hurt. When your mother left—"

Alex held up a hand. "What are you talking about? You're the one who left."

Frank sighed. "You don't remember that time in our lives. You don't know what happened. It's not my story to tell. All I can share with you is my side of things. Someday you'll have to ask your mother. But she did leave. I didn't know how to handle it so I sought comfort in the bottle. And that made me a bad man and a bad father."

Alex's heart twisted. He didn't remember his mother leaving. He remembered them fighting, he remembered the stench of alcohol. He remembered his mother holding him and telling him everything would be all right. But it never was. He always blamed his father. Alex had never considered his mother's role. In his mind, she had been the victim. But now, Alex could see that maybe... maybe they were all victims of circumstances that no one handled well. But his parents had been the adults. They should have protected him, done what was best for him, their child. He would never make that mistake. "It doesn't matter now, Dad. It's in the past."

"I wish it was that easy. But you've never forgiven me. And I can't forgive myself."

A strange feeling ripped through Alex's heart, crawling up his throat. The back of his eyes burned. His father's words opened up a deep wound, one Alex thought he'd cauterized a long time ago.

The craving for family, for a place to belong, with

people to belong to, welled up so strong that he thought he might drown in the tidal wave of emotion. He didn't know what to do or say. How did he make this over-whelming sense of hurt and pain go away?

"I hope one day you will be able to forgive me," Frank stated sadly. "But more than that, I hope you can open your heart so you can see what's right in front of you." With shoulders slumped, Frank headed back down the hall toward his room, leaving Alex alone.

His father's words assaulted him, popping against his chest with the force of a paintball gun. He flinched, rubbed at the spot over his heart and lifted his gaze heavenward. *Lord, what do I do now?*

Not really expecting an answer, Alex picked up the papers from the floor and set them on the table. He stared at the undecipherable symbols, which looked to him like scratch marks. He couldn't make heads or tails of them. But Brady had figured them out. The kid was amazing, just as his father had said.

The swell of affection for Brady filled him, and on its heels was a swell of love for Brady's beautiful sister, Maya. Alex's heart raced making him shake. He was falling in love with Maya. Falling? Ha. He'd fallen right over the cliff into the messy abyss of love. And he had no idea what he was going to do about it.

He gathered up all the pages, putting the ones that Brady indicated would show the way to the treasure on top. Tomorrow, he and Brady would map out a route and Alex would hunt down the secrets buried in the mountain, putting an end to the threat against Maya and Brady once and for all.

Then he hoped and prayed he would be able to persuade Maya to let Brady spread his own wings, as well
as convince her to take a chance on him.

FIFTEEN

Sunday morning arrived with a light snowfall. The first of the season. Maya came out of her room dressed in her favorite soft green sweater and cargo pants that were perfect for the weather. Her feet were toasty in thick wool socks. She found Frank and Brady already at the kitchen table, consuming stacks of pancakes doused with real maple syrup.

"Someone's going to have a sugar high."

"Oh, I didn't think of that," Frank said, clearly contrite.

She held up a hand. "Seriously, it's fine. He'll crash this afternoon and need a nap before church. Not a bad thing."

"I made coffee," Frank told her. "I already delivered a thermos and a stack of pancakes to Deputy Rawlings."

"I thought Kaitlyn was on duty?" Maya felt bad that the female deputy had stayed out in her car all night guarding the only road onto the ranch.

"Daniel relieved her early," Frank said.

"That was kind of you to take him a hot drink and something to eat."

Looking uncomfortable with the compliment, Frank's gaze darted away. "Just doing what I can to help."

She gave the older man a quick hug and then her brother a kiss on the head before going to the kitchen counter for coffee. Movement outside the window drew her attention. Alex riding Truman out of the barn toward the pasture. Her heart gave a little thump against her rib cage at the sight of him, so confident on the big horse. She sighed at how easily he affected her.

After putting on her all-weather boots, she grabbed her mug of coffee and went to the back porch to take in the view. Alex was dressed in worn jeans that hugged his long legs and a flannel shirt stretched against his broad shoulders. Apparently, he wasn't bothered by the cool morning.

Instead of his shiny black uniform cowboy boots, he had on scuffed brown cowboy boots and a cowboy hat. His utility belt was slung low over his hips and his gold sheriff's deputy badge was pinned on his chest.

Even on his day off, he didn't give up his identity as a sheriff's deputy. A cowboy deputy.

She liked this look on him. She'd thought him handsome in his dress uniform during the parade and his regular uniform day to day, but this look had her heart pumping extra fast.

Yes, she was attracted. Who wouldn't be? The man was more than appealing in so many ways. Her feelings for Alex ran deeper than she'd ever expected or wanted. Not just because he was good-looking but because of his honor and integrity. His willingness to fight for her and her brother. His determination to keep her safe and to prove her brother's innocence. Thankfully, that was no longer in question after the fire at the sheriff's station.

Not that long ago she'd prayed for protection and God had granted her request in the form of Alex Trevino.

Alex's gaze locked with hers and he nudged Truman toward the house. She admired the way he rode, so confident and sure in the saddle. She let out another little sigh and was glad Alex wasn't close enough to hear. She walked off the porch to meet man and horse at the edge of the lawn.

"Good morning." Alex tipped his hat in greeting.

Knowing he'd grown up in the city had her smiling at his cowboy gesture. "It's lovely out here. The world always seems more pure and fresh with a dusting of snow," she said.

"It does."

"Would you mind taking Brady and I to the evening church service?"

"That shouldn't be a problem. I'll touch base with the sheriff."

"I get the feeling Sheriff Ryder respects and trusts your judgment," she said.

Alex shrugged but didn't comment.

She thought about something she'd heard a couple months ago. Gossip bandied about the hardware store. Normally, she didn't take stock in the local chatter. But now… "Some people are saying the sheriff's going to retire soon. Is he grooming you to take over?"

Alex looked off into the distance. "I can't assume to know what the sheriff is thinking."

She followed his gaze to where the Rocky Mountains provided a majestic backdrop to the pasturelands and houses of people she'd known all her life. She loved this town and its citizens. They'd rallied around her and Brady when her parents were killed. The townsfolk kept the store afloat. She and Brady had a wonderful life in Bristle Township. She had everything she needed and wanted in life.

Except a love to call her own.

Her gaze slid to the man sitting atop the beautiful horse, then away.

Alex was fair, committed and honest. Almost dogged in his quest to find the truth. All traits that made for an honorable, respectable sheriff. Alex would make a good sheriff, she decided, and refused to consider what else he'd be good at. She looked back at him. "I, for one, will vote for you if you do run for sheriff."

Alex's gaze touched her face like a caress, sending a series of delighted shivers over her skin. "I'd welcome the vote. However, in Bristle County, the sheriff is appointed by the mayor."

"Well, if I ever get a chance to put a bug in Mayor Olivia's ear, I'll let her know that I one hundred percent support you."

"I appreciate your support," he replied with a smile that tugged at her heart. "I'm going to take Truman out for some exercise. Would you care to join us?"

"Yes." The admission came without hesitation. Remembering every thrilling moment of the last time she'd sat on the horse with him had her heart pulsating with energy. "Let me put this away—" she held up the mug in her hands "—and grab a jacket. I'll be right back."

He nodded. "We'll be here."

She hurried inside, mentally telling herself this would be okay. It's just a ride around the ranch. Nothing to get worked up about. She set the mug in the sink, grabbed her down jacket and carefully slipped it on. Her arm was already so much better than it had been after her fall from Truman, but she still needed to baby her shoulder.

On her way back out the door, she paused and said, "Hey, guys, Alex and I are going for a ride."

"Can I come?" Brady asked.

"Not this time," she said, her gaze meeting Frank's. Heat crept up her neck at his amused and pleased smile.

She left the house and hoped Alex would think the blush staining her cheeks was from the chill in the air.

Alex had dismounted and stood beside the large horse. Her heart skipped several beats at the sight of the two males. So majestic and handsome.

"Up front you go," Alex said, stepping aside so she could reach the horse.

She approached Truman and grabbed ahold of the pommel with her good hand. Alex moved behind her and placed his hands on her waist to boost her up. Her lungs stalled, and she forced herself to breathe deep because there was no way she was going to let Alex know how he affected her. The last thing she needed was for him to be aware that she was falling for him.

The thought made her foot slip from the stirrup.

Wait! What? Falling for Alex?

"Something wrong?"

His voice cascaded over her as awareness of his big body close to her shimmied across her skin, heating her from the inside out. "No," she choked out. *Yes.* She was falling for Alex big-time.

Don't think about that now, she chided herself as she allowed Alex to help her up into the saddle.

Truman held still as Alex settled on the back of the horse.

"Shouldn't I be in the back?" she practically squawked

when one of his arms encircled her waist while the other reached around her to take the reins.

"It's easier this way. Plus, I can hang on to you rather than you putting pressure on your arm to hang on to me."

Sounded reasonable. Delightful. Scary. She held herself stiffly away from him. Her sore shoulder tensing as her heart thudded in her ears. She put her hands on the pommel and willed herself to relax in the seat because she didn't want Truman or Alex to realize how completely unsettled this situation made her. As they started walking toward the pasture, she wondered what had ever possessed her to think this was a good idea.

Alex ushered Maya out of the evening church service, keeping her close as the throng of attendees filed into the night through the open double doors. She'd been subdued all day after their ride that morning.

At first, she'd been so tense in the saddle he thought he'd blown it big-time by asking her to go for a ride, but eventually she'd settled back and seemed to enjoy the outing. He'd shown her the full extent of his property. When she'd asked what his future plans for the place were, he'd had no answer but her question stuck in the back of his mind.

Coming out of the church behind them, Frank stopped to talk to Pastor Foster. The two men seemed to be old friends. Alex vaguely remembered his father saying he had been meeting with the pastor.

"Brady will meet us here," Maya told him as they stopped on the sidewalk outside the pretty white steeple church building. "It's our usual plan."

"I'd rather we found him," Alex said as he searched

the dispersing crowd. He saw mostly locals, men and women he knew, but here and there were faces he didn't recognize. Not unusual given the Harvest Festival. Some folks stayed through Sunday and traveled on Monday, when the roads would be less congested. He thought he got a glimpse of two of the treasure hunters, Roger Dempsey and Claire Owens, but they melted into the night.

"This way," Maya said, and led him around the back of the church, where there were several classrooms for various ages of children. "The room the sheriff's department commandeered is usually used for the junior high kids," she said. "But now all the preteens and teens are in the community room."

The community room was actually a gym with hardwood floors, basketball hoops and a stage set up at one end for a worship band. Long tables in the middle were being used by several kids making crafts.

Brady saw them and left his place at the table with a paper craft in his hands. "Look, we made pinwheels."

"That's wonderful," Maya said. "We'll put that in the garden this spring."

"Hey, boss." Chase approached Alex.

Shaking his head, Alex resigned himself to putting up with the moniker. "Hey, Chase. What's up?"

"I saw you walk by our new digs. I found something that might be of interest."

The need to know what Chase had discovered warring with his determination to stay close to Maya and Brady must have shown on his face because Maya put a hand on his arm. "You two talk. We'll be over there."

Grateful for her thoughtfulness, Alex smiled. "Thanks."

She turned to Brady. "Show me how you made your pinwheel."

Brady tugged her back to the table of craft supplies.

As soon as they were out of earshot, Chase said, "So after you told me about the freerunning, I did a little more digging into our five friends and discovered that each one of them has done some sort of acrobatics."

"That would lend itself to freerunning."

"I thought so, too," Chase said. "The two women were cheerleaders in their respective high schools. The Smith brothers actually are acrobats. They perform with a smalltime traveling show that is a knockoff of the one that's so famous in Vegas."

Anticipation revved in Alex's veins. The Smith brothers rose to the top of the list of suspects. He wanted to have another chat with the two men. Remembering Maya had said Truman had head butted one of the masked men, Alex was curious if either of the Smith brothers had a large bruise over their sternum.

"The last guy, Roger Dempsey, is a bit more of an enigma. He's a wrestler and track star. Even the dentist was a gymnast in his college days."

Because Weber was deceased, he was obviously ruled out as being one of the masked men, but the common thread of athletics might have been what drew these people together. What other activities did they do as a group besides hunt for buried treasure? What secrets did they hide?

"I want you to search the databases for any crimes that could be attributed to freerunning. See if you can connect anything to any of these five people." Alex had a feeling in the pit of his gut that there was more to explore with the group. "Also, check the hotel to see if any of them are still in residence. And if so, I want them in on Monday for a follow-up interview. If not, track them down."

"I'll get right on it."

Alex appreciated Chase's can-do attitude. "What about the Delaney brothers? Anything of note there?"

Chase's mouth twisted. "After their mother died, Ian and Nick went to boarding schools in Europe. Ian went on to graduate from the London School of Economics while Nick was asked to leave several colleges. Apparently, he wasn't cut out for academia. He finally managed to graduate from a small private university in Virginia after a large donation to the school from Patrick Delaney."

None of that surprised Alex. "Any connections to parkour or freerunning?"

Chase shrugged and shook his head. "Not that I can find. Ian was on a rowing team and now plays tennis. He's quite good and competed at Wimbledon. Nick's more into girls than sports, from what I can glean on social media."

"Thank you for the info." He clapped Chase on the back. "You do good work."

Chase grinned. "Thanks, boss." He turned on his booted heel and strode off, then pivoted. "Oh, I almost forgot. That sedan that tried to run you off the road was found in the next county. Wiped clean. It had been reported stolen a week ago."

A dead end there.

Alex stayed rooted to the spot, his mind going over what he'd learned. On the surface, it appeared the Smith brothers were his most likely suspects, but he couldn't rule out the Delaney brothers or the other three treasure hunters. The Delaneys had the most to lose if someone found the treasure. But how desperate were the Smith brothers to be the ones to claim the prize?

Monday morning, Maya insisted on opening the store. "I've lost too much profit by being closed half of Friday and over the weekend." Her bank account couldn't take another hit.

She and Alex stood at the kitchen sink, finishing the breakfast dishes together while Brady was outside in the garden with Frank. She liked being here with Alex and his father. Brady was enjoying it, too. She worried that when it came time to leaving later today, Brady was going to have a hard time coping with the loss of the two Trevino men.

So was she, truth be told.

But it was time to go home. Despite her realization that her feelings for the handsome deputy had progressed to a place where she feared she'd never come back from, she had to keep the situation in perspective. It was natural to develop tender emotions for Alex. All this time spent together. Wasn't there some psychological phenomena about people falling for their protectors? Or did it only happen with a person's captors?

Whatever the case, falling in love with Alex wasn't a wise decision.

"Just stay closed until tomorrow, after the security alarm is installed," Alex countered, taking another dish from her to dry.

The alarm company was sending out technicians today to the ranch, the store and her childhood home. "I need to be there when the alarm guys arrive. I might as well open."

Alex put the dried dish away in the cupboard and set the dish towel down. "I can meet them. Kaitlyn or Daniel will be here to oversee the installation of the ranch's security system and to keep you and Brady safe."

"No. Brady and I need to return to our house and our lives. He has school."

"That's not a good idea," he countered.

"You really think someone would try to harm him at school?"

He didn't answer but kept his gaze steady on her. Acid burned in her stomach. "Fine. I'll call his teacher and get his assignments. But we are going to the store. And to my house. No one is going inside without me present."

His mouth tipped upward at one corner. "You can be stubborn, you know that?"

She gave him a saccharine sweet smile. "One of my many admirable traits."

He coughed, but she had a suspicion it was to cover a laugh. "That is true."

Wait. She was being sarcastic. Did he think she had admirable traits? What were his feelings for her? The questions hammered at her, matching the frantic beat of her heart. Oh, boy. Better not to let her mind go down that twisty path.

"I—I'll go get our things packed," she stammered and backed out of the kitchen.

As it turned out, Frank also accompanied them to town, saying he wanted to pick up a book he'd ordered from the library.

On the way into town, the security company called with their estimated time of arrival. Because they were traveling from Boulder, it would be in the afternoon before they could get started on the installations.

When they arrived at the store, Maya had Alex bring Brady's smaller desk out to the front of the store so he could do his schoolwork and be within sight at all times.

"What can I do to help?" Alex asked as she went about the task of opening the store.

Having help was a commodity she wasn't used to. "Right now, all I can think of is to straighten the shelves. I didn't have time to do that before closing up on Friday."

He nodded and moved down the aisles of hardware, lining up the hammers, organizing the various sizes of screwdrivers and paint supplies. Maya tried not to watch the way he moved with agile grace. He wore his sheriff's uniform again today and she found herself missing the worn jeans and flannel shirt.

The bell over the door dinged. Ethan and Bess Johnson walked in. Glad for the distraction, Maya greeting them. "Ethan, Bess. So good to see you this morning."

Bess took her hands. She was in her early seventies but looked much younger with her dark curls and vivid green eyes bracketed by gentle laugh lines. "My dear, I was horrified to hear about your troubles. Are you doing okay?" Her gaze slid to Alex, who was arranging the birdseed.

With a smile, Maya said, "We're in good hands."

Ethan went to Brady's side. "What are you up to, young man?"

"School stuff," Brady said. "We're learning about solar energy. The sun could power our lights."

"That would be something," Ethan said.

A loud squeal of tires on pavement reverberated

through the store followed by the horrific sound of metal meeting metal.

Maya rushed to the window. Two cars were locked in a crumpled embrace in the middle of Main Street. "Alex! There's been an accident."

Alex raced to the front door. He skidded to a stop. "Don't leave the store," he instructed. "I'll be right back." He pushed through the doors.

Maya stood with Ethan and Bess, watching as Alex ran to the crash site. Her heart cried for the drivers of the cars. She lifted up a prayer that there were no fatalities.

The bell over the door dinged. She swiveled to greet the incoming customers and found herself facing two familiar faces, and one of them held a gun.

SIXTEEN

"You won't get away with this." Maya's heart hammered in her chest as she and Brady huddled together on the back passenger seat of a black SUV. The vehicle sped north, taking them out of town. She tried to keep as much distance as possible from the woman kidnapper next to her.

Ignoring them in the front seat were the man and woman who'd entered the store right after the collision. They had been a part of the group who'd helped Brady down from the mountain.

The man, who had held the gun in the store, had ordered Maya and Brady and the Johnsons to the back of the store, where they locked the poor Johnsons in the office. They'd then forced Maya and Brady into the awaiting vehicle that was now being driven by the brunette woman named Claire, the treasure hunter who'd stopped Maya and Alex on the sidewalk the night of the sheriff's department fire. Had they set the blaze?

Beside Maya, the blonde woman, Sybil, cackled. "Looks like we already have gotten away with this. Taking you two was easy."

"Alex will find us." Maya put her arms around Brady and held him close. He shook with fear.

From the front seat, the man named Roger turned around to wave the gun at them. "I wouldn't be too sure about that. He's got to be busy with the accident."

A thought occurred to Maya and horror cut her breath in half. "You caused that accident."

He grinned. "Maybe."

"Roger, where are we going?" Claire asked.

"Pull over at that turnout," he replied.

Claire brought the SUV to a halt. Roger pointed the gun at Brady. "Now, tell me where the treasure is buried. I know you deciphered Ned's nonsense in his journal."

With a sinking feeling, Maya asked, "How do you know about that?"

"We have our ways," Sybil said with relish.

Somehow, these people had been spying on them. Maya shuddered, totally creeped out.

"I won't tell you," Brady said, ducking his head into Maya's shoulder.

She tried to shield him as much as possible.

"Oh, you'll tell us," Roger said. He shifted the barrel of the gun toward Maya. "I'll hurt your sister if you don't."

"Maya?" Brady looked at her with fear in his almond-shaped eyes. Her heart hurt for him.

"Go ahead, Brady. Tell them what they want to know." The treasure wasn't worth anything to Maya. They could have it for all she cared.

"Okay." Brady explained that he thought the treasure had been buried somewhere on the back side of

Eagle Crest Mountain. Ned Weber had been looking in the wrong place.

"That wasn't so hard," Roger said. He faced forward. "All right, then, Claire. Do you know where you're going now?"

The car didn't move. "Are you sure we should be doing this?" Claire's voice wobbled with nervousness. "What if something happens? If we are caught, we'll go to jail."

"Stop being such a big baby," Sybil said, smacking the back of the driver's seat with the palm of her hand. "We won't get caught."

Maya wanted to point out that Alex would know where they'd gone. Especially once he found Bess and Ethan in the office. But she kept her lips pressed tight. The longer they thought they were in control, the better. Though it amazed her that these people were not thinking very clearly. Gold fever? They were so anxious to find the treasure they were making mistakes, which worked to her and Brady's advantage.

"Shut up and drive," Roger demanded. "I will call Greg and John and tell them to meet us there."

As the SUV took off, heading toward the back side of Eagle Crest Mountain, Maya sent up a prayer asking God to once again provide help. And this time she really wanted—no, she needed, Alex.

"What's going on?" asked Frank as he followed closely on Alex's heels into the Gallo Hardware and Feed store.

Fear cramped Alex's chest. He ran a hand through his hair as helplessness flooded his system. "Someone has taken Maya and Brady."

Color drained from Frank's face. "Oh, no, what do we do?"

"Not panic," Alex told him. But inside, Alex was panicking. What if he couldn't find them? What if something happened to Maya and her brother? What if he never got a chance to tell Maya he loved her?

Forcing back all the what-ifs, he took several calming breaths. He needed to stay focused, to think this through. It had to be either the treasure hunters, some combination of the five people, or the Delaney brothers, who had taken Maya and Brady. He reached for his radio but paused as banging echoed through the store.

"That sounds like it's coming from back here." Frank ran toward the rear of the store.

Alex followed, grabbing his father by the shoulder and pushing him behind him. "Let me."

Using caution, he approached the office door with his hand on his weapon. "Who's there?"

Frank gripped his forearm. "What if it's a trap? You won't do Maya and Brady any good if you're dead."

"Deputy Trevino!" Ethan Johnson called out. "We can't open the door."

Inspecting the lock carefully, Alex realized something had been jammed in the mechanism, keeping the door from being unlocked from the inside.

"Stand back," Alex shouted. He kicked the door open. Wood splintered, sending slivers and bits flying.

Bess Johnson and her husband, Ethan, rushed out of the office. Bess clutched Alex's arm. "Those nasty people took Maya and Brady."

"Who?" Alex asked, anxiety making his voice sharp.

"A man and woman," Ethan said. "I've never seen

them before. But Maya and Brady seemed to know them."

"Two of the treasure hunters?" Alex said.

"Yes," Bess said. "They were after some sort of treasure."

Turning to his dad, Alex said, "I'm heading to the back side of Eagle Crest Mountain. I have to go get Truman first."

"What should we do?" Ethan asked, hurrying to keep up with Alex as he headed toward the front door. Bess and Frank came along in their wake.

"Stay calm," Alex replied. Out on the sidewalk, Alex said to his dad, "Tell the sheriff what's going on. Have him round up the mounted patrol and have them meet me at the back side of Eagle Crest Mountain." He searched his memory, trying to picture the route Brady had formulated yesterday. "Tell them to go to the trail on the left."

Off the top of his head, he couldn't remember the name of that trail. But on the drawing that Brady had done, Alex remembered the main trail veering to the left and climbing upward.

With his heart in his throat, he raced to his truck parked behind the building. Every second that he drove toward his ranch was a second that Maya and Brady were in danger. When he reached the ranch, Kaitlyn and the alarm company man were about to leave. He quickly explained to Kaitlyn what was happening. She didn't waste time on questions but rather ran to her own vehicle, calling out, "I'll meet you there with my horse."

Not taking the time to acknowledge her statement, he hurriedly saddled Truman and led him to the trailer. Once he was secure, Alex jumped into the driver's seat of the attached truck and sped away from the ranch. On the road to the back side of Eagle Crest Mountain, he used his Bluetooth and dialed Patrick Delaney's estate.

Collins answered, and Alex asked for Ian, since the man seemed willing to try to convince his father to give up the treasure's location. Now, more than ever, Alex needed that information.

"This is Ian," came the deep voice of the man Alex had met a few days ago.

Without preamble, Alex detailed the situation. "I need you to ask your father if the treasure is buried on the back side of Eagle Crest Mountain or not."

Ian sighed. "I've been badgering my father for days now to get him to divulge the information you want. He's a stubborn old man, and he's finding some perverse glee in all of this. But I'll press him again." There was a pause before Ian said, "And make it my personal mission to provide you with assistance. I'll get back to you as soon as possible."

Alex hung up, forcing himself to push through his anxiety and concentrate on driving as fast as he could without doing any type of damage to his horse. He reached the back side of the mountain and parked his vehicle next to a black SUV. It had to be the vehicle that had brought Maya and Brady to the trailhead. Another vehicle was parked not far away. A silver pickup truck.

Something niggled at the back of Alex's brain. Hadn't one of the treasure hunters said that Ned Weber drove a silver truck?

Alex didn't have time to analyze how the truck came to be here. He released Truman from the trailer and led him carefully over the gravel lot to the trailhead. Just as he mounted the horse, three other vehicles came into the parking lot pulling trailers. Kaitlyn, her father, Aaron, and Leslie Quinn.

Kaitlyn jumped from her vehicle and ran to his side. "We'll be right behind you. The sheriff and Chase are still dealing with the accident site. Daniel is running point from the church."

"Thanks." Alex saluted her and urged Truman forward at a fast trot. When they reached the place where the trail formed, he nudged his horse to the left. He didn't take the time to see if there were footprints, the urgent, horrible need to get to Maya and Brady overrode all else.

"Are we sure we should trust this kid to get us to the treasure?" asked Greg Smith. The two brothers, John and Greg Smith, had joined them at the trailhead. Each man carried a bag over his shoulder with a shovel sticking out.

Maya nearly snorted. These people didn't know that Brady had no guile in him. But she decided to keep her thoughts to herself.

"Well, if he's lying to us," Roger said, "then we will just leave them both here for dead and go on about our business."

Maya's lungs contracted and she stumbled over a root.

"Hey!" Sybil pushed Maya. "Don't try any funny business."

They were hiking up Crescent Moon Trail at a fast pace. Brady was in the lead and Maya followed closely behind, keeping at an arm's length so that she could grab him if she needed to. Behind her were the five treasure hunters. The Good Samaritans that she had once appreciated had turned into deadly thieves.

She glanced back over her shoulder. "Did you kill Ned Weber?"

Sybil raised her hands, palms up. "Not me." She hitched her thumb over her own shoulder. "One of them."

"I didn't kill him," Claire said with a catch in her voice. "Ned and I…" She sniffed. "We were close."

"So close," John taunted, "that he was going to find the treasure without you or us."

"You didn't have to kill him!" Claire returned with fire. "That's on you two."

At least that answered one question. Maya filed the information away. Watching her step, she tried to gauge how Brady was doing. His foot had to be hurting him, even though he seemed okay. "Brady, slow down. I don't want you to twist your ankle again."

He looked back at her with a mix of fear and determination on his sweet face. "Don't worry, Maya. I know what I'm doing."

She sent another plea, asking God to please protect them. She hoped Brady did know what he was doing. He was smart. And she loved him beyond distraction. He was her whole world. Or had been, until a certain handsome deputy had stepped into their lives.

Her chest expanded. She loved Alex. There was no use denying the truth any longer. She prayed she lived long enough to tell him how she felt and hoped he still felt the same about her as he'd claimed earlier. She wanted more than those dates he'd talked about. God willing, she wanted a long life spent together as a family.

Brady stopped abruptly. Maya halted, putting her hands on his shoulders. Sybil bumped into Maya. "Hey! Watch it."

The others stopped.

"What's going on?" Roger pushed his way to the front, waving his gun around as if the device were some kind of baton and he was leading the orchestra.

Maya kept Brady behind her. She hoped Roger didn't accidentally shoot them.

Brady glanced around, as if searching for something, then pointed to the side of the mountain. "Up there."

"You've got to be kidding me," Sybil grumbled.

"Let's go!" The Smith brothers ran ahead, bounding through the woods.

"Lead the way," Roger said, keeping the gun level.

Trusting Brady knew what he was doing and where they were going, Maya gave him a nod.

Brady went off the path, leading them through the bramble bushes and large trees. The terrain roughened. Maya's breath came in little puffs. Behind her, the others were struggling with the exertion, as well. She glanced upward at the side of the mountain. The two Smith men were scaling the boulders with ease.

"There's no way we can get up the side of the mountain. We need rock climbing equipment," Claire said. "We should just let Maya and Brady go and forget this."

"No way," said Roger. "We are so close to finding the buried treasure."

"But what if it's not there?" Claire argued. "What if this is just another wild-goose chase?"

"Then we will storm the Delaney castle and force the crazy old man to give us the location," Sybil said. "That's what I've been saying all along."

Good luck with that, Maya thought to herself.

Ahead, the Smith brothers disappeared out of view as if swallowed by the mountain itself. After a moment, they reappeared standing on a ledge, waving their arms and shouting in tandem, "You guys, there's a cave." They disappeared once again.

Urged on by Roger, they quickened their pace over the rough terrain. When they finally reached the ledge and the cave, Maya was out of breath. The opening in the side of the mountain barely gave enough clearance to stand. The earth had been dug away leaving a tight space filled with darkness. The Smith brothers produced flashlights from their packs. The light revealed the cave didn't extend very far into the mountain.

"Okay, Brady led you here," Maya said once she managed to talk with out gasping for air. "Let us go."

"Not so fast." Roger gave her a little shove. "You stay close until we have the gold."

"You don't even know if it's gold," Claire said. "We don't even know if it's here. Or even if it's legit. For all we know, old man Delaney could be pulling our chain."

Ignoring her, Roger waved at the ground. "Let's start digging."

"I don't have a shovel," Sybil complained. "I'm not ruining my manicure."

"You start digging, Roger!" Claire shouted. "I don't want any part in this."

Roger trained the gun on her. "You are a part of this whether you want to be or not. You better start digging or I'll leave you here with those two."

Dread twisted Maya's stomach up in a knot. The man had no intention of letting her and Brady go. She grabbed Brady and held him tight.

Roger turned to them. "You start digging." He shot a menacing look to Sybil. "All hands on deck."

Afraid he'd shoot them before Alex could find them, Maya dropped to the ground and used her hands to dig in the dirt. It was hard packed and shredded her nails and palms. Brady stood rooted in place, his gaze taking in the cave walls as if he were searching for something. Maya grabbed him and pulled him to her side. "Start digging," she whispered in his ear.

"But the treasure—"

Maya put a finger to his lips, cutting off his words. "Whisper."

He dropped his voice to as much of a whisper as he could. "—isn't in the ground."

"How do you know?" She glanced behind her to make sure nobody was paying attention to them.

"The clue today."

She arched an eyebrow at him.

He grimaced. "I know I wasn't supposed to look, but I did."

"Doesn't matter now, Brady. What did the clue say?"

"Your heart's desire is at eye level."

The words tumbled over and over in Maya's head. Eye level. Brady could be right. If the treasure was in this cave, it would be in the walls not the earthen floor.

"I'll keep digging," she told Brady. "I need you to pretend like you don't understand what's going on."

"Pretend?"

She nodded. "Pretend. Like when you were in the church Christmas pageant." He'd pretended to be a shepherd herding his sheep.

"What are you doing over there?" John Smith asked.

Maya spoke loudly. "Brady is scared, I'm trying to reassure him. We are digging as best we can."

Hoping to have appeased their captors, Maya dropped her voice to a whisper again.

"I want you to pretend like you don't know what you're doing while you search for the treasure."

Brady stared at her for a moment, then he grinned. "I can do that."

He jumped to his feet and put his hands on the wall.

"Now what is he doing?" Roger groused.

"I don't understand." Brady patted the wall up and down as he slowly made his way along the cave wall toward the cave opening, away from Maya.

Maya rose and faced Roger. "Can you put the gun away, please? He thinks you're a robber. You know, put your hands up."

Roger made a face and tucked the gun into the waistband of his jeans. "Whatever." He dismissed Brady with a wave of his hand and resumed his search for the buried treasure.

Breathing easier, Maya returned to digging, while keeping an eye on Brady. Maya despaired that the treasure was not hidden inside the cave at all. Sweat trickled down her back. She didn't know how long they'd been stuck inside the cave when Brady made an excited little noise.

She swiveled to look at him. He turned around and met her gaze, his eyes as wide as they could be. He dropped to the ground where he was and crawled across the floor to her.

"I found it," he whispered to her.

Excitement beat against her chest wall. "Follow me."

Taking his hand, she rose, tugging him to his feet.

"This would go a lot faster," she said as she and Brady slowly made their way back to where he had been standing. "If we had the right equipment." She kept her gaze on Roger. "Like a metal detector or at least enough shovels for everyone. It will take forever at the rate we're going. Why don't you all come back when you're better prepared for this? Brady and I won't say anything."

"Yeah, right," said Sybil as she rose and dusted off her hands on her jeans. "Like we'd believe that."

Maya positioned herself so that Brady was against the wall. She started to stretch her arms over her head bending side to side.

"Now what are you doing?" Roger demanded, clearly exasperated by her antics.

"Stretching," Maya said. "My back is spasming."

"Mine, too," said Claire as she moved to stand next to Maya. She leaned close to whisper, "I'll help you if you help me."

Maya nodded, praying she wasn't mistaken in trusting this woman. They both did some stretching exercises, while Brady dug at the wall.

A loud roar filled the cave.

"Helicopter!" Greg Smith exclaimed. He stood at the mouth of the cave, his head tilted so he could see the sky.

Maya's hopes leaped in anticipation. Did that mean Alex was close by?

Or did this bunch still have more tricks?

SEVENTEEN

"**Y**es!" Brody clapped a hand over his mouth, obviously realizing he'd been too loud.

Maya cringed.

The other treasure hunters turned toward her and Brody, dashing her hopes that no one had heard the outburst.

"Did you find something?" Roger demanded to know, raising his voice over the loud noise of the helicopter hovering outside the cave. He moved closer to see what had Brady so excited.

Brady pulled a small wooden box from a cleverly concealed notch in the wall and hugged it to his chest. "Mine."

"Brady, set the box down," Maya told him. If they gave them the treasure, then surely they'd be safe.

"No!" The stubborn jut of Brady's chin didn't bode well.

Seeing Roger reach for his gun, Maya did the only thing she could think of to protect her brother. She shoved Roger as hard as she could, sending him backward to land on the ground. "Run, Brady!"

Ducking his head, Brady used his shoulder and

rammed into Greg Smith, sending him flying to the side and allowing Brady to race out of the cave, onto the thin ledge. "Maya?"

"Go, Brady, go," Maya yelled as she did her best to block Roger from following her brother. She could hear rocks sliding as Brady scrambled down the face of the mountain. Claire joined Maya, pushing and shoving to keep the others from chasing after Brady. Greg and John Smith darted out of the cave, giving chase.

"That was stupid," Roger hissed, the gun once again aimed at Maya. "You'll pay for that."

Claire jumped in front of Maya. "No!" she said. "We still need her. When Greg and John capture Brady, the only way we'll get the treasure back is if Maya is alive and unharmed."

For a moment, Maya feared Roger would hurt Claire for helping them, but then he growled, "Fine. Let's go." He waved them toward the mouth of the cave with the barrel of the gun.

Maya's heart tumbled and she stepped onto the ledge. Below she could see the Smith brothers were gaining on Brady. Her brother needed her help.

Knowing she had one shot at this, she took a deep breath and elbowed Roger in the gut as hard as she could before breaking into a headlong run down the steep hill. Her feet slid on the loose earth and she went down on her backside. Rocks dug into her skin. Her shoulder protested but she had to keep moving.

Ignoring the pain, she glanced behind to see Claire being restrained by Roger and Sybil. Overhead, the helicopter continued to hover. Maya raised her good arm and waved frantically, praying that whoever was up there had seen her and would send help.

"Maya."

To her right, Brady popped up from behind a fallen trunk of a tree. He must have stopped to hide.

Her heart in her throat, Maya dodged behind a clump of bushes and worked her way to her brother's side.

From above them, Roger yelled to Greg and John and pointed, giving away Maya and Brady's location.

Maya's heart sank. There was nowhere for them to hide now.

Static on Alex's shoulder radio crackled through the forest. Alex slowed Truman so that he could thumb the mic. Daniel's voice came across the static line. "Patching you through to Ian Delaney."

"Alex here," he said curtly.

"I'm hovering above the back side of the mountain face."

Alex glanced upward at the craft flying overhead. He had wondered who was piloting the helicopter.

Ian's voice came again. "Maya and her brother ran out of the cave. There are people chasing them. Hurry."

A jab of fear made Alex's voice sharp. "Where?"

"You're about a hundred feet from their position to the right of the trail."

Heart full of worry and panic hammering against his rib cage, Alex urged Truman off the path and into the woods. Undeterred by the branches attacking them, they crashed through the forest until Alex caught sight of Greg and John Smith. He drew Truman to a halt.

The two men stared at Alex for moment then in tandem veered to the left and raced out of sight.

"Maya!" Alex called at the top of his lungs.

"Here." He heard her but couldn't see her in the thick underbrush.

He jumped off Truman and dropped the reins, then ran forward, unsure from where her voice had come. "Where are you?"

"Over here."

He stopped, swiveled and saw her peeking over the thick trunk of a dead tree. He headed toward her at a run.

The retort of gunfire, followed by the *thwack* of a bullet hitting the tree trunk sent terror crashing through Alex. "Get down."

Alex dived for the tree trunk and hauled himself over the side to land on the ground next to Maya and Brady. They appeared unharmed and relief flooded his system. But he couldn't rejoice yet.

"That's Roger," Maya told him. "I believe he's the only one with a weapon."

Alex grabbed his radio to call in the situation.

A second later, the sheriff's voice came through the radio. "Chase and I are almost there. Hang on."

Maya touched his hand. "I knew you would come. I prayed you would and God answered my prayer. Again."

The retort of more gunfire echoed through the forest. The radio on Alex's shoulder came to life again. "We have Roger, Sybil and Claire in custody," said the sheriff. "Chase and the others went after the Smith brothers."

Maya latched onto Alex's arm. "Claire tried to help us. She didn't want to be a part of this. She and Ned Weber were an item."

Alex covered her hand with his. "We'll sort it out later." Giving in to the relief and love sweeping through him, Alex cupped her cheek with his hand and lowered his lips to hers to kiss her for all he was worth. Her lips moved under his, her hands gripped the front of his deputy jacket. For a moment, the world faded away. It was just the two of them.

"Ew," Brady said. "Kissing."

With a laugh, they broke apart.

Brady held up his find. "Look, I found the treasure."

"I see," said Alex.

Brady set the box on the ground and opened the lid. With a gleeful cry, Brady dug into the contents. Inside were what appeared to be gold coins and jewelry. Maya picked one of the necklaces up to inspect it and frowned. She grabbed more of the jewelry and stared at them. "They're fake," she said. "All of this is fake."

She dropped the costume jewelry and coins onto the ground. "I'm going to give that old man a piece my mind for all the trouble he's caused over nothing."

A good dose of anger burned in Alex's chest, too, but he'd found the best treasure of all in Maya and Brady.

Not appearing the least disappointed, Brady picked up the necklaces and gold coins and put them back in the box. "I'm the smartest one of all. I'm the best treasure hunter."

"Yes, you are." None of this sat right with Alex. Delaney hadn't struck him as a cheat. "May I see the box?"

Brady handed it over to him and Alex inspected the interior and the sides. Turning the box over, he noticed a notch in the wood. He ran his finger along the edge. "This has a false bottom."

He popped the compartment open and inside was an envelope. He handed it to Maya. She broke the seal and slid out a check.

A small squeak escaped her. "One hundred thousand dollars," she breathed out.

Now that was more like it. "It's yours and Brady's."

She shook her head. "No. We're giving it back to that old man. And I'm still going to give him a piece of my mind."

"We can't do it from here," Alex said as he pulled her to her feet. "Let's go home."

Two days later, nervous butterflies danced in Maya's stomach. She, Alex and Brady stood on the doorstep of the Delaney estate.

So much had happened in the last forty-eight hours. The five treasure hunters had been arrested and taken to jail. Alex and Maya had both spoken with the state's attorney who would be prosecuting the case. He promised to take into account the help that Claire had given to Maya by trying to keep Roger from hurting her and Brady and distracting Roger so the Gallo siblings could escape the cave. Claire agreed to testify against her fellow treasure hunters for their part in the sheriff's station fire. Sybil and Roger both claimed the Smith brothers had killed Ned Weber and stolen his notebook. The Smith brothers had lawyered up without saying a word.

Alex told Maya he figured one of the brothers must have stashed the notebook in Brady's backpack as a way to get it off the mountain without it being found by the police. They hadn't counted on how hard it would be to retrieve.

They were all taken out of town, and they were now awaiting trial in Denver. Maya and Brady would eventually have to testify in court later this year. But for now, she was determined to return the "treasure" to Patrick Delaney.

She didn't want any part of this horrific game he'd set in motion with his Treasure Hunt of the Century. Many people had tried to convince Maya to keep the money, but she would not be swayed. Thankfully, Alex had only said it was her choice. She'd appreciated his support.

The massive front door of the Delaney's estate creaked open. Collins stood there with a large grin on his face. "Our winners," he said and clapped his hands. "Come in, please. Patrick is waiting for you in the library."

Collins escorted them through the house toward a large set of double doors, which he opened with a flourish. When they walked inside, Maya understood why they named the room the library because the room didn't just house a few books. Three walls held floor-to-ceiling shelves brimming with all kinds of books. The fourth wall had a bank of windows overlooking an amazing view of the Rocky Mountains.

Patrick Delaney sat at the massive desk in the center of the room. Today, he wore a gray suit and a red tie. Beside him were a videographer and a news anchor from the local television station.

Maya almost felt sorry for the old man because he was not going to get what he expected. There would be no accolades today.

Beaming, Patrick waved them closer. "Come in. Come in." He turned to the camera. "These are the winners of the Treasure Hunt of the Century."

Maya glanced at Alex. He gave her a droll look, which made her smile. She stepped forward. Brady, however, remained at Alex's side, the treasure box gripped in his hands. She motioned for her brother to join her. Reluctantly, he did.

Patrick rubbed his hands together in obvious delight. "This is a banner day."

From her pocket, Maya produced the check and laid it on the desk in front of Patrick. She met his gaze. "We do not want your money. Brady is happy with the fake gold coins and the fake jewelry. This—" she tapped a finger on the check "—was not worth a man's life or all those other people getting hurt."

Patrick's rummy blue eyes widened with bewilderment. "But he won." He smiled and shoved the check back toward her. "This is yours. Yours and Brady's. You found the treasure. Only the worthy could find the treasure."

Brady set the box filled with the fake treasure inside on the desk. "I'm worthy," he said. "I'm smarter than everybody else."

Maya put her hand on his shoulder. "It's not polite to gloat."

Brady nodded and stepped back, leaving the treasure box on the desk. "Sorry, Maya."

Patrick frowned. "I want you to gloat." He gestured to the TV crew. "We are on camera. You should be proud because you finished my game."

Maya shook her head. Pity colored her words. "To you it was a game, to others it was life-and-death. We don't want your money. Good day, Mr. Delaney."

Putting her arm around Brady, they turned and walked out of the room with Alex as their escort.

A loud banging proceeded Patrick Delaney's agitated cry. "No, no, no! That's not the way it's supposed to go."

Maya didn't mind disappointing the old man. She'd

kept her integrity intact and was so proud of Brady for relinquishing the treasure. "How about we stop for ice cream on the way back to the ranch?"

"Rainbow sherbet on a sugar cone," Brady said with a happy skip.

In the entryway, they found Ian Delaney standing by the door. Today he wore a white polo shirt and navy-colored shorts. He held a tennis racket in one hand. "Good for you, Miss Gallo. I can't say I blame you for not taking the money. But I hope that you will allow me, on behalf of the Delaneys, to offer you a small token of our appreciation for finally putting to rest this whole treasure business."

From his pocket, he withdrew a folded check and extended it to Maya.

Maya's jaw firmed. Irritation swept down her spine. "I don't want the money."

Ian smiled and put the check back in his pocket. "Very well." To Alex, he said, "Rest assured, Deputy, the Delaney estate will give generously to rebuilding the sheriff's station." He held out his hand. "And anytime you need me and my helicopter, you let me know."

Alex shook the offered limb. "The sheriff's department will be grateful for your donation. And I appreciated your assistance the other day. I will definitely take you up on your offer in the future."

"Thank you, Mr. Delaney," Maya said.

He bowed slightly. "You're welcome."

She smiled and said, "And you're welcome to come in to town anytime. The citizens of Bristle Township would appreciate knowing not all of the Delaneys are as pretentious as they seem."

Ian threw back his head and laughed, "I will take

you up on that offer. I understand Christmas is quite a big deal in Bristle Township."

Alex chuckled. "You know it."

"Christmas is the best," Brady interjected. "There are hayrides and Christmas caroling and Santa comes to town. There's even reindeer. So much fun."

Ian's smiled was filled with tenderness. Maya hadn't expected to see that. She decided she liked the man after all.

"I'll take your word for it, Brady," Ian said. "Maybe you can show me around."

Brady eagerly nodded. "I sure will. I get to be the shepherd in the church Christmas pageant every year. With real sheep."

"I look forward to seeing it," Ian told him. "Now, if you'll excuse me, I have a tennis lesson." He walked away, leaving them to see themselves out.

Once the massive door was firmly shut behind them, Maya breathed a sigh of relief. "At least that's over with."

Another worry churned in her gut. It was time for her and Brady to return to their childhood home. But she didn't want to. And as they drove back through town, stopping for ice cream, then heading out to the ranch, she worked on building up her courage to tell Alex exactly how she felt about him. And she prayed that he would feel the same.

When they arrived at the ranch, she held Alex back as Brady ran inside to tell Frank about their visit to the Delaney estate. Rusty's excited barking from within the house made Maya smile despite her nerves.

Alex gave her a questioning look as she led him to the pasture fence. In the distance, Truman chomped on grass. The Rocky Mountains' majestic lines met the clear blue autumn sky. Snow still clung to the branches of the trees and mountaintops, but warmth brightened Maya's heart. She leaned against the fence and stared at the man she loved.

With her heart beating in her throat, she said, "This experience has taught me that none of us know what life holds for us. Brady or I could have easily died up on the mountain. And you could have, too." She shuddered as she remembered how close those bullets had hit. That day on the mountain could have ended very differently.

Alex put his booted foot on the bottom railing and leaned his elbow on the top rail so he was very close to her. He ran the knuckle down her cheek, sending a wave of sensation through her.

"There are no guarantees in life, Maya. You know that more than anybody. But I can guarantee you one thing." The intensity of his gaze drew her in and her breath lay trapped in her chest.

He leaned closer. "My heart belongs to you."

She took in a sharp breath and slowly let it out as her courage, her hope and her joy converged with her love to fill every cell of her being. She nuzzled his hand still resting against her cheek. "I love you, Alex." She lifted her gaze to his. The joy in his eyes gave her the last bit of courage she needed. "Alex, will you marry me?"

For a moment, he stared at her, apparently speechless with his eyes wide. Then a slow joy-filled grin spread across his handsome face. "You continue to surprise me, Maya Gallo."

He dipped his head and captured her lips for a kiss that curled her toes, quickened her breath and made her sigh with delight.

When the kiss ended, he touched his forehead to hers. "Yes, Maya. I will marry you, because I love you and want to spend the rest of my life you and Brady."

Elated, she entwined her arms around his neck. "Good." She went on tiptoe and lifted her lips to capture his in another soul-searing kiss that left her breathless.

A warm muzzle pushed in between them and Truman gave a soft whinny of approval.

Laughing, they smiled at each other as they hugged the horse.

Alex pulled back, his face growing serious again. "There's just one thing, Maya."

Her joy dampened, and wariness moved in. "What is that?"

He took her hands in his. "Brady will be sixteen soon. Old enough to go to that overnight camp next summer. Promise me you will let him go."

Tears of tenderness and happiness flooded her eyes and love for this man expanded in her chest until she thought she might burst. With him by her side, she could be brave enough to do anything. "Yes, I will let Brady go."

He waggled his eyebrows. "It would be a nice time to take our honeymoon. I was thinking Spain."

She tucked in her chin. "I don't want to wait that long. And Spain would be amazing."

Pulling her into an embrace, he whispered, "I don't want to wait, either."

And he kissed her.

* * * * *

SPECIAL EXCERPT FROM

LOVE INSPIRED SUSPENSE
INSPIRATIONAL ROMANCE

A K-9 officer and a forensics specialist must work together to solve a murder and stay alive.

Read on for a sneak preview of
Scene of the Crime *by Sharon Dunn,*
the next book in the True Blue K-9 Unit: Brooklyn series
available September 2020 from Love Inspired Suspense.

Brooklyn K-9 Unit Officer Jackson Davison caught movement out of the corner of his eye: a face in the trees fading out of view. His heart beat a little faster. Was someone watching him? The hairs on the back of Jackson's neck stood at attention as a light breeze brushed his face. Even as he studied the foliage, he felt the weight of a gaze on him. The sound of Smokey's barking brought his mission back into focus.

When he caught up with his partner, the dog was sitting. The signal that he'd found something. "Good boy." Jackson tossed out the toy he carried on his belt for Smokey to play with, his reward for doing his job. The dog whipped the toy back and forth in his mouth.

"Drop," Jackson said. He picked up the toy and patted Smokey on the head. "Sit. Stay."

The body, partially covered by branches, was clothed in neutral colors and would not be easy to spot unless you were looking for it.

He keyed his radio. "Officer Davison here. I've got a body in Prospect Park. Male Caucasian under the age of forty, about two hundred yards in, just southwest of the Brooklyn Botanic Garden."

Dispatch responded, "Ten-four. Help is on the way."

He studied the trees just in time to catch the face again, barely visible, like a fading mist. He was being watched. "Did you see something?" Jackson shouted. "Did you call this in?"

The person turned and ran, disappearing into the thick brush.

Jackson took off in the direction the runner had gone. As his feet pounded the hard earth, another thought occurred to him. Was this the person who had shot the man in the chest? Sometimes criminals hung around to witness the police response to their handiwork.

His attention was drawn to a garbage can just as an object hit the back of his head with intense force. Pain radiated from the base of his skull. He crumpled to the ground and his world went black.

Don't miss
Scene of the Crime *by Sharon Dunn,*
available wherever Love Inspired Suspense books
and ebooks are sold.

LoveInspired.com

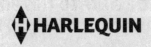